CHIEF LIGHTNING BOLT

CHIEF
LIGHTNING
BOLT

DANIEL N. PAUL

ROSEWAY PUBLISHING
AN IMPRINT OF FERNWOOD PUBLISHING
HALIFAX & WINNIPEG

This is a work of fiction.
Any resemblance to actual persons or events is coincidental.

Editing: Chris Benjamin
Design: Tania Craan
Printed and bound in Canada

Published by Roseway Publishing
an imprint of Fernwood Publishing
32 Oceanvista Lane, Black Point, Nova Scotia, B0J 1B0
and 748 Broadway Avenue, Winnipeg, Manitoba, R3G 0X3
www.fernwoodpublishing.ca/roseway

Fernwood Publishing Company Limited gratefully acknowledges the financial
support of the Government of Canada, the Canada Council for the Arts, the
Province of Manitoba, the Province of Nova Scotia and Arts Nova Scotia.

Library and Archives Canada Cataloguing in Publication

Paul, Daniel N., author
Chief Lightning Bolt / Daniel N. Paul.

Issued in print and electronic formats.
ISBN 978-1-55266-969-3 (softcover).--
ISBN 978-1-55266-970-9 (EPUB).--
ISBN 978-1-55266-971-6 (Kindle)

I. Title.

PS8631.A84964C55 2017
C813'.6
C2017-903117-1
C2017-903118-X

A novel featuring love, comedy,
intrigue, murder, compromise, war and peace,
set in fifteenth-century Northeastern North America.

In memory of my parents,
the late William G. Paul and Sarah Agnes, nee Noel,
two decent people who persevered in the face of the
racist attitudes that made paupers of Canada's Native
American population. May the Great Spirit give them
peace and tranquility for eternity in the Land of Souls.
And for my friend Dr. Joseph Randy Bowers, PHD,
whose help with this book was of exceptional value!

THE LAND OF THE MI'KMAQ

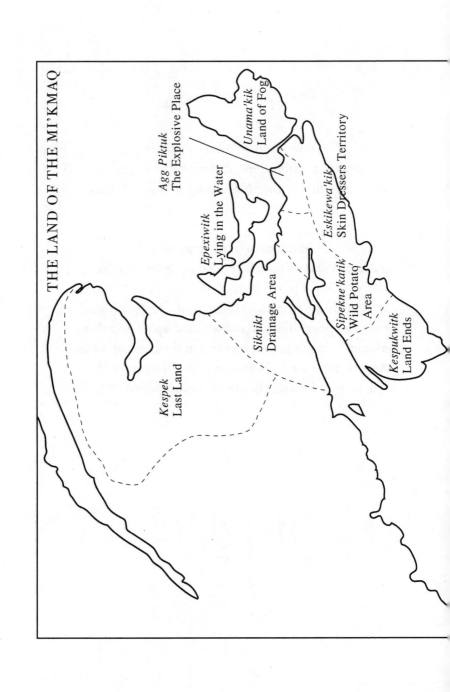

Kespek
Last Land

Siknikt
Drainage Area

Epexiwitk
Lying in the Water

Agg Piktuk
The Explosive Place

Unama'kik
Land of Fog

Eskikewa'kik
Skin Dressers Territory

Sipekne'katik
Wild Potato
Area

Kespukwitk
Land Ends

AUTHOR'S NOTE

IN VIEW OF THE FACT that before the European invasion the Mi'kmaq did not have any First Nation enemies interested in attacking them to satisfy a greedy need to accumulate wealth and dominance over others, I had to use my imagination to create a First Nation to fill the requirement for one. This fictional Nation was needed to display the Mi'kmaq adversity toward war-making activities in this novel. I endowed it with the title "Western Nations."

That the Mi'kmaq and other Northeastern North American First Nations held such views towards war is well supported by the comments left behind by scholars and colonial European officials. A few examples:

The behaviour pattern requisite of any Micmac was such as to virtually eliminate any overt and direct forms of aggression. The ideal man was one who was restrained and dignified in all his actions, who maintained a stolid exterior under all circumstances, who deprived himself of his possessions to take care of the poor, aged, or sick, or the less fortunate, who was generous and hospitable

to strangers but implacable and cruel to his enemies, and brave in war.... The Micmac developed a stoicism that would have rendered credit to the Stoics.
— Bernard Gilbert Hoffman

Our savages do not found their wars upon the possession of the land. We do not see that they encroach one upon the other in that respect. They have land enough to live on and to walk abroad. Their ambition is limited by their bounds. They make war as did Alexander the Great, that they may say, "I have beaten you"; or else for revenge, in remembrance for some injury received.
— Marc Lescarbot, French colonial lawyer
Annapolis (Nova Scotia), March 4, 1720

Committee of the Council could not accept the old frivolous excuse for outrage at Minas [fear of Indians]. Because ... their letter of excuse could not be considered as satisfaction, as the Indians rarely, if ever, commit depredations.
— Letter from the English Governor's Council to the Acadian People of Minas, in a rare admission by the English that the Mi'kmaq did not participate in crimes against civilians and were essentially non-belligerent

Later in the novel, for the purpose of showing the Chief working to end a senseless war over a perceived wrong, I created two other fictional First Nations: the Penikt and the Atikitkas.

My intention in writing this book is to offer an historical narrative that captures the essence of what and who the Mi'kmaq First Nation were prior to the onslaught of

European colonization, and what life was like for the members of a Mi'kmaq village. The story is set during the fifteenth century — a period when the Mi'kmaq Nation was strong and allied with several other northeastern Nations within the Wabanaki Confederacy. The Mi'kmaq Nation is located in what today are called the eastern provinces of Canada and part of the American state Maine.

The story of Chief Lightning Bolt is the story of how a Mi'kmaq man with leadership attributes was expected to live his life, with honour and humility. Each chapter represents a different phase of his life, the customs and traditions he was expected to observe and uphold, the actions he would take and the values he would cherish and try to always embody. In Lightning Bolt we see the adventurousness of youth, the intense nervousness of a young man trying to win the hand of the woman he loves, the commitment to serving his community in the Hunt and when absolutely necessary, in battle, and his dedication to serving his People justly and fairly through an egalitarian and democratic process.

RENEWAL AND BIRTH

The arrival of the Sunrises of Spring was rapidly turning the land of the Mi'kmaq lush with renewal. Lakes, rivers and streams, now ice free, were teeming with fish and in dens and nests hidden in Mother Earth's forests the animals and birds that provided meat for the Mi'kmaq were giving birth to offspring that would assure them bountiful harvests for many Moons to come. After they had experienced an extraordinarily cold Winter, Mother Earth, in her timeless way, was telling the Mi'kmaq that their dreams of enjoying the warmth and plenty of Summer would soon be realized.

In fact, they were in for a big treat. It was to be a spectacular Spring. The Great Spirit had decided to reward the People for their love and devotion by making the Season exceptional. Thus, as the Sunrises passed, the People's hearts were filled with awe to see the splendour of Mother Earth's ongoing renewal. Her redecorating of trees and meadows with fresh green leaves and other colourful growth was an unmatchable work of art.

In addition to renewal, Spring's Sunrises were also important for the well-being of future generations of Mi'kmaq society in a very human way. Spring was when thoughts of love and marriage were at the forefront of the minds of many young men and women. In truth, for most of them, it was a top priority to win the heart of a loving mate to spend a lifetime of happiness with and to raise many cherished children. Their excitement was contagious. Relatives and friends were looking forward with great anticipation to celebrating many exciting wedding parties.

That the current Spring would be blessed with more couples pursuing wedded bliss than normal was evident throughout the far-flung villages of the seven Mi'kmaq Nations. The happy glows in their faces made it apparent to friends and relatives that most of them would soon realize their dream of acquiring a beloved spouse.

Such conclusions were further solidified by the preparations being made for participation in the ancient romantic ritual by the smitten and their families. To help the potential lovers to move things in the right direction, loving mothers, sisters and aunts were busy designing and stitching together new outfits, which the love-struck thought essential for attracting the attention of the spouses of their dreams. Friends were also involved. They were finding excuses to bring couples into contact with each other at every opportunity.

The Elders, of course, were especially affected by the sense of happy excitement exhibited by the young lovers. It caused them to recall the Seasons long ago, when they had taken their first timid steps towards winning the hearts of their beloved. They remembered with fondness the excitement and fear of rejection, the wonderful moment when a simple yes to a shyly asked question set their world on fire and the inner bliss that made their future look like the Land of Souls on Mother Earth. In contentment they thought, "Ah, the marvelous memories of the delights of one's youth!"

The pursuit of married bliss was not without trials and tribulations. Under the Nation's ancient romantic rules, which *guided courtship, engagement and marriage, many rituals had to be followed by the smitten. First and foremost, Mi'kmaq custom dictated that the enamoured young warrior must take the first step to initiate courtship, which involved giving appropriate presents to the parents of the young woman of his dreams.*

Thus, to prepare for the ritual, the young braves and proven warriors throughout the Land of the Mi'kmaq were worriedly amassing troves of quality goods to present to the parents of their dream women. To them, because the success of their romantic efforts directly affected their future contentment, it was a traumatic experience. Each fervently hoped and prayed that the quality and quantity of his presents would be convincing evidence to her protective parents, and to her, that he had the wherewithal to be a capable and conscientious provider.

Under such pressure, the courageous young warriors were often reduced to nervous wrecks. In fact, among the many adventures that they encountered during their lifetimes, winning the heart of a young woman was considered one of the most traumatic. Many, because of the stress and tribulations they suffered, would state to friends afterward, "I would much prefer to fight, unarmed and alone, two mother black bears with cubs, than go through that again!" If not for the needs of the warrior's heart overruling the urging of his brain to avoid the daunting process altogether, Mi'kmaq society would have been hard pressed to survive.

//

CHAPTER ONE

Throughout the seven Mi'kmaq Districts, brave warriors were approaching the daunting process of courtship with much anxiety. Among them was Little Bear, a member of Chief Thunder Cloud's village, in the District of Kespukwitk. He was a handsome young man who had had his warrior's status confirmed during the last Hunt.

With fear tugging at his heart, he was marshalling up the courage to visit Chief Thunder Cloud to ask permission to court his daughter, Early Blossom, whom he was madly in love with. To his eyes, she was the most desirable young woman to have ever graced Mother Earth, which only added to his anxiety. Because of her exceptional qualities, he thought he had little chance to interest her in courtship. Thus, he began his romantic endeavour with a deep fear of having his quest for her hand rejected. It never occurred to him that Early Blossom might be waiting eagerly for him to make his approach. Like all young Mi'kmaq men, he had been taught from early childhood to be humble and shun self-aggrandizement. He was unappreciative of his personal assets. If asked to list the personal strengths and accomplishments that would make him a good husband, he would've been embarrassed to try.

His lack of self-appreciation was also the reason he had no awareness of the widely held view among virtually all the young women of the surrounding area that he was one of the most desirable young men available. He was regarded as being blessed with ruggedly handsome good looks and exceptional hunting skills. Young Mi'kmaq women, when it came to the games played between the sexes, were a match for any man. They usually succeeded when they set their heart on marrying a warrior who took their fancy, a feat they accomplished in spite of the cultural traditions that required they be very circumspect in their pursuits. Thus, they followed maternal ancestors and permitted a suitor to believe that he alone was the assertive participant in the process.

In the case of Little Bear and Early Blossom, they had much the same attitude about themselves. As a result, the game wasn't playing out according to the ancient rules. She was a shy, unassuming and beautiful young woman. Her humility was deeply embedded. She was thus unaware of her considerable charms and was full of doubts about her ability to attract a mate. It never crossed her mind that she was viewed by the young warriors of their village with very high affections. Early Blossom had for many Moons been madly in love with a person with whom she had not exchanged a single word of intimacy. In her eyes he was the bravest, the most handsome and the most desirable young man in the country. Because of this she wanted with all her heart to be the one who would end his bachelor seasons.

Her apprehension about her chances of accomplishing her goal didn't stop her from trying. Whenever she had an inkling that Little Bear might be around the village in places where she would be, she dressed in her best outfits and tried to be extra charming. But, from her perspective, regardless of what she did, he was unaware of her existence. With this outlook guiding her thoughts she began to despair that the young warrior would never, if he did find her desirable, summon up the courage needed to approach her father to ask if he could court her.

During these moments of despair, she lamented that men were so afraid and so slow to take the initiative when it came to affairs of the heart. She discussed her anxiety with her mother, Blue Water.

"Mother, can you tell me why Little Bear finds me unattractive? I make sure I'm as presentable as possible when I think I might meet him around the village. Yet, when we do meet in passing, he pays no more attention to me than he would to a fly on the back of a moose. He acts as if I don't exist, mumbles something and goes on his way! All my friends tell me that he is attracted to me but his actions don't support what they say."

Blue Water, from her own experience, knew that the pursuit of a first love was a trying ordeal for a young woman. She, like countless mothers before her, tried to use her experience, combined with the knowledge she had collected in friendly exchanges with girlfriends over the Seasons, to find a way to give confidence and comfort to her worried daughter.

"Early Blossom, my baby, you are a dependable, attractive, intelligent young woman, but you don't appreciate the full effects of your charms on men. I can assure you that Little Bear finds you very attractive. In fact, so do most of the other young men in the village, and surrounding area, who would be busy trying to convince you to be their bride if they only thought that they had a small chance to win your affection. You are beautiful, my dear." Her mother embraced her daughter, who had tears welling up in her eyes. "You are so very wonderful my dear; trust me in this one matter."

After a brief pause, Blue Water said, "Be patient with Little Bear; he is shy and like all young men, almost without courage when it comes to affairs of the heart. I can assure you, from my own experience of courtship with your father, and also from the words of wisdom collected over the Seasons from friends and relatives, that your fears are completely unfounded. Rest assured, my dear, when Little Bear musters up the courage, he will visit your father!"

Brushing the tears from her cheeks, Early Blossom said, "I hope you're right. The prospect of being a lonely old maid doesn't appeal to me."

Anyone listening closely would have heard Blue Water mumble as she walked away, "Great Spirit, give me patience and strength."

From past experience, Thunder Cloud knew that all signs indicated love and marriage were in the works for his youngest daughter. She and Little Bear were so tongue-tied when near each other that only a blind person could miss the signals. With a great deal of anticipation he was looking forward to the fun of putting on a stern and reluctant fatherly show for him. In fact, the prospect of teasing Little Bear by pretending he wasn't pleased with his wanting to court Early Blossom would be the highlight of the Season. As the father of five sons and five daughters, he had already been through the process many times and each had been equally enjoyable. His sons, of course, had been the objects of another father's fun.

In Little Bear's case, Thunder Cloud didn't have much longer to wait. With each passing Sunrise the young man was slowly but surely drumming up the courage to ask for permission to court Early Blossom, if only Thunder Cloud would offer his consent.

Finally, two Sunrises before the first Moon of Spring, after running out of excuses for any further delay, Little Bear decided to undertake the heart-stopping task the next Sunrise. He made the momentous decision, which required using his wellspring of courage, shortly after retiring to his comfortable fir-bough bed for the night. This assured that he had a fitful and restless sleep.

Family and friends sensed from how tired and haunted he looked during the next Sunrise that he had finally made the decision to ask for courting permission. They also figured correctly that the look of the condemned they saw in his face was caused by his picturing being rejected by the father and sentenced to a life of heartbreak without the company of the girl he loved. In fact, during the night he had repeatedly imagined everything that could possibly go wrong, over and over again.

He thought, "Oh Great Spirit, Thunder Cloud will never judge me worthy to court Early Blossom. After I make my request, I can see him reacting like a cranky old bull moose with porcupine quills in its hide, raging at me for thinking I'm good enough to be a provider for his daughter. Then, in a thunderous authoritative voice, which leaves no space for question, asking me to leave his wigwam forever, saying, 'Little Bear, for you to think that I would permit one as unworthy as you to court my daughter is an insult to my family's good name, to our pride and honour! Please, never come back to my wigwam with such a disrespectful and offensive request again! Go!'"

Little Bear chanted to himself during the early morning

hours, "Oh Great Spirit, how I wish this Sunrise was over!" Throughout the sunrise these thoughts tormented him, while he waited for the appropriate time to visit the wigwam of his beloved.

That evening, when Thunder Cloud saw the young warrior approaching his wigwam with the reluctance of a condemned man going to his final appointment with the Great Spirit, he sensed that responding crankily to Little Bear's proposal was going to be extra fun. But, by the obvious discomfort of the approaching young man, he knew that he would have to summon up his reserves of stoicism to maintain throughout the visit the facade of a stern and reluctant father.

Thus Little Bear, upon entering the Chief's wigwam, met a father who appeared to be the reincarnation of old Stoney Heart himself. With much trepidation he opened the encounter by offering the Chief a present of two of the finest beaver pelts he had trapped during the prime Season. The Chief accepted the presents without displaying much enthusiasm, leaving a definite impression that he was accepting an inferior gift. Then Little Bear, with much dread in his heart, opened the subject of courting Early Blossom.

He tried get the words from his lips as quickly as possible without appearing disrespectful. "Thunder Cloud, kind father, I've come tonight to discuss a matter of great importance to my future happiness. I really don't have any idea how I'm supposed begin so I'll tell you straight out. Great Chief, for many Moons I've been in love with your daughter Early Blossom. I can't tell you exactly when I began to feel this way about her, but every time I see her walking around the village and chatting with others, my love for her increases. Because of this, I can't see a future without her at my side. Therefore,

I humbly request your permission to ask her if she'll permit me to court her. If you consent, and Early Blossom agrees, I want you to know that, if this leads to marriage, I will do every thing possible to assure that she will be well provided for as long as she lives."

The Chief, acting out his part with enthusiasm, mischievously responded by reciting a list of many invented shortcomings that he saw in Little Bear's character, which might prevent him from becoming a good provider and father, even if he put his best effort into it.

With a sinking feeling, Little Bear went deep into his heart and before the Great Chief he bravely defended his honour and swore before the Great Spirit that he would work tirelessly to overcome any shortcomings he might have. He ended his pleas by restating emphatically, "With the passage of the Seasons I shall be a better provider."

Thunder Cloud, enjoying himself to the fullest, laid it on heavy, "My son, you come to my wigwam and make a present to me of inferior beaver pelts. You tell me that these are the finest taken by you during the Hunt. Such actions are not supportive of your boast that you will make a good provider. If you thought that such would influence my judgment in your favour you're mistaken. If anything, they have had the opposite effect."

Sweating profusely, dismaying of ever receiving approval, Little Beaver, with a quiver in his voice replied, "Father, please accept my humble apology for presenting you with such unworthy gifts. I can assure you that when I select presents in the future to give you, I will take much greater care to assure that they are of the best quality. I know that I have shortcomings my father and perhaps as you implied I am unworthy of Early Blossom, but for me she is the centre of the Universe and without her I have no future. I beg of you, please give me a chance to prove myself."

After many similar exchanges with Little Bear that seemed to drag on for hours, Blue Water called the Chief just beyond Little Bear's hearing. "My dear, you've had your fun, now end the torture."

Finally the Chief gave way, allowing himself to be prodded by his wife's short and decisive directive. Seeming reluctant to offer his permission, Chief Thunder Cloud said, "My son, you may ask my daughter if she wishes to engage in a relationship with you; after all, this is a decision for her alone to make."

He leaned forward and whispered, to place greater emphasis on his words, "But I must warn you, Early Blossom has always exercised common sense and good judgment when making important decisions about her future. I hope, in this case, she continues the practice." The Chief's unenthusiastic permission delivered another smashing blow to Little Bear's already shaky confidence. It had the effect of adding substantially to his dread of being rejected. When the crestfallen figure of Little Bear had faded into the darkness, Thunder Cloud, with enthusiasm, remarked to his wife, "That young man will make a wonderful husband for our baby!"

The following evening, a distraught Little Bear, dressed in his finest, with butterflies churning in his stomach, set out to see Early Blossom. Arriving at Thunder Cloud's wigwam he entered and asked Blue Water if he could speak to Early Blossom.

Blue Water, sensing his grave unease, checked with Early Blossom and asked Little Bear in a very kind and polite voice to return in the time it took to smoke three pipes. Then Early Blossom would be ready to see him. That evening Little Bear learned firsthand something that uncounted souls before him had learned — the time that it takes to smoke three pipes, when waiting to find out something important, feels like a lifetime.

With foreboding in his heart, and after walking many times around the village to pass the time, Little Bear returned to Thunder Cloud's wigwam. He was made welcome by Blue Water and Early Blossom. Then, before Blue Water had a chance to move a discreet distance away, in semi-terror, he uttered from the heart a sudden proposal of courtship: "Early Blossom, do me a great honour and permit me to come courting. I implore you to consider my request with this in mind — I've grown to love you, to the point where I cannot envision a life without you at my side. If you decide to say no, I will accept your decision, but I will have a great heaviness and an empty space in my heart forever." Later, when he had time to think about it, his boldness shocked him.

Early Blossom, after consulting her mother, told Little Bear to return the following evening when she would answer his proposal, as custom dictated. He thanked her profusely for her consideration, said goodnight, then with feelings of great uneasiness in his heart, started for home. When he was out of sight and earshot, Early Blossom abandoned her sedate demeanour and almost jumped with joy at the prospect of having the man of her dreams for her own.

The future lovers would never again see the time between two evenings pass so slowly and painfully. For Early Blossom, knowing she would say yes, the time dragged on because she wanted their courtship to begin. For Little Bear it was the opposite. In not knowing what her decision might be, his imagination ran wild with scenes of failure.

Finally, the time for the ultimate decision arrived. Little

Bear, exhibiting signs of another sleepless night, looking even more ragged but somehow more handsome, with a great apprehension in his heart, returned to Thunder Cloud's wigwam. Blue Water made him welcome and then, in order to give the young people a semblance of privacy, she moved to the far side of the wigwam.

Early Blossom, with a smile on her face, told Little Bear, "Yes, I accept your proposal of courtship with pleasure."

Little Bear appeared awestruck.

"Why do you look so surprised? I know that this might sound bold, but not only do I look forward to our courtship, I pray we will find that we love each other enough to want to spend the rest of our lives together." They passed the rest of the evening chatting and getting acquainted. When it came time to leave, he promised to return the following evening.

If ever there was a young man who floated on a cloud because of a woman uttering "yes" it was Little Bear. The word was the answer to his dreams, hopes and prayers. He walked away from Thunder Cloud's wigwam feeling so happy he almost burst with joy. When he told his parents the news of his good fortune, they feigned surprise, which was necessary because they and all the villagers already knew that it would come to pass.

The next evening, Little Bear and Early Blossom began their supervised courtship. Her mother or another female relative was always discreetly present as a chaperone when they met.

Little Bear went all out trying to convince Early Blossom and her family that he was a worthy potential husband for her. He made presents to them of the best furs and other fineries he could acquire. But being the eternal pessimist when it came to matters of the heart, he thought, "Dear Great

Spirit, I'm doing all I can to demonstrate to Early Blossom and family, should she one Sunset consent to marry me, that I will be a good provider. However, I don't think I'm doing enough. My presents are the best that a man can give, but Thunder Cloud seems unimpressed. What, oh great Father, must I do next?"

The courtship continued for an appropriate time. Then, in spite of his misgivings, Little Bear summoned the courage to ask Thunder Cloud for permission to propose marriage to Early Blossom. One evening, Little Bear arrived at Thunder Cloud's wigwam loaded down with more presents than usual. The Chief, seeing him coming with a look of hopeless despair on his face, and loaded with goodies, anticipated with pleasure the fun he would soon have at the young warrior's expense.

After Little Bear entered the wigwam and polite greetings were exchanged and gifts disbursed, with the now-expected disdain for them shown by Thunder Cloud, Little Bear asked if he could speak to the Chief in private. His request was reluctantly granted.

Little Bear, filled with fears and misgivings about his prospects for a favourable answer, after restating his belief that he would be a worthy husband for Early Blossom, asked for Thunder Cloud's permission to propose marriage.

Thunder Cloud, thoroughly enjoying himself, put the young man through the paces. Then, seeing the look of absolute dismay on Little Bear's face, he couldn't contain himself any longer and broke into howls of laughter, telling the young man, "My son, since you first came to ask if you could court Early Blossom I've had a lot of fun at your expense. The memories of the look of a losing lover on your face when I invented baseless reasons you wouldn't make a good husband for my daughter or a good father for my grandchildren, was precious. I shall remember them always. But now, my son, it is time to be serious."

With a look of compassion and kindness unfamiliar to Little Bear, the Chief said, "I'll start by disavowing the false impression that I gave you over the past Sunrises that I was full of doubts and reservations about your worthiness. This has never been the case. In fact, during the passage of the Seasons, I've watched with much happiness as you grew into a fine and courageous young man. My son, I have no hesitation in stating that throughout your short life you've displayed all the fine attributes that I consider essential in a man who asks to be my daughter's husband. You will make a fine father, and you are already an exceptional community member. Your parents, with great love and wisdom, did a wonderful job in raising you. They should be proud of their accomplishment. I consider you to be a fine and honourable young man, and will be proud and honoured to have you as a son, if my daughter agrees to marry you."

In stunned disbelief, Little Bear responded, "Father, I thank you from the bottom of my heart for your consent and compliments! I'm surprised beyond belief by your reaction. I thought, by your reactions to my presents over the past several Moons, that you would reject me at once as unworthy of Early Blossom. Father, you've made me so happy. I want to swear to you before the Creator that as long as life remains in my body, I shall remain true and faithful to your trust. I assure you with all my heart that I shall love and care for Early Blossom, if she agrees to marriage, for eternity."

Little Bear asked if he could speak to Early Blossom in private. Blue Water, in order to give the young couple all the privacy that social niceties permitted, suggested that they come with her for a stroll in the moonlight.

Walking along holding hands, about thirty paces ahead of Blue Water, Little Bear began, "Early Blossom, my love, my precious, I'm not very good at this, but I want to try to explain to you how much I love you. My darling, when we're apart, I miss you with all my heart. It fills me with joy to be with you whenever I can. To my humble eyes your beauty is like all the rainbows wrapped into one, and far exceeds the beauty of all other beautiful things that the Creator has made combined! My love, I cannot picture living my life without you. Your father has granted permission if you accept. Will you make my life complete and marry me?"

"My precious Little Bear, at times over the past few Moons I've caught myself wondering if you would ever find the courage to ask me that wonderful question. Why the hesitation my love? After putting aside all your misgivings, in your heart of hearts, you must know already that my answer is yes. My handsome warrior, how could it be otherwise? Life for me without your presence would be bleak and barren. I love you dearly and look forward with joy to a future of happiness, as your wife."

After so much sweat and fears, with the exchange of these words of endearment and love, Little Bear and Early Blossom sealed a bargain of love that assured their future happiness.

The engagement official, with the help of family and friends, Little Bear and Early Blossom set about planning their wedding. As the Sunrise for the big event approached, the villagers were also caught up in the fun. Many close friends, almost as excited about the event as the engaged couple and their families were, arranged and hosted lavish feasts and entertainment. The wedding and the following celebrations were worked out by family and community with a desire to make it perfect for the happy young couple. The highlight of the wedding ceremony, the exchange of marriage vows of love, fidelity, loyalty and devotion by the young couple, was scheduled to take place at sunset, followed by a wedding feast. The happy couple would then be led to a specially designated wigwam, erected for the occasion, to consummate their marriage.

The Sunrise of their wedding was perfect, sunshine and warmth putting all in the mood for a great time. The wedding went without a hitch. Partying and dancing continued until the sun began to rise the following Sunrise.

Late in the evening of the wedding night, after being led to the wedding wigwam by family and friends to consummate their marriage, the words they used in blissful happiness and hushed voices to express their unconditional loving commitment to each other would often be revisited. "Early Blossom, my love, our marriage this Sunrise is the true beginning of my life; it makes it complete. In comparison, my life before you was almost barren. My darling, my love for you is so intense that it is beyond my powers to describe. But, I'll try. For as long as I live, I shall hold you precious before all else. You are to me all of the beautiful things in life that are meaningful. Without you in it, my life is unthinkable. My little flower, I pledge to you my undying love for the rest of our lives on Mother Earth, and for eternity."

"Little Bear, my darling husband, your words of love are to me like the music of the sweet sound of the birds in early Spring when they shout out their joy in tribute to Mother Earth's awakening benevolent bounty. I love you, my sweetheart, with all my heart. If I were to search forever, I couldn't find words adequate to describe how much. Tonight, my darling, the Great Spirit has also fulfilled all the dreams and wishes I've ever had. To lie here in your arms, in the knowledge that we have been bonded together in marriage for our lifetimes, makes my life almost complete. The only thing missing is a child, who in time shall come. My dear, this Sunrise, and for all the Sunrises of my life, I pledge to you before the Great Spirit that I shall love and care for you for eternity also."

The young lovers then talked on until near dawn, when they drifted off into a contented and dreamless sleep. The next Sunrise, after preparing and eating a good breakfast and enduring much teasing from the community they, with the help of family and friends, set up their own wigwam. It signified the beginning of a contented domestic routine.

Within only a few Moons, the most exciting and anticipated development came to be when Early Blossom became pregnant for the first time. The course of the pregnancy seemed like eternity to Little Bear and Early Blossom. But, it seems, even eternity has its limits, because with the passage of the Moons and three Seasons, the birth was imminent. The loving parents-to-be looked forward to the approaching event with the happiness that can only be known by a young couple expecting their firstborn. Early Blossom informed Little Bear of the impending arrival with these words, "Great news my darling husband, our son has turned. This, so the midwife informs me, indicates that he is preparing to make his grand entrance into the world. It's hard to believe, at last, our wait is almost over."

"How can you, my dearest wife, be so sure that it is, and that we're having a son? To me, even though you say you feel it in your bones and some of the Elders have predicted it, it's anybody's guess what sex our child will be. But, it doesn't really matter to me my love because I wouldn't be the least disappointed if the Great Spirit blessed us with a beautiful daughter."

"No, no, my husband, it will be a son! And, I'm so confident of it that I will go one step further and predict his future. I predict that he will grow up to be one of the greatest warriors and leaders that our nation has ever known."

With just a hint of disbelief in his voice Little Bear commented, "We shall see, my sweet Little Blossom, what the Great Spirit desires for us, when the Sunrise of the child's birth arrives, if it ever does. The wait has been so long that sometimes it seems a lifetime has passed since you first discovered you were pregnant. In the interim, I could have built a hundred canoes. My love, watching the whole process has been a truly fascinating experience, but by all that is sacred it is time for the Great Spirit to end our turmoil and to permit this birthing."

Early Blossom, who could barely contain her own anticipation, tried to maintain an air of tranquility for the sake of her husband's mental well-being. With an expertly feigned air of blissful calm she responded, "Patience, my dear husband. Patience, the Sunrise for it will come."

Finally, during a raging thunder and lightning storm, three Sunrises before the first full Moon of Spring, with Little Bear bordering on the verge of mental collapse, their first son was born. He was named Lightning Bolt. He was given the name, which followed the Nation's time-honoured tradition of naming children after Mother Earth's creations, because a great bolt of lightning was seen by the community, flashing across the sky, at the very time of his birth. After the resounding thunder had echoed across the land, the next sound to be heard was the wailing cry of the new baby. He would be the couple's first of several children.

The joyful news of the much anticipated arrival of their son spread like wildfire throughout the community. The women, responding with enthusiasm, began to organize a feast of birth celebration. The birth was a special event for the entire community because the birth of a child for the Mi'kmaq was a time to be especially thankful to the Great Spirit, Who, by making the People fertile, assured the Nation's survival.

On the Sunrise of the celebration the festivities began with the community's women giving presents to Little Bear and Early Blossom. They consisted of practical things, especially blankets and cloths that were needed by parents when starting the joyful task of raising a child. And then, with happy hearts, they shared a delectable meal and enjoyed fascinating entertainment arranged by the community's musicians and storytellers.

With uncanny accuracy, the truth of Early Blossom's prediction of great things in store for their son soon became apparent. During his early childhood, Lightning Bolt began to display an outstanding intelligence and a curiosity about the world around him that seemed insatiable. At nine Moons he spoke his first words and he soon had a vocabulary that was exceptional for his age. In just a little more than eleven Moons he began to walk and, with his new mobility, he was soon investigating everything that came in sight. His curiosity soon had him asking any adult he met those hard-to-answer questions that only small children can ask.

When he passed five Springs, Little Bear began teaching Lightning Bolt the skills Mi'kmaq males needed to become warriors. As he did when he learned to walk and talk, the little man displayed an exceptional ability to pick up knowledge and to improve upon it. All this gave his parents pause for thought.

In fact, although it was Early Blossom who had predicted great things for her son, she was much awed by his outstanding progress. One Sunrise, after hearing her son's comments when engaged in a deep conversation with a passing Elder, Early Blossom commented on it to Little Bear. "My love, never in my wildest dreams did I believe the Great Spirit would bless us with a son who is so intelligent. It makes me wonder how two humble and average people such as us are ever going to cope with it. I pray with all my being that the Creator will give us the wherewithal and wisdom to raise him in a manner that will see him devoting his life to protecting and improving the ways of our Nation."

In a show of bravado he didn't actually feel, Little Bear tried to assure her by saying, "Don't worry my little flower, we can, with love, teach him to love and be humble before the Great Spirit. All else, with the passing of the Moons, shall fall into place."

Lightning Bolt, by both word and deed, soon proved to all his compatriots that he was a natural born leader, who had the charisma to inspire others to follow him. By the time he reached his sixth Spring his playmates were already enthusiastically following his lead. They did it with little hesitation, especially when he was trying to satisfy his and their curiosity about the mysteries of Mother Earth.

His quest for knowledge extended beyond geography, flora and fauna to include history and legends. In fact, his intense quest for knowledge in this area was sometimes almost too much for his Elders to bear. He peppered his parents, grandparents and others with questions that seemed at times without end. But they praised him lavishly for his initiative. In spite of this, he maintained an air of humility that was commendable.

Lightning Bolt, like most children, had a best friend. He was a boy named Crazy Moose, who was born the Summer following Lightning Bolt's Spring birth to special friends of his parents, Swift Otter and Morning Star. The special friendship their parents enjoyed brought the two boys close together as babies. Thus, in early childhood they created a friendship bond that was destined to withstand the passage of time.

The incident that gave Crazy Moose his name had caused a great deal of merriment among the People. It happened the Sunrise he was born. A monstrous bull moose, seemingly driven to distraction by black-flies and other pests, decided the best way to alleviate his torment was to take a swim in the Bay of Bear River. As it was a matter of great urgency for him, he decided that the quickest way to get to the water was a route straight through the middle of the village. Unfortunately, two wigwams happened to be sitting astraddle the straight line he had decided upon. They caused him no delay. They were sent flying like they were made of feathers. One was empty but the other was occupied by Moon Light, a very aged and beloved Elder.

At the time the tormented moose struck Moon Light's wigwam, she had just finished pouring herself a herbal tea and was moving the drinking vessel towards her mouth. As several villagers watched in amazement, the scene changed like it was caused by magic. In the blink of an eye the scene of a wigwam was replaced with a scene of a very elderly woman calmly taking a drink of tea, seemingly unfazed by the disappearance of the shelter that a moment before had shielded her. The incident became a timeless tale retold in front of countless campfires.

Due to their different personalities, one outgoing, the

other retiring, Lightning Bolt became the loyal leader and Crazy Moose the loyal follower. Their friendship was never adversarial. Although they grew up as equals, Crazy Moose was willing to follow his friend anywhere. He loved and trusted him completely. It was a most productive relationship that would amass many moments to recall and savour of danger, adventure, and mirth.

Their taste for adventure began to develop early. During the passage of their first ten Summers they had been on many enjoyable overnight and longer camping trips with their fathers. However, by age ten, they felt a need to branch out on their own. Taking the bull moose by the horns, so to speak, they initiated their first step toward independence by summoning up the courage to ask their fathers for permission to make a solo overnight excursion. After Swift Otter and Little Bear had spent some time assuring their wives that the boys would be safe on their own for overnight stays, they permitted them to go alone to pre-approved areas.

They, when travelling and camping on their own, like most boys their age, "accidentally" ran into many adventures. And they created many for themselves by trying to satisfy their insatiable curiosity or tastes. Some of their escapades were so dangerous and foolhardy that if their poor mothers had known what was going on they would have had nervous breakdowns.

One such hair-raising escapade occurred during their second solo camping trip. After selecting a suitable site and setting up camp they started to explore the area. Before long, Crazy Moose spotted a beehive. A few seemingly innocent words from him started the events which resulted in a heart-stopping and near fatal adventure for them. "Hey, Lightning Bolt, look over there, in that old tree stump, a beehive!"

This elicited a response from his friend that could be expected from a person with an insatiable taste for honey: "I see it; I see it! Oh, my brother, the sight of it sets my mouth to watering! Already I can savour the taste. I don't know about you my friend, but I must have some."

With some caution, Crazy Moose responded: "So must I, my friend, but the big question is, when one has to take it from bees, how does he get it?"

Not in the least daunted by the task ahead Lightning Bolt shot back: "Don't worry, my friend. Getting it will be as easy as crawling through that old hollow log over there. We'll wrap ourselves in our fur bedding from head to foot and then knock open the old stump with boulders. Once we crack it open, we can grab the honeycomb and escape untouched."

With the mode of acquisition settled, the boys prepared to implement Lightning Bolt's plan. As a precaution, knowing that the bees would be driven mad when disturbed, they investigated the area around the beehive to map out an escape route if needed. As the hive was located in an ancient burn on a hillside that went downwards about twenty-five paces to the river, they wisely determined that if things went wrong they could make it to the river and the safety of the water before suffering more than a few stings. With an escape route laid out, they put their acquisition plan into action.

Lightning Bolt directed the assault, "Get ready, Crazy Moose! When I say, let fly with your boulder. As soon as yours hits, I'll run in with my large one and try to split the stump open. Go!"

The well-planned assault played out like a charm. The boulder Lightning Bolt hit the stump with successfully split it wide open as anticipated and sent the honeycomb out to fall on the ground. The delicious smell of honey quickly filled the air while the bees began buzzing about in frenzy. Observing all this from a short distance was a cranky old gentleman, who in his own right was born with an insatiable taste for delectable honey, Brother Black Bear.

Brother Bear, with taste buds salivating, made his presence known to the boys with a deafening roar, which instilled a suitable amount of terror in them. As a result the leader, in a near panic, issued some astutely thought-out orders, "Run, Crazy Moose; run for your life! Head for the hollow log; we can't make the river!"

With no undo delay, into the log they swept at what seemed to be the speed of light. In the process, although in a near panic, Lightning Bolt, without conscious thought, had picked up the honeycomb as he ran past and brought it into the hollow log with them. This had an infuriating effect upon the ordinarily good-natured bear who, it must be said, in the best of times had a way about him that said, "Leave me alone!"

Thus Brother Bear, without any preliminaries, began an assault on the log that could be heard several thousand paces away. Experiencing near terror, Lightning Bolt made a firm resolution to himself. "Oh, Great Spirit! Great Father, please spare us from this horror and I swear by the graves of my ancestors that I shall never try to deprive bees of their honey in this place again." Remarkably, even at this time of great anxiety, in order to protect his obsession to gather honey in the future from other sites, he had the foresight not to make his promise to the Great Spirit all-inclusive.

Being the natural-born leader that he was, Lightning Bolt soon calmed down, began to take the measure of the problem and devise a solution. After deducing that their safety was not in any immediate peril, he calmed himself more and sought to reassure his friend. "Calm down, my brother, we're safe! Our hollow log is a safe haven because it's a dead old oak tree; consequently it's as tough as stone. But, although safe for the present, we can't stay here forever; we must find a way to escape because our friend out there isn't very happy and in such an ugly mood he isn't going to leave us alone until he gets satisfaction."

After a few moments and a jolt, Lightning Bolt said, "Hey, Crazy Moose, my brother, wasn't that a mighty swat he just gave our log, it must have moved it at least two paces. Here, have a piece of honey."

"Lightning Bolt, my brother, my friend. How in the name of our beloved ancestors can you eat honey at a time like this?"

"Easy, my friend, I love the stuff. Take it easy, have a piece and accept the fact that we're safe. There now, don't you feel better? Now let's make some plans for getting out of here. I think we can manage to do so if we break the honeycomb into four pieces and share it with Brother Bear."

Another larger jolt, and Lightning Bolt said, "Wow, when he walloped our log that time it must have moved at least three paces. All right Crazy Moose, I have the honeycomb broken; when I say go, throw a piece towards the bear."

But at the same moment Lightning Bolt issued the order to throw, Brother Bear gave the log an extra mighty swat and sent it rolling bumpily downhill towards the river. In a panic, Crazy Moose threw the piece of honeycomb anyway. Fearing that his treat was escaping him, Brother Bear failed to see it and took off in hot pursuit of the log. He, without hesitation, and with a single-minded determination to share in the honey spoils, followed the log into the river and climbed aboard it as it began to float downstream. Lightning Bolt, after surfacing from several anxious moments underwater inside the log, began to view the situation with some alarm. In near desperation he made a plan to dislodge the bear.

"Crazy Moose, I want you to hold onto my feet tightly as I go partly out of the log. While out there I'm going to try to put a piece of honeycomb in front of Brother Bear and pray that he goes for it. If he does, he may head for shore and leave us alone. If not, may the Great Spirit help us!"

Then, with desperation motivating him, and with Crazy Moose clutching onto his trembling legs, Lightning Bolt inched his way up to the end of the log. But with the shift in weight the end Lightning Bolt was heading towards began to submerge. This forced him to move faster. With a resolution born of a desire to survive, he quickly pulled his torso halfway out of the log and thrust the piece of honeycomb almost directly into the bear's mouth. Then, just as quickly, he scurried back into the log. For what seemed like eternity, Brother Bear's weight remained on the log, then was gone.

The boys crawled out of their haven to survey the situation and saw their friend swimming easily to shore with his prize. "Ah, free and safe at last!" they chimed.

Giving strength to the belief that disaster follows disaster, from behind they heard a deafening roar. Quickly turning toward the sound, they discovered that they were heading directly into white rapids.

Lightning Bolt saw Crazy Moose display panic and make ready to jump off the log. He managed to grab him and reassure him, "Stay on the log, my brother, we're safe here! Just hold on. We should be able to ride out the rapids without a problem." By acting so quickly he saved his friend's life.

After a short and exciting ride over the rapids, which stretched no more than a thousand paces, the boys once again found themselves in calm waters. They swam to shore, dried their clothes and recouped the strength they had lost from the rigours of their adventure.

That night, sitting by a warm campfire, eating honey from the two pieces of honeycomb saved, Crazy Moose asked his friend: "Tell me, my brother, I know you love honey, it seems beyond all reason. If Brother Bear had missed the piece of honeycomb you gave him, then afterwards missed the piece I had, as last resort would you have given him the last piece, yours?"

"I don't know, my brother, I honestly don't know."

Later on in life they used their youthful adventures to entertain many of their countrymen around uncountable campfires. The howls of laughter evoked by their tales of misadventure always warmed the hearts of these two friends. Neither of them was ever offended by someone having a laugh at their expense.

❧

During the formative Seasons of a person's life, one is constantly relishing the wonders of new experiences. Thus, Lightning Bolt, before the second Moon of his twelfth Autumn, and during a Hunt with his father, had the exciting and daunting accomplishment of killing his first big game animal.

As they were travelling across a woodland meadow, the hunting party had come upon a magnificent and well-antlered elk that had, as evidenced by his appearance, seen a great many Autumns come and go. Even with the edgy nerves of the novice, Lightning Bolt had aimed well and placed an arrow in a vital spot that brought the animal down almost immediately. The moment of the kill evoked two conflicting emotions in him. At once he felt exhilaration for a feat so well accomplished and a profound sense of regret for having taken a life so esteemed.

Beside a roaring campfire that night he discussed his feelings with Little Bear. "Father, this worries me; I've had problems with killing animals ever since I made my first kill of small game as a young boy. After killing them, I always felt some remorse for my actions. The same thing happened this Sunrise, when I killed the great elk; I felt regret for killing even more intensely."

Little Bear, with a touch of pride in his voice, replied: "My son, my brave son, it warms my heart to no end to hear you say that taking the life of an animal causes you pain. It's an emotion I've also experienced ever since I brought down my first kill. In fact, it's something experienced by all good hunters. It probably will never go away. But, if you always remember that the Great Spirit created these creatures to serve the needs of the People it will ease it somewhat. Killing them for food and clothing can be done with a clear conscience. However, if you ever kill for fun, you should hang your head in shame, for your action offends the laws of the Great Spirit."

"Thank you, my father, your wisdom as always lifts the mist from problems troubling me."

That Lightning Bolt took heart from his father's words was evident by his accomplishments afterward. By the age of fourteen, he had several kills of large game under his belt and was considered by his peers and adults in the community to be a very promising young warrior. To this point in life, except for some self-doubts, his experiences had been mostly pleasant.

However, with the passage of the Seasons, along with

the fun of growing up, harsh realities must at some point be faced. It was during one such time that his father, with not a little heaviness of heart, asked Lightning Bolt to sit down with him. This was during the second Sunrise of Spring, during the sunrises when Little Bear saw his son was ready to learn another aspect of life among the Mi'kmaq People. Deciding it was time, Little Bear invited his son with a gesture of the hand to attend to his words while sitting around a comfortable campfire.

Little Bear watched his son with closeness and measured his words with care. He told Lightning Bolt about the need of defending oneself, or Nation, and as a last resort that sometimes one must choose to kill a fellow human being in battle. He emphasized that this should only happen under pressing circumstances. He also explained to his son what responsibilities he would face as a young brave, if and when their Nation had to go to war with an aggressive country.

Although repelled by the thought of humans killing other humans in anger, Lightning Bolt was surprised and disappointed to learn that he and his peers would not be permitted, because of their age, to join in battle should war become necessary, except if it was an instance of dire need. But, he was somewhat mollified to learn that under the command of experienced warriors they would be expected to be part of the home guard left behind to protect the community from enemy raids during the absence of most of the men. The boys of the community viewed their potential war duties on the home front with great pride.

Being on the verge of manhood, at fourteen Springtimes, Lightning Bolt's societal responsibilities increased substantially. The humble and dignified manner in which he accepted these new tasks surprised no one because he had already displayed the courage, humility and sense of responsibility needed for almost any task. His sense of responsibility had developed early. As the oldest child, he had helped his younger siblings learn about life and was very protective of them. He had also shown a well-developed sense of respect and devotion for his peers and for other members of the community.

In later Seasons, Lightning Bolt would recall with nostalgia and appreciation the many wonderful memories of his youth — his first successful Hunt, canoe trips, winning prizes at physical contact sports. But the memories from his childhood that were most profound and would provide him with the most pleasure were those times when he felt the love, devotion and dedication shown to him by his parents and Elders. These memories guided him through youth and gave him much consolation as an adult.

He appreciated that the Great Spirit had blessed him many times over by giving him a family life that was filled with tranquility and peace. His devoted parents had taught him and his siblings how to accept and manage the responsibilities of life with enthusiasm and care.

All in all they were outstanding parents. During the many ups and downs associated with raising children, never once had they showed any resentment for the time they had to set aside for their children. Throughout his life, Lightning Bolt always emulated this unselfish love, respect and devotion. Little Bear and Early Blossom's example was deeply embedded in their children's hearts and minds and was a guiding source of strength for Lightning Bolt in the seasons ahead.

THE THREAT OF WAR

With the coming of Spring, unbeknownst to the Mi'kmaq and their allies, the worth of their alliances was about to be tested. War was on the horizon. Threatening warfare to influence the outcome of Nation to Nation negotiation was not an option used by the Mi'kmaq until all peaceful alternatives had been explored and exhausted. Even then, it was used only with the greatest reluctance. This deeply ingrained aversion to war came from the civility and respect for human life, instilled in them by learning, and holding in high esteem, the democratic tenets of their culture. Also, like most humans, the vast majority were in no hurry to face death. In fact, the Great Spirit willing, they wanted to live long and enjoy happy lives before joining their beloved ancestors in the Land of Souls.

The seven Mi'kmaq Nations, a large and powerful group of fraternal Nations spread out over a large land area, had in ancient Seasons formed a mutual defence organization capable of raising a mighty army of warriors. This army had the capacity to chastise, punish and repulse any enemy. Prior to forming the Grand Council of the Mi'kmaq, any one of these seven Nations, when suitably aroused, could raise an army powerful enough to pose a formidable threat to a potential aggressor; when combined they were practically unbeatable. One rarely bites one who can bite back hard, and almost assuredly fatally.

Although the alliance was exclusive to the Mi'kmaq Nations, whose seven leaders comprised its council, the Chiefs often permitted leaders of allied Nations to sit in on their deliberations. Most of those who were permitted came from the Wabanaki Confederacy, an alliance the Mi'kmaq countries had formed with most of their smaller eastern neighbours. Both alliances had their allotted spheres of influence and were much valued by their citizens for the protection and services provided.

In the case of the Grand Council, besides defence, it provided a forum where the Mi'kmaq Nations came together to discuss political and social problems of mutual concern. Created as an advisory body, the council had no authority to impose or implement decisions. Thus, before any decision it made could take effect in a member country, it had to be ratified by that country's own council and approved by its People.

To activate the mutual defence agreement of the Grand Council, a country under enemy attack had to request a council meeting held at the earliest possible Moon. On the appointed Sunrise, the aggrieved party or parties brought the details of their problems before the council to request military aid or other forms of assistance.

The Wabanaki Confederacy was not as structured as the Grand Council. Mutual defence was its prime reason for existence. However, from time to time, it was also used by member Nations to come together for discussion of international issues not related to war, such as a forum to settle disputes among them. Its member Nations, although close friends, had many cultural differences, including distinctive languages. But they also had many similarities. For instance, the rituals used for pipe smoking and Sweet-grass Ceremonies were almost identical throughout the lands of the Confederacy. Due to the brotherly regard these Nations had for each other, their citizens were able to socialize freely and mixed Tribal marriages were common. Related to this mutual regard, at ceremonies and celebrations throughout member countries it was common to hear many languages being spoken.

Mi'kmaq Elders had the responsibility of teaching new generations when, how and why the Confederacy was created. They had a very short story to use for the purpose:

"Back in ancient Sunrises the small Eastern Nations, because they weren't capable of defending themselves, were being constantly invaded and robbed by the larger Western Nations. The Westerners appropriated the Easterner's food reserves and other personal property as spoils of war. This left the Easterners poor and hungry. The Mi'kmaq, who had many relatives and friends among the Easterners, finally had enough and decided to put a stop to it. They didn't envision that it would be a hard thing to accomplish because our Nation's armies were more powerful than the Western armies and if they attacked us we would easily defeat them.

"To accomplish their goal, our leaders started the Wabanaki Confederacy, which was strictly a defence alliance that would enforce this rule; an attack on one was to be considered an attack on all. They asked the Easterners to join and they happily agreed. The terms of the agreement were worked out and then it was ratified.

"The Western Nations were advised by runner of the new alliance and its purpose. They, now knowing that an attack on the Eastern Nations would bring the Mi'kmaq Nations to their defence, stopped attacking them. Our Nations can be proud of this accomplishment. It's a demonstration of our humanity at *its best. We've also benefitted from the agreement. For instance, when their armies are combined with ours it forms an even more formidable defence umbrella that a belligerent Nation only challenges at its peril."*

If a member Nation attacked another without a valid reason, the mutual defence provisions of either alliance were not automatically activated. In fact, if it was proven that the member Nation engaged in battle did so without reason, its membership in either alliance was revoked. But not one had ever been evicted.

//

CHAPTER TWO

Lightning Bolt, during the last Moon of his twentieth Spring, was visiting and chatting with his father, who was now Village Chief, when a runner arrived, carrying an urgent message from Grand Chief Big Elk — who was also National Chief of Sipekne'katik — detailing a war situation developing in Kespek. The messenger related that Big Beaver, Kespek's Chief, had advised that twenty Sunrises before the last Moon of Spring, while the People still slept, warriors from several Western Nations had launched an attack on Chief Running Fox's village, causing many causalities and much destruction. The location of the sacked village was near the headwaters of the Great Salmon River. The attack was followed within Sunrises by several other random raids, the forerunner of an all-out invasion of Kespek, setting the stage for Lightning Bolt to taste the bitterness of bloody conflict between men.

Lightning Bolt told his father, "I think Kespek can handle the situation without any aid from our country. After all, they've repulsed similar attacks and thoroughly punished attacking Nations before."

Lightning Bolt was wrong. While he was relating his opinion to his father, the better prepared Western armies were attacking and terrorizing many Kespekian villages.

The Kespekian war report detailing these outrages, which would assure the future involvement of Lightning Bolt's District, Kespukwitk, in Kespek's bloody battles, arrived eighteen Sunrises after the first Moon of Summer. A weary runner delivered the oral report from the chairman of the Grand Council, Grand Chief Big Elk, to Kespukwitk's leader, Chief Big Timber.

The message was short and to the point. The Grand Chief had received a message from Big Beaver requesting that he call an emergency meeting of the Grand Council at the earliest possible Sunrise. Big Beaver wanted to relate how his country had come under full attack from the Western Nations and make an urgent request for military assistance. The meeting, which was expanded to a joint Grand Council–Wabanaki meeting, was set for ten Sunrises before the last Moon of Summer.

Lightning Bolt, Crazy Moose and hundreds of other warriors accompanied Village Chiefs and Elders for their protection. Protection was necessary because of an ever-increasing number of reports of sightings of enemy scouting parties throughout Mi'kmaq and allied Nations. It would not help the war cause to see one of their leaders killed, or worse, taken prisoner. The latter would provide the enemy with a huge psychological boost. The Chiefs, their anger over the unprovoked attacks reaching seething levels, were determined that the Western leaders would not be given any such help without first paying a heavy price.

Five Mi'kmaq Nation Chiefs and most of their Wabanaki counterparts arrived in Grand Chief Big Elk's Sipekne'katik village during the few Sunrises before the meeting's opening. However, Big Beaver, because he was delayed making many urgent decisions related to the war, looking exhausted from his hasty trip, arrived as dawn was breaking on the Sunrise of the joint meeting.

Immediately after he and his travelling companions had been made welcome and given a hearty breakfast, the meeting was convened by Grand Chief Big Elk. In acknowledgment of their respect for a higher power, he called upon Swift Eagle, the senior Elder of the community, to lead a talk with the Great Spirit before deliberations began.

Swift Eagle asked the People to stand and raise their hands with him to the Land of Souls to thank and praise the Creator for his benevolence and to implore Him to help the Chiefs make wise decisions. The prayers were followed by traditional Sweet-grass and Tobacco Ceremonies. Then the Chiefs got down to the somber task at hand.

Grand Chief Big Elk opened the meeting for deliberations with, "Big Beaver, please relate the war news, then we'll discuss a plan of action."

"Thank you, Big Elk, my esteemed noble friend, for arranging and convening this meeting so quickly. And, from the bottom of my heart, my brothers, I thank you a thousand times over for coming at such short notice. Under normal circumstances I wouldn't dream of disturbing your peace and tranquility, but the events that caused me to request this meeting are not normal; disaster is a more fitting description for it.

"Brothers, the aggression against my country that I'm about to detail is serious enough that if left unchecked it will very probably end the freedom of all our Peoples for uncountable Moons to come. The reason I make such a chilling prediction is that the war situation in my country is so bad that I'm hard pressed to find adequate words to describe it. The Western Nations, because they are so well armed and prepared, are running rampant. They must have been planning on invading our country for many Seasons.

"With grief in my heart, I will now, for clarity purposes, give a short overview of the unprovoked attacks against my country that have caused us to convene here this Sunrise. The first, as most of you are now well aware, occurred twenty Sunrises before the last Moon of Spring. Without any fore-warning or provocation a small war party of Western warriors attacked Chief Running Fox's village and killed a great many people.

"Before they began withdrawing towards their home ter-ritories they set a great many wigwams on fire and destroyed the personal belongings of survivors. They took many of our People prisoners.

"Fortunately for the well-being of our kinsmen that were taken as prisoners, when the news of the raid spread to surrounding communities their leaders hastily raised a large party of warriors and set off in pursuit. They caught up with the enemy before they crossed into their own territory, engaging them on two occasions. During these clashes our People escaped from custody and our warriors managed to take several of their warriors prisoners.

"The objective of the attack, revealed by the Western prisoners under intense interrogation, was to assess our preparedness and capability of defending our Nation. The captives also revealed a rumour circulating in their countries that a full-scale war was set to be launched against Kespek by the Western Nations within a few Moons.

"By weaving together other tidbits of information gleaned

from interrogating the prisoners, we have concluded with near certainty that their first objective is to overrun and subjugate our country. After consolidating their positions they will move against your countries with the ultimate goal being to win complete domination over all Mi'kmaq and allied territory.

"We have delivered a message to the aggressors that our will to oppose foreign aggression is intact. However, the fact is that we are ill-equipped to respond. In shame my friends I have to report, based on the information supplied by the captives, that the enemy is well aware of how we have let complacency lull us into a false sense of security. We have failed, without excuse, to keep prepared for action our tools of war needed to defend our Nations." After filling in more details Big Beaver responded to questions about the war data he had related so far.

Chief Little Eagle of Eskikewa'kik asked, "My brother, I have three questions: did the prisoners give any estimate of how many warriors were being mustered by the Westerners? Is there any truth to the rumour that they are killing a great many civilians? And what is the extent of the invasion?"

"My brother Little Eagle, there probably are as many as twenty thousand warriors involved. To your second question the answer is yes, many civilians are being killed and brutalized, many taken prisoner and many of our villages have been burned. This has resulted in panic spreading among the People. Many Elders, women and children are abandoning their homes and seeking refuge in my village."

After fielding several other similar questions Big Beaver continued, "My brothers, our situation has gone from grave to desperate. One Moon after the first attack, and in addition to several other smaller attacks, the Western Nations invaded in force. And, early this Sunrise, before we arrived, a runner from War Chief Mighty Water informed me that the enemy has taken effective control of over a quarter of our territory.

"Their assault is so intense that our forces are being pushed back rapidly on all fronts with very heavy causalities. To try to reverse their successes, we're recruiting and sending more warriors into action and will, if possible, mount a counter-offensive. However, at this point they seem unstoppable.

"As an indication of how well prepared they are, their offensive is being carried out with the same ease a good hunter displays when tracking his prey. Their attacks appear to be so well planned and coordinated, that their objective to quickly overrun Kespek and then on to their next target seems perfectly feasible. The situation is so bad that without the immediate infusion of major assistance from your countries I predict that Kespek will fall within the next four Moons. I'm sorry to report that we were unable to determine from the prisoners which Mi'kmaq or Allied country is next.

"My friends, if we are to demolish the dreams of the Western leaders to make us their inferiors, we must undertake a united effort to contain and reverse their invasion of my country very quickly. Undue delay will cost additional lives and may result in our universal defeat. Should this happen, it will be all but impossible to remove them from the land that the Great Spirit has permitted us to live on for uncountable Sunrises.

"The danger is great. In recognition of it, many Eastern Nations represented here this Sunrise have already sent in warriors to help, but their assistance is only enough to slow the tide. Therefore, my brothers, I beseech you to come to our aid and muster a great army to accomplish two things: expel the Westerners from Kespek and eliminate forever the threat they pose for the citizens of our countries. They must be informed emphatically, by the might of our collective will and numbers, that peace is their only salvation.

"Thank you my brothers. I await your decisions with much hope in my heart. My esteemed brother, Big Elk, I thank you for permitting me the honour of addressing our brothers."

"Big Beaver, my brother, your news fills my heart with great sadness. My outrage is so intense that I can barely find words to express it. My brother, the valiant efforts made by your courageous warriors, during the past Moons, to try to repulse the Western warriors in the face of such formidable odds, is truly commendable. Your brave and beloved countrymen have my heartfelt sympathy.

"Oh, my brothers, in order to control the anger raging within my soul I need to take a moment to ask the Great Spirit to help me have charity and forgiveness in my heart toward our enemies. Please join me, Dear Father of the Universe, help us, your poor children, to find forgiveness, at this time of great stress in our heart, for the excesses of our enemies."

After a few moments of meditation Grand Chief Big Elk continued, "Big Beaver, you may inform your fellow Kespekian citizens that our country stands firmly with them in these dangerous times. You and they may be assured that everything in our power will be done to free your country. And, from the comments made over the last few Sunrises to me by our colleagues, I can assure you that Kespek will have their unconditional support as well. We have come to this because the war in Kespek is an attack against all Mi'kmaq and Allied Nations and threatens the very survival of our way of life.

"My brother, your belief that the Western Nations were motivated by our weakness is absolutely correct. Because of our lack of foresight, we are collectively responsible for this sad state of affairs and must accept a large part of the blame for the misery being suffered by our brothers and sisters in Kespek because of it. Because of this negligence they've concluded that we're cowards and thus can be defeated without much resistance.

"However, soon they will learn they should never take the Mi'kmaq and Allies for cowards. Our Peoples will quickly overcome the sad state of our defences and we shall preserve our land and freedom.

"This must also be a hard-learned lesson to us. To assure that our Nations never again face such a threat and be put into such mortal danger, we must vow this Sunrise to never again permit our defensive capabilities to lapse into a state of disrepair. The loss of so many of our beloved people in Kespek will always lay heavy on my conscience for our sin of omission. I now pass to Chief Big Timber."

"Thank you, Grand Chief Big Elk, my brother. I also wish to express my absolute outrage in regards to these attacks by the enemy against our brothers and sisters. This is, I can assure you, also the feeling of my countrymen. When they first heard the bloody details about the magnitude and unprovoked nature of the Western assault, they reacted with indignation and revulsion. I can state with near certainty that we will be moving a large army of warriors into Kespek within one Moon. The enemy's aggression shall be brought to a halt and they shall be taught convincingly to court peace forevermore. I pass to Chief Little Eagle."

"My beloved brothers, I concur that we must take responsibility and shoulder much of the shame for this aggression. I have no doubts that we invited attack by being ill-prepared to forcefully respond. To assure that this never happens again I propose that we ask the citizens of our countries to enshrine, as part of the laws of our Nations, this oath to be sworn to by leaders before they assume office:

"'I, before the Great Spirit, do solemnly declare, to prevent foreign aggression that I will take all steps deemed necessary to assure that the defences of our country shall be kept in top condition. I further acknowledge that failure to do so will result in disgrace and loss of office.'"

Without debate or discussion, Little Eagle's proposal was endorsed by the Chiefs.

During the rest of the afternoon the remaining Mi'kmaq and Allied Chiefs offered comments. After all had spoken the meeting was adjourned by Grand Chief Big Elk until the following morning, in order to allow the councils of the other six Mi'kmaq countries and Allied Nations sufficient time to consider Big Beaver's urgent request. Because of the major threat posed by the invasion of Kespek and the fact that its citizens were Mi'kmaq in distress, the result of their deliberations was predictable.

The next morning after reconvening, Big Beaver was informed by all Grand Council members and allies that they had decided to send volunteers to Kespek as soon as possible as an interim measure to slow the advance of the Westerners. He was further informed that to implement their decisions, their War Chiefs had been given instructions to start the process of marshalling volunteers immediately. The Chiefs of Unama'kik and Eskikewa'kik, because of threats to their territories posed by other unfriendly countries, regretfully advised the council that they could only provide modest voluntary contingents. The Chiefs of the Eastern Nations also advised that they would take immediate measures to help.

The Chiefs began to lay their individual plans for getting their countries fully involved in the war effort before the meeting. Chief Big Timber, anticipating that his People would quickly approve full-scale participation in the effort to end the war, informed his peers that he had already instructed Kespukwitk's War Chief, Grey Eagle, to begin to make plans for travel to Kespek's War Chief Mighty Water's headquarters, with a sizeable army for deployment. One by one, after Big Timber's presentation, the other Chiefs presented their preliminary plans of action. It was decided to defer final planning and decision-making to a War Council meeting to be convened as soon as possible at Mighty Water's headquarters in Kespek.

Because of the graveness of the situation, the Chiefs, as soon as they arrived home, sent runners to villages to arrange meetings to discuss with the People the proposals to end the war. Such meetings were required by the laws of the culture, because in the land of the Mi'kmaq, the People were the ones who made the final decisions in matters of this magnitude.

While Kespukwitk's National Chief Big Timber was arranging village meetings, War Chief Grey Eagle sent word to villages in close proximity to the village of Little Bear asking for volunteers. They were instructed to gather in Little Bear's village fifteen Sunrises before the first Moon of Autumn, so that they could depart for Kespek by the following dawn. Volunteers from more distant villages were advised of places they could join up with the main party along the way. By the time of its departure, the volunteer force was equivalent to the strength of a large army contingent.

Lightning Bolt and Crazy Moose, prompted by a deep

sense of indignation and anger over the invasion, were among the first in Little Bear's village to offer their services. The dusk before departure, Lightning Bolt discussed his forthcoming journey into battle with his parents. "When Grey Eagle asked for volunteers to travel with him to Kespek to fight the Westerners, I immediately volunteered without informing you of my intentions. In haste to help, I completely forgot that being considerate of the feelings of others is a most important social responsibility. You have my humble apology for this oversight. It was inconsiderate and inappropriate. The only excuse I can offer is that the war so outrages my moral sense of justice that it caused me to react in a positive manner to the volunteer request without thinking. In any event, I can't wait to get there to help end it."

His mother, to erase his feelings of remorse, responded, "My son, my brave warrior, an apology isn't necessary because what you did is what we fully expected of you. We knew with certainty, from the time we first heard of the atrocities being committed in Kespek, that it would fill you with a sense of indignation and outrage that would compel you to volunteer. My precious son, your volunteering to serve a great cause was expected and we know it was done with a very generous heart."

Little Bear added, "My heart, my brave son, is filled with love for you and for all the other young men who have so selflessly volunteered for war duty. This demonstrates that you and they have a firm belief in the righteousness of the noble cause for which many of you may give up your lives.

"Kespek's agony, my son, must be in good conscience ended. It will take time but I know in my heart you and your fellow brave warriors shall eventually evict the attackers. You deserve nothing but praise for what you did. Fear not, you did not hurt our feelings. Indeed the quick response to the call to arms by our warriors makes me feel very confident and secure about the preservation of the values of our way of life. The young people must be complimented about how well they learned to be staunch defenders of liberty, justice and equality. This commitment by successive generations to protect and preserve our country's democratic tenets is the key to its survival. I'm sure that our ancestors in the Land of Souls are very proud of the commitment by their descendants to the perpetuation of their remarkable handiwork.

"For the democracy they created for the enjoyment of their children's children, we must never forget to be thankful. When I talk to the Creator, every Sunrise, I always thank Him for providing our ancestors with the wisdom to accomplish what they did. The excellence of their work is no better stated than by the unselfish willingness of their descendants to defend it with their lives and thus preserve it for the enjoyment of future generations.

"My beloved son, when I embark on this subject I'm like a fiery old comet streaking across the sky; I go on forever. Before I stop, I want you to know that I shall pray and ask the Great Spirit every Sunrise to protect you and all the other brave men that will be fighting beside you, and ask that if possible He permit you all to return home safely. During the trials that lie ahead, if you ever begin to despair of them, remember that we're with you in spirit. And so is the Creator.

"My son, I love you dearly. At times such as this, when a child is leaving home to encounter danger, a father realizes he has neglected to say this enough times. To rectify this omission I want to restate what I just said, from the depths of my heart: I love you dearly. Please carry that always with you in your travels. I know in my heart that you shall be honourable and above reproach in battle, and when needed, be forgiving of your enemies. I also feel strongly that the Father of the Universe shall see you safely home."

With tears in his eyes Lightning Bolt responded, "My honoured Father, I thank you warmly for your words of love and confidence. It warms my heart to hear you say what I already know, that I have the good fortune to have the undying love of my wonderful parents. It will comfort me constantly during the uncertain Sunrises ahead.

"Now, my beloved Mother and Father, it's my turn. I want you both to hear this, because it may be the will of the Great Spirit that I not return to your warm embraces, that for everything you've ever done for me in life, I thank you. You have proven your love for me a thousand times over with your dedication to my well-being. I love you both dearly and shall miss you constantly during the Sunrises ahead.

"While away, my beloved parents, I shall dream that perhaps at a future Sunrise, partings of people who love each other dearly such as us, because of war, will be only memories. It can happen! When men learn to respect life and use their intelligence to promote the common good of all People, rather than using it to seek power, war will end.

"Wars give no one pleasure. The fact that this war will take me away from you for an unknown period of time fills my heart with anger and sorrow. The only thing wars beget is human misery, and all participants lose, even the winner. The damage they do to the soul of nations and their citizens is almost irreparable.

"There isn't any doubt in my mind that this conflict will leave deep marks on both sides. It breaks my heart to know that the many deaths that have already occurred, and shall continue to occur until it's over, will leave empty spots in the hearts of so many decent people. I find no solace in knowing that our side has a legitimate and just excuse for taking military action, because I believe that we would not be fighting a war if our leadership had shown more foresight and kept our Nations well prepared for defensive action. What were our leaders thinking when they neglected to keep our Nations well prepared for defensive action? The danger signals were there. The unfriendly conduct of the Western Nations over the Moons alone was ample warning that they were not to be trusted. I don't think anyone needed an eye into the future to know that they had designs upon our lands.

"This is verified by the number of times they have over the past few decades conducted unprovoked raids into our territories, then pretended that the culprits were bandits outside of their control. Why our leaders kept hoping that their words of reconciliation, which they offered so readily after each incident, indicated that they would change, is beyond me.

"My beloved parents, when I look at our situation through the eyes of the enemy I can only conclude that we must have appeared to them like ripe fruit ready for picking. Our willingness to forgive their aggression as the acts of individuals, which they were not able to control, fortified their belief that we were soft when it came to defending our civilization. From this, it isn't any wonder that they drew the erroneous conclusion that we are cowards and as such would not make the necessary sacrifices to defend ourselves. Displaying weakness to an enemy such as the Westerners is not a virtue. It's suicidal.

"Never again should we permit our defence capabilities to become decrepit. As Chief Little Eagle said at the Grand Council meeting, 'We must never again leave our guard down, for by doing so we encourage a potential enemy to lose his reason and attack us.' I know in my heart, my beloved ones, if a Nation wishes to remain free and live in peace it must always be prepared to go to war to defend its way of life."

His Father replied, "My son, the wisdom of your words is unquestionable. They make a father proud! I can assure you that I too stand fully persuaded to the belief that in unity, strength and preparedness rests peace. The mistake we've made must never be repeated, because the cost of lives is too great."

Lightning Bolt then swore to them that he would use his best effort during his lifetime to help find peace. "I pledge this Sunrise to you, two of the people whom I love most dearly on Mother Earth, that I shall devote the rest of my life to promoting peace through strength. If during my lifetime there develops a tendency to let down our guard, I shall be the first to tell the People that we court disaster."

Impressed by the sincerity of his son's words, Little Bear replied, "The wisdom of your words this evening convinces me that you will do it some Sunrise. But now, as it's getting late and we have to get up well before dawn, it's time to go to bed."

"Are my brothers and sisters getting up to see us off?"

"Yes. Everybody in the village will be getting up to see their loved ones off. Many, especially the younger ones, with lots of sleep in their eyes. I can see it now, small children staggering and stumbling around half-asleep, only half-recognizing the beloved brothers and friends they're wishing a safe return."

"My dearest Mother and Father, I don't feel that it's going to do any good to ask you not to worry while I'm gone, but I feel I must ask anyway."

With a serious face, his Mother responded, "My son, there are no assurances that anyone can give a mother that will ease her mind in times such as this. Until I see a canoe come over the horizon bringing you safely home and unharmed, I can assure you, my precious baby, I shall worry."

Early the next morning, with sadness in their hearts, Little Bear, Early Blossom, their children and neighbours all watched as their beloved sons rowed off into the darkness of the bay to meet their destiny in far-off Kespek. They knew in their hearts, although they maintained an air of cheerfulness, that they had seen many of their relatives and friends alive and well for the last time.

The warriors, as they rowed out of sight, although already missing their loved ones, were full of expectation and excitement. Even the travel route to Kespek, selected by the leaders, offered an exciting diversion. It included traversing over some land, but most of it would be by canoe over sea, river and lake. The leaders told them that the trip, under ideal conditions, would take approximately twenty Sunrises. The boys saw this as a challenge and decided to try to knock off approximately three Sunrises and do it in seventeen. In fact, it took them eighteen.

Upon arrival in Kespek, the warriors were greeted by the impressive sight of several thousand warriors making preparations for war. Mighty Water, Kespek's War Chief, and peers from the allied Nations held many planning councils during the ensuing Sunrises to map out strategy for the deployment of warriors on the field of battle.

To help implement their plan, the War Chiefs selected many young warriors who had already displayed leadership abilities, including Lightning Bolt, to lead small groups of warriors. With this detail taken care of, deployment began.

Meanwhile, unknown to the volunteers from Kespukwitk, their brothers and sisters back home had given Chief Big Timber's request for a declaration of war speedy and almost unanimous approval. Approval had been given so swiftly and enthusiastically that within half a Moon a large contingent of warriors had been assembled, equipped and supplied to follow the volunteers to the warfront.

These men and their allied comrades constituted the visible heroes. However, in carrying out a war, there are many unsung heroes, particularly those who put themselves in jeopardy behind enemy lines to gather information about enemy movement, numbers and so on. Their inputs are crucial to the efforts of those mapping out effective long-term war strategy. The allied war effort was helped by those carefully selected warriors involved in the intelligence-gathering system, which War Chief Mighty Water had set up a few Sunrises after the first attacks. Positioned around strategic areas inside enemy territory, the intelligence supplied by these heroes was invaluable to the cause.

Just how critical to the success of the Allied war effort these individuals were was demonstrated two Sunrises after the arrival of Kespukwitk's warriors. Several scouts sent reports that they had seen a formidable force of Western warriors travelling down the River That Drains the Big Lakes towards Kespek by canoe.

This critical information provided time for Mighty Water to devise a plan to nullify the Westerners' long-term intention, which, he correctly deduced, was to eventually link up with their warriors already occupying large tracts of Kespek. He proceeded to make plans with this in mind. He knew if such a linkup occurred, the battle to eject them from his country would be much more difficult and longer, and would cost hundreds of additional lives. To assure that did not happen and, being a polite man, to greet them properly, Mighty Water deployed a large contingent of warriors in a prime riverbank location with instructions to hit the enemy hard and fast as they disembarked from their canoes. He fully appreciated that winning the coming battle was of vital importance.

Before the Sunrise of the morning of the strategic battle, in keeping with long-established traditions, the opposing Nations sent emissaries out to meet and arrange a conference between the Head War Chiefs to explore the feasibility of a truce. The allies were hoping for an end to the carnage but the Westerners viewed the meeting as an opportunity to regroup and prepare. Within a few Sunrises a meeting of War Chiefs was arranged and convened. After the opening ceremonies were completed, Roaring Rapids, the Head War Chief of the Western Nations, the eldest, spoke first.

"Mighty Water, my friend, I wish to inform you my brother that my heart is heavy because of the loss of life this war has caused your People. Our compassionate, kind, humanitarian leaders are full of remorse for any hurt they may have inadvertently caused anyone because of their need to take military action against your country. But, as you well know, we were forced into taking such drastic action by the illegal incursions into our territory by Kespekian renegades. We don't fault your councils for being unable to stop these outrages because we know this was caused by the vastness of the territory that they try to police with inadequate forces. This unfortunate and regrettable state of affairs is the root cause of your People's grief, pain and sorrow.

"However, my brother, now that we have forcefully removed the troublemakers from along our common borders and assumed your policing responsibilities in problem areas, we view things to be under control. Therefore, in good conscience, we firmly believe that constructive peace talks between us can now take place. With this in mind, and as a demonstration of our sincerity, we've decided with generous hearts to make an offer for peace that your country, in view of its present circumstances, should find very equitable and just. Above all it will alleviate the distress that you, our friends, are suffering.

"My brother, in view of the fact that your situation shatters our hearts and pains us beyond words, with humble hearts and the utmost compassion, we pledge to agree to lay down our arms and live in peaceful coexistence with you forever, providing that the leaders of your Nation agree that they have more land than they can responsibly manage and cedes the troubled areas that we have already pacified to us."

Many among the allied contingent sat in stunned disbelief at Roaring Rapids' unmitigated gall.

He continued his incredible recital, "My brother, our compassionate offer to accept these areas will provide border stability and solve your land management and policing problems for all time. As you can gather from the generosity of this offer, the leaders of our Nations have nothing but the best interests of the People of Kespek at heart. They truly desire to arrange an honourable and just peace with your country. May we have, my brother, your response to our compassionate and generous offer?"

Not a person to be knocked off course, nor shocked by anything he heard, Mighty Water calmly responded to the outrageous proposal. "Roaring Rapids, my true brother, seldom in my life has my heart been so touched by the compassion, generosity and kindness of others. To know that your great leaders love us so much that they are willing to make such a generous sacrifice on our behalf is truly heartwarming. It soothes me to know that they are so willing to remove from our shoulders the responsibility of controlling and managing a large tract of the land that the Great Spirit permits us to use. It is a sign that they are endowed with kindness and generosity beyond comparison. Your leaders are truly men of good will and blessed with much wisdom.

"Oh, my dear brother, in the face of the humbleness and generosity displayed by your great leaders in their offer, I'm almost overwhelmed. But, with a heavy heart, I must inform you that it would be deemed by the Great Spirit as an act of selfishness and unkindness beyond description for us to burden your kind, humble and generous leaders with the problem of controlling and managing the portion of our land which has proven to be so unmanageable in the past for us, from your viewpoint.

"Therefore, my true friend, please inform them that it grieves me beyond description to refuse an offer that I know was made with kind hearts. But, I truly believe that the Great Spirit would never forgive us if we were unkind and burdened your humble and generous leaders with our problems."

"Mighty Water," Roaring Rapids said. "My dear brother, I hear the kindness in your words and humbly accept and acknowledge the fact that you cannot bring yourself to burden us with additional problems." The Chiefs, after going through the other civilities demanded by protocol, ended the meeting with the continuation of war assured.

Having confirmed what he already knew, Big Beaver instructed the armies of Kespek and its allies to make an all-out effort to get the Western Nations interested in peace. With the die cast for more war, three Sunrises later, after making their peace with the Great Spirit, the allied warriors engaged the enemy in battle. At first, because the Western warriors had come across the river further upstream than expected, thus denying the Wabanaki warriors the opportunity to take them by surprise, the battle was going badly for the allies. However, with the extraordinary courage and effort displayed by such individuals as Lightning Bolt, they took heart and began to turn matters around. In fact, it became a rout. By the time the sun was halfway to the horizon they were forcefully driving the enemy back towards the big river and victory was soon theirs.

Many allied heroes emerged from the war, but the courageous effort of one of their number was adjudged exceptional by both his peers and leaders. During the heat of his first battle, in total disregard for his own well-being, Lightning Bolt single-handedly fought off and killed many enemy warriors, often while they were in the process of trying to snuff out the lives of one or more of his comrades. The men who owed their lives to his intervention numbered in the dozens.

His performance that Sunrise, as related by his peers, was so outstanding it became almost instant legend. Because of the magnitude of his bravery and valour, it was destined to be talked about with awe around many a campfire for generations.

Lightning Bolt didn't take much pride in his actions. The words he exchanged with Crazy Moose by the campfire that night were laced with remorse. "Crazy Moose, my brother, I feel so very sad about the loss of so many men today, that I want to weep. Perhaps if I'd been more resourceful, many of their deaths could have been prevented."

Trying to give him cause for cheer, Crazy Moose replied, "Lightning Bolt, my beloved brother, I saw you perform miracles in battle. Your acts of bravery were almost supernatural and were awesome to friend and foe alike. Because of your exceptional gift for hand-to-hand combat, many deaths of comrades were prevented. Your efforts saved many from certain death; for this they shall be forever in your debt."

But Lightning Bolt wasn't to be swayed. "Please, my dear brother, don't flatter me, I'm not worthy of it. There are others who deserve praise far more than me. For instance, you did more than your fair share to turn the tide of battle. Without your inspiration and presence, I would have been without support and lost."

Crazy Moose responded to the self-deprecating comments emphatically. "No, my brother, you were my inspiration. You fought with the ability of at least ten men, well witnessed by the four enemy warriors you sent to the Land of Souls. If not for your outstanding effort, the battle may well have been lost. Your leadership this Sunrise, my friend, clearly demonstrates that when it comes to fighting an enemy, you are without equal."

In response Lightning Bolt bared his soul. "Well, my dear brother, I guess we will have to agree to disagree about this because I firmly believe that others, including you, exceeded my humble efforts. You must remember, my brother, before you award me so much credit, that battles are won by the combined efforts of many men not just one. For example, a multitude of brave men fought valiantly this Sunrise and won a strategic battle that will probably change the course of the war in our favour. If not for them the army we defeated would now be well on its way to dealing our cause a perhaps-mortal blow by linking up with the main body of occupiers. I was only a small part of the action. Our combined efforts were the reason we won.

"And, in regards to the four men I killed, I take no pride from it. The death of these brave souls gives me no satisfaction whatsoever. In fact, for the loss of them and their soon to be heartbroken families, I truly grieve. They fought bravely and died for nothing except the sad desire of their leaders to acquire land and control over others. May the Great Spirit welcome them home to the Land of Souls.

"When you consider it, it's so sad that they had to die for such an ignoble cause. The men who lead the Western Nations caused their deaths. There is no justification for what they've done. They certainly can't use an excuse such as needing more land to help feed their People, because they already have enough land to last their People for thousands of Moons

"My fondest hope, my dear brother, is that we always will remain vigilant and wise enough to prevent the sickness that motivates their leaders and warps their minds, from ever afflicting our civilization. The envy and greed they nurture are the root cause of all the troubles of mankind. It breeds many evils. And, without question, the worst that stems from it is war. The heartbreak for Peoples victimized by wars is unimaginable. This was certainly true for me. Before this Sunrise, I could only imagine what it would be like to see a man perish at another man's hands. I imagined it would be horrific, but in reality it is far worse. Pitting man against man to brutally cut one another down is truly a senseless thing.

"No one, my friend, should ever take pride in causing the deaths of fellow human beings. The men I killed in battle this Sunrise will forever be on my conscience. This is so even in the knowledge that our cause is just."

Crazy Moose draped his arm over the shoulders of his friend and they sat in silent contemplation for a long time.

CS

Following the victory of the battle of the River That Drains the Big Lakes, the allied forces rallied with their confidence reinforced. They became more determined than ever to eject the invaders in the shortest time possible. This objective was moved along considerably by the arrival of multitudes of reinforcements from the homefronts. The allied offensive soon became unstoppable.

By late Spring, the Western armies were driven out of Kespek and were being hotly pursued into their own territories. However, hoping for a miracle to reverse the tide in their favour, the enemy leadership did not sue for peace until their defeat was virtually assured. Only when the complete occupation of all their Western territories was no more than a few Moons away did they admit the need for talks to abate their demise. Completely humiliated, they finally sent out emissaries to Mighty Water's encampment to ask for peace talks.

The Western emissaries arrived at Mighty Water's encampment, located on the shores of beautiful Lake Loon, deep within Mi'kmaq territory, just before sunset, three Sunrises after the last Moon of Spring. The next Sunrise, shortly after dawn, following ceremonial rituals, the War Chiefs sat down for discussions. Mighty Water, deferred to by the Elder Roaring Rapids, opened the discourse with the utmost civility.

"Roaring Rapids, my brother," he said. "It's a treat for my poor eyes to see you once more. Since our short visit last Autumn, I've spent many moments wondering when I would have the happy experience of visiting with you again. Therefore, I must say that when you requested an opportunity to come to our camp and chat with an old friend it was truly my pleasure to agree."

Roaring Rapids responded in kind, "Mighty Water, my brother, my friend. I too have missed the pleasure of seeing and talking with you. It's unforgivable that old friends allow so much time to pass before renewing brotherly friendships. We must endeavour, my brother, to ensure that it doesn't happen again."

Mighty Water then got to the point, "Your words, my brother, are like the music of songbirds to my humble ears. I will make every effort to ensure that in the future we have more opportunities to meet and renew our brotherly relationship. But now my friend it's time to get down to the business at hand. What say you now, my friend, about our land management problems?"

Not missing a beat, nor projecting any sign of the pressure he was under, and with a tinge of irony, Roaring Rapids replied, "The last time we met, because of the difficulties Kespek was experiencing in this endeavour, I made an offer to take over and manage some of your territory for you. Now it seems your leaders have taught themselves so well how to manage your territory properly that they may be in a position to manage some of ours also. My brother, give me your views about this."

Being always the refined gentleman, Mighty Water sympathized with the Westerners, then made a gesture of kindness, "Roaring Rapids, my friend, brothers must come to the aid of each other in times of need. This may seem mean and stingy to you, but we don't want to permanently manage your land for you. However, we will help your leaders overcome their newly acquired territorial-management problems by sending advisors to help them for an interim period. It's truly regrettable that we can't do more my friend and I apologize most profusely for it."

Roaring Rapids, accepting the humiliating fact that the Western Nations were destined to be managed by strangers for many Sunrises, responded with resignation. "My brother, I'm truly brokenhearted that you will not be able to find time to stay and manage our land for us indefinitely. However, we, with profuse thanks, accept your generous offer to send advisors to teach us how to better manage neighbourly relations and how to implement a new management style."

Without gloating, but with a granite-like determined resolve, Mighty Water responded, "Dear Roaring Rapids, my friend, my brother, your unconditional acceptance of our offer is most welcome. I want to assure you that sending advisors to teach your leaders a new way to manage their territory will be a great pleasure for us. However, with the greatest reluctance, I must tell you that if at a future time we determine that your leaders haven't learned to manage their lands properly, and to have respect for the right of their neighbours to live in peace and security, we will indeed come in and manage all Western lands permanently. This, my friend, is a promise you can be assured we shall keep."

Without any sign of the rancor he must have felt, Roaring Rapids replied, "My dear brother, you can rest assured that your kind words have not fallen on deaf ears."

Mighty Water then turned the conversation to details. "That's good, my brother," he said. "Now let's talk about how we shall implement the truce and word the Peace Treaty…"

With the armies of the allied Nations occupying a large tract of their territory, the Westerners were in no position to negotiate for anything beyond the unconditional peace dictated to them. Negotiations were completed in short order.

The following terms were submitted to the councils of both sides for ratification:

Agreed,

1. That each side will release unharmed all prisoners captured during the war.
2. That our original borders will constitute each side's territory and that from this Sunrise forward the territorial integrity of both countries shall be respected.
3. That for an unspecified period of time allied advisors shall supervise Western Government.
4. That a mediation committee will be struck to provide a mechanism to settle all future disputes.
5. That the hatchet be buried for all time between the Nations.
6. That suitable presents be exchanged to seal the agreement.
7. That Western war criminals, alleged to have committed atrocities against innocent Kespekian civilians, be turned over to Kespek for punishment.

Both sides speedily assented to the pact. Once again peace reigned supreme throughout the lands of the Mi'kmaq and their allies. Mighty Water and his countrymen, in a show of appreciation for the heroic efforts made by the allied forces to free them, decided to award honorary Kespekian War Chieftainships to allied warriors who had shown extraordinary bravery during the conflict. Lightning Bolt was among those chosen to be so honoured. It was also decided that the presentation ceremony was to be accompanied by a great feast and much partying — a going-home party for the Allied warriors.

In accordance with Mi'kmaq custom, which demanded that one honour and pay respect to the bravery of those who had been met in combat and defeated, the former enemies were also invited to attend. Early morning, two Sunrises later, festivities got under way. It started with thanks being offered to the Great Spirit for His generosity in helping them to restore peace. Then the People turned their attention to celebrating, dancing, chanting, pipe smoking and other entertainments.

As the sun hit its high mark, Chief Big Beaver called a break in festivities and requested that the People gather around for the awards ceremony. After he finished thanking and praising the Allied forces for their selfless help in freeing Kespek, he asked War Chief Mighty Water to begin making awards to the designated warriors. Each honouree was allotted a moment to say a few words after receiving his award.

When Lightning Bolt's turn came, he paid tribute to all those who had fallen during the war, comrades and enemies alike. With humility, he ended, "My brothers and sisters, the brave men who fell during the war, never to warm the arms of their loved ones again, must also be remembered and honoured this Sunrise. They deserve all honours that can be bestowed; therefore my brothers and sisters I accept this award in their memory."

The following Sunrise, Honorary War Chief Lightning Bolt and his countrymen began to assemble their possessions for a triumphant return home. As the need for speedy travel was no longer a consideration, they decided to stop and visit with some of the people in several Mi'kmaq countries along the way. To enable them to do so, a route was selected that would take them across the water to Epekwitk, then to Unama'kik, up the Musquodoboit River in Eskikewa'kik, through Sipekne'katik via the Sipekne'katik River and out to the Basin of High Tides, then home to Kespukwitk. They estimated, with allowances made for visiting, it would take upwards of thirty Sunrises for the party to reach home, just after the second Moon of Autumn, which would allow plenty of time to prepare for the pre-Winter Hunt. With news of the allied victory preceding them, the warriors were greeted by the People as heroes at each stop. They showered them with presents and feted them with parties. Most warriors secretly basked in the glory, but as their upbringing required, they tried to maintain an air of humility and dignity while enjoying the praise.

Lightning Bolt enjoyed the effusive welcomes but also reflected upon his experiences in battle. It left him with no doubts that warfare was an affront to the Great Spirit's laws and to the dignity of humanity. Because of this he re-swore before Him the oath that he had sworn before his father and mother — that he would dedicate his life to finding peaceful solutions to disputes between Peoples and Nations. To begin the task, he also pledged to deal with all Peoples in the future with the utmost courtesy and diplomacy, while keeping a deep regard for the dignity of friends and opponents alike. He became a preacher for peace. In future Seasons, when circumstances beyond their control forced his country and allies to go to war, he fought vigorously and valiantly for the right of his People to remain free, but he never took any joy in ending another human's life.

Although they were enjoying time with the citizens of the countries visited during their homeward trek and the tributes and festivities provided, the warriors were becoming anxious to see their loved ones again. Late in the afternoon of the thirty-second Sunrise of their travels, from out on the waters of the Basin of High Tides, they saw the encampment of District Chief Big Timber. Soon, they could also see gathered along the shore a huge crowd of families and friends who had journeyed from the far reaches of the country to give them a boisterous welcome home.

When they landed, the greetings were thunderous and joyful. Mothers, fathers, brothers, sisters and other relatives and friends embraced them and thanked the Great Spirit for their safe return. Many wept with joy at having their beloved sons once again safely in their arms and many sons wept with joy to be there.

Lightning Bolt's parents and siblings gave him many gifts, including a new outfit, made by his mother and sisters, befitting his new designation as an Honorary War Chief of the Kespek Nation. But no gift surpassed the value of the thing he most desired and missed during his absence, their warm embrace.

To show heartfelt appreciation for a job well done and to welcome the warriors home, the Nation had prepared a great feast for its sons and had set aside three Sunrises for celebrations. But, before it began, they paused to remember the brave men who had not returned. Lightning Bolt was chosen by his peers to give a eulogy.

"My brothers and sisters, the evils of war have robbed us of many of our beloved brothers. During the conflict they fought bravely, and they willingly gave their lives to help assure that we could continue to have the democratic rights to enjoy justice and equality and to live in freedom and peace. Their sacrifices were not made in vain, for the right of our cause has prevailed. May they enjoy, with the Great Spirit and our ancestors in the Land of Souls, peace and rest for eternity. For giving their lives to assure the right of our

People to be free we shall always be in their debt."

Other members of the community also made eloquent speeches in praise of the fallen. Then the People turned their energies with gusto to celebrating the accomplishments of the living. During the celebrations, the valour of all returned warriors was lavishly lauded by family and friends. While they enjoyed the praise, they had not forgotten the debt they owed a brave and humble compatriot. Unbeknownst to him, they made plans for special recognition of Lightning Bolt's outstanding battlefield accomplishments and leadership. They asked the People, keeping it secret from him, to award him an honour that had never before been awarded to some-one his age, a Chieftainship.

The People arranged a public meeting for noon, on the third Sunrise of the celebrations. Chief Big Timber called upon Crazy Moose to propose to the assembly the appoint-ment of Lightning Bolt to the office of Junior War Chief. Crazy Moose's motion was quickly seconded and Chief Big Timber asked for the consensus of the assembly, which was given with a mighty roar. If any had thought to oppose the appointment they were drowned out by the enthusiastic majority.

For the second time in a few Sunrises, shy and retir-ing Lightning Bolt was called upon to make a speech. In accepting his appointment, he made an impassioned plea to his countrymen to follow whenever possible the path of peace. In humility, he informed them that he was not worthy of their esteem because the praise and honours they were heaping upon him were out of proportion to the deeds he had accomplished. His self-depreciating statement only increased the People's esteem and respect for him.

HUNTING STORIES

After the conclusion of the celebrations the People dispersed to their home villages and began preparing for the Hunt, an event essential to the very existence of the country. They would soon, after securing their freedom and enjoying a fitting celebration, with the benevolence of the Great Spirit, reap Mother Earth's bounties.

Because the Great Spirit had blessed the Mi'kmaq Nation with a healthy environment, which produced a reliable, nutritious and plentiful food supply, its citizens considered themselves a truly favoured People. In fact, the bounties that Mother Earth provided from her forests, meadows, rivers, streams, lakes and ocean seemed almost inexhaustible. Hunger, caused from food shortages, was unknown. If one source proved unproductive for a Season, the others filled the void. Favourable weather conditions were responsible for creating this almost idyllic environment for producing food. Above average rainfalls assured that fresh water was always plentiful. Destructive conditions such as droughts, a hardship that often afflicted their brethren from inland Nations, were rare, only lasting a Moon or so when they did occur. Hurricanes and tornadoes were practically unknown. For the good life the Creator had blessed them with, the People gave profuse thanks.

During the proper Seasons, the People found harvesting the bounties of Mother Earth a most enjoyable and anticipated activity. Thus, over the passage of thousands of Moons, they had developed a special festival for each Seasonal harvest. But, the one that caused the most celebration, for warriors in particular, was the Hunt. The annual harvest of caribou, moose, elk, bear and other large fur-bearing land animals was filled with adventure and was very important for community survival. Clothing and bedding material was made from warm furs.

Just how important it was to the People was reflected by the actions of the fathers, who began teaching their eager sons in early childhood the skills needed to participate in the Hunt. As they grew older, the appetites of the boys for the adventures and the honours that came with hunting were whetted by the tales and legends they heard around campfires, told by Elders and older hunters. Properly primed by these stories, young men looked forward to the exhilaration of their first Hunt with barely contained anticipation.

This training was very productive for the Nation. The desire to become an esteemed hunter motivated adult warriors to excel in the Hunt. Being considered an excellent hunter was the dream of every man and leadership ambitions could not be realized without it. Thus, competitions to amass outstanding hunting reputations and the lure of the forests in hunting Seasons were to these men an annual taste of paradise on Mother Earth.

Visual and audio effects also contributed substantially to the paradise effect. The colourful beauty and exotic sounds of the forest during the hunting Sunrises of Autumn were well appreciated, especially by the young. They viewed with awe the spectacular panoramic vistas created by Mother Earth as she turned the leaves of the trees and underbrush into nearly every colour of the rainbow. The fresh crisp air was filled with the whispers of the wind flowing through the branches of dry colourful leaves, blended with the sounds of moose, elk and other animals engaged in the rituals of mating. To all their ears, it was music of contentment.

Living in this marvellous and serene environment blessed many of the Mi'kmaq with long lifespans. Consequently, it was common to find among them Elders who had passed their eightieth and ninetieth birth Seasons and several who had seen their hundredth.

This had its rewards for the Elders. The achievement of great age in Mi'kmaq society was rewarded with great respect. Age and wisdom were viewed as compatible companions. Thus, Elders were consulted on matters affecting the welfare of the state and by individual citizens trying to resolve personal problems. They also acted as keepers of history for the Nation. In this capacity they educated and entertained the young by relating tales and legends of the exploits of current great heroes and those of their ancestors during past Hunts, and other activities such as war and travelling.

A favourite legend the Elders often related was how Glooscap had in ancient Sunrises helped a young man named Little Storm single-handedly bring down enough game to feed his people for a Season. Although the saga was entertaining, its most important function was to educate.

The Elder sharing the story would start by relating how the People long ago, in an ancient age, in a place known as Little Storm's village, had come down with a mysterious debilitating ailment. The disease wasn't usually fatal but it was long lasting and sapped the strength and will of the individuals afflicted. For the remaining able-bodied villagers it was a chore to get them to drum up enough energy to even feed, clothe and clean themselves. The only individuals who had escaped its ravages were

Little Storm and two young women, Doe Eyes and Small Fawn. Thus, the responsibility for the community's survival fell to them.

As the only adult member left with his health, Little Storm felt the weight of a great responsibility fall upon his shoulders. Here he was, barely into his manhood, holding the destiny of the community in his hands. Whenever he thought of it, he had moments of pure panic. He was often heard muttering to himself as he went about the chore of trying to keep the community functioning. "How, dear Creator of the Universe, will I ever find a way to acquire food to prevent starvation among the People? Please help me, my Father, find a way."

He, in spite of being overwhelmed by the hopelessness of the situation, intended to do his best to prevent disaster. In desperation, as he lay one night in the snugness of his sleeping furs worrying, he prayed to the Great Spirit for guidance, strength and assistance. Feeling compassion for the sick villagers and knowing that Little Storm couldn't accomplish the daunting task alone, the Great Spirit decided to answer his prayers by instructing Glooscap, His helper, to provide aid without revealing Divine intervention.

Unaware that the Great Spirit had decided to help, Little Storm began to put together the gear he needed to undertake the seemingly impossible task. When he had this chore completed, he had to take care of another one of equal importance before he started to hunt. He had to make preparations to preserve, transport and store the harvest. To acquire the knowledge of how to do it, he had to ask the sick women for help. With much prodding, they were able to communicate to Little Storm, Doe Eyes and Small Fawn the required know-how. Little Storm set out to complete his impossible task.

Unbeknownst to Little Storm, Glooscap accompanied him. Following the Father's instruction to keep his presence a secret,

Glooscap decided that he would help by guiding most of Little Storm's arrows to each animal's vital spot. With this help, Little Storm was able to bring down the biggest caribou, moose, elk and bear with uncanny ease. Within a Moon, the disbelieving young warrior had harvested enough meat to see the People through to the Spring.

The villagers, with plenty of nourishing food and the passage of many Sunrises, eventually recovered their health. In recognition of the outstanding efforts made by him to save them, they praised and toasted Little Storm lavishly. They showered him with many gifts and honours and made him Chief of the village. He, at first, thanked the People for their praise, but soon began to get a big head and view their tributes as his right. Many began to refer to him, with a touch of sadness, as Chief Big Head.

Unforgivably Little Storm, who was blinded by egotism, neglected to do some very important things. He forgot to offer thanks to the Great Spirit for the help He had given during the crisis, and in a spirit of meanness and without honour he forgot to share recognition with the young girls who had worked unceasingly to bring in and store the meat. Contrary to the tradition of the Mi'kmaq, he wasn't showing the generosity and humility expected of a leader.

As Moons passed and Little Storm's pompous behaviour worsened, the People grew increasingly weary of his arrogance and lack of respect for their dignity. They accepted, with sadness in their hearts, that drastic action had to be taken to restore his sense of balance and humility. But how could they show the young Chief, to whom they owed so much, the error of his ways without removing him from his post as leader? They prayed to the Great Spirit for assistance.

The Great Spirit answered their prayers by instructing His helper to intervene. Glooscap decided that the best way to shrink the young man's head was to make him look incompetent for one Moon. Thus, in his invisible state, Glooscap began deflecting Little Storm's arrows in the Hunt and caused him to display a very unusual tendency for clumsiness and ineptitude, tripping over his feet, tipping his canoe, often slipping and falling, and so on. He bungled the simplest tasks with the same regularity as the sun rises and falls. Soon his ineptitude began to generate uncomplimentary remarks among the villagers about his competence. This, along with being rarely sought for advice and company, was swiftly undermining his self-confidence.

In desperation, Little Storm once again turned to the Great Spirit for help. One Sunrise before his period of humiliation was due to end, Glooscap visited him in his dreams. "My son," he said. "When in trouble, you quickly beseech the Father for help and promise to repay Him by being eternally grateful and respectful. However, after He helped you save your village you failed to do so. Instead, you got a big head and began to treat your fellow citizens as if they were worthless and mindless inferiors. You praised your own accomplishments constantly and put self-interests before those of others. Now you ask for more help! Your behaviour befouls the ways of the Mi'kmaq. If you want to make peace with and regain the favour of the Father, you must regain your humility."

Glooscap then laid out three things that Little Storm had to do in order to make peace with the Creator. First and foremost he had to sincerely thank Him for helping him during his Sunrises of need. Second, he must call his People together and apologize publicly for the disrespectful arrogance he had shown in his relationships with them. Third, he must give public praise and recognition to Doe Eyes and Small Fawn for their labours during the village's crisis. If this was not done with remorse for his sins, the Great Spirit and his fellow citizens would forsake him and leave him to live alone in a world filled with loneliness and unhappiness.

Upon awakening, Little Storm felt an overwhelming sense of shame for his bevaviour. Immediately, with humility restored, he raised his hands to the sky and begged the Creator for forgiveness and promised with the utmost sincerity that for the rest of his Seasons on Mother Earth he would always remember to be humble and offer thanks for favours granted. Then he promised that he would go to the People, before the sun set, to confess and apologize publicly for his sins and humbly beg them to forgive him.

Shortly after Sunrise, Little Storm began moving around the village asking the villagers to gather at noon for a meeting. At the meeting, with downcast eyes, he made a humiliating public accounting of his misdeeds. "My brothers and sisters, I stand before you this morning in deep shame because I have, with superb arrogance, violated almost every one of the most basic values of our country. The worst and most unforgivable among them is that I didn't thank the Great Spirit for the help He gave me during the Sunrises that the sickness afflicted our villagers, which assured our survival.

"During the crisis caused by the sickness, in helpless desperation, I asked the Father to help me find a way to harvest enough food to see us through to the Spring Season. He answered my pleas and permitted me to bring down the largest of beasts and fill the larders. Without His help we would have been lost. Yet, knowing it was the Great Spirit who was responsible for our salvation I allowed and even encouraged you to believe that I had done it alone. Without humility I accepted all your praise.

"But, this is not all that I have to be ashamed of. I have another terrible act that I must confess and repent for. My brothers and sisters, if you don't already know why I say this, then let what I'm about to say shame me further in your eyes. While the sickness was rampant in our village, Doe Eyes and Small Fawn worked hard and without complaint from dawn to dark to bring in the meat and properly store it. For their hard labours I've never so much as given them one word of praise. Before another Sunrise passes, I want to set matters straight, because without their devoted help, I couldn't have completed my task. They are true heroes! Please, Doe Eyes and Small Fawn, I beg of you, forgive me for my selfish and ungrateful ways.

"Now my People, I must detail and ask forgiveness for what I've done to you. I've treated you, including the Elders, with contempt and disrespect. I have by my actions mocked and betrayed your trust. Because of this, I'm not worthy of being your Chief. In such a position of trust I was honour bound to protect your rights as human beings and I did not. Instead, I put my petty self-interests before yours and wallowed in unearned feelings of self-importance and superiority. My transgressions, my brothers and sisters, are truly great. The unkind and ungrateful things I've done to the Father and to you, my People, are almost beyond redemption and are truly unforgivable. But, humbled by the shame of what I've done, I'll ask for forgiveness with hope in my heart.

"Before you, my sisters and brothers, in atonement for my sins, I raise my face in humble shame, up toward the Land of Souls, and ask the Great Spirit to forgive me for the unforgivable contempt I have shown Him and you. However, I must confess my friends that I know not why He should.

"From you my friends, in view of the seriousness of the wrongs I've committed, I'll gladly accept any punishment that you find fit to give me. Whatever it is, it will be well deserved. In order to give you time to decide upon a fitting punishment for my dishonourable ways, I adjourn this meeting until next Sunrise."

The following morning, with much joy in their hearts, the People reassembled to give their verdict. Great Owl, the senior Elder, delivered it. "Little Storm," he said, "your words of apology and remorse last Sunrise for your sins were like the sweet songs of the meadowlark to our ears. Therefore, my son, we've decided that your public repentance was punishment enough. We consider the matter closed. However, we do want to emphasize for your future benefit that if there should ever be a recurrence of your big-headedness, it will lead to your being condemned to a life of disgrace as a deposed Chief, because my brother, depose you we will.

"Now, my beloved Chief, we wish to take a moment and thank the Great Spirit for answering our pleas to help you see the error of your ways. Great Spirit, we your children humbly give thanks for the return of our leader and with joy acknowledge your generosity in answering our pleas." Great Owl went on to praise the Creator of the Universe for all the blessings received by the People.

When Great Owl finished, Little Storm addressed the People. "My bothers and sisters, in view of the magnitude of the wrongs I've done, your kindness in forgiving me is more than I deserve. In return for it, my beloved friends, I pledge to you this Sunrise, with the Great Spirit as my witness, that I shall never again dishonour your trust and that I will always treat your human needs with dignity and respect. I also want to thank you from the bottom of my heart for your charitable gesture of permitting me to continue as Chief of our village. May the Great Spirit always be with you, because you are deserving of his love."

Little Storm lived up to his promises. For the rest of his life he served the People diligently. In return for the dedicated, wise and intelligent way he served them, the People grew to love him above all others and promoted him accordingly. By the Sunrise of his fortieth Summer he had served them as Village Chief, their Chief of the Hunt, War Chief and then as part of the Mi'kmaq Grand Council. As a Grand Council member he wisely used his knowledge to help citizens and Nations solve problems. After he served with distinction for many Moons, his peers on the Grand Council paid him the ultimate honour. After the Grand Chief died, they appointed him to the office. When he died at the age of one hundred and four, he was the most honoured and revered man in living memory among the Mi'kmaq. So the story is told by the Elder.

Such stories were used extensively to instill a deep sense of respect for the Great Spirit and the rights of others in Mi'kmaq children. They were also used to implant a strong desire in them to use decency, humility, generosity and tolerance in their Sunrise-to-Sunrise human exchanges with each other.

The culture's philosophy of sharing was a product of these values. From long practice, sharing was as much part of their daily lives as survival functions. To be accused of being a stingy person was a source of deep shame for an individual. A person guilty of such an accusation suffered a loss of honour that was almost irreparable.

To avoid ever being identified as stingy, Mi'kmaq people were beyond generous with everyone. In all aspects of life, members of the community shared equally. Those who were physically able also shared equally in the labours of the village. This value was well demonstrated during preparations for the Hunt.

By the middle of Autumn all healthy men, women and older children throughout Mi'kmaq country were caught up in communal preparations for the Hunt. In order to get and keep everybody in the right frame of mind these chores were always accompanied by a few celebrations. In Kespukwitk, Little Bear's village was a hive of activity. Lightning Bolt and his peers, once again comfortably installed in the wigwams of their loved ones, barely containing their excitement, pitched in with gusto to complete preparations. Possible adventures from the chase and friendly competition were looked forward to with the utmost anticipation.

Just thinking of these activities was like nectar to the men. During the Hunt, they would strenuously compete with one another to bring down the most, the biggest and the fattest animals. This good-natured competition provided a healthy vent for the young and mature men alike to burn off excess energies. But, its most significant benefit was that it filled the village's larders with meat for Winter, by spurring the warriors on to greater efforts.

//

CHAPTER THREE

With equipment in excellent condition and ample supplies packed in carrying bags, the hunters, two Sunrises past the second Moon of Autumn, departed the village at the first light of dawn to set up a central hunting camp. Little Bear's two youngest sons were among them. Raging River, fourteen Springs, was making his third trip, and Little Beaver, twelve Summers, was making his first.

Because his youngest was a novice hunter, Little Bear's plan was to keep him by his side during the Hunt. Raging River, with two hunting Seasons' experience behind him, would be permitted to hunt with his friends under the light supervision of an experienced hunter. This practice was to give the older boys opportunities to develop skills to work the Hunt in concert with mates. Implanting the desire to work in harmony in complex situations was essential to the success of future Hunts and thus the Nation's existence.

Lightning Bolt and Crazy Moose, now in their twenty-first hunting Seasons, had teamed up during their sixteenth birth Season, and were by now regarded by peers as a very successful team. They seemed to know instinctively what move the other was planning when on the trail of a moose or other big game and they reacted accordingly. They often brought down more meat than two other teams combined. Whereas Lightning Bolt was seen as the leader of the duo, he had already at his young age been appointed the prestigious position of Chief of the Hunt.

The air of excitement that hung over all the hunters as they journeyed to the hunting grounds affected all participants. But, it was the young boys who were looking forward to participating in the hunt with the greatest energy and impatience. Coping with this had been a challenge to fathers since fatherhood began. From their own experiences they knew that to help their sons become successful adult hunters it was essential to teach them to check their energies and appreciate the value of patience.

Like their peers, Little Bear's two youngest sons had their expectations of adventure worked up to almost a fever pitch. He, like countless fathers before him, often had to respond to an ancient question asked by his youngest, "Father, will we ever get there?"

That evening, after travelling about three thousand canoe lengths from the village, the hunters set up camp in a pine forest by a small spring-fed stream near the great Stoney River. The aroma of food cooking, mixed in with the fresh scent of pines in the cool air, was a treat. After dining on delicious freshly caught brook trout, the men and boys gathered around a huge campfire to be entertained by spellbinding storytelling.

Through the course of the evening, tales were told about the exploits of legendary figures and the true adventures experienced by hunters, but the products of great imaginations were also a delightful part of the night's entertainment. Wise Owl, one of the older hunters, grabbed their rapt attention with this short fictional tale:

"One beautiful warm and comfortable late Summer Sunrise, with the invigorating smell of Mother Earth's ripening produce in the air, an unarmed and self-possessed young warrior called Stoney River left his village for a walk through the forest. Eventually he came to a meadow that had a small stream meandering through it.

"In no hurry to go anywhere in particular, he stopped to soak in the warmth and appreciate the scenery. He decided to sit down with his back against a boulder, to reflect and do some serious meditation. In spite of the burden of the seriousness of his thoughts, he soon fell into a peaceful, trouble-free and deep sleep.

"After a considerable interval had passed, he awoke feeling greatly refreshed. When his eyes cleared of sleep he scanned the scenery and discovered an enormous black bear contentedly eating ripe blueberries from nearby bushes. This, of course, gave him quite a shock.

"However, being a brave warrior he managed to keep his wits about him and remember what he and his peers had been advised to do in such situations by the Elders when he was still a young lad. Their advice was that if they had no way of making a dignified and safe retreat, do exactly what the animal did. They were assured that this would keep them out of harm's way. Being a person who had learned his lessons well, Stoney immediately began to emulate every move the bear made.

"He got down on his hands and knees and copied as near as possible the bear's dining practices, eating blueberries by holding the bush with his hands and chewing them off with his teeth. The Bear, after feasting for a considerable period and comfortably filled with blueberries, decided he was thirsty and went to the stream to ease his thirst.

"For the span it took the sun to fall halfway from its zenith to the horizon, young Stoney copied all actions of the bear with unflinching devotion. When Brother Bear rolled around in the water of the stream, he did too. When Brother Bear ate more berries, he ate more berries. When Brother Bear relieved his water, he did so as well, and so on.

"As the Sunrise wore on, or from Stoney River's perspective, dragged on, Brother Bear decided to sit and sun himself for a spell, which activity the young man copied with unfailing devotion. After lazing around for a good part of the remaining Sunrise, Brother Bear arose and moved off somewhat to move his bowels. This caused Stoney River to blurt, 'Ah, Brother Bear, I'm way ahead of you on this one, because I did that when I first saw you.'"

Late in the evening, after being treated to many other great tales, the hunters retired to their beds, made from fresh aromatic fir boughs, with contentment in their hearts. The Seasoned went to a night of peaceful bliss, the young to a night of restless anticipation.

The next morning, after enjoying an early breakfast, Little Bear and Little Beaver set out by canoe to scout for game around the headwaters of the mighty Stoney River. By the time the sun was well up, they had travelled against a strong current upriver a substantial distance to the White Rapids, where they had to traverse around the rough stretch. After treating themselves to a quick rest, they hoisted their canoe onto their shoulders and began the traverse.

Little Bear cautioned his son, "My son, the heavy rains have caused the river to swell to the lips of its banks, making the rapids an extremely dangerous obstacle. The survival chances of anyone who falls into it would be very slim. Therefore, my young hunter, because the rains have also made the moss-covered clay stretches along the trail very slippery and treacherous, I want you to be very careful when walking over places that come close to the rapids."

"Don't worry, my dear father, I'll watch my step with the caution of a wildcat."

Within fifty paces of the end of the trail it narrowed against the river. Little Beaver, stepping on a piece of slippery moss, lost his footing and slid into the raging current. Little Bear plunged into the powerful waters to try to save him. He quickly located his Little Beaver but found that the current was too strong to escape while carrying him. Rather than abandon his baby to meet his destiny with the Great Spirit alone, Little Bear wrapped him firmly in his arms and became a victim of the rampaging Stoney River with him.

At the main camp that night, the hunters attached no importance to the fact that Little Bear and Little Beaver hadn't returned. It wasn't uncommon for a scouting party to spend a night away from it. However, with the arrival of another nightfall with still no sign of them, some misgivings were expressed about their safety.

That evening, the Hunt leaders, although not expecting to find that anything unusual had befallen them, decided to send a small party upriver the next Sunrise to determine their whereabouts. Grey Owl, a Seasoned hunter and a lifelong friend of Little Bear, was appointed to lead the search. He, before retiring for the night, sought out Lightning Bolt and Crazy Moose and asked if they would like to accompany him the next morning. Because Lightning Bolt felt a deep sense of foreboding about the welfare of his father and brother, they quickly agreed. At the first light of dawn, upon arrival at the riverbank, Grey Owl found them waiting impatiently beside a canoe holding their supplies. He quickly secured his provisions and they shoved off.

As they paddled out onto the river, they noted how high it was and the swift current running because of it. They soon realized fighting against the current would make the upriver trip much longer than usual. However, by putting their backs to it, they reached White Rapids by midmorning and put ashore. Disembarking without taking a rest, they took the canoe upon their backs and began to traverse around the rapids. They soon came upon Little Bear's canoe lying seemingly abandoned across the trail. The discovery deepened their foreboding because they knew that an experienced hunter such as Little Bear wouldn't leave his canoe in this way without being forced to do so. Upon closely examining the ground, they found evidence of broken moss leading directly into the river. In dread of what they would discover, they followed the river's course back downstream. At a dead fall of trees extending well out into the rapids, they spotted entangled in the branches the bodies of the missing hunters.

They could see from the shore that Little Bear had his son locked firmly in an embrace. The sight told them that he had tried to comfort his beloved baby to the end and that he had consciously decided to accompany him to the Land of Souls. It also told them that Little Bear, a strong swimmer, might have saved himself if he had chosen to do so.

With the initial shock over and the bodies recovered Grey Owl, leaving Lightning Bolt and Crazy Moose with the remains, started downriver to deliver the shocking news to their brothers and to get help to bring the bodies back to camp.

After Grey Owl's departure, Lightning Bolt expressed his agonizing grief to Crazy Moose. "Oh my brother the pain in my heart is unbearable. How can I ever bear such a great loss? My father and baby brother gone forever. Oh tell me, my brother, why has the Great Spirit failed me? What have I done to deserve such pain? Oh, my friend, how can I ever be happy again?"

Placing his arm around the shoulders of his sobbing friend, Crazy Moose comforted him. "Lightning Bolt, my brother, I love you as a true brother and share your grief profoundly. But, my friend, you must understand that the Great Spirit has not forsaken you. Although He took away two people you love dearly, He has left you with a loving family and a multitude of friends who hold you dear. By no means, my brother, has the Creator left you alone in your time of need and sorrow.

"Although it will be a hard thing to do at this time of heartbreak, you must keep in mind that when our time comes to go to the Land of Souls, we have no choice in the matter; go we must. My beloved brother, one Sunrise, when we are called home, our families and friends will also have to accept the finality of the wishes of the Creator. In the case of Little Bear and Little Beaver, although we will miss them dearly, He, in His wisdom, decided He wanted their company and called them home. This is something we cannot reverse. But they are not lost to us forever, because when we are called some Sunrise we will know once again the joy of their company. But, my friend, until that Sunrise arrives, we must remember that even with the passing of our loved ones, life continues without pause and waits for no one."

Crazy Moose finished with a reminder that those left behind have wonderful memories to comfort them. "To help console us at occasions such as this we have memories of the happy times we had with our departed loved ones. And, as our grief ebbs into the reality of knowing that what has happened is only the beginning for them, we shall be happy again."

Lightning Bolt, visibly moved by the eloquence of his friend, replied, "Thank you, my dear brother, your words of comfort and wisdom speak the truth. I must not doubt the love of the Great Spirit. For He is with me."

Until Grey Owl returned late that afternoon the two friends reminisced about the fond memories they had of Little Bear and Little Beaver. They found, as the afternoon passed, that talking about them was like a salve, because it slowly eased the pain caused by the disaster.

Back at the main camp, after Grey Owl had finished relating the dreadful news, the Hunt leaders met and began making preparations to return home for the funeral. They decided, in order to permit the family and community adequate time to recover from the shock of the tragedy and hold a proper Feast of the Dead, to suspend the Hunt for seven Sunrises. When they had finished making the arrangements needed to do so, with much sorrow in their hearts the leaders retreated to their personal camps to offer private prayers to the Great Spirit for the repose of the souls of their beloved brothers.

While this was happening, Grey Owl rounded up several warriors, including Little Beaver's older brother, Raging River, to accompany him upriver to help bring back the remains. When they arrived at White Rapids, Lightning Bolt allowed his brother some time to view the remains of their loved ones in private. Then he took him around the shoulders and led him off from the main party for consoling.

Once out of sight and earshot of his fellow hunters, the

boy began to sob uncontrollably. Lightning Bolt comforted his brother as Crazy Moose had comforted him. "My precious brother, I know the extent of the heartache you're feeling so don't feel embarrassed about showing it. Let the tears flow until you've cried yourself dry. Don't try to stop them. It helps to ease the pain."

The devastated boy, tears flowing freely, replied, "Oh Lightning Bolt, I feel so empty and sad. I find it so hard to believe that our precious father and brother are both gone forever. How could it happen so quickly? When they left camp the Sunrise before last they were so full of life. I shall weep forever! Why, oh why, my brother, has the Great Spirit forsaken us?"

Raging River went on for some time before Lightning Bolt was able to politely intervene to console him. "Excuse me for interrupting my little brother, but when I was alone with Crazy Moose, baring my innermost feelings, I said many of the things you've said. In his company I also cried and lamented about the Great Spirit deserting us. But Crazy Moose, in his wisdom, would not long permit me to think that way. He reminded me that being parted from Father and Little Beaver is only a temporary thing that will some Sunrise be ended when we are reunited in the Land of Souls.

"He also reminded me that during this time of sorrow we have our memories to help console us. This is absolutely true. Our wonderful recollections of the good times we had with Father and Little Beaver will comfort and warm our hearts for the rest of our Sunrises on Mother Earth. And, my brother, there is something else we must remember. Our father would be sad and unhappy if he saw that we did not accept and rejoice in the fact that he is home in the Land of Souls and joyful in the company of our ancestors."

"Oh Lightning Bolt, my beloved brother, just hold me tightly for a while until I can begin to deal with my sorrow." After a short period Raging River continued, "I know at first it will be hard to accept the Great Spirit's will, but as the Sunrises pass the hurt will fade and life will begin to take on a new meaning for us. But, now we must be strong for the sake of Mother and our sisters, for in the Sunrises ahead they will need our love, strength and support."

"See, my little brother, the healing process has already begun for you. In a few Sunrises, with the help of the Great Spirit, we shall begin to recover our zest for life. By doing so we will assure the happiness of our father and brother in the Land of Souls."

The brothers talked for a short while longer and then returned to the company of the other men. After respectfully wrapping the remains of their beloved Chief and Little Beaver in furs, the warriors began the trek downriver to camp. As they rounded the last bend in the river, before the campsite came into sight, Lightning Bolt suddenly felt the heavy weight of full responsibility for his family's welfare that was now his alone to carry. The realization caused him to briefly wonder about his ability to meet the challenge. However, it was overshadowed by the future chore that fate had bequeathed him in this very moment, of telling his mother and sisters the tragic news.

The thought of telling his mother and sisters caused him the utmost apprehension. His feelings of dread were intensified by his memories of the broken hearts shown by families and friends after the late war. During that difficult return home, he had to tell them the heart-wrenching news of the deaths of loved ones and had the painful task of trying to console them afterwards. It had been the hardest and saddest thing, up to that point, he had done in his life.

Upon landing at the hunting camp he quickly sought out the Hunt leaders to tell them that he, Crazy Moose and Raging River were leaving for home to deliver the tragic news to his family. After securing their equipment, they got underway. Unhampered by equipment and supplies, the trip home was speedy. Afterwards, Lightning Bolt would tell Crazy Moose that he couldn't imagine ever making a sadder trip. In his mind, during their walk home, Lightning Bolt recalled the matchless love his parents had enjoyed. The extent of it had been evident to him since he was a little boy. He saw then that the obvious pleasure they took from each other's company followed them everywhere. Their intense love affair was almost legendary in the community. If there had ever been two people who had loved each other more dearly, they were unknown to him. In view of this, the thought of the impending chore of telling his mother that the man she loved so dearly had died in an accident, filled him with apprehension. It would be like pronouncing a death sentence upon an innocent. The news that her baby boy had also perished would grieve her beyond comparison.

With this foreboding still troubling his mind they arrived home. When they entered their wigwam, they could tell by the look on their mother's face that she had already sensed something dreadful had happened. Not knowing any easy way to break such horrific news, Lightning Bolt simply told her and his sisters that Little Bear and Little Beaver had perished in a canoeing accident.

Early Blossom reacted with serene dignity and almost supernatural control. Her words and actions afterwards reflected her strong character. However, her eyes from that Sunrise forward always betrayed the hurt, grief and loneliness she held within. During the ensuing Seasons she would finish raising her children with loving care, but soon after the youngest had left the nest she asked the Great Spirit to permit her to join her beloved Little Bear in the Land of Souls. He consented. Afterwards, family and friends alike would say that she had died of heartbreak.

Because he had been the Chief of the community, and a much admired and revered man, Little Bear's funeral would take place amid much ceremony. Little Beaver's ceremony, because of his age, would be part of his father's. This was the family's desire because they felt that it would be fitting to have a father and son, who had died giving comfort to each other, praised and interred together. Within a few Sunrises, the tragic news had been circulated throughout the country. Thus, by the fifth Sunrise after the tragedy, Kespukwitk's National Chief Big Timber, Village Chiefs from surrounding communities and a multitude of people were gathered in Little Bear's village to conduct the Feast of the Dead.

At the feast, Big Timber was the first of a long procession of relatives and friends to recount the accomplishments and feats of the departed. He praised Little Bear's bravery and courage, his wisdom and knowledge, his dignity and humility, and mentioned the possibilities that might have been, but now would never be, for Little Beaver. Then he humbly beseeched the Creator of the Universe to keep in comfort, in the Land of Souls, His two sons. He closed by calling upon the community to pray to the Great Father for the family, who in their sorrow would need strength to overcome the loss of two dearly beloved family members.

Then other members of the community, one after the other, stood and respectfully took their turns expressing their admiration and respect for the departed. With sadness, at the end of six Sunrises of mourning, the father and son were, with great dignity, laid to rest.

After the Feast of the Dead was over and they had some time alone, Lightning Bolt told Crazy Moose, "My brother, I find this strange to say, but after going through the Feast of the Dead I feel as if I know my father and brother better now than I did when they were alive. This feeling comes from the new stories I heard from relatives and friends about Father's adventures and accomplishments, and my brother's antics. I had thought that Father had told me everything about himself during our times together, but it appears from what I heard over the past few Sunrises that he still had so much to tell.

"Hearing them praise and speak of him so well was very pleasing to me. To have half as many people say such kind things about the honourable manner in which one had lived his life would be a major accomplishment. I only hope, my friend, that I can live out my life nearly as well as father lived his. My brother, because of the things I just mentioned, and many other things that happened during the Feast of the Dead, I've become more appreciative of the privilege of being part of a loving community like ours. If I live a hundred Springs I'll always remember and appreciate with a grateful heart the kindness shown by the People to my family and friends during our time of sorrow."

"Lightning Bolt, my beloved brother, over the last few Sunrises I've wanted to say something to you about your father that I felt needed saying for quite some time, but I was always too timid to say it. Now I'm going rectify this. Little Bear was for me a role model in life. I've always felt he was a truly great and honourable man and I strongly believe that if fate had not intervened in a future Sunrise he would have been our Nation's leader, and probably later on appointed Grand Chief. I should have said this to him, and to you, a long time ago.

"While on the subject of saying nice things about people whom I deeply admire, love and respect, I want to include your mother. My brother, I've never seen anyone carry so much pain with such dignity and poise as she. That she is a strong woman there is no doubt, but, my friend the hurt she carries is almost visible. To see it causes me much pain. I pray that some Sunrise she can partly fill the empty spot left in her life by the loss of Little Bear. However, we must accept that to love another as dearly as she loved your father is not part of her future, for a love like theirs is almost unique. In recognition of this we must support and cherish her, for she suffers a loneliness that will not leave her until she is reunited with Little Bear in the Land of Souls."

"My friend Crazy Moose, as always in these matters, you're right. I know from experience that mother will try her best to be happy with the knowledge that father is at peace in the company of our ancestors. But I also know in my heart that true happiness will not be hers until she is again in his arms. I want you to know that the comments you made about them were deeply appreciated. Without hesitation I can say that your feelings about them were mutual. They always loved you dearly and considered you part of our family. Father, my dear brother, would have been very proud of how you've helped us carry our sorrow.

"Therefore, on the family's behalf, I want to thank you from the bottom of my heart for the help you've given since the accident. I'll express the extent of my appreciation in this manner. Until the Great Spirit calls me home some Sunrise, I shall love and cherish you as a blood brother and will, whenever humanly possible, be with you when needed. This I swear by my ancestors.

"Now, my dear brother, I want to say a few words, which are about the future but rooted in the past. We have known each other since we were little more than babies and have derived a great deal of pleasure doing many things together. But, now that we are men, soon we shall seek out and separately share the love of women who meet our fancy, and have children. I'll pray each Sunrise that our children can establish bonds as strong as ours. To have known your friendship, my dear brother, is something I thank the Great Spirit for. I cannot imagine what my life would have been without it."

"Lightning Bolt, my brother, I thank you for the praise and with a humble heart I accept it. But I also want to say that because of you, and your friendship, my life has been enriched beyond measure. I tell you, my friend, that as surely as I'm sitting here this Sunrise, the adventures we've shared together will always be a pleasure to my soul. And, I sincerely hope we shall share many more pleasant things together in the future. I also cannot begin to imagine what my life would have been like without your presence. I venture to guess that it probably would have been very dull."

"Crazy Moose, my friend, there is another matter I wish to discuss with you before the Hunt resumes. Raging River needs my help in the coming Seasons to finish learning the ways of a warrior. I was wondering if you would mind helping me for the next several Seasons to take up where Father left off in teaching him the skills he still needs to learn by making him part of our team."

"I'm glad you brought it up because it saves me the trouble. It'll be a pleasure. I'm already looking forward to the fun of having a young guy like him on our team and teaching him.

Also, it will be good practice for the Sunrises ahead when we have to do the same for our own."

With the sad task over, and with Winter fast approaching, the need to get the Hunt back into full swing had taken on an air of urgency. Already, on several occasions, heavy frosts and a few dustings of snow had covered the ground. From experience the men knew that a Hunt conducted under severe Winter weather conditions was, if possible, something to avoid. The added workload was enormous.

Lightning Bolt and Raging River, who were aware that the needs of the community had to come before their grief, also returned to the Hunt. They soon discovered that the concentration the Hunt required diminished the hurt and helped renew their fond memories of Hunts past, in the company of their father. They came to fully appreciate that their father's comforting presence would always be with them in their memories. With this in mind, they rejoined with renewed vigour. The Hunt was a tremendous success and completed in record time. It seemed as if the Great Spirit was compensating the community for the loss of its loved ones.

Lightning Bolt would always remember this Hunt, with its sad and joyful memories. Both he and Crazy Moose thoroughly enjoyed taking Raging River under their wings and watching him, filled with the enthusiasm of the very young, learning and growing before their eyes. Under their tutelage, Raging River very quickly displayed the stuff that would one Sunrise, with his skills fine-tuned by experience, see him recognized by the People as one of the great hunters of the Nation.

However, during this Hunt, it was Lightning Bolt who surpassed the best efforts of his peers. He brought down the most animals and bagged the biggest. The young Junior War

Chief showed his peers that in addition to the skills already displayed in war, he had the potential to become one of the greatest hunters in the memory of the Nation. When commended for his skills, he replied, "With men on my team such as Crazy Moose and Raging River, how can I be anything but successful?"

Blinded by his humble views, Lightning Bolt didn't realize that the extraordinary abilities he had shown during the Hunt, and his outstanding record in war, combined with his passionate pursuit of peace, were already generating a desire among the People to launch him upon a lifetime career as their leader.

DICTATORS AND DEMOCRACY

With the end of a very successful Hunt, and the first heavy snow of the Winter Season covering the ground, the village leaders turned their attention to the chore of administering the community's routine political and social affairs. At their first meeting without Little Bear presiding, tears of remembrance came to many eyes. They had one important item on the agenda that was not at all routine. They needed to set aside a Sunrise for a village meeting to nominate and select a new Village Chief. They settled on a Sunrise that allowed everyone enough time to engage in the social processes involved in electing a new Chief, and sought the People's agreement during the next Sunrise.

With the nomination and selection meeting agreed upon, excitement began to build in the village. Who would replace the beloved Little Bear? Who could carry this honour and responsibility? These were the questions on most people's minds. As if they were of one mind, the People began preparations for the election with enthusiasm. They were excited because such events also included celebrations, which gave them a welcome opportunity to get together again with beloved relatives and friends for lots of reminiscing, dancing and games.

However, this didn't diminish the seriousness with which they approached the responsibility of selecting a new Village Chief. The exercise would be carried out with the greatest dignity and respect. Such care was demanded by the Nation's laws that required citizens, before selecting a Chief for any office, whether for National, Village or War purposes, to engage in debate and reflect deeply upon the character and other qualifications of the men proposed or offering for office. Extensive discussions occurred before electing someone to their term of service. Such was meant to assure that they picked the most qualified man for the position. Such vetting of candidates made it a rare occasion when they had the distasteful exercise of removing a Chief from office because he had failed to live up to expectations.

As ancient custom dictated, before the Sunrise for Village Chief selection arrived, an important chore demanded immediate attention. As a precaution against a food supply shortage arising because of contamination or spoilage, the hunters had to repair or replace broken equipment for a possible emergency Hunt. The root for this diligence was an ancient disaster, caused by neglect that had befallen their ancestors of a far off time.

These customs reminded the People of the Legend of the Lazy Warriors, a story used to teach young people important lessons during their formative Sunrises. At the core was the message that they must never permit men without honour to come to power. The Legend depicts in horrendous detail how the People in those ancient Sunrises had almost perished from the effects of famine, caused by the brutality and laziness of their hunters. The teller, usually an Elder, always began by describing the shortcomings of the warriors

⋐⋑

The men of the village, which was then part of a cruel dictatorship, avoided their community responsibilities with the diligence *that only the truly lazy can muster. Just how completely the evil had taken over their souls was demonstrated fully by the fact that they forced their women and children, in order to give them more time for their lives of leisure, to do much of the work that was traditionally done by men. With very few exceptions, they were only interested in enjoying the pleasures of life and providing for personal comfort.*

As a result of their laziness, hunting equipment and other gear was not kept in good condition. This meant that the community continually lived on the edge of disaster. Even when necessity demanded that they prepare for a Hunt, they did just the bare minimum. As a result, even in good Seasons, they barely brought in enough meat to last a Winter. No preparations whatsoever were made to guard against an unforeseen emergency.

The warriors also made no effort to drive the animals they were preparing to slaughter to sites that were easily accessible, which would spare the women and children additional hard labour when bringing in the harvest. In fact, they often did the opposite and endeavoured to slaughter the animals in the most difficult places, just to enjoy the spectacle of watching them slave. Their cruelty was without equal.

During the current Hunt, they had barely brought down enough meat to last the Winter before they hurried back to the village to laze about and feast. And, as was customary for them, no effort was made to prepare for an emergency situation. A rare and unSeasonable heat wave struck without warning. Within a few Sunrises most of the harvested meat had spoiled before it could be preserved. This setback could have easily been corrected by an additional Hunt, except most of their equipment was in an advanced state of disrepair and almost useless. Even with this, if they had made an immediate and vigorous effort, enough could have been repaired, or replaced, to enable them to make a reasonable try at acquiring a new meat supply.

However, even with hunger now a very real possibility for the community, they procrastinated and put only a half-hearted effort into preparing for another harvest. By the time they had made barely sufficient repairs and got their reluctant efforts under way, Winter had descended with a vengeance. Within a few Sunrises, snow had piled up in huge drifts and made a further Hunt very difficult. However, if they had made the effort, with a great deal of determined hard work, it would still have been possible to bring in enough food to sustain the community.

But, displaying their meanness to the fullest, instead of taking up the challenge, they settled on a cruel and easy solution to sustain their life of leisure. They cut back food rations to bare subsistence levels for their dependents and saved the best for themselves. Within a few Sunrises the children, women and Elders began suffering the pangs and ravages of near starvation.

The Great Spirit, viewing all this from the Land of Souls, went into a seething rage. He instructed Glooscap to intervene and help the women, children and Elders, and to cause the guilty men to suffer greatly for their behaviour. Glooscap obediently caused an illness to occur in the men that prevented them from eating, becoming violently ill even at the sight of food. The only thing they were able to retain was some water. After twenty sunsets had passed, many of the offenders were near death from starvation. In desperation they called upon the Great Spirit for help.

In response, the Creator instructed Glooscap to visit them in their dreams and inform them individually that He was outraged and repulsed by them because they had been so cruel. That night, after each drifted off into a fitful sleep, Glooscap intoned,

"The Great Spirit has directed me to inform you that your behaviour has been so monstrous and evil that it is almost beyond redemption. But, there is a slight chance for you to find

forgiveness. If you wish to have Him consider forgiveness for the terrible deeds that you have committed against humanity, you must first atone. If not, the punishment will be great. Upon death, you will not be permitted to enter the Land of Souls, and your death will not be long in coming because your inability to eat will continue.

"To persuade the Great Spirit to consider forgiving you, this is what you must do. He demands that in a public forum you beg the forgiveness of the village's women, children and Elders for the harm you have caused them. Then you must convince Him that you will live your remaining life with deep humility and will, without the slightest deviation, have the utmost respect for the rights and dignity of your fellow human beings. I strongly recommend, if you hope to live, that you begin your act of contrition when you awake."

Immediately upon awakening each man solemnly and tearfully promised the Great Spirit that he would from that Sunrise forward live his life fully devoted to the welfare of his fellow citizens and never again place in danger their lives by being lazy and irresponsible. The Great Spirit, believing they spoke with sincerity, instructed Glooscap to assist the few men left standing, who had been spared the ravages of the virus, with a Hunt. They alone had survived because they had refused to follow the cruel decision of the vast majority of men who kept food from their dependents. With Glooscap's assistance, they were able to harvest enough food to return the repentant men and their dependents to health.

With their health restored, the men called a village meeting and finished making peace with the Great Spirit by publicly begging their brothers and sisters for forgiveness. Even after they had apologized and the People had forgiven them, these same men could not completely shake off their feelings of guilt and shame, even with the passage of many Seasons.

❧

The lessons taught by this legend helped assure that the Mi'kmaq People were never again burdened by hunters without honour and integrity. Ever afterward, the goal for hunters was a great matter of honour, to meet or exceed the superhuman effort that was made by the few men who had brought in enough food to save the People, even with the help of Glooscap. Any man who displayed a tendency towards laziness from then on was considered a man without honour. He was shunned by the community until he mended his ways. Thus, the preservation of one's honour became a matter of the highest priority among the People, and laziness and self-centred meanness became all but unknown in Mi'kmaq society.

Lightning Bolt, Crazy Moose and their peers had all learned this message well. In manhood they were very protective of their honour and would have felt the depths of shame if it was tarnished.

With their equipment in top shape for the next Hunt, the men got down to the chore of finishing preparations for selecting a new Village Chief. Because of the extensive democratic require-ments of the Mi'kmaq Nation, the process to elect a replacement, which had been set in motion by the death of the Village Chief, was normally slow and cumbersome and sometimes took several Moons to complete. This was especially so when the People had a multitude of candidates that they needed to assess, to assure that the eventual winner would be possessed with a high degree of honour, wisdom, intelligence and all the other characteristics required to provide the community with wise and dependable leadership.

The search to find qualified candidates was not difficult. The office of Chief was the prerogative of males only, so the education *young boys received from Elders and parents in early childhood was structured to develop in them high ideals of character, in preparation for the possibility of one Sunrise being considered for office. Thus, as they grew into manhood, Mi'kmaq young men strove to live in a manner that would engender the People's trust by supporting loyally the laws of the country and devoting their lives to assure the welfare of others.*

Two of the most important skills the People looked for as regards political office were the ability to communicate and use logic to persuade. These characteristics were very important because the man selected to fill the office had to be extremely capable of using oration, logic and persuasion. Indeed, there was no other option to get people to follow your ideas and guidance, save for demonstrating through your actions and words the strength of your resolve. The use of force by a Mi'kmaq leader to compel others to carry out his wishes was not an option open to him. Mi'kmaq society was a democracy; the People's will was paramount.

As a tool to help assure that their young people grew into adulthood with great respect for the democratic practices used to select leadership, the Elders used the legend about the Despotic Dictators. This is how they told it:

The Mi'kmaq Nation, in ancient Sunrises, was governed over by cruel and uncaring men. They forced citizens on pain of death, or barbaric punishments, to obey and carry out their commands. For the slightest infraction people were tortured, and a favourite pastime was ordering the death penalty for minor as well as major infractions.

Thus abused constantly, the People lived in terror and silently prayed to the Great Spirit for deliverance from their tormentors. Generation after generation they kept the faith and continued to believe that some Sunrise the Father would respond. However, after the passage of thousands of Moons, many were despairing of ever being rid of them.

The Great Spirit, after watching with a heavy heart the mistreatment of succeeding generations of the People, and hoping that they could find a way to revolt and overcome, finally decided they would never be rid of their persecutors without His help. His decision was not taken lightly, because He felt it was up to men to make their own way. He had hoped that somewhere along the line of succeeding generations of Dictators that some would see the grievous error of their ways and adopt a more humane approach towards the People. To limit interference, His help was not to be in the form of Divine physical intervention but human, with the possibility of failure.

Thus, unknown to the People, He caused a boy to be born during a severe Winter storm. The boy was destined to help lead them in revolution against their heartless Masters. As a big blizzard raged during his birth Sunrise, he was named Big Blizzard. To assure that he would have a very good chance in adulthood of unseating the Dictators, the Father endowed him with exceptional human intellectual abilities and a caring conscience. He also, knowing that strength and courage would be needed, assured that Big Blizzard was without a peer in strength and courage.

Not known to any human, including his parents, the Great Spirit's hand was apparent in the boy's early childhood. By the arrival of the first anniversary of his birth he was already displaying an exceptionally high intelligence and courage of conviction. The Dictators, recognizing Big Blizzard's outstanding abilities, took him under their wings when he was three Springs old and began to indoctrinate him with their *ideology, grooming him to become one of them.*

Big Blizzard, as is typical of many young people, enjoyed the trappings of power and partook of its benefits freely. The daily suffering and degradation of the People were noticed by him, but initially caused him no concern. However, as his birth Seasons passed, the pervasive suffering and misery of the People began to instill in his conscience a dislike for what he saw. This caused him to think about ways to alleviate their suffering. However, his progressive ideas of making peaceful revolutionary changes to the system were replaced by plans for violent change, following a horrific event during his eighteenth Winter. It brought home to him the full extent of the suffering of the People.

The thing that turned him completely against his mentors was the horrific policy that they implemented to cope with the minor discomforts they were suffering because of the severe Winter weather that settled in and stayed. The snow was deep, the cold was bone-chilling and the winds seemed to blow without end. In the midst of it, to assure their own comfort, the Dictators forced the People to give up most of the warm furs that they had set aside for Winter clothing and bedding. Because of this heartlessness, the citizens were suffering the rigours of the severe Winter in abject misery. Many were dying from malnutrition, diseases and exposure.

Then, as if this weren't bad enough, they decided to tax the will of the People to survive even further by issuing an edict requiring that each wigwam give them one-third of their food stores. This demand condemned many of the remaining people to almost immediate death.

As he watched the results of this inhumanity, Big Blizzard felt great revulsion. This caused him to hatch in his mind a plan to unseat the Dictators. But they were supported by a well-fed and fully equipped army. He knew this would be a difficult task that involved great personal risk. In addition, he also knew that the People, his hoped-for allies, had nothing of substance to offer or contribute to the effort except a strong desire to be free. However, he prayed that when the revolution began, it would impel the People to find the courage to rise up.

In the Land of Souls, the Great Spirit was viewing the development with pleasure. To help assure that Big Blizzard's revolutionary plan would work, He caused His helper Glooscap to visit him in a dream and offer reassurance. To this end, Glooscap told him that night that the Great Spirit would not openly use His formidable powers to dislodge the Dictators, but He was in complete support of Big Blizzard's plans to do so. Because of these encouraging words, when he awoke, Big Blizzard felt a great surge of confidence in the rightness of the path he had chosen.

He started feeling out some very carefully selected friends in the ruling class to determine if they felt any compassion for the People's hardship. To his relieved surprise, several spoke out in private about the pity and shame they felt because of the horrible suffering they saw every Sunrise. He also discovered that they believed in their hearts that all human beings were created equal and that everyone should receive equal treatment. When asked if they would join him in attempting to overthrow the Dictators, they readily agreed. The Great Spirit, watching the progress, was overjoyed that the first seeds of democratic principles had finally taken roots in the minds of some of the ruling class.

The inspired conspirators, under Big Blizzard's leadership, organized a small secret society to finesse plans for the struggle to unseat the Dictators. They also started to rough out the democratic tenets needed to establish the free society envisioned. For this task they used three principles: equality, honour and sharing. The idea was that laws enacted from such a base would in time make dictatorships, dishonourable conduct, intolerance and greed all but obsolete in the new society.

Because of the danger of being caught, they worked together in the knowledge that speedy actions were in the best interest of starting a revolt with any chance of success. They completed the planning stage in only ten Sunrises, recruiting carefully selected warriors to take on the task of recruiting more.

Although it increased the danger for them substantially, more men had to be brought into the core group from the ruling class to support the magnitude of the operation. As expected, the recruiting soon led to rumours of the plot spreading among the citizens. At the same time, the mounting tensions generated in them an undercurrent of excitement. When the Dictators were made aware of the rumours, they decided to take immediate, and if necessary, forceful action to determine their validity. However, having absolute control of the Nation's powerful army, they were supremely confident and didn't feel threatened.

Big Blizzard, because his name had been mentioned in connection with the rumours, was summoned to appear before them. They, knowing that petty jealousies were rampant among the upper class, and that many among them constantly tried to curry favour, tended to treat the whole matter as a figment of someone's vindictive imagination. This was a very feasible assumption; it was an open secret that many among the aspiring ruling class deeply resented Big Blizzard's imminent position in the Dictator's list of preferred leaders. Because of this, ugly rumours about his character and loyalty *had been floated before, and more could be expected.*

When questioned, Big Blizzard, with the conviction of the righteous in such situations, convincingly denied knowing of a plot and stated a belief that the rumours were indeed the product of jealous peers. The Dictators, accepting the explanation without reservation, dismissed the charges.

However, the encounter brought home to Big Blizzard the fact that the time for full implementation was at hand. He reported the details of his meeting with the Dictators to his inner circle. He also shared with them his conclusion that they must put their plan into action immediately. They concurred and the revolt began. They decided to do so by first bringing the plot out into the open at a face-to-face meeting with the Dictators.

Thus, armed with not much more than their determination to change the political and social environment of their Nation, they arranged, with great apprehension in their hearts, a meeting with the Despots. The meeting, they knew, with almost complete certainty, would quickly result in a sentence of death for all participants. Without regard to this certainty, they met with the Dictators and delivered their message. As expected, their proposal to reform the system was immediately rejected and they were all sentenced to death. Upon hearing the response, they speedily implemented a previously devised escape plan and were out of the village and into the forest before they could be arrested. Once into the forest they speedily made their way to a previously selected secret location from which they quickly began the recruitment of a volunteer army.

Their call for more volunteers to unseat the Dictators spread like a fire throughout the country and ignited in the population an unquenchable thirst for freedom. The response exceeded all expectations. Within a few Sunrises hundreds of warriors, in many cases with nothing much to offer than their determined bodies, began arriving in the dozens as if out of nowhere.

Such an enthusiastic response was heartwarming to Big Blizzard and his colleagues. They had thought, because of their long oppression, that the People might be too timid to risk the retribution of the Dictators by openly giving support to a rebellion. However, their enthusiastic response indicated to them that success for the revolution was within grasp.

Within half a Moon, the ragtag army of freedom fighters numbered in the thousands. With makeshift and meagre weapons, they were strategically dispersed to attack from locations across the country. With their army in place, the leaders picked a Sunrise to begin the war for freedom.

By this time, the Dictators were well aware of the planned uprising. However, related to their remarkable overconfidence, they all but ignored what was going on around them. In their supreme arrogance, they believed that their overwhelmingly superior army would crush the rebels, like so many maggots, in a few Sunrises, if rebellion actually broke out. They were so contemptuous of the threat the rebels posed that they didn't order the army to take any extraordinary defensive actions. Because of their contempt, it was impossible for them to consider that the forces opposing them were motivated by something that would make them unstoppable, a determined thirst for freedom.

When the Sunrise of the uprising arrived, the warriors prepared themselves for battle by making their peace with the Great Spirit. Soon after dawn, they attacked key strategic locations as planned and met with unexpected success. Resistance in many places, including the headquarters of the Dictators, was at most nominal.

Big Blizzard, who led the attack on the headquarters of the Dictators, was shocked and pleasantly surprised by the lack of organized resistance. It quickly became apparent to him that the army the Dictators had relied upon for protection had become fat and lazy over the passage of hundreds of Moons. They were ill-prepared to mount any kind of defence. They could not muster even a fraction of the mighty force everyone had expected. The People arose en masse in open support and the vaunted army that the Dictators had relied upon to retain power dissolved quickly. By the following Sunrise the fight for freedom was won with very little bloodshed.

The victors arrested the Dictators and put them on trial. To no one's surprise, given the overwhelming evidence against them, they were quickly convicted of committing crimes against humanity and sentenced to be executed at the end of two Seasons if they did not repent. They were told that their death sentences would be commuted if they begged the People for forgiveness and mercy, accepted responsibility for their sins and undertook to live the rest of their lives in humility and in the service of the Great Spirit and the People.

All but two were eventually rehabilitated and went on to become respected and trusted members of the community. After they had come to fully appreciate the benefits of living in a democratic society, they became some of the new order's most ardent defenders. The two who continued to refuse to repent had their sentences commuted. They lived the rest of their lives as shunned outcasts in the community. The People, who had suffered grievously under the Dictators, never again permitted individuals to rule them autocratically.

It is no wonder that the Mi'kmaq People do not suffer fools when picking leaders.

//

CHAPTER FOUR

Leading up to the nominating and election Sunrise, several of the village's most honourable and respected men were being actively considered by the People for the post. Most were actively promoting their causes in the low-keyed Mi'kmaq fashion. But one, who didn't know he was among those being considered, was getting a lot of attention. Unbeknownst to Lightning Bolt, although he still had several Moons to go before he passed his twenty-second birth Season, he was considered by most of his peers to be the top contender for the office.

His credentials were impressive: Honourary War Chief of Kespek, Junior War Chief of his own Nation, a great hunter, a person eager to learn, a brilliant strategist in the Hunt and in warfare, a young man with a high degree of intelligence, an ability to innovate, who was trustworthy and loyal.

Lightning Bolt, when he became aware of the activities of his family and friends in support of a candidacy for him, tried without success to dissuade them from it. However, after much debate, he reluctantly agreed to allow them to put his name forward.

As scheduled, on the twenty-fourth Sunrise of Winter, the nomination and election meeting was called to order. In the absence of a Chief, the village's senior Elder, White Dawn, presided. She opened the meeting by asking Elder Swift Otter to lead a talk to the Great Spirit.

He responded eloquently, "My brothers and sisters, please stand and raise your hands with me to the Creator. Great Father of the Universe, we your humble children implore you to give us the wisdom to choose a leader with the qualities needed to lead us into a prosperous and peaceful future." Swift Otter went on to thank the Father for the kindness He had shown the People and finished with, "Dear Father, we your humble and obedient children acknowledge Your supremacy!"

White Dawn then requested they assume proper formation for a Sweet-grass Ceremony. Smoke from smouldering sweet-grass braids was offered by the Elders to the People who then symbolically took the smoke and washed their bodies with it to cleanse their spirits. Afterwards, White Dawn asked for the Pipe-Smoking Ceremony to begin. It was performed by the village's senior male Elder, Black Bear.

Elder White Dawn then opened the meeting for business. "Brothers and sisters, we will now begin the process of electing our Village Chief." During her discourse she reminded the People of their responsibilities in the process, and then continued, "I open the meeting to nominations. Crazy Moose."

"My brothers and sisters, I respectfully nominate a warrior who is my friend and brother. He is a man whose lifestyle and performance of duties have earned our utmost respect. He has great intelligence, courage and wisdom, and is very humble. I believe that if we make him our leader he will lead our People in a responsible manner and work diligently to assure the future prosperity of our village. My dear friends, I nominate Lightning Bolt." Crazy Moose's nomination was seconded by Storm Cloud.

White Dawn then asked if there were any further nominations. "I recognize Mighty Eagle," she said.

"My brothers and sisters, the man I propose for office is a person who has displayed many times over by his outstanding performance during Hunts and in warfare that he has all the attributes necessary for leadership. His intelligence and wisdom are unquestionable. I respectfully nominate my friend and brother Red Fox." This nomination was seconded by White Cloud.

White Dawn then asked for further nominations. After a reasonable wait, with none forthcoming, she closed the process. Then, she invited the nominees to come forward and address the People. Lightning Bolt, as the first nominated, led off with a speech that he hoped would enhance Red Fox's chances. "My beloved brothers and sisters, I humbly stand here before you this Sunrise and wonder, what am I doing here? I, a man of only twenty-one Springs, being proposed for the office of Village Chief, over a man with such an illustrious background as Red Fox, is inconceivable to me. He has seen twice as many Moons as I. Therefore, he has twice as much experience in practically everything. I cannot favourably compare to him in this area.

"In addition, he is a great hunter and has established a record fighting in war that is impeccable. His wisdom is widely acknowledged and his advice is sought by many. How could I, a young unlearned child in comparison, possibly hope to have you realistically favour my pitiful attributes in comparison to a warrior as brave and wise as he? It seems almost disrespectful to even contemplate that I could.

"When I ask myself, what have I done in life to deserve such an honour from the People, I have to honestly answer, not very much. Then when I ask my friends the same question, they respond by relating things that I did during the Kespek War, during Hunts, and so on. This isn't right. I've tried to tell them that the only reason I performed well is because I was fortunate enough to have working with me the most capable partner that a man could ever ask for, Crazy Moose. Without him I would be lost.

"Yet, in spite of these shortcomings they insisted that I allow them to nominate me for the prestigious position of Village Chief. Reluctantly, I acquiesced to their wishes, and now stand before you nominated. Therefore, if for some reason beyond me, you decide to make me Chief over Red Fox, I will undertake to perform the duties of office in as humble and conscientious a manner as my father did before me. I'll serve with the knowledge that the dignity of the People takes precedence over all else. However, after saying this, if you were to wisely choose Red Fox over me, I would agree that you have made the right choice. Thank you."

Red Fox was then asked to address the People. His words were long afterwards remembered for their eloquence and wisdom. "Brothers and sisters, during my lifetime I have heard many great speeches and some not so great. Some lasted for what seemed like Seasons and some for what seemed like only blinks of an eye. The wisdom shared in the messages has been savoured and appreciated, or, sometimes rejected. Not once over my forty-one Summers have I ever made a public comment about any of them. They were received in the generosity in which they were given and the kindness of the giver was acknowledged.

"But, my friends, this Sunrise I will alter my practice and make a comment about the one just made. The speech made by my brother Lightning Bolt, although short, was for me the greatest speech I've ever heard. His humility overwhelms me. He claims because of his age that he has very little to offer the People, but you and I know that he has already given us much. He belittles his performance in battle, yet I have seen his performance and I know it knows no equal. He says that in the Hunt, it is because of the labours of his noble friend Crazy Moose that he is successful. I have seen him hunt. His success stems from his own ability as a great hunter. He has shown compassion to friend and foe alike. He advocates peace everywhere he goes. When it comes to possessing wisdom he has few equals. In short, my friends, he has the makings of a great leader.

"My brothers and sisters, over the passage of my Seasons I have striven to live my life in a manner that would at some Season make me worthy in the eyes of the People for the office of Chief. This, as you well know, is the dream of most men in our society. Most of us know that we shall never realize our dreams, but yet we continue to dream. Sometimes with luck they do come true. Until Lightning Bolt spoke this Sunrise, I thought this was the time when mine would be realized. But after hearing his humble speech, I know that it is not the time for me.

"Brothers and sisters, I humbly withdraw my nomination and ask that you give unanimous consent to the appointment of Lightning Bolt as our Chief!"

With a mighty roar of approval, the People made it so. Lightning Bolt became the youngest Village Chief in the history of the Nation.

Red Fox spoke again. "My People," he said, "we have chosen wisely. Before stepping down, I wish to thank all who supported me. I'll forever be grateful for your generosity and kindness. Brothers and sisters, may the Great Spirit always be with you and may He always guide the actions of our new leader."

White Dawn, when the noise died down to a level where she could be heard, asked the new Chief to step forward and take over her duties. He thanked her profusely for her invaluable services and requested that the People give her a big hand in recognition of a job well done. They did with enthusiasm. He then invited Red Fox to come forward. The brothers embraced and Lightning Bolt thanked him for his support:

"Red Fox, my brother, the words you spoke in favour of my appointment show that you have a generous and kind soul. You mention a dream of being Chief. Well, my brother, to me you are a Chief among Chiefs, and shall always be, because only a strong and wise man could have said what you did this Sunrise. I only hope that I can live up to your confidence and expectations. To assure that I have constant access to your wisdom, I respectfully ask the People to agree to appoint you Chief of the Hunt." This position had been held by Lightning Bolt and he was happy to pass the responsibility along to someone as experienced as Red Fox, so that he could focus fully on his new duties.

The People roared their approval and Red Fox's dream of being rewarded with leadership came true. During his acceptance speech, Lightning Bolt thanked the People who had, in spite of his age and efforts to dissuade them, given to him their confidence. He pledged before the Great Spirit that he would do everything in his power to ensure that their confidence and trust were not misplaced and that he would uphold the Nation's laws in administering village affairs with unwavering diligence.

He recalled the memory of his father and promised to faithfully follow his example of dedication to the People. Then, above all, he thanked the Great Spirit for blessing him with a loving family and a multitude of friends. He did not mention the fact that in spite of his outward signs of confidence, he harboured within him serious doubts about his ability to deliver what the People expected. After the meeting, the People turned their energies towards celebrating his election, as an excuse for getting together with loved ones. It would be a major celebration, with people from across the Nation and beyond.

With the thought of friends and relatives visiting from faraway villages, who they hadn't seen for many Moons, the People became involved in planning preparations with undisguised enthusiasm. Even small children got caught up in the excitement. The Elders, in consultation with Lightning Bolt's family, set the anniversary of Lightning Bolt's birth Sunrise to begin the festivities. The guest list was to include the leaders from the other six Mi'kmaq countries as well as relatives and friends.

The women, to keep the guests well fed during the party, started preparing a feast of delicacies that would tickle the taste buds of the most discriminating of appetites. Sweets were made from honey and maple syrup. Choice meats and fish were delicately smoked over oak fires with the greatest of care and devotion. And, as an extra bonus, they already had available an abundant supply of moose butter they had made from the bones of last Season's Hunt. There was no doubt that the People would savour this delight. The preparations held the promise of a feast to be remembered for a multitude of Moons.

To allow plenty of time to prepare for travel, runners were sent to deliver invitations to the leaders of their sister Mi'kmaq countries and to their Eastern Allies. The leaders were asked to spread the word around that any of their citizens who wanted to come would be welcomed with open arms.

Big Timber and most of his country's Village Chiefs and other Chiefs had already advised of their intentions to attend in the company of many of their countrymen. The runners also delivered invitations throughout the region asking teams to come compete in games such as canoeing, archery and moose calling. In short order, positive responses began rolling in from far away places. The party was shaping up to be the awesome event desired.

In the midst of all the hectic preparations, Lightning Bolt, feeling a need for peace and tranquility, asked Crazy Moose to accompany him for a few Sunrises on a snowshoeing and camping trip. His friend, also feeling a need for some relief from the hustle and bustle going on around him, quickly agreed.

In anticipation of the rest and relaxation awaiting them, they departed shortly after dawn the next Sunrise and snowshoed for several thousand canoe lengths before setting up camp late in the afternoon at an idyllic location they loved, high up on the side of a small mountain. That night, sitting by their warm campfire with a vista before them of a moonlit valley covered in snow, the friends had a serious discussion about their futures.

Crazy Moose began by asking Lightning Bolt, "My brother, have you summoned up the courage yet to approach

Spring Flower's father to get permission to ask her if she would consent to a courtship with you?"

"Yes, my brother, I have. As soon as the celebrations are over, I plan to do so. How about you, will you soon be asking Silver Fox for permission to court Little Moonbeam?"

"Yes, my friend. I've also decided to make my move after the celebrations are over. However, I think it will be a waste of time. I would move mountains for her, but I don't think she could ever love someone as unworthy as I."

Lightning Bolt stated: "My feelings exactly."

In this negative frame of mind, these two brave men, who would lay down their lives without hesitation to protect their country or a friend, spent a beautiful late Winter moonlit evening sitting before a warm campfire comparing notes on the terrifying subject of preparing to take a wife. Like their fathers before them, they had put off the heart-stopping task as long as the yearning in their hearts would permit. But, also like their fathers, they would get the job done. They were madly in love with women with whom they had not shared one word of intimacy. However, they were very fortunate, as back in the village were two lovely young women in the very same situation. They too were wondering if the handsome young men would ever come calling.

Meanwhile, the women of the community, mindful of the need to have their men and children well clad for the festivities, were spending a great deal of time designing and stitching together well-decorated outfits for the celebration. When these products of their imaginations were ready, made from the finest moose, elk, beaver and other animal pelts, they were among the finest anyone could hope to wear. The one they produced for their new Chief to wear the Sunrise of the celebration was awesome in its splendour.

Finally, after what seemed like an extra-long Winter, which seemed that way only because of the wait for the celebrations, the party Sunrise was near. Many guests began arriving and the excitement increased substantially. Kespek's Chief, Big Beaver, accompanied by a large contingent of warriors and villagers, was among the first. They were greeted with traditional Mi'kmaq hospitality and made welcome in the wigwams of their hosts.

Finally, Lightning Bolt's birth Season Sunrise had arrived, the third Sunrise before the first full Moon of Spring. The colourful splendour that poured over the landscape as the sun rose over the horizon filled those who saw it with renewed appreciation for Mother Earth's wonders. The People hoped that it was a sign that the Great Spirit would bless them with good weather for the entire celebration. To this end they gave humble thanks for the great beginning and prayed that for the next three Sunrises He would let the fine early Spring weather continue. He answered their prayers. The weather for the event was the nicest, warmest and clearest anyone could remember for a Spring Season.

The list of leaders arriving from other countries to join the celebrations was impressive. Even their neighbours, the Atikitkas and Penikt Nations, halted their seasons of warfare with one another in a truce so that both could join the celebration. Normally, because villages numbered in the hundreds, the turnout of National Chiefs and allied leaders for celebrating an appointment of a Village Chief was nominal. The usual attendance came from the leaders of the country where the village was located and sometimes the Grand Chief. The difference in Lightning Bolt's case was that he was already recognized far and wide as an outstanding leader and warrior, with an impeccable reputation for bravery and honour.

The makers of the colourful clothing celebrants wore on the first Sunrise of festivities were profusely complimented. They were treats for the eyes. But the makers of the outfits were especially pleased by the oohs and ahs uttered when Lightning Bolt turned out in his new outfit. The sight of the handsome young Chief in all of his glory was enough to warm the hearts of the coldest young women.

Big Timber, as Kespukwitk's National Chief, automatically presided over any meeting held in the country when he was present. He opened the celebrations by asking senior Elder White Dawn to lead a prayer to the Great Spirit. When she finished and the Sweet-grass and Pipe-Smoking Ceremonies were over, Big Timber extended a warm welcome to the guests and wished them an exciting and happy visit. He then asked Grand Chief Big Elk to say a few words.

The Grand Chief began by extending greetings to the several thousand people in attendance. "Brothers and sisters, on behalf of Sipekne'katik and the Grand Council, I bring you greetings! It gives me great pleasure to be here to help an outstanding young man celebrate his appointment to office. Adding to the pleasure is the opportunity it provides to renew relationships with beloved relatives and dear friends from far away places who we haven't seen for many Moons. To see their smiling faces again is like a taste of honey. My friends, I can tell by the excitement that these next three Sunrises will provide us with sweet memories that will last into eternity.

"My friends, partying is a wonderful way to celebrate with our brother Lightning Bolt his elevation to the office of Village Chief. But he has another reason to celebrate this Sunrise; he is also celebrating his twenty-second birth-Spring. Please join with me in extending best wishes to him on reaching this landmark in his life."

The wishes came from the crowd in a mighty roar.

Grand Chief Big Elk continued. "Brothers and sisters, our brother Lightning Bolt is a young man who has demonstrated to all during his twenty-two Springs on Mother Earth that with determination and dedication to duty one can achieve great things in life. He is an inspiration to all young people. The fact that the villagers have made him their leader at so young an age is a testament to his abilities and potential.

"Already, even at this tender age, he has shown wisdom far beyond his Seasons. As a result, many are seeking him out for advice and guidance. And he has demonstrated beyond challenge that he is a man of honour who carries out responsibilities with dignity and humility. He has indeed displayed all the qualities required of a great leader.

"My friends, I want to make a prediction this Sunrise that I firmly believe will come to pass. I predict that Lightning Bolt will one Season lead his country, and later be appointed Grand Chief. Further, he will live to see the passage of his hundredth Spring in good health. In great age he will be greatly respected and loved by all. During his lifespan, he will become renowned for his efforts in bringing people to appreciate the folly of war. As a matter of fact, he will be widely known as "the Peacemaker." Upon his death he will be honoured as one of the greatest Chiefs our People have ever known. Now, my children, have a wonderful time and may the Great Spirit be with you."

Several other Chiefs and Elders took turns in wishing Lightning Bolt well and showering him with praise. Then, with great ceremony, the symbols of office were presented to him. Afterwards he addressed the People.

"My friends, I thank you from the bottom of my heart for your confidence. I'm still bewildered by it all, and have some doubt about the wisdom of appointing a person of only twenty-two Seasons to an office that would normally be filled by someone with far more experience in life. However, my fellow villagers have spoken and as a man of honour it is my duty to serve them.

"I want to confess that at the time the villagers appointed me their Chief, I had some serious misgivings. To try to deal with them I decided shortly after getting elected to take seven or eight Sunrises and revisit many of the places in the forest where Father and I had camped when I was young. These places, as you can appreciate, brought back fond memories of our loving relationship and many of the enjoyable Sunrises we had together.

"During our lives most of us find places on Mother Earth, or in our imaginations, where we can enjoy peace and quiet, and to meditate. Father's favourite was deep in the forest at the head of a spring brook, surrounded by gigantic pine trees. The exhilarating scent those mighty trees give off is wondrous. And the taste of the sparkling spring water that feeds the brook is wonderfully refreshing! Even during the hottest Sunrises of Summer the springs produce water that is icy cold and refreshing. This beautiful spot has also become my favourite.

"Because of this I decided to camp there for a few Sunrises to contemplate my future. During my first night, surrounded by the peaceful stillness that sometimes settles upon a forest, I retired early to the coziness of my bed of fresh boughs. Snugly wrapped in sleeping furs, I drifted off to a deep and untroubled sleep. Some time during the night my father visited me in my dreams.

"He told me, 'Son, when you return home, please tell your mother that although I miss her dearly and greatly anticipate the Sunrise when we will be reunited, I'm very happy in the Land of Souls. My happiness is sustained in this magnificent land by the wonderful memories of the loving life we had together. However, my son, sending a message to your mother is only one of two reasons I came to visit with you tonight. The second is to help you overcome your doubts about your ability to honourably lead our village. These misgivings are, my son, without foundation. You have within you all the essential qualities needed by a man to provide strong and wise leadership. Our People have recognized these qualities and with confidence have entrusted their fate to your hands.

"'You must have faith in yourself my son. When striving to fulfil their expectations, you won't fail if you take up the challenge and go forward with honour, wisdom, bravery and confidence. But, when doing so you must always remember that the Great Spirit is the guiding hand behind all our accomplishments, and thus we must always be humble before Him. Have peace of mind, my son, and may the Father be with you always.'

"After my dearly beloved Father's words of encouragement, I drifted back into a deep and untroubled sleep. When I awoke at the crack of dawn to the sounds of birds and the wind singing in the air, I felt a sense of peace and renewal. It was in this state that I spent the rest of the Sunrise drinking in the beauty around me and meditating about the future. I have, my friends, with the help of the Great Spirit and my father, overcome as much as possible my misgivings.

"However, I don't believe they have dissipated to the extent where I could live up to the predictions that my beloved Grandfather Grand Chief Big Elk has made. But I do thank him and all of my other friends who spoke for the kindness of their words. This Sunrise has given me memories that shall provide comfort to me for the rest of my life.

"In closing, my brothers and sisters, I wish to offer my humble and heartfelt thanks to those of you who have come from near and far and honoured us in our wigwams with your presence. I also wish to thank the People of our village who have expended so much of their time and effort to make sure that everything needed was in place to make the party a resounding success. Most of all I wish to thank the Great Spirit for giving us the means to come together and bask in the glory of His creations and benevolence.

"Stay with us, my friends, as long as it pleases you, and during your stay be part of our family. We cherish your company and will miss you greatly when you leave. Now, my dear brothers and sisters, please enjoy in peace the excellent food and make good cheer."

With the end of his speech began a party that would be talked about for many Moons afterwards. The food was succulent and great entertainment delighted all. With this atmosphere of mutual love and admiration surrounding him, Lightning Bolt, at last, began to feel comfortable with his appointment as Village Chief.

//

CHAPTER FIVE

The Sunrise after the Chief-installation celebrations ended, Lightning Bolt and Crazy Moose made arrangements to meet in the evening with the fathers of the women they had secretly loved for some time. They would ask for courtship permission. Although these meetings held the promise of future happiness, they each were arranged with a great deal of pessimism. The fear these warriors carried regarding their ability to win the love of their chosen brides filled them with trepidation. The obviousness of their feelings also promised to provide their prospective fathers-in-law with many Sunrises of fun.

That evening, with despair in their hearts, they approached the fathers. The fact that they did this at the same time, during the same evening, was a feeble attempt at bolstering each other's resolve. At least they could dare each other on toward their dreaded goal of facing these fathers and their almost certain demise. But when they faced each father of their special dream and their beloved, they were completely alone. As if standing stark naked and exposed, each entered the wigwam of the father of his beloved feeling as if this encounter was bound to be a battle he would lose in great humiliation and despair.

As if like clockwork, both fathers appeared with a great deal of disapproving grumpiness. Lightning Bolt's heart raced. Across the encampment, Crazy Moose felt the same panic rising to his throat like bile threatening his ability to breathe. As if by some fate of the stars, they each mysteriously remembered that the other was facing the same trial by fire. This did not help them much, but it did give them a form of solidarity.

The fathers put them through the paces. In reality, Lazy Beaver and Silver Fox were as happy as loons in Spring with nests full of eggs in the security of marshes. They were overjoyed at the prospect of having a proven young man as their son, knowing full well how tested these boys had been and how they had both displayed the highest qualities of personhood anyone could hope for in a son-in-law.

The two boys did not yet know the hidden skills of reading hearts, nor did they foresee the age-old ways that father-in-laws tended to behave, because this knowledge tended to remain hidden within the traditional culture. And even if they were aware, such awareness could too easily be registered as a false sense of self-assurance. Because, after all, the right of the father of any girl remained firm; he could refuse the courtship for any number of reasons and many a father had done so. Regardless of how many battles were won or how many Hunts brought home with success, every young man who came asking for permission to court a young woman had not two legs to stand on. And it certainly felt like legs turning to pine sap when it came to such an uncertain undertaking. After sweating them out for several grueling hours with an appearance of great reluctance, each father gave his prospective suitor permission to ask his daughter if she would see him.

Afterwards, with hearts thumping at the thought of it, they met each other in the middle of the village. Their eyes were afire. Their hands waved in the air with large gestures of victory. Anyone looking on would have been astonished and would think they had just won a great victory in war. They quickly described the events that each had endured, making it sound as if each had suffered the greater humiliation. But their hearts were aglow with passion, so they quickly decided to approach the ladies of their dreams the evening of the next Sunrise. Their bodies went limp and silent. Anyone watching might have thought they had come to the part of any story of conflict where the warriors remembered their fallen comrades. A solid two moments of silence was respected between them. They each knew, with little doubt, they would be rejected. They each knew they had never summoned the courage to speak to their beloved before this moment. To give each other courage, and as moral support, they agreed to also face this trial at the same time.

When the moment of truth was near, as the next Sunrise arrived, they were in a near panic and approached the daunting task with an air of the condemned. If someone had stepped forward at this crucial moment and given them a valid excuse to disappear, they would have done so immediately with gratitude. However, shortly after arriving at the wigwams of the ladies of their dreams, they posed the question and were told to return the following evening for answers. This increased their agony and tension tremendously.

When the heroes returned the following evening, after Spring Flower and Little Moonbeam had accepted their proposals with enthusiasm, they were completely flab-bergasted. In great relief, and filled with happiness, they exchanged news. "Crazy Moose, my brother, how goes it? You look as if you have just realized every pleasant dream you've ever dreamed. I gather that Little Moonbeam said yes."

"She did my friend, she did! The Great Spirit had pity on me and answered my prayers. I was so happy when she said yes that I had to use all of my willpower not to dance with joy. But, my brother, you must feel the same way because I can tell by the happiness showing on your face that Spring Flower has also said yes. What say, my friend, we have a double wedding?"

"My brother, my brother, yes Spring Flower answered my prayers to the Great Spirit and agreed to see me. As a matter of fact, when she said yes, it felt as if the weight of the world was lifted off my shoulders. In fact my friend I still find it hard to believe, but she seemed enthusiastic. You know, I believe she really likes me and looks forward to our courtship with as much enthusiasm as I do. However, I think it's a little early to be discussing a double wedding. After all, we haven't even spent one Sunrise with them yet. But, if things go well, and they agree to it, I can't think of anything more pleasing than to be married at the same time as you."

With the same exuberant enthusiasm that they applied to everything else they did in life, they courted the ladies of their dreams and eventually were rewarded with acceptances of proposals of marriage. And, as hoped, the women agreed to a double wedding. The fifth Sunrise after the first Moon of Summer was chosen for the ceremony. Their families and friends helped them plan a wedding party that they believed would be rated a great event by attendees.

Planning for a double wedding was a new experience for the community. Making it even rarer was the fact that one of the parties was Village Chief. Under normal circumstances a few relatives and friends from other Mi'kmaq Nations and most of the villagers would be expected to attend. In this instance, where the grooms were two esteemed young men and the brides were two of the most beautiful, intelligent and sought after women in the Nation, the wedding was expected to attract a very large crowd of well-wishers from most of the Mi'kmaq and allied countries. Therefore, plans had to be made to feed as many as a thousand guests, or more, for several Sunrises. A daunting task!

A few Sunrises before the big event, guests began arriving in Lightning Bolt's village from far away places for the second time within four Moons. The villagers welcomed them back with open arms. Some visitors, in mock anger, teased their hosts that they were not able to do without their company.

When Kespek's Chief Big Beaver arrived, even though he was very pleased to have another opportunity to visit with beloved friends and relatives, he, with mirth in his eyes, remarked to Lightning Bolt in an exaggerated crabby manner, "My son, I love you like one of my own, and thus receive news of your accomplishments and successes in life with pride. But, as an act of kindness to an old man, can't you put a little space between celebrating your milestones in life? It seems, on account of your achievements, I've been in travel constantly for the last several Moons. I had just arrived home and barely had time to greet my family properly before I had to start preparing to return here for your wedding. In the future please try to put at least twelve Moons between such events. If I keep travelling at this pace, I'll soon be nothing but a faint memory in the minds of my grandchildren."

Lightning Bolt, with love for his aged friend showing clearly on his face, responded in kind, "Welcome back, my beloved father! Your presence and caustic comments bring me great joy. If I could manufacture a thousand reasons to keep you coming back here constantly, I would, because when you're gone, I pine for your company. Just the thought that I can look forward to sitting around a campfire with you tonight, if you feel up to it after your long journey, to hear more of your wonderful tales, fills me with anticipation. And, I promise you my father, that I will, if your absence from Kespek makes your image grow foggy in the minds of your grandchildren, with joy in my heart, travel to Kespek and reintroduce you to them."

"My son, you make me feel welcome and at home."

The weddings were a resounding success. The rites, food and celebrations were enjoyed tremendously by all. The happy young couples thanked the Great Spirit for their happiness and their family and friends for their generous love and support. That night, after consummating their marriage, the love Lightning Bolt and Spring Flower had for each other was reflected in the vows of undying love they made as they lay in a cozy embrace, covered by warm furs in their fir-scented bed of soft boughs. Lightning Bolt made his straight from the heart. "My precious Spring Flower, if it was even possible to love you more, I would, but my love for you already knows no bounds. To put in words how I feel is probably impossible, my sweet flower, but I'll try. Having you in my arms this night is like having a wonderful magical dream come true for me. If in reality it proves a dream and you are lost to me forever when I awake, my heartbreak would be inconsolable. My darling, knowing that we will now share in the most intimate way our lives, and be there always to comfort each other through both good and bad times, this is my idea of the Land of Souls on Mother Earth. I promise you, my little flower, that I shall love and cherish you forever."

Spring Flower's response was equal in heartfelt intensity: "My husband, they say the pleasures that our ancestors know in the Land of Souls far outshines any we can ever know on Mother Earth. If such is the case I truly look forward to going there for I can't imagine knowing more happiness than I know tonight. My love for you, my darling, is also indescribable. I promise, my precious, that it will remain so for all eternity." With more such words of endearment tickling their ears and warming their souls, the young lovers talked until the first light of dawn about their hopes and dreams for the future.

The following morning, installed in their own wigwam, they settled into a comfortable and loving homemaking routine. Two Springs later, while a storm sprinkled snowflakes of many shapes and designs over the countryside, Spring Flower gave birth to a beautiful girl. But it was a long and challenging birth, a true struggle for life, during which Lightning Bolt's admiration and love for Spring Flower grew even greater. When he first held his little girl, he could think of nothing more perfect on Mother Earth. They named their daughter Snow Flake, inspired by the snow that fell during her birth.

Because of complications encountered during her birth, Snow Flake was to be the only natural-born child Lightning Bolt and Spring Flower would have. Like most fathers, Lightning Bolt had dreamed of having a son some Sunrise, but accepted it as the will of the Creator. He thanked the Great Spirit profusely for giving them a daughter who was as dear to him as life itself.

In happy coincidence, on the same Sunrise, Crazy Moose

and Little Moonbeam welcomed to their wigwam a baby boy. The storm clouds that produced the snowflakes that gave Snow Flake her name were an inspiration to the happy parents, and they named their son Storm Cloud. Friends teasingly asked the couples afterward if they had deliberately timed things to have the children at the same time.

Being close friends, the young families spent many contented evenings feasting in each other's wigwams and enjoying the pastime and entertainment of spinning tales invented with much imagination. They also spent many vacations travelling together, exploring the panoramic and awe-inspiring wonders of their country, and others.

One of their favourite spots, and one they visited often, was Blomidon. On a clear Sunrise they could see from the top of its cliff across the Basin of High Tides to the lands of neighbouring Mi'kmaq countries. The vast scenery of water and land was often bathed in the glory of spectacular sunrises and sunsets. It was something that can only be truly appreciated by being there.

As time passed their children, Snow Flake and Storm Cloud, became inseparable. This led many to assume that in adulthood they would marry. It was not to be, because the loving friendship they forged was that of sister and brother, of comrades and confidants. In fact, when they did marry, their mates accepted their loving friendship without reservation and became a part of it.

For the next ten Springs, things changed little in village life. The Seasons came and went and the community lived a life of contentment in concert with the Great Spirit and Mother Earth. During these Seasons, Lightning Bolt matured in his roles as Chief, advisor and mediator. Because of his roles and growth in wisdom, the esteem in which he was held continued to grow. As he aged, his ability to find fair and just solutions for problems large and small, between brothers and sisters, friends and Nations, was becoming legendary. Under his able and competent leadership the village prospered.

Shortly after the second Moon of Lightning Bolt's thirty-third Spring, an event occurred that altered the lives of many people. At dawn a foreign ship, about five hundred canoe lengths off the coast of Kespukwitk, floundered and sank during a raging storm. All hands, except one, were lost. The disaster occurred almost directly off the point where Lightning Bolt's People set up their Spring and Summer village.

The deliverance of the survivor from the jaws of death was miraculous. His ordeal had started when the rigging came loose and smashed into him with such force that it knocked him unconsciousness. He and Lightning Bolt later reasoned that somehow, after the blow had struck, the force of its movement had flung him atop a piece of wreckage, which acted as a life-raft.

Before he was discovered, around midmorning, he had floated and floundered for quite some time in the roiling wash of the huge waves crashing into the shore as a result of the storm. He later learned that he owed his life to the curiosity of some village children walking along the beach, admiring the powerful show Mother Earth was putting on. They had spotted him amid the debris in the wash and ran to tell their parents. If not for them, he would have been carried back out to sea at the turn of the tide.

The parents at first listened with amusement to their tales, thinking the children were letting their imaginations run wild. However, after hearing them universally describe the thing as part-man, part-beast, with white skin and hair the colour of blood growing long and covering over half of its face, they relayed the story to Lightning Bolt.

Lightning Bolt, though skeptical, decided to investigate. He was in company with several curious young warriors who tagged along uninvited, but were welcome nonetheless. To their amazement, there was indeed something that appeared to be part human, part beast, being battered around on a huge piece of driftwood in the wash of the still raging waves. After retrieving the badly wounded thing, they carried it back to the village and placed it in Lightning Bolt's wigwam.

Spring Flower, with several other women assisting under the watchful eyes of the warriors, cleaned its wounds and set two broken legs and a broken arm. When they had it as comfortable as they could make it, they left the wigwam, leaving this thing in Lightning Bolt's care.

Lightning Bolt, on closer inspection of the survivor, changed his first conclusion. This was not half human. This must be some kind of strange man. However, he would have a hard time convincing his fellow villagers to accept his new conclusion. This was evident from the tone of the alarmed comments about the origins of what they deemed to be a beast. Lightning Bolt heard these and other similar comments from those who stood outside his wigwam. He deduced from their tone that he needed help from a Seasoned Elder to calm them down. To this end, he sent for senior Elder White Dawn. A young warrior was sent to ask her to come and help, post-haste.

Then he stood before the wigwam and tried to calm the worried People by telling them that the strange apparition was not a beast but a man. "My brothers and sisters, please rest assured that the thing plucked from the arms of the raging sea this morning is not a monster but some kind of strange man. Although he has white skin and has hair over much of his body, he is human and poses no immediate danger. To substantiate my opinion and ease your fears, I've sent for White Dawn to come and give her opinion of the birth origins of the prisoner." To the Mi'kmaq, he was a prisoner until they knew they could trust him.

Lightning Bolt's words of assurance only somewhat mollified the People, who had imagined that upon regaining consciousness the thing might be vicious and uncontrollable. Some, in the name of self-preservation, were openly advocating that it be put to death as a precautionary measure. Playing for time, to permit White Dawn to get to his wigwam, Lightning Bolt continued assuring the People by pointing out to them that they were in no immediate danger because the strange man, in his condition, with two broken legs and a broken arm, could pose no threat to anyone. It still didn't have the desired effect; they remained highly agitated.

Thus, when White Dawn arrived she was greeted with a huge sigh of relief by the Chief. "My sister, thank the Great Spirit you're here!" Without any preliminaries, he whisked her into the wigwam to view and examine the strange apparition.

After finishing her examination, White Dawn emerged from the wigwam and found a sea of anxious faces awaiting her verdict. She could tell by the looks on their faces that wild thoughts about the future were going through their heads. They were probably mulling over with dread the unsettling prospect of entertaining the strange apparition for many Moons to come. Thus, without any delay, she told them that Lightning Bolt's words were true, confirming that the thing they thought a monster was indeed a human being, and that such humans were not entirely unknown in Mi'kmaq history. This had the effect of calming them down considerably.

To allay their fears further, she related some of the rare

occasions when white people, who proved to be harmless, had before appeared from the sea. "After getting used to their strange appearances, the People who found them in ancient times adopted them into their communities. Most of them later married, raised families and generally lived out their lives in contentment." She explained that these incidents were rarely talked about because of the adoption custom of the Nation, which mandated that once adopted the person became known as the natural born of the adopters. Thus, it would have been extremely impolite not to accept them as such. Accepting without challenge her explanation, the People calmed down and went back to their normal routines.

The following Sunrise, when the white man regained consciousness, Lightning Bolt and Spring Flower were with him. By using sign language, they tried to communicate to him that he was being held prisoner until the community decided his fate. But, in spite of it, he would be given the best medical care available. It was apparent from his lack of response that it was going to be extremely difficult to communicate with him.

After this initial session was over the prisoner, whose name was William, surveyed his surroundings with apprehension. Then, with clarity, he recalled, painstakingly with sign and body language and sound effects, his last conscious moments before the ship sank. There was the wild sea, the howling wind and waves like mountains. He saw again the mountainous wave that hit the ship and caused her to start breaking up. Then, at almost the same instant, the ship's spar broke loose and swung in his direction. At this point, before it hit him, he commended his soul to God. The excruciating pain he felt for an instant upon contact was the last thing he remembered.

Now here he was being cared for by a strange copper-coloured People, who spoke a strange language, wore clothes made from leather and lived in conical homes made from birch-bark. His wildest imagination couldn't have prepared him for it.

Slowly, he began to recall the events that had brought him here to this unknown destination. The fishing vessel he had been assigned to by his master had been in trouble for several days prior to the storm. Its captain, navigator and several crew members had come down with an unknown fever and died during their third week out. None of the remainder of the crew had any knowledge of how to set a course for a ship. Thus, they had erroneously set sail in a direction that brought them to the coast of an unknown land. Without having any notion of where they were, and not seeing any familiar landmarks, they had begun to sail along the coast. Eventually, they had encountered the rage of the storm which brought their ship to grief.

After a few Sunrises, taking stock of his circumstances, William, not schooled, but very intelligent, surmised from the nice way he was being treated that he was safe. He relaxed and started to think about the future. The immediate problem was communication. He recognized, from the mostly unsuccessful attempts they were making to communicate with him by sign language, that his need to communicate had to be attended to quickly.

He did not envision that this challenge would be too hard to overcome because he was a natural-born linguist. He had to his pleasant surprise during his nine years of indentured service to the ship's master learned with little effort many of the languages of the foreigners among the crew. This had a spinoff effect; once able to communicate with them he learned a great deal about the customs and habits of the Peoples of a large number of European, African and Asian countries. Surprisingly, to his hosts, within a few Sunrises of regaining consciousness, he began to pick up Mi'kmaw words and soon was able to crudely communicate verbally with them.

Within fourteen Sunrises, with the aid of crutches provided by the Chief, William was making his way around the community. The People still found his appearance strange but slowly began to accept him. However, when visitors came, the villagers were very amused by the look of shock on their faces when they first saw him. His efforts to fit in and learn the language pleased the People of the village. Thus, when he stopped to talk they took the time to teach him more with good cheer.

By the end of the Autumn Season, William had almost completely mastered the language and felt well enough to begin to ponder his future relationship with the Mi'kmaq. Would they help him return home? During the first Moon of Winter, with his health almost back to normal, William decided it was time to talk to the Chief about his future. The most pressing decision that he had to make was whether to try to return to Europe or try to make a life in this land. The option, if it was offered, of staying in this free, loving and carefree Nation was one he found pleasant. He had, by socializing with them extensively, developed a warm fondness for the People. However, because he was still torn between two cultures, he wasn't completely sure he wanted to stay.

After the annual Hunt was over and Lightning Bolt had some free time, William arranged to meet with him on the evening of two Sunrises before the second Moon of Winter. The Chief greeted him that evening with his customary friendliness. "Welcome to my humble home, William. For a man who only a short time ago looked as if he had lost a vicious battle with a crazed bull moose you're looking very healthy. When I think of the terrible wounds that you had, I can't help but marvel at what good care and good food can do for a broken human body in such a short time."

With the deeply instilled European trait to show deference for authority guiding him, William replied, "Sir, thanks for taking the time from your busy schedule to meet with me to discuss my future options. But, before we start, I want to take a few moments to thank you for all the other times that you've sat and chatted with me since I came. They were some of the most enjoyable and interesting conversations I've ever had. These and the many other enjoyable experiences I've had since I arrived here have given me a new outlook on life. The excellent food and care given to me so expertly, and freely, by these wonderful women, and the friendliness of the People, have all been revelations to me. I didn't know such compassion and generosity existed.

"For everyone sharing so willingly, openly and freely, for me this is astonishing. I trust and like people far more than I ever did before. This brings to mind what an old sailor once told me. He said, 'Having a good attitude is as much a healer of the body as medicine.' He was right. Being treated so kindly and respectfully by your People has not only helped heal my body, it has done marvels toward healing my soul."

Lightning Bolt, quite pleased with the compliments, responded, "My brother, I'm delighted to hear that you've enjoyed your stay so much. As for our talks, I've also enjoyed them, but I must confess that at times I also found them depressing. Hearing about so many people in the place called Europe existing under such deplorable living conditions makes me very sad. This is especially so for me, because I know I cannot do anything to help them. Living under the conditions you describe must try their will to live, and burden their poor souls with grief.

"However my friend, this is not the purpose of your visit. Deciding your future is. But, before getting to this, there is another matter I want to settle with you. This is the matter of your freedom. I'm pleased to inform you that as of this Sunrise your life as a prisoner is over. This decision was made because we now view you as a friend. We know in our hearts that a friend does not hold their friend prisoner. I hope regaining your freedom pleases you."

Astounded, William exclaimed, "Master! If in fact I've been a prisoner of yours, this is the best-kept secret I know of! How could I have possibly been a prisoner here? You and your compassionate countrymen have not put any constraints on my movements whatsoever since I so unceremoniously arrived. Never have I ever enjoyed so much freedom."

"Well, my friend, your stay has also been an enjoyable experience for us. We've noted with delight that you've conducted yourself in an honourable and civilized manner, and made a very successful effort to learn our talk and live our way of life. Because of your civilized behaviour, the vast majority of the People now view you as a brother. They would not be displeased if you were to decide to stay with us always.

"This brings us back to why you are here, your future. Staying with us is one option, but, whether you do, or move on, is your decision to make. You have plenty of time to decide. No need to make a hasty decision. But, before you begin to think about it seriously, I have to tell you that you do not have many other options. In fact, I can see just two. To be very honest with you, there is not any safe way for us to help you return to your home in Europe.

"This, I hasten to add, is not because we would not want to help you return, if you wanted to do so. This is simply because we do not have the means. As a matter of fact, the only way that I know, which might have some remote possibility of your safe return home, is by travel over the Northern Frozen Land. But the weather there is so harsh that your chances of survival are very slim. If you were to do so, you would be travelling over a country inhabited by our northern cousins and into lands of other Peoples unknown to us, who are used to the harsh conditions. But long before you even met these Peoples you would most likely die amidst the extremes of weather and scarcity of food. Even with great preparation and endurance, our strongest warriors would not venture into these lands except under the most dire of circumstances and then only to return to our beloved country as quickly as possible.

"Your only two viable options are: stay here with us or leave and see if somewhere in this vast land to the west you can find another Nation that is more to your liking. Your choices are not limited in this regard. There are many hundreds to choose from. However, if you do decide to stay with us, it is mandatory that you agree to live by our customs and agree to be adopted by a family. After they do, they will give you a name suitable to our society.

"All this, my friend, must be approved first by the People. If you ask and they approve, from then on you will enjoy all the rights that any other citizen enjoys. The choice is yours. Go in peace. And may the Great Spirit be with you."

William, somewhat awed by what he had just heard, returned to his wigwam for meditation. His thoughts covered a wide range of comparisons of his present life with his past experiences in England. For starters, he found the fact that he had been a prisoner since he arrived unbelievable. At no time had he ever been restricted in his activities and movements. There hadn't been any hint whatsoever in the Sunrise-to-Sunrise conduct of the People towards him that would have given a clue that he was a prisoner. In fact, given the mainly brutal way in which he had been treated prior to coming here, he believed that he had been treated like an honoured guest. He thought to himself, "Prisoner status? If only, in youth, I had been lucky enough to have been a prisoner with these kind People."

In comparison to what he had heard about prisons from European friends and workmates, who had languished in dismal conditions, this was heaven. They had described without any doubt the worst kind of hellholes, of almost unbelievable squalor, where torture, depravation and brutality prevailed. The difference to him between the way the two societies imprisoned people was like night and day.

In general, the leaders of his country seemed to enjoy making the peasant's life as miserable as possible. People in the main only enjoyed limited freedom of expression, and few civil rights. It was a life of hard and unceasing labour. If his countrymen had a chance to exchange their present lives for the life of a prisoner in this enlightened society, the lineup would be endless. William was quickly coming to a decision. His former life did not compare well with the life he had known since fate had brought him to live among the Mi'kmaq. This subconscious comparative exercise had started when he began to tell Lightning Bolt, during their first few meetings, about the sad conditions under which many Europeans lived.

When he had first awoken to find himself in a bed made of

boughs, in a strange house, being cared for by a strange People, his only thoughts had been for survival and the time when he would be able to return home. Then, with the passage of time, he had learned much about the civilization his rescuers enjoyed. He had not, by any measure, found it wanting.

William's own childhood had effectively ended at the age of seven, when his father had pressed him into farm labour. He then worked for five years, ten hours a day, six days a week. He remembered his father as a cruel man. Shortly after his twelfth birthday, his father had placed him into bondage with a sea captain for an unknown monetary consideration. He had not seen his family since.

He had a few fond memories. He knew in his heart that his mother and siblings loved and missed him. They had wept when he was sent away, indentured for an unknown length of time. Decisions fathers made were not open to question. For his father, money and status came before family. William now recognized, as an adult, that if his mother, whom he loved dearly, had tried to interfere with his father's decision to indenture him, she would have received a vicious beating. In fact, he could still recall vividly and with a great deal of anger and sorrow, that he, his mother, his brothers and sisters had all received terrible beatings from his father for no apparent reason. As he reflected back from this new place of freedom from fear, the actual frequency of these physical assaults seemed to fill his heart with dismay. He recalled how the right to beat your wife and children occurred because of the laws of most European countries. Women and children were without assistance. Anyone without financial means or the status of a man held nothing more than the status of property and captured farm animals. A father's word was unquestioned law.

William mused over the many other differences between the two societies. They were profound. In Mi'kmaq society, Elders were shown the utmost respect and held in high esteem. No poorhouses existed for them to be consigned to by their children. He recoiled when he remembered how elders in his own society had to live out their remaining years in dire straits and abject poverty. Here in this new land, the physically and mentally ill were also given the best of care. There were no lunatic asylums. Nor were there hospitals hiding the sick away from everyone else. In Mi'kmaq society, each individual appeared to be genuinely loved and cherished regardless of status or condition.

He noted that leadership was also completely different. In Mi'kmaq society, the People controlled the agenda, as opposed to the iron-fisted control of the aristocrats throughout so much of Europe. And women, although not permitted to hold the office of Chief, were in no other way denied. The way they were esteemed because their childbearing capabilities made them far more influential in the affairs of the community than most men cared to admit.

The way the Mi'kmaq selected their leaders impressed William as compared to European societies, where most had assumed their positions by way of birth, and high offices automatically came with lavish perks regardless of personal conduct. He had been astounded to learn that no special perks came with an office. An incumbent, if he received any advantage, had to earn these each through his actions.

Even more unbelievable, William reflected that a certain value appeared very strong in the Mi'kmaq way. He had noted very early in his stay how this society was strictly governed by the principle of "one for all and all for one." And he thought to himself how these people enjoyed the freedom of speech and assembly. He wondered if they even knew how much they might be taking for granted. In sharp contrast to his birth country, which had a system that relegated people into a multitude of different social classes, he had witnessed no different classes of people in Mi'kmaq society. His old life was led by the titled, followed closely by the wealthy, then those in the different trades and so on. He was at the bottom of this order of things.

Considering all this, William realized that he was not leaving much behind. The tenets of the society from which he came did not compare favourably in any respect with Mi'kmaq society. He imagined how his conclusion might sound offensive to the ears of his European leaders, while those in lesser roles might jump at the mere thought of becoming free, at last.

Of course, technology was more advanced in Europe, he had to admit. But he found that the tools used by the Mi'kmaq served the needs of their society more than adequately. Perhaps the Nations of Europe had advanced so fast in this field due to their lust to kill each other. To wage war, to try to dominate their neighbours or steal their properties, they continually spent vast sums of money to develop more efficient tools of war. Many European countries had been locked in wars for so long no one could remember when they started. William could see no virtue to war in a community of nations whose means to wealth and prosperity was assured. In most cases he felt their wars were not fought for noble purposes, but based on greed and thirst for power over other's lives. He knew this from the information that he had gathered, by listening to the tales of many old sailors and other well-informed acquaintances he had encountered on his travels.

As he considered his options, William recalled and reviewed several conversations he'd had with Lightning Bolt about European civilization. "Tell me, my friend," Lightning Bolt once said. "As a child did you love the man who made you work like a man when you were only half-grown, and sold you into what you call indentured service?"

"Master, when I was very small I did. But, as I grew older and began to realize how he was exploiting us for wealth, my love turned to hate. Try as I might, I still cannot find any charity in my heart for him. I don't know if I can ever forgive what he did, just thinking about it turns my heart to stone!"

"My heart turns to stone just hearing about him. Do other fathers where you come from do the same thing?"

"Yes, many. Children are used for many different things: farm labour, factory hands, chimney sweeps and so on. Also, many are turned out into the streets at very young ages and taken in by individuals called pimps, who sell their young bodies to perverts for sexual pleasure. And I've heard about young boys, placed in choirs when their voices are at their sweetest, who are castrated to assure that they retain their sweet voices as long as possible. Such abuses are common."

"My friend," Lightning Bolt said, "when I think about how you — your mother, sisters and brothers — have suffered at the hands of men like your father, this breaks my heart. Such heartless men would not be permitted to do such things in our country. Beating women and abusing children is one of the worst crimes a man can be accused of. If convicted and he refused to mend his ways, we would probably shun him for the rest of his Seasons, or give him the death penalty.

"We have provisions in our system that provide an honourable way for individuals who might be inclined to indulge in such abuse to transfer their children to other families for care. Adoptions are very easy and give those who find they haven't the patience for parenthood a civilized way out of their dilemma. No one is bothered when a child is raised by a new family other than its birth parents. If we were to ostracize them, none would come forward and many children would suffer because of it.

"Divorce is also easy. After marriage some people find they can't abide each other. It doesn't make sense to force them to live unhappily together for the rest of their lives when they could find compatible mates to be happy with. But divorce and child abuse are rare.

"Now my friend, back to the subject of your father, would you consider killing him for his crimes against you, your mother and siblings, if you had the opportunity?"

"Master, what I missed as a child was brought home to me when I heard you describe your relationship with your family. My heart yearns to have known the same. When I look back on my youth and see how my bothers, sisters and mother and I suffered at the hands of the man whose seed I come from, I know that in reality I never had a father, nor my mother a husband. What we had was a master. He owned us. He didn't love us and he treated us worse than most human beings treat animals. Yes, if I was to come face-to-face with the monster today, I would without any hesitation dispatch him to his Maker for judgement.

"But I don't lay all the blame on him. His behaviour is common throughout many European countries. Our leaders must accept much of the blame. They enacted the laws that give fathers ironclad control over wives and children. Now that I know that abuse can be outlawed by a caring society I cry for the sufferings of the women and children of Europe."

"William, my friend, our society has a legend about a group of men who ruled our Nation in ancient times in a manner that was almost identical to the way your leaders rule yours. The cruel things that these men did to the People always seemed to me almost impossible to comprehend. I even had doubts about the truth of it, until you told me about the world you come from. I'll tell you the legend of the Dictators…" When he finished, Lightning Bolt continued, "My friend, I've nothing but heartfelt pity for most of the people from whence you come. Living without human rights, equality or justice is a nightmare to me.

"Do Europeans really not know that at birth everyone is born naked and that when we die we return to dust? Equality is there from start to finish. I know of no one who is immortal and therefore better than his brothers and sisters. Do you know of any such person in your society? I won't wait for an answer to that question, because the answer is obvious; of course you don't.

"The Great Spirit gives us only a short time to reside on Mother Earth. During it, except for the innocents He calls home early, we are expected to demonstrate to Him, by being kind and generous to our fellow human beings, that we are worthy of residing in His presence in the Land of Souls. There are no exceptions made for anyone. "In the Land of Souls there are no special perks for anyone. A leader is treated the same as the canoe maker, the basket weaver and so on. No preferential treatment is given because of the position a person held on Mother Earth. Leaders are not the People's superiors.

"How could a leader believe his position makes him better than his People? How can they permit themselves to be called such things as your gracious majesty, your worship, your most sacred majesty, master and so on, and then force the People to bow down and crawl before their presence? Such behaviour seems sacrilegious. They put themselves above the laws of their God and do terrible injury to those they think below them. To me, such an attempt by men to take up the trappings reserved only for the Great Father is sure to offend Him.

"Another thing that bewilders me about Europeans is the thirst you tell me they have for the thing you call money. Using it to buy such things as power, property and sometimes titles, and other perks, so that a person can say, 'This is mine. I own this.' I don't see the sense in this idea. To us, a person with an aptitude for making canoes does so. When he finishes making one, he freely gives it to another who needs it. The same philosophy of sharing applies to all material things. For the life of me, I can't see why a canoe maker would want to sit around looking at all the canoes he made during his lifetime, saying 'I own these,' when he can make others happy by giving them away. After all, when he dies, he owns nothing.

"I've tried, my friend, to sort out in my mind how these things called money and personal property can be useful. To be honest, I cannot. From what you've told me they hinder the establishment of good relationships between brothers and sisters. In your society, as you have explained, even the religious leaders compete for money, property and power. How this kind of activity by them would please the Great Spirit is another thing far beyond my powers of comprehension.

"In our society, hard work, generosity, compassion and humility earn the love and respect of the People. In yours, the ones who own money and property get what your People consider respect. How can a leader expect thanks and respect from people who are forced to work like slaves from sunrise to sunset, to the end of their Sunrises, for only bare sustenance? It sounds like madness.

"What makes the whole thing even more inconceivable for me is that the desire to acquire wealth seems to infect all these different levels of your society. From the king down to the lowest peasant, like your father who is, although at the bottom, still deeply involved in the competition for this wealth. I think, in contrast, and with great respect not withheld to your People, that the true wealth of nations has not yet been discovered by Europe.

"Therefore, my sympathy for the plight of the peasants is lessened moderately by the fact that many do stoop to the same self-serving and mean-spirited level as do the rich. I say moderately, because I can understand that the choice between working for the leaders for so little or starving could impel a weak person to do wrong.

"When you told me that these peasants need their master's permission to marry, go to school or to look for other jobs that might give them a higher station in life, I was incredulous. But still, this mistreatment is not justification for selling children into indentured service. It sounds as though in your society the desire for money is so strong that it even extends to buying unfortunate people called slaves as work animals or human sex toys. It grieves me completely to know that at this very Sunrise, there are people in countries being forced to parade naked in front of buyers, fondled and poked by them as if they were canoes, to see if all their parts are working properly. That many female slaves will be taken and sexually abused by their masters, that any children born from these forced encounters will be considered animals and sold by their fathers. Such, my friend, is horror without equal.

"We don't have this kind of activity in our society, and I don't think we've ever had it. For this I praise the Great Spirit with all my heart! Even our prisoners of war are only required to share equally in the chores of the community. We have, on rare occasions, especially when it was concluded that peace could not be secured with an enemy for some time, ransomed them back to their own Nations for furs, but never have we considered trading them to a third Nation to be used as slaves. In fact, we offer any prisoners, if they don't want to return to their homelands, the option of becoming a citizen. I don't recall, nor have I ever been told about any instance where someone was repatriated to their Nation against their will."

William recalled with amusement Lightning Bolt's incredulous reaction when he told him how some Europeans lived permanently in large villages and depended on others to harvest Mother Earth for them. Then, when he told him about some of the huge homes, many with a hundred rooms or more, that were owned in these villages by the titled, or the rich, and that only a few people lived in them, his reaction was disbelief incarnate. The Chief wanted to know what purpose these huge monstrosities served. When told that they were for a thing called prestige, and having explained what prestige meant, William thought Lightning Bolt would die laughing.

He would always remember with glee the Chiefs comments, "But what, my friend, do these crazy people do in these places? Do they entertain themselves by chasing themselves through the rooms? It conjures up in my mind an image that tickles my funny bone. Can you imagine how ridiculous it would look if we lived in the same kind of society, me having a hundred wigwams at my disposal? I could see myself now, foolishly trying to live in all at the same time. And you say they do it for this thing called prestige, which is being able to tell another I have something bigger and better than you. May the Great Spirit spare me from ever having to deal with such utter folly."

Of all the things he had told the Chief about his former life, the thing that shocked Lightning Bolt most was the way Europeans worshiped their God. Lightning Bolt responded, "My friend, you sit there and tell me things that astound me. Why on Mother Earth would they build huge structures to go into, in order to pay homage to the Great Spirit? Why ever would they only take a little time on certain Sunrises, which they call Sundays, and Holy Days, to give thanks to the Creator of all things? Why build any buildings in the first place? You don't need a building to worship and respect the Great Spirit. It can be done always. And anywhere.

"William, my friend, the differences between our Peoples, who live their religion and the Europeans, who practise theirs for only a little time on special days, is irreconcilable with common sense. And, for this, I thank the Great Spirit. In our society, we don't have priests or hell. Why should we? The Creator needs no interpreters to spread his word, nor a place of punishment to threaten us with if we don't live our lives the way another man says we should.

"The power your religious leaders exercise in your society is baffling. To presume you have the power to tell others how to worship the Great Spirit, that if they don't do it your way when they die they will go to this place you call hell to be tormented by eternal burning. It seems an affront to the compassionate and loving nature of the Great Spirit.

"When I think of the powers of the Councils of Inquisition you describe, where religious leaders convict a person of a thing called heresy and sentence them to be burned at the stake, I shudder. Fire is the most painful thing a human can come into contact with. I could never, in all my life, picture the Great Spirit being cruel enough to countenance burning anyone for one moment, let alone eternity. I will for the rest of my life ask the Great Spirit to have mercy on the persecuted and oppressed Peoples of Europe. I feel the greatest pity for them."

This last statement stood out in William's mind the most. Imagine, him arising from the soils of Europe, arriving in this mysterious and unknown land. Imagine this Chief of the Mi'kmaq spending his hours in prayer for the oppressive nature of European societies. This Chief owned absolutely nothing and yet was surely the most enlightened and wealthy man William had ever met. The revelation was moving and made him wonder why on earth had he been so blessed as to become so free that his very way of thinking about human relationships was changing in such remarkable ways? He wanted more of this kind of change. It must be good. He felt a pleasure in each day that had never existed before. His inner world was being transformed by joy just by being present in the lives of those around him.

William, without any more reflection, made a decision about his future. He concluded that upon his arrival in the land of the Mi'kmaq he had come home, and that he would stay. It was, to his surprise, a very easy decision. After becoming accustomed to freedom, there was no way that he could picture himself willingly returning to the life of bondage and hardship he once knew. He would miss and hold a soft spot in his heart for his mother and cherish in memory some members of his family. For the rest of his life he would carry this sweet burden of love. But he knew, in his heart of hearts, that even if the means were available to return to Europe, he would not. He could not. Unless he was absolutely forced to do so at the point of a sword, he would never return to his old life.

With his future decided, he returned to Lightning Bolt's wigwam early the next morning. Lightning Bolt greeted him, "Welcome again to my home my friend. Did you forget something, or have you reached a decision already?"

"Yes, Master, I've made my choice."

"William, my brother, for many Moons I've been patiently waiting and hoping that you would, on your own accord, stop calling me Master. I hate the sound of it. It makes me feel that you think I'm better than you, which I'm not. Using a title is something you had to do in Europe. It isn't the case here. We're all equals, and treat each other as such. Sometimes, if people feel like it, they call me Chief. But mostly they call me Lightning Bolt, my brother or my friend. I like it that way. Please start addressing me the same way."

"Thank you Master, I mean … my brother! Don't be surprised if for a time I occasionally use my old way of addressing you because such a deeply ingrained habit of scraping to authority will be hard to break. It was something we learned at a very young age because not to have done so would have been a fool's way to disaster. But, I pledge that I shall leave my European habits behind."

"I'm sure that time and lack of use will erase them. Now, what is your decision?"

"Lightning Bolt, my friend, allow me to put it this way. By allowing fate to bring me to this land, the Great Spirit has brought me home! It is with a feeling of peace and contentment that I humbly request, please will you ask the People if they will consent to have me as a citizen of their great country?"

Honouring his request to be considered for citizenship, the next afternoon the Chief called the People together to discuss and consider the issue. Without much discussion the proposal was approved, with the provision that he had to be adopted by a family and given a Mi'kmaw name. Early Blossom, knowing that her family had become quite fond of William, solved the problem. She stood and adopted him as her son and renamed him Flaming Hair.

Lightning Bolt, extremely pleased with the outcome, welcomed Flaming Hair into the Nation with a short but moving speech. "Brothers and sisters, this Sunrise I have another thing to be thankful to the Great Spirit for, a new brother! An unusual looking one I must admit, but one who I sincerely believe will become a true Mi'kmaq at heart. A good omen for this to happen is that he has already accustomed himself to many of our ways and shows respect for one and all. And, since coming among us, he has never consciously shown a lack of respect for the laws of the Nation. What more does one want from a citizen? My brothers and sisters, thank you from the bottom of my heart for accepting and welcoming Flaming Hair as a brother. To have so generously cared for and helped heal a stranger in need, and then accepted him as a brother, shows that you are a true People of compassion. I'm very proud of what you did and I know that the Great Spirit will be greatly pleased.

"Flaming Hair, my brother, we welcome you home as a member of our family and Nation with warmth and love. This Sunrise you've left your old life behind and become one of us. My brother, we have only love and loyalty here. From this Sunrise onward you are part of us; we are part of you. We share all our material possessions equally. As of this Sunrise these possessions are also yours. Use and enjoy them to the fullest. May the Great Spirit always be with you my new brother and may He let you know peace and happiness."

Lightning Bolt then embraced his new brother and, to the cheers of the People, asked him to say a few words.

Flaming Hair turned to the People and said, "My brothers and sisters, how can I ever thank you enough for your gift of freedom? It seems so unreal to know that there will never be another master in my life. As a person who has lived under the iron fist of one, and who has only known leaders who I had to bow before, I can tell you that I never imagined in my wildest dreams that a society where love, devotion, generosity, justice and freedom prevail could exist on Mother Earth. In fact I keep thinking that I'm dreaming and will awake some Sunrise to find myself back in my old life. I shudder to think of it.

"But, I will eventually overcome this and fully realize that I'm home to stay. My friends, my brothers, my sisters, thank you from the bottom of my heart for taking me in as one of your own. I ask myself how can I ever repay these wonderful People for this great gift? In truth, there isn't any way that I can.

"However, I will, before the Great Spirit, promise you this, my brothers and sisters. As long as the Great Spirit permits life to remain in my body I shall without care for my personal safety help to defend the wonderful society that you inhabit. With diligence, I shall always strictly obey all the laws that govern our Nation. Above all else, I acknowledge the supremacy of the Great Spirit's will in the governance of our Nation and shall always be grateful for His kindnesses. I thank Him now and forever for the kindness of permitting me the opportunity to become part of this great Nation. To you my newfound mother, family and friends, I pledge my eternal love and devotion."

The villagers then set about arranging a huge feast to celebrate the occasion. Flaming Hair found the tradition of taking every opportunity to dance and feast, especially Sunrises which marked the passage of landmarks in the lives of beloved friends and relations, one of the most endearing traits of his adopted community. He became one of its most enthusiastic participants, often encouraging family and friends to let down their hair and get into the swing of the moment by his example.

While making preparations for the party, Early Blossom and her children took pains to make Flaming Hair feel comfortable, as part of the family. Besides filling him in on its intimate details, they discussed with him the amusing prospect of introducing him as a natural-born son, and brother, to visiting relatives and friends from other countries.

Little Blossom, watching her children going through the acceptance procedures with Flaming Hair, felt proud and pleased to have him as a son. She felt certain that her departed beloved, Little Bear, would have shared the family's joy in welcoming a new member and known that her heart's intention was right.

During the Winter Season, with Flaming Hair now fully recovered, the men undertook to teach him the ways of the Hunt and how to harvest the sea in the Mi'kmaq fashion. He proved an astute student who quickly learned how to harvest the gifts of Mother Earth with great skill. He embraced the traditions of the Hunt with a passion reserved for the true believer, and as time passed he became one of the Nation's greatest hunters.

Many things about his new country's practices fascinated Flaming Hair, but the way hunters carried out the harvesting of nature's bounty was always a particular pleasure for him.

To watch them acting with the greatest of care to balance the needs of the animals with theirs never failed to impress him. In his old age he would look back over the Seasons and not once recall an instance where the People had abused Mother Earth's bounty. They took only what was needed, or what Mother Earth could afford to provide. Not a bit was ever intentionally wasted.

With the arrival of the first moons of Spring, Early Blossom had the pleasure of seeing her youngest daughter married to a young man who worshiped the ground she walked on. This was the Sunrise she had been waiting many long Seasons to see. All her children, except Flaming Hair, were now happily married and could do without her presence. Feeling confident that her new son could make his way in life with the assistance of family and friends, she asked the Great Spirit to reunite her with her beloved Little Bear. Two Sunrises before the second Moon of Spring, the Great Spirit honoured her request and welcomed her home.

During a Feast of the Dead, people visited and extended sympathy to the family for its loss of a dearly beloved family member, and offered heartfelt homage to her memory. But, although the People dearly loved and respected the departed, they didn't grieve too long. Some Sunrise in the future, with the will of the Great Spirit, they would meet her again and enjoy her company in the Land of Souls. Flaming Hair was deeply touched to find that Early Blossom's family and friends put her wishes first and prayed for her speedy return to Little Bear's arms.

Flaming Hair discovered over time that each person mourns and respects the memory of their ancestors in their own ways. Some felt the loss over many years. Others seemed able to move on, but remained very respectful to the memory of their dearly departed. All partook at one time or other with the tradition of offering the best gifts of food, prior to many feasts and ceremonies, to their ancestors who had walked before them to the Land of Souls.

Flaming Hair, at first, found the direct and honest way that the Mi'kmaq lived their lives, so devoted to the Great Spirit, as slightly disconcerting in its simplicity. Before coming to his adopted country, faith in the goodness of God had always been tempered by the words and actions of many religious leaders who were supposed to be God's disciples on Earth. They often lived in large dwellings and engaged in some of the most corrupt practices known to man — preaching fire and damnation for sinners, while at the same time being among the worst sinners on Mother Earth. One of their biggest sins, in his humble opinion, was exhorting poor people to donate most of their meagre funds to the church to escape the eternal pain of hell. The rich and the mighty received special services and treatment from the religious establishment and special dispensations were given them when they made large donations.

In contrast the profound simplicity of offering food to the Sacred Fire, in honour of eternal rest for a dearly departed family member, was one of the most beautiful acknowledgments he could imagine. At certain times when the Sacred Fire was unattended, he was observed visiting in prayer and remembrance. He would bring with him secret offerings from the Hunt, and things he had helped the women gather during the height of Seasonal picking. With great care, he would select only the choicest of fruit and berry, leaf and flower, flesh and bone, and bring them to the Fire, or place them under a special remote tree outside the village. During these times, Flaming Hair always held in his heart an intense gratitude for his new mother, Early Blossom, who had given him his rebirth as a child of the Mi'kmaq People.

Perhaps it is understandable. For a former child of the European nations to be reborn as a Mi'kmaq warrior and a true man of the People, he must surely undertake a serious transformation of nearly every part of his being. This is why the directness, honesty and simplicity of the beliefs and worship that the Mi'kmaq People gave to the Great Spirit became for Flaming Hair such a soothing Sacred Medicine for his soul. The innate beauty, balance and harmony that these teachings and ways of life provide to the People eventually made Flaming Hair one of the most devoted followers of the ways of the People. His complete acceptance and practice of the simple method the People used to honour their Maker made Flaming Hair a true Mi'kmaq. And by honouring these ways with good heart and good cheer, he paid a great respect to the Mi'kmaq nation.

//

CHAPTER SIX

Lightning Bolt, early in his thirty-sixth Spring, was enjoying a few Sunrises of rest and relaxation at his favourite forest retreat. He reviewed the state of his life and concluded that he was a very fortunate man. In his heart he felt a sense of gratitude and he thanked the Great Spirit for many gifts of people, places and experiences.

The People were prosperous and contented with their lives. His leadership was not questioned and he had very little trouble persuading the villagers to undertake new initiatives. Life with Spring Flower was contented and filled with love. Helping to raise their daughter, Snow Flake, had given him wonderful memories, and his brothers and sisters had produced a multitude of loving nieces and nephews whom he cherished. And, miraculously, the Big Pond had given him a dearly beloved new brother, who, even though he had already reached his twenty-first Autumn when adopted, was an addition to the family that fit in so well it now seemed as if he had been born to it.

In retrospect, he took immense pride in the way the People

of the village, who had been beyond generous in accepting Flaming Hair, had helped him with the utmost patience to adapt to his new homeland. Fitting in completely had taken him a remarkably short time. In fact, considering the most unusual circumstances of his case, it seemed incredible to Lightning Bolt that with the passage of only three Autumns since he arrived, although his appearance still engendered startled comments from visitors, his foreign origins had almost been forgotten by the community.

This happy state of affairs had a lot to do with how Flaming Hair had so wholeheartedly embraced the Nation's traditions, including marriage. He had, during his second Autumn with them, sought out and won the hand of Spotted Fawn, daughter of Big Burn and Blue Moon. The feasting and entertainment that the boisterous happy young couple's relatives had put on to wish them much happiness on their wedding Sunrise was still talked about.

Their union was almost a perfect match. They had personalities so perfectly suited to each other that it seemed as if the Great Spirit had, with foresight, created them for each other. The bride, who was a fiery, well-developed and big-boned woman, matched the shape, size and nature of her husband. Flaming Hair and she were good natured, playful and could be vocally combative when excited.

Their mischievous personalities assured that things were rarely dull with them around. It was especially so when they, in a playful mood, showed their love for each other. It was far different from what the Mi'kmaq were accustomed to. Watching them enjoying the fun of teasing and affectionately carrying on was a sight to behold. When in the mood, they would sometimes wrestle, upset the other in canoes, dunk the other into the water of a river or lake when least expected and do whatever else came to mind to amuse themselves.

Even in communications, their different approach to life stood out. Both had tempers that sometimes erupted like wildfire. This sometimes caused arguments between them, or debates, that could be heard across the entire village. However, there was never rancor afterwards; the argument was soon forgotten. They were exceedingly generous with each other. The great love they nourished was open for all to see and appreciate.

Then came the Sunrise when they made Lightning Bolt an uncle again. The birth occurred during Flaming Hair's twenty-fourth Autumn. Early in the morning of that mist-en-shrouded Sunrise, Spotted Fawn had presented Flaming Hair with a rusty-haired son. Even though his hair was not as red as his fathers', they decided to call him Little Red. He was blessed with many of the good characteristics of both parents. Like them, he had a playful nature and his antics, even in early childhood, delighted all who came to know him.

From the time he was born, Little Red was the centre of his father and mother's universe. They delighted in the progress he made and described over and over to family and friends the many accomplishments of their pride and joy. Lightning Bolt took almost as much pride in his nephew's progress as the boy's parents. This had a lot to do with the fact that Little Red, by the middle of his second birth Season, had taken a shine to his uncle that was remarkable. As soon as he could walk well enough, he began following his uncle around the village, trying to imitate his actions. His hero worship lasted his lifetime. He was also, like all children in Mi'kmaq society, cherished and loved by the entire community. In time he returned the affection with enthusiasm.

Most children born into this mutually responsible social

environment grew up, because of its teachings, to be caring, compassionate, loving and productive citizens. However, into every community at one time or other is born an individual so malevolent in spirit that the Great Spirit Himself would be hard pressed to find a justification for his existence. The Season after Little Red was born, such a person was born into Lightning Bolt's village, to Rolling Thunder and Misty Moon, on a foggy Sunrise during the first Moon of Summer. His parents named him Running Elk. The name was inspired by the antics of a huge Elk that had come running out of the fog that dawn and down through the village at breakneck speed.

As he aged, Running Elk gave the appearance of a perfectly normal child, exceptionally obedient, following every request made by his parents and Elders without question. From the time he was old enough, he was first to volunteer for community projects and offered his considerable talents to help organize sport events. He appeared to thoroughly enjoy competing in them. In every respect his outward behaviour towards family, friends and community was impeccable.

However, as time passed, and without much notice by others at first, when he was around bad things often happened, sometimes even causing death or injury to a member of the community. The explanation for it was simple. Running Elk was the cause. Unfortunately for the community, he was able to do these things in a stealthy manner such that no one had a sliver of suspicion that he was the culprit.

In the early Summer of Lightning Bolt's forty-second Spring, sad tidings were delivered to him by a runner from Chief Big Timber's village. Their beloved and esteemed Kespukwitk National Chief, at the age of eighty-eight Summers, had peacefully passed away in his sleep. Lightning

Bolt, accompanied by many villagers, left immediately for Big Timber's village for the interment service, which took place two Sunrises later.

The family, knowing the Hunt was approaching, set the date for the Feast of the Dead for two Sunrises after the first Moon of Autumn. By the time it arrived, in spite of the short notice, the crowd that assembled for the service in Big Timber's village was immense. Included among the thousands of mourners were the leaders of the other six Mi'kmaq countries, the Eastern Nations and many non-associated Nations.

The service began with the usual Sweet-grass and Pipe-Smoking Ceremonies. After these, Grand Chief Big Elk was called upon to begin the testimonials. He paid glowing tribute to the character of his beloved departed brother.

"Dear brothers and sisters, we are gathered here this Sunrise to pay tribute to the memory of a brother whose company the Great Spirit got a hankering for and took home. Big Timber's absence will leave an empty space in the lives of so many of us, which cannot be filled. However, we can be consoled by the knowledge that when, some Sunrise, we also make our own journeys home to the Land of Souls, we will meet with him again.

"My friends, our beloved brother Big Timber was a great and humble man. He generously devoted his life to the services of the People. Never once during our long friendship did I ever know him to put personal interests before ours. And, he was one of the friendliest men I've ever known. He never failed, wherever he went, to stop and chat with people about their families, health and other matters. He loved us dearly and served with dedication, distinction and honour in all the offices he held.

"I, my brothers and sisters, was fortunate enough to have witnessed all of his successes. Sixty-four Summers ago, when we were not much more than boys, I attended the ceremonies that made him a Junior War Chief and, afterwards, all the other ceremonies that took him from there to the leadership of Kespukwitk. Even though he served his People extremely well in the many offices he held, he often wondered if they had made the right choice in selecting him to do so.

"In this regard, many times he told me about the qualifications of others, who he thought might have served the People better. But my friends, as you well know, the choice of Big Timber as leader by his People was a wise one for all of us. He excelled in service to his own countrymen and others who needed it. His knowledge and advice were of great assistance to many and shall be sadly missed.

"For me, my children, Big Timber's passing leaves an especially empty space in my heart because, from the time we were small children, he and I were brothers and friends who played and worked together. We became friends because our parents were also lifelong friends, who spent a great deal of enjoyable time visiting each other. They also took many happy and memorable vacations together. In their loving company, Big Timber and I saw a great deal of Kespukwitk, and especially Sipekne'katik, when we were young.

"Thus, when we were old enough to travel on our own, we started a practice of travelling together that lasted until our old bones couldn't tolerate it anymore. However, every time we've met since, we've rehashed old times. These wonderful memories are my comfort this Sunrise.

"Ah, my brothers and sisters, when I think of it, the Seasons have flown so fast since Big Timber and I were young and getting into mischief, it seems as if only a few Sunrises have passed since then. I'll tell you about some of the wonderful Sunrises that happened more than seventy Seasons ago. During those Seasons, we did many exciting things together: canoeing, swimming and so on. But, my friends, it was our hunting and fishing trips that often put us into exhilarating and sometimes dangerous situations. In fact, they were the source of some of our most memorable exploits, with which we often entertained many of you around campfires during celebrations, Hunts and other events.

"From among those memories I've picked one as a treat to tell you; it'll tickle your funny bones. It's about an amusing adventure we had in youth, which was embarrassing for him, that we never told anyone about before because we agreed afterward to keep it secret until he died. Thus, if I had gone first, it would have remained a secret forever. The incident happened while we were hunting near the mountain of Blomidon during our twelfth Summer.

"We were amusing ourselves tracking an elk, pretending we were great hunters. We had just come out of the forest under the look-off, from which one has a panoramic view of Changing Valley, when we lost his trail. Not being all that interested in the elk anyway, as we had no intention of trying to harvest it, we decided to find another diversion.

"It wasn't hard to find. The steep and almost treeless cliff, which stretches almost three-hundred paces straight up to the look-off, presented a challenge to climb that we figured would be entertaining if we dared. We debated the pros and cons back and forth of tackling the dangerous climb for some time. But, without giving the cons very much thought, decided that the climb presented a challenge that could not go unanswered.

"With our foolish, risky decision made, we quickly began

to climb. Things were going quite nicely until we got about halfway up. I still recall so clearly every detail of what happened next. Just after I had traversed a particularly dangerous section, I stopped to warn Big Timber to be extra careful when he followed. I had just begun to speak when he lost his footing and plunged to our starting point, his fall only partially broken by branches on the way down. With my heart in my mouth, I hurried down the mountain as fast as I could and found him unconscious from a bump on the head.

"After frantically checking him over for broken bones and finding only a few bruises and scratches besides the bump, I relaxed somewhat. Fortunately for him, the small bushes that grew on the face of the cliff had broken most of his fall. However, unfortunately for him, a porcupine had provided an extra added cushion at the end of his undignified descent.

"My friends, when I rolled him over to view the damage the porcupine had caused, I knew with dead certainty that his immediate future held a lot of pain, and that he would not be sitting around very comfortably for several Sunrises. His bottom was a quill worker's dream. At least half the quills from the porcupine's back were stuck in it. At this point, my friend began to moan and groan and soon regained consciousness.

"Then the painful ordeal of quill removal began. I tell you my friends, from the middle of the sun's descent until dusk, I pulled quills from his hide. With the exit of each he screamed, and then giggled because of the ridiculousness of the situation. Although I felt much compassion for my beloved friend, I was laughing so hard at his alternate laughing and screaming that all the while I removed quills, tears were streaming down my face.

"The reason we agreed to never tell anyone about it was very good, in fact, essential for his future happiness. Can you imagine, my brothers and sisters, going through life with the nickname Quill Ass?"

It dawned on people as they looked each other in the eyes that the very story about laughter and pain raised the same, even greater, grief and loss within their hearts. But they did not stay stuck in grief, they transformed it into loving kindness, and if you were there you would immediately see this amazing shift in the eyes and gestures of those gathered around.

Grand Chief Big Elk fondly recalled several other stories about his adventures with Big Timber. Then he listed and praised the outstanding feats and accomplishments his late friend had performed during his lifetime. After he concluded, other members of the Grand Council took turns relating some of their fondest memories. They were followed by the leaders of the allied Nations, Elders, relatives and friends. The ceremonies were spread over the next four Sunrises. On the fifth, Big Timber was ceremoniously commended by the People to the company of his beloved ancestors.

Afterwards, before they returned to their villages, the Village Chiefs of Kespukwitk met and picked a site and Sunrise for meeting to choose Big Timber's successor. Because of the importance of the position and the fact that the Hunt was fast approaching, it was determined that the meeting should be held as soon as possible. Thus, they set the meeting for ten Sunrises before the second Moon of Autumn. In appreciation of the fact that the People from distant parts of Kespukwitk would be travelling mainly by sea to the event, the site chosen was where the Bear River falls into Bear Bay. To expedite matters, the leadership appointed a committee of Elders and other citizens to oversee the logistical arrangements to accommodate the many hundreds expected to attend.

Without any delay, the committee immediately set to work planning and was presided over by Kespukwitk's senior Elder, Little Dove. They also planned the accompanying celebrations. To spread the work around fairly, it was decided that each village would bring provisions and prepare delicacies. Schedules for dancing and other forms of entertainment were worked out with an eye for giving the People the utmost enjoyment.

When the Sunrise for choosing Big Timber's successor arrived, the process began early. Senior Elder White Dawn presided over the meeting. The agenda for taking nominations and for the election had been worked out the Sunrise before in consultation with the Village Chiefs.

No one knew how long the process would last. In Mi'kmaq democracy the procedure used by the People to select a National Chief could be, depending on the circumstances, short and simple, or long and complex. If a number of well-qualified candidates were nominated, it could well go on for several Sunrises. An elimination process would ultimately reduce the number to two candidates.

White Dawn, shortly after Sunrise, convened the meeting by calling upon Brown Bear, Kespukwitk's senior Village Chief, to lead a prayer to the Great Spirit. After he carried out the honour with fitting dignity and eloquence, and the rest of the traditional ceremonies were over, she advised the People how nominations would be received and how much time each nominee would have to make a speech. Then she recited the rules that the election process would be run by.

With the preliminaries over, White Dawn opened the meeting for nominations. Immediately, almost as if it had been prearranged, several people jumped to their feet at once and nominated Lightning Bolt. The din of approval that followed the nomination drowned out the voices of the seconders for several moments. From the reaction it was evident that no others would be nominated. This was affirmed when White Dawn asked several times for more nominations with no response. She then closed the meeting for nominations and asked the People to declare Lightning Bolt elected National Chief of Kespukwitk by acclamation. It was done with a loud roar, indicating an overwhelming consensus. White Dawn, her duties ended, turned the presiding post over to Lightning Bolt. Their new Chief humbly addressed the People.

"My friends, with a humble heart, I find myself standing here this Sunrise acclaimed as National Chief of Kespukwitk. To be acclaimed to such a high office is to me the highest privilege and greatest honour citizens can bestow upon a man. I thank you deeply for the faith and trust you've shown in me. I pray, my brothers and sisters, to the Great Spirit, that I can live up to your expectations. For the trust you've shown in me, I pledge before the Creator that I will do my utmost to assure that you shall never be disappointed. And I promise you faithfully that I will carry out my duties as Chief of Kespukwitk with dignity, diligence and what little wisdom the Great Spirit has endowed me."

After he finished making his inaugural address, he asked Grand Chief Big Elk, Chief Big Beaver and others who had come home with him for an extended visit after Big Timber's Feast of the Dead, to come forward to say a few words. When they finished, he ended the meeting with a command that everyone gladly obeyed, "Let the festivities begin!"

When Lightning Bolt became the Nation's Chief, as was dictated by Mi'kmaq custom, his formerly normal, quiet, little village became the country's capital. Until his death, the name of the capital of Kespukwitk was "Lightning Bolt's village," and it became a beehive of people coming and going. There was a positive side to this practice — it didn't entail any dislocation for his family. However, the burdens of responsibility that the office carried changed his lifestyle drastically. The increased duties would reduce significantly the quality time he had previously enjoyed with friends and relatives, especially his wife and Crazy Moose.

The scheduled festivities got under way early and with great enthusiasm, and continued almost nonstop for the next three Sunrises. Friends and relatives partied and reminisced far into the nights. Games were played, triumphant winners declared and prizes claimed. Delectable food was plentiful, as was good music and dancing. The People were having a wonderful and memorable time.

However, their happiness was tempered towards the end by two horrific incidents that occurred late in the afternoon on the third Sunrise. An infant of only two Moons had been mysteriously scalded around the feet and was in much pain and misery. The People considered many possibilities for what caused it, but couldn't come up with a logical explanation. Some ventured that it might have occurred while the mother was walking among the crowd during mealtime. Others thought that someone might have accidentally spilled hot liquid on the baby's feet as they walked by. These explanations were not given much credibility because the baby had not cried out in pain until she was left alone in her mother's wigwam for a nap. It was an unexplainable mystery.

The second incident involved a child of three Summers. It appeared the boy had fallen into the estuary of Bear River and would have drowned if not for the quick response of several nearby youths, who had heard his cries for help and saved him. When later questioned about how it happened, he said that he had felt someone push him in. As he was very young, the leaders and Elders were inclined to think that the shock had triggered his imagination and they did not take his allegation seriously.

The Sunrise after the celebrations ended, life in the community quickly returned to normal. But Lightning Bolt now had a new definition of normal. Besides the citizens of his own village coming for advice, there was now a constant stream of delegations from other villages and countries, burdened with problems or carrying suggestions for improving the quality of life for the Nation. The only time the routine varied was when the family of Crazy Moose and his own family would spend fourteen to twenty-one Sunrises exploring the wilderness together each Summer. These sunrises of leisure and shared activity with loved ones were for Lightning Bolt the spice of life and much anticipated.

Flaming Hair and Spotted Fawn also enjoyed going off on vacations with their family and friends, Rolling Thunder, Misty Moon and children. Blomidon and Cape Sable were two of their favourite destinations. From this relationship, Little Red and Running Elk became close friends, almost like brothers. As they grew older, it appeared from their behaviour that they were very normal children, establishing bonds to last them through the trials of time. For Little Red this was true but for Running Elk, the appearance belied the truth. Strangely, he felt a genuine fondness for Little Red. This, however, was the only exception, because he held an unreasonable hatred for all others, including his parents.

This hate begot and nourished in him almost uncontrollable desires to cause people and animals pain. His decision to kill a child by drowning did not happen in the spur of the moment. He had been stewing and planning how to accomplish this dark deed since his first failed attempt to push a child into the tidal waters of Bear Bay during the celebrations when Lightning Bolt was elected as National Chief. Running Elk decided to try again when the opportunity arose. The only unknown factors were who would be the victim and when the occasion would present itself. The opportune moment arrived when he saw two children playing alone, unsupervised, in a canoe that was partially resting in the river. He approached the canoe with stealth and shoved it into the current so quickly the children didn't see who did it.

Because of a howling wind, their pitiful cries for help went unheard. As soon as the canoe hit rough current it capsized and the poor babes were silenced forever. Running Elk, as he did after his previous "accidents" had been successful, inwardly felt a surge of elation and perverted satisfaction when he watched the innocents being claimed by the rushing water. The tragedy was declared a terrible accident.

The villagers were overwhelmed by grief, heightened for them by a belief that if they had exercised a little more care and kept closer watch over the children, the deaths could have been easily prevented. As atonement for what they thought was their sin of neglect, they prayed fervently to the Great Spirit to forgive them for not keeping the children safe.

During the aftermath, enjoying his monstrous deed to the fullest, Running Elk gave every appearance of being among the most genuinely saddened of the mourners. He attended every rite related to the children's Feast of the Dead and wept profusely with their parents, family and friends over the tragic loss. For him the acting, while watching people suffer, was part of the fun.

Fortunately for the villagers, Running Elk's brutal nature was satisfied for eight Seasons, reliving in his mind the experience of his latest killing. However, as he grew older, his lust for blood increased, needing to be satisfied in shorter periods of time.

When the mourning was over, the villagers slowly returned to normal routines. Flaming Hair and Rolling Thunder resumed spending as many pleasurable Sunrises as possible teaching their boys the Nation's legends and history and how to hunt and fish. Both progressed well, showing promise of becoming exceptional warriors. Running Elk, despite his almost continuous intimate contact with family and friends, continued to conceal his evil nature.

On the national scene, several Springs passed without any major crises occurring, and tranquility prevailed. This was changed dramatically after the second Moon of Lightning Bolt's fiftieth Spring. He received news from Grand Chief Big Elk that the Western Nations had again attacked Kespek without warning or provocation.

A few Sunrises later, he received another message informing him that Big Beaver had requested an emergency Grand Council meeting to ask his peers for military assistance. The Grand Chief tentatively set the meeting fifteen Sunrises before the first Moon of Summer, pending agreement of the Chiefs.

Lightning Bolt anticipated that most citizens of each country would eagerly agree to help the Kespekians. The attacks were a blatant breach of the terms of the Peace Treaty. He asked each Village Chief to consult with his citizens to determine if they would agree to declare war and send warriors to Kespek.

Lightning Bolt's personal reaction to the news of the unprovoked invasion of Kespek was, as could be expected from a man of his peaceful nature, indignant outrage. To control it, he asked the Great Spirit for help with a prayer. "Dear Father of the Universe, I hate war with such passion. Knowing we're being pulled into it again outrages me almost beyond reason. Please help me to have charity for an enemy filled with treachery. It will be hard. Forgive me, my Father, for at this point in time I hate the leaders of the Western Nations passionately for the death and destruction they are causing our People, and theirs. I want to see them all dead. Feeling this way I know is dangerous. Please, my Creator, help me overcome this feeling through my actions."

With meditation, the Chief controlled his anger and recovered his charity.

The following Sunrise, he sent word back to Grand Chief Big Elk that the Sunrise chosen for the meeting was okay with him and that he was in the process of carrying out his second request. To this end he had sent his own runners to the villages asking that the People, because of time constraints, might meet with him at several central locations to discuss the war.

At the appointed times, the meetings were convened. Lightning Bolt relayed to the attendees all the details he knew of the war and spelled out the possible negative repercussions should the Westerners not be stopped. He told of his personal outrage and asked the People for permission to declare war.

The news also outraged the villagers. They granted near unanimous approval to his request for a declaration of war, then authorized him to raise a large army of warriors to lead to the warfront at the earliest possible Sunrise.

With the declaration approved and issued, every Kespukwitkian village began marshalling resources for the coming war effort. They, with their anger driving them, quickly prepared and packed arms, extra clothing, food and other supplies needed by the warriors for the battles ahead.

Within a few Sunrises, well-equipped men from all corners of the country were on their way to Lightning Bolt's village to await departure. By the time the Grand Council met with Big Beaver, the army was ready to move at Lightning Bolt's command.

At Grand Chief Big Elk's village, the leaders began discussing the war immediately after opening ceremonies. Their collective anger was pervasive. After Big Beaver provided details about the attacks and invasion, Lightning Bolt asked to speak. Big Elk assented.

"My brothers, thirty Springs ago I attended, as a spectator, the peace conference that ended the last war that the Western Nations started. At that meeting our late brother, War Chief Mighty Water, and the Head War Chief of the Western Nations, Roaring Rapids, worked out an agreement that included provisions that stipulated that the Western Nations would never again attack us, nor would they try to seize the lands that the Creator reserved for our use.

"At the conclusion of the peace conference, Roaring Rapids swore before the Great Spirit, and on his honour, that the commitments they made would never be violated. He also asked for our assistance to help their leadership learn how to manage the affairs of their Nations in a more productive and responsible manner.

"In response to his request, War Chief Mighty Water made a statement that included a promise in plain language that could not be misunderstood, which I will now repeat to refresh our memories." Because of the significance of Mighty Water's words, all present had committed them to memory so that the peace agreement could be known to everyone, then and in future.

Lightning Bolt recited: "'Dear Roaring Rapids, my

friend, my brother, your unconditional acceptance of our generous offer is most welcome. I want to assure you that sending advisors to teach your leaders better ways to manage their affairs will be a great pleasure for us. However, with the greatest reluctance, I must tell you that if at a future time we determine that your leaders have not learned to manage their lands and other affairs properly, and to have respect for the desire and right of their neighbours to live in peace and security, we will indeed come in and manage all Western countries permanently. This, my friend, is a kind and generous promise you can be assured we shall keep.'"

Lightning Bolt continued, "Now, my brothers, due to the Westerners breaking what we thought were honourable commitments to live in peace, we must uphold a solemn promise made to them by our late brother. And, my friends, my Nation shall be at the forefront in keeping this promise on Mighty Water's behalf. The prospect of doing so doesn't make me happy. In fact, as a man of peace, being forced into fighting another war outrages me. It does so to such an extent that I am willing to fight to the end to defeat the invaders of Kespek and to capture and punish the men who started this outrage.

"To this end, I have already begun fulfilling Grand Chief Big Elk's request, through meeting with our People. I proudly report that they have readily approved a declaration of war and, with speed, we've raised a considerable army of well-prepared warriors who are now waiting at my village for deployment. They won't have long to wait. One Sunrise after I return home, I will travel with them to Kespek for battle duties. Marshalling our resources in such short order wasn't hard because the vast majority of our People are as outraged as I and they did not rest until preparations were finished. My brothers, this time I don't expect to be fighting the Western armies very long because in this instance we are well prepared to go to war and, with the Creator's mercy, we will quickly win.

"Thanks for letting me state our position. But, before I yield back to the Grand Chief, I have one other item to discuss. My father, Big Beaver, has asked me if I would, upon arrival in Kespek, assume the overall command of the allied forces. I have, pending your agreement, agreed to his request." Without any discussion they unanimously agreed to the appointment.

Other Chiefs made their positions known. To Lightning Bolt's pleasant surprise, they informed their peers that actions similar to those taken by his country already had been taken in theirs. The new commander asked the Chiefs to send their War Chiefs and advisors to meet with him to plan the campaign. They were to meet at Kespek, Big Beaver's village, two Sunrises before the last Moon of Summer.

As requested, they arrived and convened their meeting on the appointed Sunrise. They quickly, but meticulously, worked out a plan designed to end the war speedily. It was simple. Part of their army would strike at many strategic enemy locations inside Western territory, with the intent of stopping supplies and reinforcements from reaching the part of the enemy's army already occupying much of Kespek. The bulk of the warriors would mount a massive attack against the occupying army, with the intent of dealing them a mortal blow.

The next Sunrise, warriors moved out to take up positions to implement the plan. Fourteen Sunrises before the first Moon of Autumn they were ready. The initial attacks went exceptionally well, enemy positions fell quickly and within two Sunrises they were in full retreat. By the end of one Moon, the allied offensive measures were so successful that the Western armies were already driven out of Kespek and were being relentlessly pushed back deep into their own territory. Final victory was within sight.

A half Moon later, at his camp deep inside Western territory, Lightning Bolt received by runner a message from Head War Chief Big Eagle, the military leader of the Western forces, asking for a meeting as soon as possible to discuss terms of surrender. He accepted the request and sent by the returning runner an invitation asking Big Eagle to meet him at Lake Loon, the site used by War Chief Mighty Water for peace talks thirty Springs before. On the appointed Sunrise, shortly after dawn, the opening ceremonies began. Lightning Bolt, though he was enraged, welcomed Big Eagle and advisors to the peace circle.

"My brother, I bid you and your colleagues welcome to this circle of peace. Let us first pray together and ask the Great Spirit to give us the wisdom to make it a success." After the Chiefs finished making their supplications to the Creator, and other ceremonies were over, Lightning Bolt continued. "My friend, before we start talking specifics, I want to inform you of my intention to use blunt and plain language in my talks with you. I am going to do so because I want to assure, as much as humanly possible, that you and your colleagues clearly and fully understand and appreciate the true meaning of the terms of the agreement being worked out this sunrise. Through our agreement we will demand that your aggressor Nations will accept these terms in fullness, in exchange for an end to this war. The terms we have prepared are so comprehensive and inclusive that they will assure as far as humanly possible, when implemented, that we will never again have a need for a peace conference to settle a war between our Nations.

"I shall, in order to avoid misinterpretation of the provisions that we will insist on, explain every small detail until everyone fully understands its implications. This approach may seem crude and rude, and probably is, but when one takes into consideration that we are indeed repeating what was done here thirty Springs ago, because the kind and diplomatic language that was used then by my late and beloved brother, Mighty Water, appears to have been misunderstood by your leaders of that Sunrise and the Sunrises since. These proceedings are therefore entirely necessary, and will not be misunderstood by kind nor diplomatic talk. However, I assure you, in my heart is the deepest form of kindness, love and forgiveness that sees through to the truth of this situation, and of the very spirit of my late brother's words and his intentions for both of our Nations.

"Before getting further into discussions about the details of how we are to achieve our goals, I want you and your colleagues to know this about me. I am a man of peace who hates wars with a passion. Because of this, I feel strongly that wars are the tools of men devoid of compassion. My brothers, your leaders claim to be civilized, but civilized Peoples do not start wars to satisfy greed. By their excesses, your leaders have left you without civilized roots to build on. Their madness has led them to do irrational things: attacking us, knowing that our military situation wasn't weak like it was thirty Springs ago. Perhaps after the last war, when we let them walk away with most of their powers intact, they were led to believe that if they failed again to achieve their objective, their actions would entail no long-term consequences. If this indeed is the case, they have made a fatal mistake; mercy will not be shown to them, as was warned by my beloved late brother, Mighty Water.

"The Mi'kmaq firmly believe that everyone deserves a second chance. Our charity, in their case, was given because we believed the sincerity they projected in agreeing to a just and permanent peace. In fact, their sincerity was so profound that there were no disbelievers on our side.

"This time I will not, under any circumstance, consider a proposition that your leaders have been so humbled by their defeat that they would never again let their greed overrule good judgment again. If I were to do so, I would be as insane as they are.

"Now, my friends, let's get down to basics. Because of this war, your Nations are on the edge of oblivion. Their future existence is ours to decide. Whether we will permit them to survive will be determined by your responses to our demands, which will be harsh. I hope that what we are about to do to your Nations will cause any future potential aggressors to take note that attacking a very powerful alliance such as ours has grave consequences.

"My friends, as the Great Spirit is my witness, I state to you unequivocally that your rulers will not trouble any Nation again after this war. They have caused all the pain and suffering for our People and yours that they are ever going to cause. Without exception, we will depose and punish them. This shall be done in remembrance of all their past victims. The present conflict is their last.

"With the utmost forcefulness and sincerity, we shall now tell you what our conditions are for permanent peace. These conditions not complicated. There are only three, very short, and clear conditions that I put to you this sunrise:

"First and foremost, the democratic laws that govern

our countries shall be adopted by yours. Second, the soon-to-be-deposed leaders of your Nations shall be replaced by civilized men appointed by your country's citizens. Third, we will govern your countries until the first two conditions are implemented and functioning. The end result will assure that love and respect for the cultural differences and territory of other Nations are the guidelines for the future conduct of the affairs of your Nations. We shall consider nothing less.

"Big Eagle, my brother, if you will unconditionally accept the terms for a peace and friendship agreement that I have just laid out for you we will eventually withdraw from your territory and leave your countries intact. If not, although owning your land has no special interest whatsoever for us, we will continue the present war and take complete control. When achieved, your countries will be subdivided into smaller Nations that will have Mi'kmaq governors ruling over them for hundreds of Moons to come.

"Lastly, and I want you to listen very closely to this promise, because the future existence of your Nations as independent bodies will be tied to this: you and you colleagues are to relay this promise word for word to the present generations of your Nation and instruct them that they in turn must, without fail, relay it to future generations. This, be assured, is a promise that we will faithfully keep. If we, or our allies in the Wabanaki Confederacy, are ever again drawn into war with your Nations it will be for the last time. Because, after it is all over, your countries shall no longer exist. Understand?"

"Lightning Bolt, my brother, you state with the utmost sincerity that you are a man of peace. From what I have heard about you from friends during my travels, I do not doubt the truth of it. In view of the present situation you may be very surprised to hear this, but I also abhor the death and destruction caused by war, and I consider myself to be a man who craves peace between brothers.

"In this regard, I truly believe that in the eyes of the Great Spirit we are all brothers; thus it is absolutely wrong for a brother to fight, maim or kill a brother. I also sincerely believe that the Great Spirit must find the sight of one brother killing another, simply to take his property or freedom from him or to cause him physical harm, very offensive.

"My esteemed brother, with the before mentioned in mind, I've listened attentively to your words of wisdom, appreciating and understanding the truth of them perfectly. As you spoke, my heart felt nothing but shame and sorrow for the pain that our leaders have caused the citizens of our Nations. I include our citizens because, at peace or at war, they have suffered.

"My friend, you have done an excellent job of describing their behaviour. The thousands of deaths they have caused among the citizens of the alliance and our Nations is unforgivable. There is only one word that adequately describes the trail of death and destruction they have caused: 'horrific.' My brother, when I think of the extent of the sorrow caused to so many innocent people, my heart breaks!

"Oh, my brother, the blood of so many innocents shed in the war was for nothing that can be considered honourable. It was only started by our leaders to try to satisfy a desire for land and a craving to have control over your People. Certainly not to eliminate a threat to our countries.

"There is not a reasonable defence for the actions of our leaders. My brother, it was a deed without honour when they violated the terms of the last peace and friendship treaty between our Nations. The concept of keeping an honourable peace agreement or, for that matter, any kind of agreement, is to them quite unknown.

"My esteemed brother, I want to emphasize that when the present campaign was being planned by our leaders, I and my fellow War Chiefs spoke out against it. However, our voices were like a drop of rain in the vastness of the Big Pond. They scoffed at our concerns and ordered us to prepare our warriors to do their bidding. With their decision, I knew that again many innocents were about to die for nothing, because defeat was unavoidable. Yet, in the society I come from, it is obey or die.

"In case you are wondering why the Hereditary Chiefs started a war that was almost certain to end with our defeat I will enlighten you. They did this because they deluded them-selves into believing that the defeat we suffered during the last war was nothing more than a quirk of fate. These men never gave thought to the proposition that our defeat prob-ably occurred because of the negative attitudes of our citizens toward such a war in the first place. The feelings and needs of our People do not count when deciding matters such as war. If the aforementioned revelation has not shocked you enough there is more. They assumed the success of your armies in defeating us to the blind luck of fate. It wasn't possible for them to comprehend that the successes of your warriors were based on the total support of your citizens, who love their free way of life with all their hearts, and who are willing to give up their lives to defend it.

"It will please you to know that I have taken heart from the example your People give. I have no intention of obey-ing our leaders any longer; death would be preferable. This position is that of my colleagues also. We apologize sincerely for the great pain and sorrow that we have helped to cause, and bend our heads in shame before the Great Spirit for these offences. My brother, we wish to make amends for our grave mistakes by assisting you in any way possible to implement a peace that will be comprehensive, effective, completely enforceable and as far as humanly possible, permanent.

"To achieve this we place the War Chiefs of the Western Nations at your service. And, we pledge to you, my brother, that upon leaving this site, our two Peoples will have a peace in principle that will withstand the test of time."

"Big Eagle, my brother, your sincerity and openness in admitting the weaknesses of your leaders impresses and moves me deeply. I believe, when you spoke, you did so from the heart. This tells me that I can trust you. I was also pleased to learn that you too abhor the horrors of war and wish to see that it never again causes hurt and damage between our Peoples. To this end, we are willing to work diligently with you and your colleagues to achieve these ends. In fact, as I've already stated, we have developed a plan that will assure it.

"But, before we begin to build a new tomorrow, there is one matter of the utmost importance that must be taken care of first, because peace cannot be achieved without it. As I have stated, without exception, the Hereditary Chiefs of your Nations must be removed from office immediately and forever. They will be tried and punished. Until you spoke your words of contrition so sincerely my brother, we intended to do the honour ourselves. But now, knowing your attitude, perhaps we can work something out that will involve you and your colleagues in the process.

"I will tell you how we had planned to fill the leadership vacancy. After the end of the war, as an interim measure, we intended to replace your leaders with Governors from our Nations, until such time as your People were in a position to appoint new leaders by election. However, I would now consider appointing you as temporary leader of all Western Nations, while the democratic procedures are implemented. How say you?"

"Brother, could I have some time alone with our War Chiefs to discuss your words in a private meeting? If you are agreeable, we will return when the sun begins to fall with an answer. Do you consent?"

"Yes, my brother, go and meet in private, and may the Great Spirit be with you in your deliberations."

Shortly after the sun began its descent the peace talks reconvened and Big Eagle relayed the results of the Western Nations War Chiefs' discussions. "Lightning Bolt, my brother, we have discussed your proposals thoroughly and found them very generous. I say this because we are well aware that you are now in a position where your army, if you and your colleagues wanted it, could easily overrun all our villages in a matter of a few Sunrises and impose whatever you want on our People. If we could find the heart for it, we could probably delay the inevitable for a few Sunrises, but for what purpose? To see more decent and innocent people die?

"My friend, our People do not want war, they want their beloved fathers, brothers and friends home and safe with them, not fighting to fulfil the dreams of madmen. And, I believe that they fervently want to live in a country where they have the same kind of freedom from tyranny that your People enjoy. The fact that your country's citizens live in freedom, without fear of their leaders, is well known among our citizens. This is why, during this and the last war, they viewed your warriors as liberators, not conquerors. Warriors that the People consider enemies are not welcomed that way.

"My brother, you may not remember seeing me there, but

thirty Springs ago I was present with you at the peace circle, and heard the words of hope. But, unlike you, knowing my leaders, I didn't have much optimism for long-term peace. Therefore, I wasn't surprised when they decided to start this war. Neither were our People. When they heard the rumours of it, knowing that they were probably true, they reacted with hopeless resignation. It caused no joy in their hearts.

"Now my friends, here is our response to your peace terms. First, I will reply to your demand that the Hereditary Chiefs be removed. In this regard there is no need for you to do anything, because we have already made arrangements to have this taken care of. By next Sunrise large contingents of warriors will be on their way to their villages to inform them that they are deposed and to arrest them. We will, with your permission, try them for crimes. Should they resist, their arrest will be done by force.

"However, I already know it will be done peacefully because they are almost devoid of support. Very few, if any, will defend them. This was reflected by the reaction of the runners we sent to advise our field commanders of what we had decided, and to ask them to send warriors to do the job. They were so overjoyed at the prospect of seeing the end of the tyrants that we could hear them hooting with joy as they sped on their way.

"Now, for your request that I act as temporary leader of the Western Nations, the answer is yes, with three conditions. First, I would like to appoint the War Chief of each Western Nation as a temporary leader of their respective Nation until appointments by the People can take place. You will no doubt agree about the importance of allowing the People to carefully select men to fill their National Chief positions. Second, to see the election part of our first condition implemented properly, we want your Nations to agree to devise an electoral process for us, and then help us run it until we learn how to do it ourselves. Third, help us set up and run the democracy you spoke about. How say you my brother?"

"My brother, your conditions are most joyfully accepted. To celebrate this marvellous occasion, let us, with joy in our hearts, smoke a pipe of peace. This will help us begin to enjoy our new status as brothers in peace and friendship."

"Lightning Bolt, my brother, before we do, I propose, until the peace and friendship treaty is ratified, that our temporary truce be made permanent. Then, we can really begin to enjoy true peace with the Great Spirit's blessing."

"It is agreed. You and I can send runners to spread the word. Now let us smoke and savour the future mutual benefits of the brotherly relationship we are entering into."

Several Moons later, when the allied leaders and the newly elected leaders of the Western Nations met to officially end the war, they participated in a Burying of the Hatchet Ceremony. During the ceremony, Lightning Bolt and Big Eagle spoke on behalf of their respective Nations and allies. Lightning Bolt spoke first.

"My brothers, by ratifying the terms of an honourable and enforceable peace pact between our Nations this Sunrise, we have set out on a new path together. It is a noble path that can, if we work hard at it, lead to true brotherhood. The ratifying of our pact demonstrates fully that when people are guided by the Hand and Laws of the Great Spirit, as we appear to have been, they can accomplish great things. I predict the peace made between us will be lasting and will be enjoyed and supported in the future by our children's children for thousands of Seasons to come.

"The reason I make such an unconditional prediction

is this. With elected people now in charge in the Western Nations, and democratic laws in place, leaders only make war with the approval of their citizens. As is well proven by the record of the Mi'kmaq Nations, the Members of the Wabanaki Confederacy and many other Nations who govern by democratic principles, very rarely do a People of good will and conscience opt for war over peace.

"My brothers, let us thank the Great Spirit that we have put war behind us. We must, in the name of the Creator, and in memory of our beloved departed ancestors, who died in the unnecessary conflicts between us, resolve, while burying this hatchet, that we shall, as long as the sun rises and falls, never again raise our bows, lances or war clubs against each other in anger.

"To bind our pact, let us stand and swear an oath before the Great Spirit, with dignity, honour and love, that from this Sunrise forward we shall go hand in hand into the future with respect for each other. Let us further pledge before our Creator that the human dignity of all our Peoples shall be held paramount to all other considerations when disputes arise among us. And, last but not least, let us pledge that resolution of our disputes from this Sunrise forward shall be done in a manner that relies on well established practices of negotiation, discussion and resolution.

"Let us promise to the Great Spirit that we will respect and uphold both the notion of peace and the practice of peace, for both are essential to keeping a just peace for all parties. Such adjudications, being based upon these practices, have been shown to be respected, even when the outcomes of such discussions are difficult to bear. Here, this sunrise, we stand together, and before the Creator of us all, we give our lives to the assurance of a lasting and permanent peace."

Everybody stood and duly pledged.

Lightning Bolt, comforted by the brotherhood being displayed, continued, "With humility and respect, my brothers, I bury the harm that the past wars have caused us with this hatchet, and vow that I shall be diligent in assuring that affairs between our Peoples shall henceforth be conducted with brotherly love. May the Great Spirit shine His love down upon us, His humble children, and forgive us for our shortcomings."

In a strong, convincing voice Big Eagle made his address, "Lightning Bolt, my esteemed brother, I cannot add much to what you've so eloquently said. The truth of your words is beyond dispute. My feelings are virtually identical. There is nothing I could add that would make your message stronger.

"However, I do want to apologize once again for the fact that our country started these wars. I will recoil, my brothers, for the rest of my Moons on Mother Earth, from the memories of what our Nations visited upon our Peoples. The part I played will haunt me forever. The only thing that consoles me is that this time we were largely successful in keeping our warriors from committing the same kinds of crimes committed by our side thirty Springs ago.

"To assure as much as possible that atrocities wouldn't occur, I swore to the Great Spirit in front of my men that if any of them slaughtered innocent civilians and burned their villages that I would personally execute the perpetrators. Very few did. For this I fervently thank the Creator. My brothers, we owe it to our children and our children's children to see that these kinds of men never again come to power.

"Therefore, in the name of the Great Spirit and of my revered ancestors, I pledge that with the burying of this hatchet the greed our leaders promoted shall be buried with it for time immemorial. And I vow that I will devote the rest of my life to the pursuit of peace for all Nations. May the Great Spirit bless and keep you, my brothers, and may He always provide us with the humility and wisdom to love and cherish each other. Let us now embrace and celebrate our victory over the evil spirits that have caused us so much pain and sorrow."

The Chiefs embraced and smoked another pipe together. The warriors followed their example and with much jubilation began the process that would, in time, permanently bind these Nations together as friends. Both victor and defeated celebrated and feasted as equals, and parted as brothers. The strength of such bonds was demonstrated when, from that Sunrise forward, these brothers and their families were warmly welcomed in each other's wigwams. Wisdom and humility had effectively smothered the evils of war between their great Peoples.

The war produced many heroes. One in particular made Lightning Bolt feel very proud of him. His brother Flaming Hair, with the conviction of the wronged motivating him, had given an outstanding performance while carrying out his war duties. Because of his demonstration of outstanding leadership and dedication, he had been put in charge of a large contingent of Kespukwitk's army, which occurred within Sunrises of the initial battlefield encounters. The courage he displayed was inspiring. He had, at great risk to himself, taken extraordinary measures to protect his men from harm.

The Chiefs of the allied Nations and warriors returned home to heroes' welcomes and great celebrations. Fitting homage was paid to the valiant men who had died during the conflict. Eventually life returned to the contented, peaceful and normal existence they enjoyed previously.

Lightning Bolt, now in his fifty-sixth Spring, like most men in positions such as his, often used social visits with relatives and friends to discuss business. Thus, he and Flaming Hair, three Sunrises before the second Moon of Autumn, after eating a delectable supper of fresh salmon they had caught shortly before in the Bear River, began to discuss the details of trading transactions they had been involved in while on a visit to Sipekne'katik, six Sunrises before.

Eventually, Flaming Hair changed the subject by asking: "Lightning Bolt, my brother, may I use your medicine pouch tomorrow? I plan to go next Sunrise for a long walk to enjoy some quiet time alone and can't find mine."

"I have a spare one that I'll give you, but whatever happened to yours?"

"Thank you. I don't know; it seems I mislaid it somewhere, but I can't figure out for the life of me how it happened. I'm so sure, my brother, that I put it in the same place where I always put it, when I go to bed at night, I would swear to it. I distinctly remember removing it from my waist and laying it at the head of my bed. Spotted Fawn says she would also swear before the Great Spirit that she saw me do it. However, this morning, it's nowhere to be found."

Lightning Bolt, knowing his brother was not forgetful, responded, "I know that it's highly unlikely you didn't do as you say, but, just in case, did you and Spotted Fawn thoroughly search your wigwam and the clothing you wore last Sunrise?"

"Yes, we tore the place apart. It seems as if it grew legs and walked away under its own power."

Lightning Bolt alluded to the mysterious things that often happened around the village: "It's strange my brother that it would disappear into thin air. I guess we'll have to classify it as one of those strange and seemingly unexplainable incidents that happen. However, when I come to think of it, many unexplainable things have been happening in our village, ever since the tragic drowning deaths of those two poor children — it was 15 years ago now. Sometimes I wonder if there isn't a human hand in it. No, forget I said such an unkind thing. They just happen from time to time in any community."

"My brother, don't shrug it off too easily. I have had the same suspicion occasionally running through my mind. The reason I mostly reject it is because I think that if the horrible incidents — like those drowning children you mentioned — that have happened around our village without logical explanation are actually done by a human being, the person would have to be a fiend. Which we don't have in our village. No one I know seems capable of that. Anyway, forget it. While I'm away next Sunrise, I will ask Spotted Fawn if she would kindly make me another medicine pouch; then I'll have another to fall back on if I should lose the one you just gave me."

The next Sunrise a horrible crime was committed. The bodies of a brutally murdered mother, Morning Mist, and her two young daughters, aged five and seven, were found just before dusk by Little Red and Running Elk in an old burn where she and the children had gone to gather berries. Their thoroughly mutilated remains indicated that they had been extensively tortured and sexually molested before being killed.

A possible clue to the identity of the murderer was found at the crime scene. Flaming Hair's blood-spattered medicine pouch was discovered under the remains of the mother. The fact he had gone off alone that morning to enjoy a Sunrise of tranquility added to the suspicion centred about him. He didn't have a credible alibi for the timespan when the crimes were committed.

The villagers were in an uproar over the horrific murders and wanted the culprit severely punished. In view of what seemed like compelling evidence against him, they were demanding that Flaming Hair be brought to justice without delay. Upon his return late that night, warriors put him in bonds and brought him before Lightning Bolt for examination.

After hearing his brother plead his innocence, Lightning Bolt informed him that he would fully investigate the matter and arrange for him to have a full hearing, witnessed by his fellow citizens, the following sunset. He then instructed the warriors, for his protection from the angry crowd who wanted swift justice, to hold Flaming Hair unbound in his wigwam until he sent for him late the next Sunrise.

At first light the next Sunrise, Lightning Bolt began gathering evidence and soliciting information from individuals who might have witnessed something that could be relevant in proving the guilt or innocence of his beloved brother. That dusk, with inquires completed, he convened a meeting of Elders and advisors and asked them to sit in judgment upon Flaming Hair; he then had him brought before them and assumed the position of examiner.

"My brother, I want you to feel assured that you will be given every opportunity to prove your innocence. During the hearing you will be permitted to examine any witnesses brought before us. And, if there is anything you need to help prove your innocence, it will be made available. Do you have any questions in this regard before we commence?"

"No, my brother, I haven't."

"Very well, let us begin. My brother, you have been accused of committing the heinous crimes of torture, rape and murder. How say you, guilty or innocent?"

"My brothers and sisters, as the Great Spirit is my witness, I have no knowledge of these horrible crimes. I could never have done something so loathsome. I loved Morning Mist and her children like my own. I feel the deepest sorrow in the knowledge that they must have suffered beyond endurance at the hands of the contemptible person who did these things to them. My friends, other than the oath I've made, I don't know what else I can say in my defence. The evidence found at the scene seems damning, but all who know me know that I could not perform such horrors as have been done."

Lightning Bolt prodded: "My brother, tell us how you spent your time last Sunrise?"

"After rising, Spotted Fawn helped me prepare for a walk I planned through the forest for a Sunrise of reflection and meditation. She, as she always did when I wanted to be by myself for a time, joked about me becoming weary of her company and preferring the companionship of the birds and other beasts instead. After I ate breakfast, I started walking through the village, stopping to say a few words to Broken Canoe when I passed his wigwam.

"He cracked a joke about me needing someone to save me if Spotted Fawn kept dumping me in the river as she had a few Sunrises ago. During that frolic, which he had witnessed, I swallowed a great deal of water and needed some fairly strong slaps on the back to get my choking and coughing under control.

"He then asked if I was going off on one of my walks to meditate. I replied yes and told him the general direction I was taking. He related that Morning Mist and their two girls were heading off shortly in the same direction to pick berries at the old burn. After we exchanged a few more pleasantries, I set off in an easterly direction into the wilderness. When I came to the old burn, I picked and ate a handful of berries and continued on my way.

"Brothers and sisters, how do I explain the rest? I can tell you what I did, and thought about, during my walk through the forest. I savoured the wonders of Mother Earth. I smelled the fresh scents of trees, grasses and flowers while thinking about my wonderful family, friends and country, and how the Great Spirit has blessed me with a bountiful life. I walked and rested at times, meditated and thanked the Creator for His love and benevolence. Other than repeating that I had absolutely nothing to do with committing the sick crimes I find myself accused of, my brothers and sisters, I have at this time nothing more to say."

Lightning Bolt responded, "Thank you, Flaming Hair. Broken Canoe, please come forward. My beloved son, it saddens me to be forced to intrude into your time of grief for the loss of your precious family. However, in order to get to the bottom of these horrific crimes, I must ask you to bear with me and answer a few questions. Are you ready?"

"Yes my father; however, if I occasionally weep, please bear with me because my sorrow is so overwhelming."

Gently, feeling great pity for the young father, Lightning Bolt requested, "My son, tell us briefly about what happened early last Sunrise."

"My beloved father, first I'll tell you why Morning Mist and our babies were at the old burn. At supper, two Sunrises ago, the girls told us that they had a craving for some of their favourite desserts made from blueberries. Morning Mist, with a twinkle in her eye, responded that a craving for something as essential to the joy of a person as a delicious dessert should not go unfilled. Then she suggested that we all get up early the next Sunrise and go to the old burn and pick berries. The girls, in their excitement, went off to tell their friends.

"To my everlasting sorrow, in the absence of the girls, I declined. The reason I did was that several friends and I were working on a new Big Pond Canoe and wanted to finish it before the next fish harvest. Later, after telling the girls I wouldn't be going, as a way to ease their disappointment, I told them that I would get up early the next dawn and help them prepare for their trip.

"The next morning I had just come out of our wigwam to go to the stream to wash when I saw Flaming Hair coming. We stopped for a short time and passed a few pleasantries. He told me about his plans for the Sunrise and I told him that Morning Mist and the girls were soon heading in the same direction to pick blueberries around the old burn. He replied that if he came back that way early he would look for them. After a few more words, he set off and I continued to the stream for a wash.

"Returning to the wigwam I roused Morning Mist and the girls. After they dressed and washed, we ate and they got under way. They were laughing and waving goodbye to me as they walked into the forest. That is how I saw my darling wife and precious babies for the last time. Oh, my father, why oh why wasn't I there to protect them. How can I ever forgive myself for not going?"

"My dear son, the Great Spirit sometimes works in strange ways. Perhaps He didn't want you to go along because He wanted to take Morning Mist and the girls home with Him. I know, my son, that you will continue to blame yourself for a while, but eventually you will overcome your grief and come to accept the will of the Creator. Please take some comfort from knowing that we all love you and want to help you through this terrible ordeal."

Reluctantly, because of Broken Canoe's heartbreaking grief, after a few more words of solace Lightning Bolt continued, "I have just a few more quick questions to ask, my son, and then you can go. Did you see anyone else up and around besides Flaming Hair when you got up? And, can you recall what he was wearing, and did you find his conduct unusual in any way?"

"My father, Flaming Hair was the only person I saw. The best I can recall about his dress was that he was wearing an old outfit. He was acting his normal good-natured self, nothing out of the way; there wasn't anything unusual about him or his conduct. That is all that I can say about it, but, before taking my leave, my father, I want to say emphatically. I've known Flaming Hair since I was very young, as a matter of fact I was one of the children who discovered him washed ashore that time so long ago. Since then, he has treated me and everyone else around our village with the utmost kindness, generosity and love. I continue to view him as a respected and beloved uncle. I know the evidence indicates that he tortured and murdered my precious family, but I can't bring myself to believe that he, such a gentle and compassionate man, could ever have done such a horrible deed."

"Thank you my son; may the Great Spirit be with you in your time of sorrow.

"Little Red, please come forward and tell us how you and Running Elk discovered the bodies."

"My uncle, last Sunrise Running Elk came and asked me if I wished to accompany him on a hike through the woods. As I wasn't doing anything of any great importance, I agreed.

He suggested that we go in the direction that my father had taken when he left the encampment earlier that morning. Not being present at the time my father departed, I had no notion of which direction he had taken and I told Running Elk so. However, he said he had seen him leave that dawn and knew the direction we should take.

"We then set off in the direction of the rising sun and walked for some time before coming to the old burn. Upon seeing it, pleasant memories of the wonderful taste of blueberries came rushing back, and I sought out a place to pick a few. I had just started picking when Running Elk, in a horrified voice, yelled for me to come. He had discovered the mutilated bodies of poor Morning Mist and her girls."

"Please describe, my son, what you saw and found at the scene in detail."

Although his father's fate was on the line, Little Red spoke as honestly as he could. "The naked remains were badly mutilated. Oh, my uncle, the sight of those poor souls so badly mutilated still horrifies me. Please bear with me and I will try to keep control, and be objective about it. But, when I think of the monstrous things that were done to them it makes me want to weep. The crime scene indicated quite clearly that Morning Mist and the girls had struggled hard to escape before being tied and tortured beyond endurance by their attacker. By their appearances he had literally butchered them alive. I will relive the pain of discovering and seeing the horrific crime until the Season I die."

With compassion in his voice for the nightmare that his beloved nephew was reliving over and over, Lightning Bolt continued, "Tell us my son, did you see, hear, or find anything unusual at the scene?"

"The only thing we found, my uncle, that didn't belong

there was a medicine pouch, which Running Elk identified as belonging to my father. We didn't find anything else."

"Did you recognize the medicine pouch as your father's?"

"No, my uncle, I'm sorry to say that I can't describe the size or the shape, or for that matter anything else about my father's medicine pouch. I've seen such personal items around our wigwam and around the wigwams of our brothers and sisters in the village thousands of times, but I can't, except for a few revered personal relics that I've seen, identify any specific personal item as belonging to an identifiable person other than to me."

"Thank you, my son, for your help. The information provided is most helpful.

"Now, Running Elk, please come forward. My son, tell us your version of the discovery."

"My father, I can't help but weep while I talk to you about last Sunrise. It seems almost as if whoever committed the crimes has no conscience. The pain he inflicted upon Morning Mist and her children before slaying them was evident by the ghastly scene of brutal torture we saw. The horrible sight of their tortured bodies shall always live in my memory, always!

"I won't go into a detailed description of the horrors that we discovered because most of you viewed the scene firsthand. I will, however, verify that my uncle Flaming Hair's medicine pouch was found at the scene."

"My son, Little Red stated that you told him you saw Flaming Hair leave the camp last Sunrise. Can you tell us if this is true, and if so, describe what he was wearing?"

"Yes, my father, I had slipped out of our wigwam for a drink of water and saw Uncle Flaming Hair talking to Broken Canoe, then walking eastward through the village. I recall clearly that he was wearing his favourite hunting outfit and had, attached to his waist, his medicine pouch. After he started walking away, I saw Broken Canoe start toward the stream, as he stated."

With a touch of incredulity in his voice, Lightning Bolt responded, "My son, your powers of observation truly amaze me. For you to recognize the medicine pouch of Flaming Hair, and to know what he regards as his favourite hunting outfit, is almost unbelievable. Just to be sure that I heard you right, I will ask again. Can you state positively that he was wearing his medicine pouch when he left camp last Sunrise?"

"Yes, father, I am as sure of it as I am sure the sun will rise again tomorrow. I can close my eyes and see him walking through the village dressed in his favourite outfit, with his medicine pouch attached to his waist, as easily as I can see you before me now."

With a feeling of disbelieving horror, Lightning Bolt commented, "My son, I have known you all your life, and can say that your devotion to the community has been impressive. I long ago concluded, by seeing you volunteering for community duties and taking a lead role in promoting positive activities around the community, that you were an excellent role model for the younger children to follow. Your truthfulness has never been disputed; you've always appeared to be a humble and honourable young person. Therefore, it pains me to no end to call you a spreader of lies before this assembly."

Those assembled were shocked by Lightning Bolt's words. In feigned injured innocence, Running Elk retorted, "Fathers and mothers, brothers and sisters, I swear before the Great Spirit, and on the graves of my ancestors, that what I've revealed to you this Sunrise is the truth."

Lightning Bolt, thoroughly repulsed, replied, "My son,

you now add to your other crimes by defiling the name of the Great Spirit and of the dead. I must tell you that I have solid information that does not support your story."

Acting out his part as the aggrieved innocent to the end Running Elk, in tears now, answered, "Oh Great Chief, my father, I swear again, I've told the truth."

Lightning Bolt then ended it by revealing the truth. "Then explain to me, a simple man who does not believe in the unexplainable, how you could have seen Flaming Hair wearing his medicine pouch when he had misplaced it, and I gave him an extra one I had?"

Before anybody could recover sufficiently from the shock of Lightning Bolt's revelation, Running Elk had the Chief by the hair, and had a war club raised high in a position to deliver a death blow to his skull. The hate and spitefulness his face revealed was unbelievable to those who thought they knew him. Suddenly the gentle considerate young warrior's facade was replaced by that of a villain.

He addressed the crowd, "Before I kill this scum to whom most of you seem so devoted, I want to give you a list of my noble accomplishments in life. I have rid this world of many of the most miserable and useless souls who belonged to this village." He listed with pride the horrible crimes he had committed since early childhood.

The People were paralyzed by revulsion and shock at the revelations.

Running Elk added, "To continue with my practice of ridding Mother Earth of its human lice, I will soon rid the world of a man who, by his very existence, is an affront to my sense of dignity. Lightning Bolt, you thoroughly evil man, do you wish to speak before I send you on your way to the Land of Souls?"

With the utmost sorrow, but no fear in his voice, Lightning Bolt replied, "My son, may the Great Spirit forgive you for your unspeakable crimes against humanity. What horrors you have done to your own."

Preparing to deliver the mortal blow, Running Elk screamed, "My father, may the Great Spirit speed your soul on its way to its final rest."

However, before he could bring down the war club he fell to the ground dead with a spear through his chest. Little Red, who at first had recoiled in horror at the revelations of his friend, had quickly recovered his wits and managed to grab a spear. Knowing before he threw the arrow that this was the only chance Lightning Bolt, his great-uncle, his father and his hero had for survival, Little Red threw this arrow with the strength of the desperate, which saved Lightning Bolt's life at the very last moment.

But the trauma of finding the bodies of the innocents, then learning the truth about his friend and then delivering the blow that ended his miserable life, nearly undid him. He fell to his knees and wept enormous sobs that echoed through the whole village. Lightning Bolt himself fell to his knees, weeping and with the face of horror, dismay and shock. He looked at the body of Running Elk with the strangest expression anyone had ever seen. His eyes were hollow, as if he had seen a dreadful ghost who had managed by some feat of evil to steal away his very soul. His hands lay limp on his knees and the tears dried up in his eyes, and would not fall. These events would haunt Little Red and Lightning Bolt for many Moons afterwards. But, the Creator, with the passages of the Sunrises, helped each man slowly but surely recover the joy in life once again.

The following Sunrise, Lightning Bolt delivered an oration

at the Feast of the Dead for Morning Mist and her children. "My brothers and sisters, the horrors that we learned about last Sunrise have caused our community so much pain that it defies description. The hurt from Running Elk's deeds runs so deep that its presence can be physically felt. But, beloved friends, we must begin to deal with it and begin the process of reinforcing the love and trust we have for one another.

"To begin the healing process, we must put the horrors into perspective. They are, as far as I can determine, almost without precedent in our country. Thus, knowing that they are such leaves us with the comfort of knowing that such horrible things will probably never happen again.

"Now, my brothers and sisters, to help heal the hurt in our hearts, we must ask ourselves many questions; some are unanswerable. For instance, how can a person's mind be so twisted with madness that he can actually believe he did his community a favour by killing and maiming its loved ones? As the question is unanswerable, we have to accept it for what it is, an evil thing that happens out of nowhere, and for no reason."

Lightning Bolt continued with his reassuring words for some time, then concluded, "My beloved friends, we must in our prayers also remember with kindness and love in our hearts, that Running Elk was the son of our beloved brother and sister Rolling Thunder and Misty Moon. They have also suffered greatly from this tragedy and must be comforted. Their grief for the devoted son who disappeared so quickly last Sunrise is as genuine as any grief we may have for the loss of a loved one. They cannot be condemned for the acts of a son who, until his confession, was a beloved and respected member of our community.

"And my friends we must, when passing moral judgment

on him, keep in mind that the enormity of the crimes he committed signifies that Running Elk was possessed by a spirit so evil that only his death could deliver him from its clutches. He is now delivered, and may the Great Spirit in His mercy welcome him into the Land of Souls with an open heart."

After Lightning Bolt finished his oration and the funeral was over, the community came together and, led by Flaming Hair and Spotted Fawn, comforted Rolling Thunder and Misty Moon as well as the family of the victims. With time, the wounds healed, but the enormity of the crime would never be forgotten.

//

CHAPTER SEVEN

Five Sunrises after he passed his sixtieth birth-Spring, Lightning Bolt received a runner from Grand Chief Big Elk's family with a message that, in the near future, would drastically alter his lifestyle. The runner informed him that ten Sunrises after the first Moon of Spring, Grand Chief Big Elk, at ninety-two Winters, had passed away peacefully in his sleep, and that his remains had been interred. He further advised that the family had set the Sunrise for his official Feast of the Dead Ceremony for eight Sunrises before the last Moon of Spring. The news was sent immediately by runners to Kespukwitk's villages in order to give people who could travel to Sipekne'katik ample time to prepare.

The Grand Chief's death, due to his great age, would not engender much sadness among the People. It was their belief that the calling home to the Land of Souls by the Great Spirit of a person who had spent a long lifetime generously serving and compassionately helping his People should be celebrated, not mourned. In recognition of his status as a man of great reputation, the Grand Chief's Feast of the Dead would be the best the citizens of all the Mi'kmaq Nations could provide. As word of his death spread throughout the villages of the many countries of the Wabanaki Confederacy, many thousands of their citizens began to make preparations to accompany their head Chiefs on the long journey to Grand Chief Big Elk's village.

The vast crowd, on the Sunrise set for his funeral, with utmost respect and joy, began Grand Chief Big Elk's Feast of the Dead. The senior Elders started the rites by offering prayers to the Great Spirit. They invited all the Elders present, from the many countries represented, to jointly perform with them the Sweet-grass Ceremony. This was followed by the head Chiefs sitting in a circle and passing a pipe around in commemoration of their brother.

After they finished this aspect of the rite, Lightning Bolt, because of his close personal relationship with the family, was given the honour of speaking first. His glowing tribute would be the first of the hundreds that would be, over the next three Sunrises, offered by relatives and friends in memory of the late Grand Chief.

"Brothers and sisters," Lightning Bolt said, "I am truly grateful and honoured to be asked to be the first to praise the memory of Grand Chief Big Elk, our beloved father. In my poor fashion, I will try to describe his remarkable character. If my words seem to be inadequate, it's because my mind is clouded by the memory of his multitude of great achievements, accomplishments and his outstanding personality.

"Big Elk, my friends, was a man with a great heart, who loved and respected all people. He was brave and fearless. When it came to protecting us from our enemies, he would have, without hesitation, given up his life to do so. His performance during peace and war, the Hunt and all other things he was involved in was always above reproach. The even-handed manner and wisdom he used when assisting people and countries to find solutions for their problems was legendary. He was to me a hero and a role model. His lifetime achievements were, and will remain, a shining inspiration for us all. In spite of his outstanding accomplishments and the acknowledgements he received for them he was a very humble man.

"In fact, my brothers and sisters, his humbleness was limitless. In his golden Winters, despite all that he had done for us, he believed that his inability to hunt, because of age, had made him an undeserving burden upon his family and friends. Even with assurances to the contrary he would state, 'It is I who should be providing, not taking.'

"There are, my brothers and sisters, so many wonderful things to say about Grand Chief Big Elk that one could go on for Sunrises. Words do not exist that can adequately describe his generosity and kindness. Without fail, he assisted all who came to him for aid. Not one of them was ever turned away empty-handed from his wigwam. My brothers and sisters, when the Great Spirit welcomed Big Elk home, He welcomed home a man who had served his People to the end unselfishly, without concern for his own comfort.

"It is very difficult to find the right words to describe the love and respect I had for our brother, Big Elk. Perhaps I can best do so by simply stating that I am eternally grateful to the Great Spirit for permitting me the privilege of enjoying his company. His many visits to our wigwam were such a treasure that I can recall them vividly. They were for us the highlight of a Season. He entertained with his witty stories and then, all too quickly, his Sunrises with us would be over.

"When he left us for home it always seemed as if a

cherished member of the family had taken his leave. In future Sunrises, his visits will be missed profoundly. However, I rejoice in knowing that in a future Sunrise I will be reunited with him in the Land of Souls, enjoying his company. In the meantime, it gives me comfort knowing that he is at peace enjoying the company of the Great Spirit and our beloved ancestors.

"My brothers and sisters, when the Creator decided to take him home, He took with Him a man who had, during his sojourn here on Mother Earth, touched all our lives with his love, devotion, kindness and strength. He was a great and wise man, whose wisdom shall be sadly missed."

Lightning Bolt continued with his oration for some time, then ended it with, "May the Great Spirit grant Big Elk, our father, eternal peace and rest, and may He permit us the honour and privilege some Sunrise to enjoy his company again, in the Land of Souls."

Elder Big Bear, the late Chief's best friend and confidant, spoke next. "Brothers and sisters, the friendship I had with my brother Big Elk spanned our lifetimes. Even our births were very close. We were born ninety-two Winters ago on the fourth and fifth Sunrises before the last Moon of Winter. Our mothers and fathers, who were also the best of friends, told us about our times together as babies. They proudly recalled for us our first talk, first walks and all the other things we did alone and together.

"Therefore, I have memories of our happy relationship that cover the entire ninety-two Winters of our lives. Because we were so close I shall, now that he is at home with the Creator before me, miss his company greatly for my remaining Winters on Mother Earth. However, I will have, besides the comfort of family and friends, my memories of him to keep me company. Then, of course, there is the comforting knowledge that at my age, the time for me to join my beloved wife, Grand Chief Big Elk and other relatives and friends, in the Land of Souls, is not that far off.

"Now, while he watches and listens from the Land of Souls, I'll share with you some of my most delightful memories of the adventures we had together. Big Elk was the leader in our friendship. I can't give any reason why it was so, maybe because he liked to make decisions and I was just a little lazy in that regard. However, even in youth, with a great imagination, he was very good at it. Using his leadership inclination, he easily found ways to get us into lots of trouble during those early Winters. In fact, the predicaments were so challenging they often stood our hair on end. But they provided us with much laughter afterwards.

"One of the funniest tight spots occurred when we were about thirteen Winters old. Feeling as confident about our survival and camping abilities as young people can, we were off alone on an early Summer camping trip to Kejimkujik when it happened.

"After enjoying a pleasant but sweaty walk from the village we arrived at the lake where the River of Many Rapids begins its journey to the sea, and we found a nice spot to set up camp. It didn't hold promise of being a comfortable experience. This assessment was due to black-flies and mosquitoes being out in droves because of the wet, humid and damp weather, and they were very hungry. In fact, so hungry that they seemed motivated with a vengeance reserved for the deprived, determined to drain us of our blood. Combined with them, the heat and humidity were enough to whip up the tempers of some of Mother Earth's creatures to a frenzy.

"Big Elk meditated about our discomfort for a while, then

came up with, as I expected, an imaginative solution to ease the pain. He decided we should build a raft out of driftwood and float it to the middle of the lake, where the flies wouldn't venture. Then we could swim a bit to cool off and laze about in comfort.

"The plan sounded great to me. In fact the thought of getting some peace from the starving flies and relief from the sweltering and suffocating heat sounded like being offered a bit of paradise. With this in mind, I quickly pitched in and helped collect pieces of driftwood to use and patch together a raft, which we did with little skill or polish, but with a great deal of enthusiasm. Motivated by the thought of relief, we had it ready for launching in record time. Then off came our clothes, and we began to tow it toward the middle of the lake. When we were no more than two hundred paces offshore, we heard this great snorting and crashing coming toward us through the woods. Out into the open charged a thoroughly upset and raging, gigantic bull moose. His antlers were the biggest and most threatening I've ever seen.

"The froth running out of his mouth, because of his mad rage, didn't help to improve his image in our eyes. He was looking for a fight and wasn't too fussy about whom or what he had it with. He looked out towards us pushing the raft on the lake, and without the slightest hesitation he came charging into the water with what we deduced correctly as mayhem on his mind. To this Sunrise I can't decide if he thought we were another moose infringing on his territory or if he was simply being cranky. Either way, he decided to do us in. Whatever it was, he didn't waste any time getting out to where we were.

"As if it was only last Sunrise I can still hear Big Elk yelling, 'May the Great Spirit help us! I think that crazed beast has it on his mind to do us in!'"

"That was about all he got out before Brother Moose came up to the float and tried to come aboard. Well, my friends, I tell you the scene for the next few moments was one of mass confusion, with a lot of yelling and hollering and, on the moose's part, snorting and grunting. Making a huge lunge, Brother Moose managed to get his front end up onto the raft, which immediately caused it to break up around us. With this occurrence, Big Elk and I made haste to get to shore, with, of course, Brother Moose following closely in our wake. We managed to confuse him a bit by diving underwater several times, which gave us about a fifteen-pace lead when we came ashore.

"Then a scene occurred that I can still picture in intimate detail. Imagine it, my friends. Two boys, as naked as the Sunrise they were born, running headlong for the woods with an enormous and thoroughly cranky bull moose in hot pursuit. Big Elk, who was running a few steps ahead of me, yelled as we approached a gigantic pine, 'Swing into that big pine, my friend, or one of us, or maybe both, will be having supper with the Great Spirit tonight.'

"With the agility of squirrels we flew up the tree to what we thought was complete safety. I tell you emphatically, my brothers and sisters, Brother Moose was not amused with this turn of events. He backed off a bit, let out snorts that would scare the heroics out of the bravest man, and charged. The thump he made when he hit our sturdy tree was awesome. Of course, being a sturdy pine, our tree withstood the assault with impunity. However, the moose's head didn't receive the blow too well. He staggered back, then wobbled off a few paces and hung his head for a while. The tree encounter had the positive effect of cooling his temper a bit, but not enough to make him call it a Sunrise. He decided to wait us out.

"In the meantime, the black-flies and mosquitoes had joyously discovered our naked and delectable bodies, which presented a source of a feast for them that one can only describe as a flies' Land of Souls on Mother Earth. They were hungry and let me tell you, my brothers and sisters, they had no intention of leaving their feast until they were gorged. We were swatting and slapping at them as if our lives depended on it. Our efforts were as futile as trying to use a few blades of grass to dam a mighty river. The torment continued unabated for quite some time, which drove us to consider some crazy measures to seek relief. In desperation, Big Elk put forward one of the looniest suggestions that I've ever heard in my life. But, I have to admit, in my torment I gave it some serious thought. He said, with the pain of a thousand fly bites reflected in his voice, 'Big Bear, the only place where the moose can't get us, other than up here, is on his back. To escape the torment of these flies we may have to try to drop down on it.'

"However, before we could put such a crazy plan into action fate stepped in and added to our woes. With resounding grunts, an exceedingly large and thoroughly disgruntled male black bear stepped out of the forest into the clearing to see what was going on. It was beginning to seem to us, in our agonizing torment, that all the beasts in the forest, large and small, had woken up with mayhem on their minds and had picked us to be their victims.

"Now, Brothers and Sisters, Brother Bear spotted the moose first, and a few moments later saw us up in the tree. There ensued some decision-making on the ground that made us hold our breaths with great anxiety and dread. The moose eyed the bear and I swear to you that for a few moments, before better judgment took over, he actually considered charging him. The bear in turn, in indecision, eyed the moose, then us. After what seemed like forever, Brother Bear decided he would go with something that he had tasted before and not something new like us. With this, he took off after Brother Moose. The last we heard of them was snorting, grunting and crashing sounds moving off through the woods.

"Well brothers and sisters, we came down out of the tree with the speed of a driving wind and soaked our bleeding, fly-bitten hides in the cool waters of the lake."

After the laughter and good cheer settled down, Elder Big Bear launched into another story of adventure. "Then there was the time..."

After Big Bear finished, other leaders, relatives and friends paid their respects. As had Lightning Bolt and Big Bear, they recounted many highlights of their fondly remembered encounters with Big Elk. To all of them, he had been a mountain of a man and his company and wisdom would be missed immensely.

After three Sunrises, the rites and celebrations of the Feast of the Dead were concluded by Early Robin, the most senior Elder present, with these simple words, "He served us unselfishly while on Mother Earth and is now with the Great Spirit enjoying eternal peace and rest. Let us rejoice in his good fortune and pray that some Sunrise we will be fortunate enough to once more know his company in the Land of Souls! Go in peace and contentment my brothers and sisters, and revere his precious memory."

Before returning home to their countries, the six remaining Grand Council Chiefs met and appointed Lightning Bolt to act as interim Grand Chief. They decided to meet and select a permanent replacement on the first Moon of the next

Spring Season in Lightning Bolt's village. The exact Sunrise to hold it was left up to Lightning Bolt. The reason they opted for a Moon so far in the future was to give the People of Sipekne'katik plenty of time to select a new National Chief. With the time and date settled, the People returned to their own countries to begin to prepare for the exciting process of selecting a Grand Chief.

Late that Autumn Lightning Bolt and many of his country-men returned to Sipekne'katik for the official celebrations of White Water's appointment as its National Chief. When the celebrations ended, many guests began to take leave of their friends and relatives to return home. However, having some additional matters to attend to before he returned home, Lightning Bolt asked Flaming Hair to stay behind and travel with him. Spring Flower and Spotted Fawn, yearning for the home fires, accepted Crazy Moose's invitation to return to Lightning Bolt's village with them.

A few Sunrises later Lightning Bolt and Flaming Hair prepared to leave for home. Not in a big rush, they decided to add a few extra Sunrises to the trip by visiting some of their favourite places along the way. To this end they laid out a course for their canoe trip that would keep them close to the shoreline of the Basin of High Tides. With great anticipation of seeing again the wondrous places that neither had savoured for many, many Moons, caused by increasing responsibilities, they, excited as two young boys setting out on their first camping trip alone, began their journey early the next Sunrise. The rugged beauty of the landscape and its continually changing vista, combined with the power of the huge tides of the Basin of High Tides, was a fascination for them that could be traced back to the first time each had viewed the impressive sights.

While travelling slowly along, soaking in the sights, each privately recalled memories of instances during their past travels around and over the Basin where sunlight or moonlight, combined with spectacular scenery, highlighted Mother Earth's glorious splendour. But, unbeknownst to them, their past experiences would pale in comparison to the beauty of what Mother Earth had prepared for them to view on this journey. It was to be the most awesome that the Great Spirit would ever give them the privilege of seeing.

Some time later, as they were leisurely paddling their canoe along the coast, Lightning Bolt commented, "Brother, look at the beauty of the colours of the leaves. It's as if the Great Spirit has this Autumn joyfully decided to celebrate with His people the change of Seasons with an extra flourish. I've never before seen the forests looking so beautiful and majestic."

With awe in his voice Flaming Hair replied, "I agree, my brother, the Great Spirit has truly done wonders. The sight of His work in the colour of the bushes and trees is comparable to viewing at one sitting all the colourful and glorious rainbows I've seen in my lifetime. You know, when I view this magnificent scene, I can't help thinking about, and comparing, the splendours of the world I saw before the Great Spirit sent me here to live. I've seen the White Cliffs of England, and admired the majesty of the Alps, the Rock of Gibraltar, and other splendid places, but none can compare with what I've seen here during my many camping trips over the Seasons. And, particularly, if I live to see a thousand more Autumns, I shall always recall the beauty of this Season, because I've never seen an equal for splendour."

That evening, after dining on freshly caught eels and bass, the brothers sat before their cozy warm campfire on a cliff overlooking the basin, watching the magnificence of the scenery transforming around them. They sat in awe as they talked and watched the full Moon slowly moving up over the horizon, spreading its pale light over the world before them. The beauty of it all almost overwhelmed them. Flaming Hair, unable to contain his joy, in trance-like wonder commented, "My brother, there can never be an equal on Mother Earth to with what we're seeing this Sunrise. It's so majestic and breathtaking that it seems as if we're glimpsing what awaits us in the Land of Souls."

Equally transfixed, Lightning Bolt whispered, as if he was scared to break the spell by talking too loud, "Flaming Hair, my brother, perfection seems to be the work of the Creator at these moments. How fortunate we are that He permits us humble mortals to view His wondrous labours."

Completely caught up in the splendour unravelling before them, Flaming Hair responded in kind, "Perhaps my friend it's an omen of things to come. Over the passage of the Moons the Great Spirit has been very generous with our People and provided us with the means to live a good life, for which we all are very grateful. Maybe this Sunrise is a sign that He is happy with our humility and will continue to reward us. At any rate, He is permitting us to glimpse a touch of what awaits us in the Land of Souls. May He, my brother, continue to bless us with His loving benevolence."

"Flaming Hair, my brother, my friend, you're probably right, the Great Spirit often rewards us for how we live. When I think of the wonderful family and friends I've been blessed with, I know He has shown me much kindness. For all His wondrous gifts, I'm humbly thankful."

Later that night, still subdued by what they had seen, the conversation turned to things controlled by mortals. Flaming

Hair began to speak of the future, "My brother, the talk around the campfires during the Feast of the Dead for Grand Chief Big Elk, and during the celebration of White Water being appointed National Chief, was that you will probably be asked by the National Chiefs at the next meeting of the Grand Council to accept the responsibilities of Grand Chief. How do you feel about it?"

"I haven't heard any rumours. However, if such an eventuality was to come to pass, I don't relish the thought of it. Where will I get the time? Already, my duties as Chief of Kespukwitk take up most of it, leaving me with precious little with family and friends. Adding the responsibilities of Grand Chief to my present National Chief duties would leave me with almost no time to do them. Indeed, when I think of it, I have almost none now. This is evidenced by the fact that Spring Flower and I haven't seen our beloved daughter Snow Flake in Kespek for more than three Summers. My brother, I miss her sometimes so badly it hurts. The hurt sometimes leads me to have ungenerous thoughts about my beloved son-in-law. Occasionally I wish she had married someone a little closer to home. Kespek is such a long way off. I then feel guilt for my unworthy thoughts.

"To make amends I thank the Great Spirit for giving her a wonderful husband and blessing me with fine grandsons, who are growing into fine warriors, and also for blessing me with a lot of other loving family members to keep me company."

Teasingly, Flaming Hair commented, "My brother, you are indeed blessed with a fine family! After all, I am part of it. And, with such a fine a specimen of a man as me in the family, how could you have said anything less?"

"Right, my big-headed brother!"

"Now, Lightning Bolt, my humble brother, getting back to the possibility of your being appointed Grand Chief. Myself, and most others that I've discussed the matter with, think that the title would be a fitting tribute paid by the Grand Council to you for your conscientious labours on behalf of the People. In saying this, my brother, I speak from the heart. I feel that if the position is offered, you should accept, because in my humble opinion no other has your qualifications for the honour, or deserves it more."

"My brother, you flatter me with your words. But there are many men who are far more worthy of the position than I. To name just one there is Big Beaver. Think about his record. He is a man of impeccable honour; he is brave and caring and has unselfishly donated his life to the People's cause, has fought valiantly in many wars to preserve our liberty and his prowess in the Hunt is legendary. In view of the inspiring record of men such as him, I don't agree with your assessment, my flaming-haired brother, that I might be the best and most worthy candidate for the position."

With his convictions not swayed, Flaming Hair cut in, "My beloved brother, I stand by my statement and predict that you will be our next Grand Chief. It may be said that I'm prejudiced in your favour, but my ears have heard what is appearing to be the wish of the vast majority of the People."

"My brother, in case you're right, although I fervently pray you're not, I will probably use the rule that my mother and father and Elders taught me when I was growing up — respect the wishes of my brothers and sisters. Therefore, if at the meeting in the Spring the People choose to burden me with the office, then I will probably accept. For their will must take precedence over mine. But, because Spring Flower's life would be gravely affected by such an appointment, my acceptance would be subject to her consent."

The brothers continued to talk far into the night. When they finally tired and retired to their robes for sleep, the first early rays of dawn were appearing in the East. However, Mother Earth was not quite through with exhibiting her splendours. Shortly after falling asleep, they were abruptly awakened as the sun began to peek over the horizon by the cries of marauding seagulls in search of food. As a gift for being denied their sleep by the gulls, they were rewarded by witnessing a spectacular Sunrise that sent them on their way home with more awe than ever in their hearts.

For the rest of their Seasons, Lightning Bolt and Flaming Hair recalled in wonder to family and friends the sights they had seen displayed by Mother Earth during these few Sunrises. But, they always felt that their words were inadequate to truly describe the wonders they had beheld.

Safely back in their village, and the Hunt finished, the People saw Autumn quickly fade into a long dreary Winter, filled with an abundance of cold and snow. Then, at last, the arrival of a beautiful Spring. With its arrival came the first of many of the thousands of visitors that would arrive over the next several Sunrises to see the new Grand Chief selected by the National Chiefs.

The Winter past was harsh. The severe and long Winter was interlaced with sunrises that were colder than anyone remembered, and snow drifts to the tops of their wigwams. After bearing with stoicism the boredom of being confined for long stretches in their wigwams, the People were looking forward to the celebrations with great anticipation and excitement. Sharing time while being free to laugh and tell stories combined with all of the magic of the Spring renewal of Mother Earth and was nothing less than a welcomed relief.

Lightning Bolt, now in his sixty-first Spring, had spent a lot of his leisure time during the Winter mulling over the prospect of being chosen by his peers as Grand Chief. And how he might influence his brothers, without seeming disrespectful, to appoint another with the title. As the designated Sunrise loomed ever closer, seeing no sure way he could divert the honour elsewhere, he had one final discussion with Spring Flower, seeking her advice about what to do if the offer was made. "My love, together we've seen Mother Earth renew Herself forty times since we were first married. Our union has brought us much happiness and contentment, some sorrow, and we've seen our love grow stronger with each passing Season. Because of this, my love, I pray to the Great Spirit that He will be amiable to granting us another forty of the same. My precious darling, I thank you a thousand times over for the wonderful Summers of wedded bliss you've given me.

"My darling, don't try to stop me. I want to say many things that I don't say often enough. Like that the rewarding life I've lived would not have been complete, or possible, without your presence at my side. If I live to see a hundred Springs, I could never tell you in all that time how much I've valued your advice and loyal and dependable support over the past forty Summers. For our wonderful marriage and your loyal support, I humbly thank the Great Spirit.

"I also want to tell you how grateful I am for the wise advice you've always given me when matters tended to elude resolution for me. It was invaluable in helping to solve problems. Now, as you know, I have a new one that I need your help with.

"But, before we get to it, I want to tell you that over the Seasons it's been your unqualified love and support that gave me the courage to agree to serve our People in the offices of our country. But, accepting them has had its drawbacks. The increased duties that each succeeding office brought have cut deeply into the choice time I've always cherished and set aside to be with you and the rest of the family, which, when I come to think of it, must have seemed neglectful to you and them. However, through it all, I've never heard you or they complain once. Instead, I've received nothing but support and devotion. Without such, the tasks of my offices would have been unbearable and unrewarding, but, because of you, it has been worthwhile. For instance, the multitudes of treasured friends we've made from everywhere. For this and all our other blessings I often lift my eyes up to the sky and give the Great Spirit humble thanks.

"Saying that reminds me of the time that Snow Flake, when she was a little girl, asked me why I often did so. I told her that doing it was being true to the teachings of our traditions, which tell us that the Great Spirit must always be acknowledged for His benevolence. She asked if I really believed there was a Great Spirit. I told her that I've always accepted the Creator's existence as the truth because of His creations. To this Sunrise I would say to any doubters, look around you and see the wonders of Mother Earth; how can one speak to the contrary?

"Shortly before she got married, Snow Flake recalled our conversation in a nice little chat we had. She told me that our People were very fortunate because the lessons taught to us as children about the Great Spirit were so logical and reasonable that they instilled a strong faith in Him. This was followed by her joining me with hands upraised to offer thanks and to acknowledge Him as the Creator of the Universe and the Giver of all good things.

"Because of our strong beliefs, most of us try to serve the Great Spirit in our lifetimes in a manner that's most comfortable to our personalities. For me, this has not been the case in many instances. Instead, the People have, by insisting on placing me in unsought leadership positions, been largely the architects of my destiny. However, I always felt that the Great Spirit works in His own way and therefore, if it was His will that I serve in leadership positions, I was honour-bound to do so.

"Which now brings me to the item I need some advice on. First Flaming Hair, then Crazy Moose, and since then a few others, tell me that another unsolicited position is being offered to me. They report that my peers on the Grand Council will, in concert with the wishes of the People, ask me to accept the honour of serving the Nations of the Grand Council as Grand Chief. For me to even consider it, should it be offered, there is a major question I have to ask myself and have your advice on. It's been troubling me for some time. If I accepted the position, could I serve the People effectively?

"If I use the past to try to answer it, I can say that I've always served the People in the positions entrusted to me with the best of my ability, and, I believe, at least adequately. But when looking at the responsibilities that are entailed with the position of Grand Chief, I can't help but wonder if I have the wherewithal to effectively carry out the duties of such an important position. Now, before I give any further thought to accepting the Grand Chief position, if offered, or to whether I have what it takes to do the job, I need your advice and consent."

Holding hands and staring into each other's eyes, the two held that gaze that can only be known between best friends and lovers after many many seasons of devotion. "My dearest husband," she said. "I also have things to say that I don't say often enough. I can't think of a better way to begin than by saying that the forty Summers of love and happiness we've had together have passed for me as if they were wonderful sweet dreams. In fact, my darling, my life has been so blessed that I sometimes wonder if I might awake some Sunrise and discover that it has all been a dream. As you've so eloquently stated, my dear husband, the Great Spirit has been exceptionally good to us. His wonderful blessings are uncountable.

"But, my love, of all the wonderful blessings He has given us, the most wonderful of all for me is our marriage. During it, my darling, I've known a happy existence that is reserved only for the truly blessed, and for our ancestors in the Land of Souls. During our thousands of Sunrises together your love and devotion have been my greatest comfort and treasure in life and I thank you a thousand times over for them. I've collected uncountable marvellous memories over the Sunrises; for these treasures, my love, I'll always be grateful.

"Then there is the dignified and respectful manner in which you've treated me during our marriage. Your example is an excellent role model for all spouses to follow. I don't recall one instance in our forty Summers together where you didn't treat me with the utmost courtesy, dignity, equality and respect.

"But, we must never forget, there is another important blessing that we must thank the Great Spirit for, perhaps the most important, the ability to communicate so perfectly with one another. There are, of course, a few exceptions to this. One is the fact that you are so considerate of me that you sometimes forget that it also gives me pleasure to be considerate of your needs. It pains me, my husband, to hear that you think your duties to the Nation have denied me and the family in any way. This isn't so. If you hadn't done the things the Great Spirit had asked you to do, your life would have been without meaning, and without such there is no life.

"I can state emphatically my dear husband that there has never been a time in our married life when I resented the loss of your time to the affairs of state. I will, however, admit that more time together would have been welcomed and thoroughly enjoyed. But we must keep in mind that nobody forced us to do what we did. We had choices, but followed the path we thought honourable. I have no regrets! If we had chosen to put our personal interests first we would have felt guilt before the Great Spirit and had no happiness.

"As for your leadership, I know, as you know, in the overall scheme of things, that no one is indispensable, or holds a monopoly on anything in life. Of course there were other men who could have governed the affairs of our country instead. But none, in my opinion, could have done it with the same love, devotion and dedication to duty as you have.

"As for the feelings of the family in this matter, we've talked over your career on many occasions and I can relate to you, my love, that they have nothing but love, admiration and respect for you and will support whatever you decide. Therefore, if the Chiefs decide to ask you to become Grand Chief, you will, as always, have my love and support in whatever choice you make."

"Thank you, my little flower. Hearing your words of love and encouragement makes my heart swell with happiness."

"My precious husband, if the offer is made and you accept, I know that you will make one of the finest Grand Chiefs our People have ever known." Without pause, this couple of forty Summers retired to their cozy sleeping furs and continued with their intimate chat far into the night.

The following Sunrise, the opening ceremonies began with the People being called together at dawn to hear the Elders implore the Great Spirit to assist their Chiefs in their deliberations. The prayers were followed by traditional Sweetgrass and Pipe-Smoking Ceremonies. Then a delectable feast, followed by dancing and other forms of celebration, filled the rest of the Sunrise. At noon the following Sunrise, the Chiefs got down to the duty they had gathered for; the Grand Council meeting was convened. Lightning Bolt, as interim Grand Chief, was the host and presided.

"Brothers, we welcome you and your countrymen and invite you to share with us the love, bounty, hospitality and warmth of Kespukwitk. I hope your stay among us will be joyful and rewarding. My dear friends, I tell you straight from my heart that your presence here among us is like Spring itself, delightful, refreshing and renewing. We must, as family and friends, find occasions to get together more often. The truth of this is no better illustrated than by me looking across the circle and seeing my father Big Beaver, whose presence fills my heart with anticipation and happiness knowing that I will have his loving company for a few Sunrises and be entertained with tales of his adventures.

"However, before we get to the enjoyable pleasures awaiting us by renewing old acquaintances, we have a solemn duty that must first be fulfilled. We must, my brothers, from among ourselves, over the next few Sunrises, select a worthy man to fill the office of Grand Chief. For the benefit of the young and visitors from fraternal countries, allow me to give a short history of how the Grand Council started and its purpose." He provided the overview and said, "Our council has withstood the test of time and produced many beneficial results. Before proceeding, let us take a few moments to humbly ask the Creator to guide us in finding ways to assure that it will continue to serve our children and their children's children for infinite Moons to come."

After the Chiefs prayed and meditated for a few moments, Lightning Bolt continued with his address: "My brothers, when we select a Grand Chief, we must remember the past and use its lessons. This has enabled past National Chiefs to pick leaders who have much wisdom and foresight. With the Great Spirit's help this will be the case this Sunrise."

He tried, in a subtle way, to divert their attention from himself. "My brothers, I've had the pleasure of counting most of you among my dear friends since I first became involved in politics forty Springs ago. Over that period I've enjoyed the benefit of your wisdom and knowledge when making some very hard decisions. By often benefitting from this vast wealth of knowledge and wisdom, I have come to appreciate your capabilities as great and humble leaders. With this in mind, I will be very comfortable in supporting whomever among you is selected Grand Chief." His polite attempt to have his peers refrain from considering him for the office only reinforced the certainty that he would be the choice. "Respectfully asking the Great Spirit to guide us, I now open the meeting for deliberations. I recognize my father, Chief Big Beaver."

"Brothers, our lives have been entwined in Grand Council affairs since we were entrusted by the People with our National Chief positions. Many of us have seen, because of our close personal contacts with each other, members of our families meet and develop intimate relationships. This has happened in the case of Lightning Bolt and me. My grandson had the good fortune to meet his daughter Snow Flake and win her hand in marriage about twenty Summers ago. This union has produced many fine great-granddaughters and great-grand-sons for me, and grandchildren for him. But, the first time I met Lightning Bolt by far predates this happy event; our family contacts go back a few seasons after he was born. It happened around fifty-seven Springs ago when I came with my father to Kespukwitk to visit with his father Little Bear. He was then a lad of four or five Springs. Over the passage of the Seasons there were many other visits between our families and I watched as he grew into a fine young man.

"Even when he was very young, my brothers, he impressed me with his intelligence and command of matters far beyond his Springs. From talking to him and observing his behaviour my father would say in his wisdom, "Watch that boy; I predict he will lead us some Sunrise." As a young warrior I somewhat agreed with my father's observation about the boy. However, what really convinced me happened forty-one Autumns ago when he journeyed to Kespek as a young warrior to lend us a hand in repulsing the armies of the Western Nations.

"I knew at the time from our prior family associations that he was a young man who hated wars and believed they shouldn't be fought just to win, but to stop them as soon as possible. This is what he did when he came to help us. War Chief Mighty Water told me afterwards that because of Lightning Bolt's dedication to the goal of ending the war with all haste, he fought like a small army alone. You are all aware of his exploits in that war, and in the most recent one, and his accomplishments in other matters, so I won't retell them here.

"Suffice it to say that over his Springs he has not only served his own country well, but has served us all well. If I thought it necessary, I could easily list a good example of his many outstanding accomplishments, but it would just eat into the fun times we'll have after this meeting and we don't want that do we?" A hearty laughter spread through the Chiefs as they looked at each other with a feeling of contentment and purpose. "Therefore, I will stop rambling and make my nomination with haste and few preliminaries. As Lightning Bolt has already stated, our alliance has served us well and has withstood the trials of time. With good will among us and devotion to its principles, the alliance will continue to serve us and our children's children well for thousands of Moons to come. To assure that our children's birthrights are protected, as our traditions demand, we must select the best man possible to fill the honourary position of Grand Chief.

"In this I completely agree. It is our responsibility, when selecting a successor for Grand Chief Big Elk, to weigh carefully all the good and bad qualities of the individuals we are considering for the position. Over the past several Moons, I have given much careful consideration to the matter and, after discussing it in-depth with the People, have settled upon a candidate. My brothers, there has been a great deal of gossip in the wigwams and councils of our countries in regards to whom our choice will be. In the case at hand, I sincerely hope that for once the gossips are right. My honoured colleagues, I respectfully place before you for consideration the name of a man who I believe has no equal when it comes to leadership: Lightning Bolt."

In turn each Chief in the circle rose and spoke. They praised Lightning Bolt's strengths and virtues and spoke in favour of his selection as Grand Chief. When the circle returned to Lightning Bolt, he responded, "Brothers, I'm sure that any one of you would make a better Grand Chief than I. When you speak you never talk of my failings in life, of which there have been many. Before making your final decision, I urge you to examine those."

Big Beaver responded, "We, as fellow human beings, recognize that you like us have failings. Only the Great Spirit is beyond a fault. You may rest assured my son that I, and I assume my brothers, weighed all factors including your weaknesses when making our decisions. You've passed the test in all our minds, and if you're willing, we will make you Grand Chief."

"If this is your will, then I accept."

The Chiefs responded in unison, "It is our will."

"Brothers, in having the confidence to give me this honour, I have to say that your trust in my leadership abilities are far beyond what I think my actual limits are. However, in spite of my self-doubts, I swear before the Great Spirit and you that I shall fulfil the duties of Grand Chief with utmost diligence and devotion. I pray that I prove worthy of your trust."

Thus, in the time-honoured tradition of the Mi'kmaq, Lightning Bolt became Grand Chief. Although the office had no powers attached to it other than ceremonial, it was very influential. The men who filled this role had great stature. The Chiefs smoked a pipe. Grand Chief Lightning Bolt, after making a short speech, ended the meeting and urged the celebrations to begin.

Lightning Bolt, taking leave from his colleagues after quickly explaining why, headed for his wigwam to enjoy in privacy the company of a very special person whom he had not talked to for many, many Moons, his precious Snow Flake. She had arrived late the Sunrise before, in the company of his beloved son-in-law and his darling grandchildren. Because of her late arrival and the excited confusion abounding, they had prior time only for a quick hello. Upon entering the wigwam, after much hugging and kissing, they both started talking at once, but Snow Flake deferred to her father, who put his love into it, "My baby, when we're apart, I miss you with all my heart. To see your face again gives me so much pleasure that I don't know if my old heart can withstand the joy it feels."

Snow Flake reciprocated with words reflecting her devotion, "Dear Father, I feel the same. Our being here to visit with you and Mother for the next three Moons is something that I've been looking forward to for a long, long time. Although I rejoice in knowing the love of my husband, children and friends, there is no love that is the same as that of a loving mother and father, and I've missed it constantly. Oh Father, you and Mother look so well, it's as if time has stood still for both of you."

"My beloved daughter you still have it in you to flatter your old father. So tell me about your life."

Snow Flake related the joys of her life with Eagle Feather and their children for the rest of the afternoon. When Spring Flower, her son-in-law and grandchildren returned for the evening meal they found a perfectly contented father and daughter filling in the gaps of their three Summers apart. After eating, Lightning Bolt retired to sit beside the shore of the village's stream to enjoy in solitude a pipe and some pleasant reminiscing.

"Oh Great Spirit," he said. "It's so good to see my Snow Flake again. It gives me so much pleasure to know that she has made a wonderful life with Eagle Feather and the grandchildren they've given us are vibrant and loving.

"My Father, I want to share a little secret with you. It's something I can never tell anyone else. Although I love all my grandchildren as dearly as life itself, I can't help but have just a little extra regard for the boy named after me. He has passed his thirteenth Summer and even looks a lot like me. But, they are all wonderful children and your generosity in giving them to us is humbly appreciated.

"I also, my Father, enjoy recalling for the pleasure of it some of the funny mistakes I've made when helping raise our daughter. One incident in particular, related to her courtship, stands out above the rest. When I look back and relive the mess I made of a father's traditional responsibilities when Eagle Feather was in the process of becoming part of her life, I still chuckle about it. Although it happened twenty-one Summers ago, after Big Timber's Feast of the Dead, I remember it as if it happened last Sunrise. Eagle Feather had accompanied his grandfather to the funeral for the great Chief and afterwards came to spend an extended visit with friends in our village. I must take the prize as the most naive person alive when it comes to matters of the heart, for it never crossed my mind that the real reason he was in our village was to try to capture the hand of our daughter in marriage. I still feel a little embarrassed when I think about how inept I was when Eagle Feather came to ask permission to court. To this Sunrise I don't know whether it was he or I who was more surprised by the way I reacted when he arrived at our wigwam, bearing many gifts and shaking in his moccasins, asking if he could speak to me.

"Oh, my Father, how blind I was to what was in front of my nose. I didn't even notice right away his nervousness. However, after we exchanged pleasantries, it finally did sink in that he was exceedingly nervous, but I just saw it as the nervousness of youth in the company of someone older. Then he asked me if I would hear a request he had to make. I told him by all means.

"These were his exact words: 'Oh great Chief, my father, how does one as humble and as unworthy as I, begin to ask a person of your standing for such a great indulgence as I'm about to ask? Being a man of simplicity, there is no other way for me to do it than to just do it. Father, I've come to ask for your permission to court Snow Flake.'

"Without a thought to traditional practices in such matters I blurted out, 'Why Eagle Feather, my son, if my daughter agrees I would be very pleased to see you two courting. I can't imagine anything that would please both families more than to see the grandson of my beloved father Big Beaver and our daughter considering marriage. What a blessing!'

"Then I caught myself. But, by then it was out and I couldn't retract it. Being the good man that he is, Eagle Feather agreed to pretend, for the sake of propriety, that I didn't blurt out my assent. Knowing that he was a good sport I continued with the pretence of being less than enthusiastic about his proposal."

Lightning Bolt watched the clouds and the forms of light upon the water. He sat with a blade of grass in the fingers of his right hand, while gently his mind wandered in contemplation of the Moons past. When Spring Flower came out later that dusk to keep him company, she found her husband sitting beside the stream with a look on his face of absolute contentment. It was obvious to her that he was lost in a world of pleasant dreams. He soon became aware of her presence and with a smile began to tell her about his thoughts. "My darling…"

//

CHAPTER EIGHT

While chatting with Spring Flower the evening before his sixty-fourth birth-Spring, Lightning Bolt noticed for the first time the lines age had etched into her beautiful face. It suddenly dawned on him that his Seasons had melted away like ice in hot water. They had passed so fast that it seemed as if he had gone from childhood to Elder status in a few Moons. This by no means depressed him, only intrigued.

As he contemplated how fast time now passed for him, he recalled what he had often heard Elders saying about the phenomena, "As one grows older, it passes at an ever increasing pace." To his ears, especially in his younger Seasons, this had seemed incredible. Now, in his senior Seasons, he could empathize with what they had said. His Seasons over the last several Springs had passed so fast that four now seemed no longer than one. He thought, "Perhaps the demands of my position have something to do with the speed in which life seems to be trickling away from me?" In this he was right.

In fact, the duties of the office of Grand Chief had changed their lives completely, just as he and Spring Flower had predicted three Springs earlier. Right from the first Sunrise after he became Grand Chief, most of their Sunrises were filled with what seemed an endless stream of private citizens and leaders from Mi'kmaq and other countries seeking his advice and guidance.

This ever-increasing volume was caused largely by his remarkable ability to come up with fair and equitable solutions for seemingly insolvable disputes. Also contributing substantially to the length of the lineup of callers was the fact that the Grand Chief and wife were renowned throughout allied territory for being two of the most entertaining, delightful, genial and generous hosts a visitor could spend a few pleasant Sunrises with.

Never complaining about the imposition on their personal time, Spring Flower, true to her word, continued to give her husband her full and loving support. However, during one of the rare evenings they had alone, she was moved to say in a moment of nostalgia, "Lightning Bolt, my dear husband, I miss the very enjoyable times we were able to spend together travelling and visiting with friends and family. Seeing them again and the beauty of some of Mother Earth's wonders at a leisurely pace would be wonderful. I can, by just thinking about it, feel the warmth of a campfire, under a moonlit sky, warming us against a cool breeze coming off the Bay of High Tides at Blomidon. Ah, my love, just the thought of it warms my soul."

Her comments sparked a yearning in Lightning Bolt for the more leisurely times of the past. "My little flower, your talk also conjures up in my mind some of the wonderful memories we gathered in our younger Moons. Yes, my love, it would be wonderful to sit again before a campfire under the conditions you describe. The memories of those past cozy campfires are so clear I can almost smell the smoke. Are you, my precious wife, beginning to regret our decision to assume the time-consuming responsibilities of Grand Chief?"

"No, my dear husband, I have no regrets. However, I don't have any desire to see you work yourself to death either, which you shall surely do if things don't change quickly. What you need to do, my darling, is to accept that you, as a mortal, need to have time for rest and relaxation the same as other humans do. When I think of how your schedule has been all but continuous since you took office, I cringe. Even when you were much younger, such would have been a heavy burden. At your present age you can't continue with such a pace without harming your health. To rectify this, I have a suggestion. Let's send out runners to all the countries and tell them that we'll be away in Kespek for the three Moons of Summer visiting Snow Flake and her family."

"I hear you loud and clear my little flower. The truth and wisdom of your words are indisputable. Ah, to see our baby again. Yes, my precious wife, the time has come for us to relax and enjoy some of the simpler pleasures of life. A leisurely trip to Kespek, with many a romantic campsite in between, is one of the most enjoyable things I can think of doing. Already, besides the pleasure of visiting our family, I can envision the pleasure of sitting around a campfire after we get there and listening to the exciting stories my father Big Beaver will entertain us with."

Spring Flower, in wonder at the easiness of his agreement and their new plans exclaimed, "May the Great Spirit help me, if I had thought for a moment it was going to be this easy to get you away for a short while I would have suggested it long ago! Now that it's settled, I'll send a message to Snow Flake with the next group of people travelling to Kespek, to advise her of our plans, and then start preparing for the trip. Oh, Lightning Bolt, I'm so happy I could cry, laugh, sing and dance all at the same time."

"Well, my darling wife, I don't feel like doing all those things at once but now that we've decided to go I look forward to it with great eagerness. I can envision it now, camping in scenic spots and snuggling up at night in our cozy furs like we did in those long ago Sunrises when we travelled to so many wonderful and interesting places. Ah, my darling, I often look around our wigwam and see the many relics we acquired during those Sunrises. They always bring back feelings of happy contentment.

"Oh, my little flower, it just occurred to me. Let's bring some of the old furs we used to snuggle up in during those long-ago trips. They will help us recall and enjoy reliving those happy Sunrises. Their comforting memories will be music to the heart.

"My darling, my darling, I'm so excited, just thinking about the pleasures that await us during our vacation, that I am sure sleep will elude me tonight. However, I won't waste it. While I lie wide awake, excited just like a little boy going on his first hunting trip, I'll work out the wording of the messages that I want runners to take to the Mi'kmaq National Chiefs, and the Chiefs of the Allied Nations. As the time before we depart is short, I want to get the messengers on their way at the first light of dawn. If anything urgent has to be taken care of before we depart the Chiefs will have ample time to get the information to me before we go. If not, it will have to keep until our return.

"But, my beloved wife, before we retire for the night, I want to apologize for only thinking of affairs of state for the past three Springs and not thinking of our personal needs.

It's unforgivable of me to have neglected them. Tell me my love why do you tolerate my inconsiderate nature? To have let all this time pass by without thinking of taking some time out for ourselves is completely selfish of me. After all, we are only human and as such we need time in our lives for family, friends, rest and tranquility.

"To assure I don't neglect this necessity in future Seasons, I will include in the messages to our brothers that hence-forth, we shall be taking the first twenty-eight Sunrises before the first full Moon of Summer as time for an annual vacation. Does that please you?"

Spring Flower in jubilation replied, "Nothing could please me more, my darling. The knowledge that you won't make me a widow by working yourself to death makes me as happy as a robin with a nest full of eggs. To celebrate, my loving husband, let's go snuggle in our bed and have one of our long talks."

As they left on their journey, Spring Flower and Lightning Bolt seemed more like a young couple setting off on a honey-moon than that of elderly parents going off to visit their daughter's family and some friends. The villagers, getting into the romantic mood they exuded, sent them off as if they were. The route they had chosen to take was selected with an eye to making it as enjoyable as possible. Thus, after leaving Bear River, they followed the coastline along the Basin of High Tides until coming to the Sipekne'katik River, where they visited with friends for a Sunrise. They then travelled upriver until coming to Sipekne'katik Lake.

After spending an enjoyable Sunrise at a favourite spot on the shore, they leisurely travelled down Rocky Lake River to Mi'kmaq and Banook Lakes and the Big Pond. They went up the sea coast to the mouth of the Richibuctou River in

Kespek, where Big Beaver's village was located. It was a long but extremely pleasant journey for all. They were given a lively welcome by the citizens of Big Beaver's village. To make sure they would be at ease while visiting, they were shown to a comfortable wigwam erected especially for them. That evening, Snow Flake told her parents about her life since they had last seen her, and they did the same.

Big Beaver and Lightning Bolt, as Lightning Bolt had envisioned, spent many happy evenings sitting around warm campfires swapping tales of travels and adventures. During one particularly enjoyable session, Big Beaver told a story about a time when he and his cousin had taken on the elements while they were out on the Bay. "When I was a boy of fourteen Summers, some of our relatives from Siknikt came to visit. They had with them among their children a son named Lazy Bear, who was the same age as me. We got on very well because we had a lot in common, especially an insatiable need to eat lots of good food and explore new territory.

"Now, my son, if my old memory serves me correctly I think the Sunrise the incident happened was the second one after they had settled in with the family for their visit. It began after we ate an enormous breakfast. Wanting to demonstrate to all that I was a good host I invited my cousin on a canoe trip to a small island out on the bay. As the water was calm, and it was a beautiful bright sunny warm Summer morning, I decided, because it was much easier to handle, that we would take a small river canoe instead of a large ocean one.

"Without bothering to tell anyone our plans, we set out with much enthusiasm on our excursion. I knew we were breaking one of our sacred rules of conduct, because a child leaving the mainland without telling an adult in the village where he or she was going was strictly forbidden. It occurred to me that we were going to be in a lot of trouble if we were found out. But, being very confident of returning without anyone knowing, and without incident, I didn't worry.

"After a routine trip across the Bay, we landed on the island shortly after the sun had climbed about halfway to its zenith. As the sun moved across the sky we had a very interesting and pleasant time exploring coves, swimming and fishing. Lazy Bear was an excellent companion to while away a nice Summer Sunrise with, or for that matter, any Sunrise. He thoroughly enjoyed life, clowning and joking around. I still remember so clearly, even after the passage of so many Summers, many of his pet sayings. For instance, at the ripe old age of fourteen Winters, one of his favourites was, 'When I was a decent young man in my moccasins.' He also had a wealth of funny stories he could tell with a lot of expertise.

"Now comes the point where things started to get interesting. Returning to our starting point, around mid-afternoon, we decided to head back to the mainland to get home in lots of time for the evening meal, and, very importantly, to not get caught. But it was food that was the main concern as our bellies were already rumbling." He paused to laugh and said, "It seems when you're a young boy eating tops the list of all the things of importance. In Lazy Bear's case, it was so far ahead of anything else, it was out of sight.

"Shortly after we left the island my cousin pointed out, in the direction in which we were heading, some very black and threatening looking clouds appearing on the horizon. As they appeared to be at least a lifetime of canoe lengths away, they didn't give me any concern. I calculated we would be safely back on the mainland for a long time before any effect from them was felt.

"This calculation was so far off the mark it wasn't even in the same country. Suddenly, you could see that storm bearing down on us with the speed of a bolt of lightning. I will never forget the icy terror I felt as I watched it coming lickety-split across the water towards us. I tell you, my son, I don't recall anything in my eighty-three Summers moving as fast as that storm did.

"When it hit us, it hit with such force that everything was instantly changed. One moment, relative calm, the next, a raging nightmare. In a blink of an eye we were among mountainous waves and soaked to the skin by a deluge of rain and spray from white-capped waves. Lightning was streaking the sky and the thunder claps were deafening. The wind seemed strong enough to blow us off the face of Mother Earth.

"Wallowing in the tumultuous sea our river canoe was taking on water as if it had a thousand leaks. As I tried to keep our canoe facing into the wind I kept yelling to my cousin, 'bail my brother, bail for your life!' Strangely enough, after the first shock was over, our humour returned. Lazy Bear yelled back to me, 'Not to worry, my cousin! With the appetite I have the Great Spirit will find a way to protect His food supply from my ravenous appetite and let us live!'

"By this time we were only about four-thousand paces off the shore of our village. Miraculously, someone on shore had spotted us in trouble out on the bay and spread the word. Thus, when we crested a huge wave we could see a large crowd gathered in the wind and rain, standing by the beach waving their arms frantically. They were probably shouting encouragements, though we could not hear them with the raging storm. The deafening sounds made by the elements nearly chilled us to the heart. We were profoundly humbled. We had to fight for our lives.

"With determination born of desperation, we managed to keep crawling ahead until finally we were almost within reach of safety, about seventy-five paces offshore. I lifted my head, which was not an easy thing to do when completely focused on keeping the craft steady and firmly set on course. I quickly glanced behind us, my gaze set out to sea. It was in that moment I commended my soul to the Great Spirit. Heading towards us with a mighty force was the biggest wave I have ever seen. A split-second later it hit our canoe like a gigantic war club.

"The next seconds determined our fate. Our faithful canoe was not as lucky as we. Our tiny craft, which had performed far beyond its capacity by bringing us so close to safety, was quickly swept under the waves; it was like a mountain had descended upon us. We were tossed into the sea like specks of dust flung around in a windstorm. The last thing I remember was swallowing large mouthfuls of seawater. Then, mercifully, everything went black."

With the dignity of his many seasons, Big Beaver paused and looked over to the pipe set respectfully in its place. He rose and collected the pipe and tobacco. Nothing was said, as he sat and recollected his memories. He slowly filled the pipe and picked a slender stick next to the fire. He lit the stick by placing its end close to the burning embers and lit the pipe, taking the sacred smoke into his mouth. He let the smoke go to the four directions and passed the pipe to his companion. When the pipe was finished, Big Beaver continued his story.

"The next moment will live forever in my memory. When I opened my eyes again, I thought 'The Land of Souls isn't much different from Mother Earth, everything looks the same.' Then I heard my cousin, who had regained his wits before me, mutter in muffled words that I barely understood,

'See, my dear cousin, I told you that the Great Spirit would help us to safety in order to keep us from the spirit world and protect His food supply from me.'

"Our parents told us afterwards that the big wave had thrown us almost on shore. Then before the sea could claim us for its own, with the receding wave that immediately followed, two young warriors with precise timing had dashed into the water and pulled us to safety. We had one piece of good fortune that Sunrise. In all the excitement of pounding the water out of us and bringing us back to life, the Elders and our parents completely forgot to be mad at us for scaring the life out of them with our reckless behaviour."

When enjoying oneself, time goes by as if propelled by magic. This is how Lightning Bolt and Spring Flower felt about how fast their vacation melted away. They, with the sadness of leaving the company of loved ones in their hearts, began to prepare and pack their belongings for their return trip to Kespukwitk. Shortly after the last Moon of Summer, amid much embracing and tears, they and their warrior escort set off for home.

On their return trip they followed the coast from Kespek to where the Muddy River flows into the Sea in Siknikt, and they took the river route across Siknikt into the headwaters of the Basin of High Tides. After completing the first leg to the headwaters, because of the special memories it held for them, they travelled along the Basin's coast and enjoyed its spectacular scenery. It added tremendously to the enjoyment of their travels.

The memories they collected during this happy and carefree interlude would be recalled with pleasure and relived with the same kind of joy that only two lovers could find while entwined in each other's arms. In fact the young warriors who travelled with them to keep them safe teasingly told them for many Moons afterwards that it was the most pleasant honeymoon they would ever have.

Back home, and safely resettled in their wigwam, Lightning Bolt's work routine quickly returned to normal. However, without fail, each Summer thereafter he and Spring Flower would pack their things and set off under the watchful eye of a large group of protective warriors for their time alone. Reflective of the love and esteem they were held in by the People, a pact was made among them that they would never disturb them during their vacations for anything other than a national emergency.

Lightning Bolt, during the passage of his Springs, without aspiring to the position of being a mediator, had often found himself mediating disputes among neighbouring countries. Shortly before his seventy-fifth Spring he became involved in a memorable one that would change forever the relationships between the Nations of the eastern coast. His involvement started during separate Winter visits to his wigwam by the leaders of the Penikt and Atikitkas Nations, Chiefs Lone Wolf and Sleeping Bear. They asked him, with good will in their hearts, if he would kindly consider mediating the dispute that had seen their Nations involved in a war for uncountable Moons. The prospect of helping these well-respected personal friends end their war was a challenge he couldn't resist. He accepted it with enthusiasm and informed both leaders he would arrange a suitable time and place for negotiations to commence.

After pondering it for a few Sunrises, he settled upon the first Sunrise of Summer for a date and tentatively selected Reversing Falls on the River Goes Backwards, a site in Maliseet territory where the river drains into the Basin of

High Tides, as the place to hold it. His preference for the site was that it was easily accessible for all parties concerned and was on neutral Maliseet territory, a Mi'kmaq ally of long duration. With the site settled in his mind he contacted Big Mountain, senior Chief of the Maliseet, and asked for permission to hold it there.

Not surprisingly, with Lightning Bolt's still humble view of himself, he waited with more than a bit of apprehension for a response from Big Mountain. He was the only individual doing so. All others knew with certainty that any reasonable request made by the Grand Chief would without question receive a positive response from the Maliseet Chief. Their certainty was based on the fact that the Grand Chief was viewed as a beloved father figure by the citizens and leaders of the Nation. Whenever they needed his help or advice, he never hesitated to respond to their needs. And very often, over the passing Seasons, he had visited with them just for the sake of enjoying their company. In due time, he was given an open invitation to sit in on their councils. From these encounters had grown in the hearts of the Maliseet a love and respect for the man who knew no equal. Therefore, to give any request of his anything but a positive answer would have been unthinkable.

Ten Sunrises later, a message arrived back from Big Mountain extending a welcome. Lightning Bolt sent word by runner to the Atikitkas and Penikt Chiefs that he had arranged a peace meeting between them for the first Sunrise of Summer at the estuary of the River Goes Backwards. He asked if the time and place was acceptable. They sent word back that they looked forward to the event with enthusiasm.

On the appointed Sunrise, the participants and their hosts assembled, arrayed in their finest and most colourful clothing and ceremonial symbols of office. The meeting-place over-looked the magnificent Reversing Falls, where the waters of the bay and the river collided. With greetings exchanged, the historic event got under way. It was almost unbelievable to many to see Penikt Chief Lone Wolf and Atikitkas Chief Sleeping Bear, with their respective delegations, sit down together to talk for the first time in their lives.

Lightning Bolt, opening the historic event, intoned, "Welcome, my Atikitkas and Penikt sons, to a circle of peace! My sons, over the next several Sunrises of negotiations, with the help of the Creator and good will, I pray that you will find the wisdom to heal your differences and find brother-hood and love for each other. But, before negotiations begin, I want to ask Maliseet senior Elder Little Stone to kindly lead us in praise of the generous and good works of the Great Spirit." When Little Stone finished, the Elders performed a Sweet-grass Ceremony and a peace pipe was passed around the circle. Then Lightning Bolt resumed, addressing the combatants and their Maliseet hosts.

"My sons, first, I want to express our thanks to our hosts, and point out how very fortunate we are to have the privilege of enjoying the benefit of their excellent food and very com-fortable lodgings. In addition, Big Mountain and his advisors have kindly agreed to sit in on our councils and give us the benefit of their wisdom. Big Mountain, my son, on behalf of all the participants gathered here this Sunrise, I thank you and your People for their generosity from the bottom of my heart. For being so kind I pray that the Great Spirit will continue to shine his love and benevolence down upon your Nation for all time. Please honour us, my friend, by saying a few words and leading us in prayer."

"Thank you, my father, and welcome home. To you my

brothers, Chiefs Lone Wolf and Sleeping Bear, I also extend, on behalf of the Maliseet Nation, a heartfelt welcome. We hope, because we view you as visiting brothers, that during your stay with us that you feel at home. If at any time anything is needed to help make anyone's stay more comfortable don't hesitate to ask. If available, it will be forthcoming. My friends, before I ask the Great Spirit to assist us in making this peace circle a success, I want to say a heartfelt thanks to our father, Grand Chief Lightning Bolt, who has, by holding this historic conference on our land, shown a great deal of confidence in us. On behalf of my People, my dear esteemed father, please accept our thanks for giving our Nation the honour and privilege of hosting these peace talks. The confidence, faith and trust you've shown in us swells our hearts with great pleasure.

"When I mention this, my father, it occurred to me that the faith and trust we have between our Peoples and leaders, which has so closely bonded our Nations together in an alliance that goes so far back in time that no on knows when it started, is a model that our Atikitkas and Penikt brothers could consider using in their deliberations. If they do, and are successful, they can form a relationship between them that has built into it the same trust and faith in each other that ours has.

"That such a relationship is invaluable is proven by this: not once since our alliance was formed, either in peace or wartime, has either side failed to respond to a request for help from the other. This is a wonderful record and accomplishment. The Great Spirit, my father, has truly blessed our Peoples. For such kindness we owe Him our most humble thanks.

"Come, my friends, stand and raise your hands with me

to the sky and pray that the Great Spirit will help our brothers, the Atikitkas and Penikt, find the way to peace during their historic meeting, and afterwards enjoy the love and respect that spills from it. Oh Great Spirit, we your humble and obedient children ask that You fill us with the wisdom we need to find a solution that will end the dispute that has caused our brothers to spill the blood of their loved ones for so long. I know in my heart great Father, that these Nations have wearied of war and wish to turn their energies instead to peace. With Your help great Provider they will find their way. Thanks, Father of us all, for Your indulgences."

In an attempt to prepare the ground for what he thought would be hard negotiations, Lightning Bolt resumed speaking, directing his comments mainly to the combatants, beseeching them to have open minds during the process. "My sons, after the heat of the moment has been cooled by the passage of many Moons, if we look for them with open minds, we can find solutions for what seem to be insurmountable disputes between brothers. And, despite how impossible it may appear at first, we can find enough common ground during our search for solutions to help begin the process of healing the wounds that are left by such disputes. Thus, I feel confident in this case, that enough common ground can be found between your Nations during our negotiations to help us find a just solution for your dispute, and heal the wounds.

"And, my sons, I want to emphasize that in good moral conscience we must find a just solution for your dispute quickly. The carnage and destruction caused by it has been a heavy burden for your Peoples to carry for much too long. Because of this, it's immoral to permit it to continue, and an affront to the Great Spirit. Oh, my sons, it grieves me so much to say this, but ever since I was old enough to remember, I've heard an uncountable number of stories about the terrible bloody vengeance your Nations have exacted upon each other. To contemplate that this pursuit of vengeance will continue indefinitely is very sad for me because I've come to know and love, through our enjoyable visits together over the Moons, the Peoples of both your Nations as brothers and sisters, and it breaks my heart to think that many of them will die in war. Especially so, when I know they are kind, loving and generous people who have always treated me and my countrymen with brotherly hospitality when we visit.

"In fact, my sons, and I'm not just saying this to flatter you, the memories of my visits to your countries are among my fondest. And the same can be said about the numerous occasions when you've separately been to my wigwam as guests. In fact, since you started coming, whenever word came that either of you was on the way, I looked forward to your arrivals with the greatest of pleasure because you're both very good storytellers, and most interesting and entertaining company. I've come to look upon you as beloved sons. Because you are such to me, I want one Sunrise to have both of you come visit with me and Spring Flower at the same time. Such a future visit is possible because I know in my heart that when you come to know each other intimately, as I know you both, there will develop a brotherly love and respect between you that you will enjoy for the rest of your Sunrises on Mother Earth.

"I firmly believe that seeing such an eventuality come to pass will be much easier than everyone thinks. It's already begun in many ways between your citizens. Such is witnessed by the fact that many of them often come to our villages at the same time to visit family and friends, especially on special occasions. For instance, when I was first elected Village

Chief, many Springs ago, your Nations declared a truce and set aside differences for a short time to permit leaders, and many citizens, to come for a visit with us. During those few Sunrises your Peoples exchanged pleasantries with each other and no recriminations were made. These are not the actions of brothers and sisters who cannot overcome their differences; they are the actions of brothers and sisters looking for a path to reconciliation.

"Another positive factor that should help us find a way to your reconciliation, my sons, is that the cultural differences between your Nations are very few. In fact, there is so much in common between them that either of you could live in the other's village without much adjustment. My sons, because of such positives, and with the Great Spirit guiding us, we will finish our negotiating labours at this meeting with a Peace Treaty that will stop the senseless killing and preserve the honour and dignity of both your Nations. Neither one, my sons, will suffer any loss of face by reaching out to the other.

"If you feel a need for assurances of the truth of this, review what our brother Big Mountain just said about the Mi'kmaq and Maliseet countries. Ours have nothing to regret by being partners in a brotherly relationship, where blame is never apportioned and problems are worked out with give-and-take and dialogue. This is the way of the Great Spirit, and civilized Nations. It can be so in your situation; in fact it has already started.

"This is witnessed, my sons, by your sitting down together this Sunrise. By this simple act, you've taken a huge step towards finding peace between your Nations. And, I know in my heart from talking to each of you separately that the will is in your hearts to end the war. I firmly believe the Great Spirit loves you equally as His children and wants you to love and respect each other, not fight. Therefore, I ask you to participate in these proceedings with a burning desire to realize success. Now my dear sons, let us begin the process by examining the ancient disagreement between your Nations. I want to start by asking each of you to give an overview of the reasons for the dispute. Sleeping Bear, as the eldest you have the honour of speaking first. Please proceed my son."

"My esteemed father, I'll start by extending to you my People's sincere thanks for agreeing to mediate our war with our brothers, the Penikt. Your agreement to so generously give your time to help put a stop to our conflict demonstrates once more that you are a man with a warm and generous heart, and great wisdom. In fact, my father, it's because of your humble wisdom that we're here this Sunrise to talk in the first place. If it wasn't for you prodding me by educating me about the evils of war and the benefits of living in peace, something I now really want, I and our War Chiefs would be plotting how to exact more revenge upon the Penikt instead of trying to make peace with them. You probably don't realize this, my humble and esteemed friend, but you've changed a great many attitudes about war in many countries since you started convincingly preaching against it so long ago. Your pleas for peace have always been so convincing and logical that I've never found them wanting. Because of this, my father, I've become one of your strongest converts.

"My father, this will please you, there is positive change occurring in many countries in attitudes toward war that are derived from your antiwar crusade. Because of your teachings, many who once thought that war was the only way to settle disputes, are now viewing peaceful negotiations as the preferred and honourable way. Now, my wise and noble father, in light of what I've just said, I swear by the Great

Spirit that I want to see our Nation at peace with the Penikt. This is especially so when I see nothing but a future of blood-letting if we continue to follow the path of blind hate. When I review our situation, it breaks my heart to think about the needless suffering the citizens of our Nations have endured for so many Seasons because of this conflict. With just a little humility and brotherly regard before the war started, a peaceful solution could have easily been found. But, instead, a war was started, motivated by hate, which, my father, blinds men to everything, including the horror they pursue. In our case it completely blinded us to the hurt we were causing and the positive example of the Mi'kmaq and Maliseet Nations living side by side, prospering in glorious peace.

"Why, I ask my father, does it take so long for men to see the folly of their ways? It has finally happened to me, but it took uncountable Moons of warfare and streams of blood to do it. Facing the truth, my friends, makes me feel nothing but shame for the way that we've spilled enough of the blood of our loved ones to fill a river. Related to this senseless course, and this is something I'm really ashamed to admit: the war has been going on for such a long time that it seems like a natural part of our lives. To have come to this is inexcusable.

"But, my father and brothers, what I'm about to reveal is even more shameful than what I just said. It's bad enough to go to war with a neighbour and carry it on when there are clear cut and identifiable reasons for doing so, but this is not true in our case. In ours, the root cause of it goes so far back, in endless Moons, that the details of how it started have become blurred. Even the Elders have only vague memories of it.

"And yet we've carried on as if we were pursuing reasonable justice for a terrible wrong. It must seem incredible to you, my father, that a Nation, supposedly populated by intelligent people, is involved in such deplorable foolishness. I see some of you looking a bit shocked. But, my friends, it's true. We're carrying on with fighting a war that no longer has a valid reason. And possibly never had.

"To demonstrate how incredible this is, I'll tell you the one tale of the origins of this war that still has some credibility. It's thought that uncountable Moons ago a Chief from one of our Nations — it's not known which one — was killed by a blow to the head from a war club. The blow probably was delivered in revenge for some kind of insult. Afterwards, the person who delivered the blow claimed that it was an accident and that he had no intent in his heart to do his brother harm. The other side didn't believe him and declared war.

"My father, it's reprehensible and indefensible before the Great Spirit that our Nations have continued to spill the blood of our loved ones over something that is no longer relevant. Therefore, my father, we ask you to review all the real and imagined wrongs of the past and come up with an honourable way for us to end it forever. Our people want peace."

"Thank you, my son. Lone Wolf, my beloved son, please enlighten us with your views."

"My esteemed father, I also wish to thank you for agreeing to mediate and for prodding me to want to find peace with our neighbours. If anyone can come up with an honourable solution it's you. I echo the words of my brother Sleeping Bear, who has so eloquently laid out the cause and effect behind our dispute, and rightly described it as folly. While I was listening to him, my father, I hung my head in shame. It's undisputable that blind hate is the only thing motivating us to continue with the war, because in reality continuation of it has no defensible justification. Thus, I solemnly pray that the Great Spirit will, through you, show us the way to peace and unity and end our state of madness.

"And, my friends, the madness of it came home to me with force when I heard Sleeping Bear talk about what might have been the cause behind the war, which is identical on our side. In fact, if I didn't know it was the truth, I would have found it unbelievable. For us to be fighting over something we have no recollection about is foolishness. We have, over the past hundreds of Moons, exacted a terrible revenge upon each other. But my father, not all is lost, because of what I've heard so far this Sunrise I know in my heart we shall find a way and the Great Spirit will probably forgive us. How can we do otherwise? To carry on with a war without meaning, to kill our children over nothing, is an affront to the Great Spirit and to all mankind. With great enthusiasm we second Sleeping Bear's plea for you to review the facts and help us find an honourable way to end our foolhardiness. Our people also want peace."

"Thank you, Lone Wolf, my son. In view of what you and Sleeping Bear have just said my task will be so much easier. This is how I intend to proceed. Over the next two Sunrises I plan to interview all people present in camp who have any knowledge of the history of the war and get ideas from our brothers on how we might resolve the issue. Then on the morning of the third Sunrise, I shall present a peace plan for your consideration. Please ask the Great Spirit to light my way."

During his interviews with knowledgeable individuals, Lightning Bolt heard a multitude of versions of the incident that gave birth to the war and recounts of many of the retaliatory actions taken by both parties afterwards. From these, by the sunset of the second Sunrise, he had compiled all the information needed to fashion a just solution. He then joined the gathering for a delicious supper.

Afterward, to permit him to develop a peace proposal for the combatants to consider, he decamped for the night and set off for an isolated cove, along the shores of the Basin of High Tides, to camp alone for the night. After asking the Great Spirit to guide him, he worked out a peace proposal that he thought would work.

Early the next Sunrise, with a bounce in his step and confidence in his heart that his proposal would be accepted, he returned to the main camp and ate a hearty breakfast. Afterwards, with an air of good expectations pervading, he called the parties together to hear his solution. With the end of traditional ceremonies he began. "My sons, I've verified during my investigations that for uncountable Moons your Nations have spilled the blood of the other to right a wrong that no one can recall to memory. The hate from the original bloodletting, the bloodletting afterwards and a fear of loss of face are the only motivating factors for the continuation of the war. Thus, to continue it cannot be justified by either Nation under any known set of civilized standards or circumstances.

"The facts I've just mentioned almost leave me at a loss for words. I beg of you my sons not to be insulted, but I cannot help say this. The behaviour that your Nations have indulged, for countless Moons, is the epitome of the follies of humankind. I pray that you, in the name of your Nations, will take this opportunity and lay down your arms and embrace each other in peace forever. I have great confidence that you will do so because in your opening statements you both agreed that you want an honourable end to the conflict.

Therefore, my sons, I expect, perhaps incorrectly, that what I have to offer will be well received.

"I firmly believe that it is an ideal solution for healing the rift between your Peoples. My sons, the solution I've worked out is very simple and will, if accepted, leave both parties with their honour intact. Because only the Great Spirit knows who started the war, and because all agree that this war does not hold any ongoing just purpose or need from either party, that both of your Nations will simultaneously agree to accept the premise that both of your Peoples were jointly responsible for starting the conflict, and that both Nations consequently share equally the blame for the pain and destruction this war has caused. Then, to begin in earnest the healing, your Nations will apologize to each other for the bloodshed caused and agree unconditionally that the war is over. I can't see any reason why adopting the suggested solution should not be acceptable, because it doesn't require either Nation to lose face by admitting to being the sole instigator.

"Brothers, you now have a workable solution to ponder for resolving your dispute. Go in search of peace and return at sunset with your answers. May the Great Spirit be your guide."

As Lightning Bolt sat resting and sunning himself by the banks of the River Goes Backwards that afternoon, watching the phenomenon that gave the river its name, he talked to the Great Spirit about the shortcomings of mankind. "Great Father, how many people have died since the beginning of time to satisfy the efforts of men trying to erase bruised egos, or to seek revenge for what was perceived to be a wrong? The number must be uncountable. In this instance, it boggles the mind to contemplate that the action of one man, in a moment of heated anger, caused a bloody war between two previously friendly, fraternal Nations that has lasted so long and cost countless lives. If the citizens of the Nation whose Chief had delivered the fatal blow and that of the victim had acted responsibly, and opted for an independent adjudicator from another country to come in and pass judgment upon the survivor, so much pain and sorrow for the Atikitkas and Penikt could have been avoided. But, by seeking blind vengeance, they've visited great sorrow upon their children's children trying to heal bruised egos.

"But, my Father, such folly is not only applicable in this instance because, as you well know, men fight over practically anything. I've seen them go to war to try to acquire material things, territory and power they don't need. For what purpose? They are only mortals and must some season leave it all behind. Dear Father, to know the peace that living in a country where all people put the welfare of their fellow citizens before their own is the most secure and comforting feeling one can ask for. Perhaps, Great Spirit, one Sunrise these unfortunate Nations will find the way." Lightning Bolt continued for some time in his talk with his Maker, and slowly dozed off into a peaceful sleep.

That evening, after dining on fresh lobster and other delights from the bountiful bay, the warring Chiefs and their advisors reassembled to give their verdict on Lightning Bolt's peace plan. The Grand Chief reopened the proceedings with a short prayer. He then invited Sleeping Bear to speak for his Nation.

"Father and brothers, my colleagues and I have reflected upon the tragic dispute that has so long caused war with our brothers the Penikt. With grieving hearts we have come to appreciate the full extent of the horrors and tragic losses that it has caused us and our neighbours. Lightning Bolt, my father, you come from a Nation that has not initiated an aggressive action against another Nation since time immemorial. Your Nation has a wonderful record for keeping the peace, accomplished because your People are happy and satisfied with their lot in life and do not desire anything belonging to others.

"Further, and equally important, your People do not strike out in blind rage to try to exact vengeance upon another person. Instead they can ask for conciliation by an esteemed person or persons and abide by their judgments. Such a sensible practice has not been our way of life but I wish to tell you with the utmost sincerity that this, if Lone Wolf is willing, will change.

"My father, this will please you greatly, I've been authorized by my colleagues to apologize to our brothers and sisters the Penikt for the ages of hurt we have caused them and to accept that both our Nations are equally responsible for causing the war. I will do it now. Lone Wolf, my brother, I offer to you and your country's citizens our deepest apologies and accept our equal share of the blame. With this I wish to inform you that from this Sunrise forward we fully intend to live in peace and cooperation with your Nation, if such is agreeable to you.

"We must do this, my brother, because the hurt caused by the war is history and nothing can erase it, especially how we have killed each other over countless battles. I know in my heart that what our Nations have done in the past to each other in the name of false pride must have been extremely displeasing to the Great Spirit. But, if during this Sunrise we seek to mend our ways and make a pact to live in peace and friendship with all our neighbours, because of His love for all of His children, I know He will eventually forgive us.

"With great hope for peaceful future relations between

our Nations we lay before you Lone Wolf this proposition for ratifying the peace between our Nations. We propose that two Sunrises before the first Moon of Autumn we, with permission from the Maliseet Nation, and in the company of the Mi'kmaq and all Eastern Nations which might want to join with us, meet once more here by the banks of the River Goes Backwards to bury the hatchet between us forever. I further propose that after we've ratified our Peace Treaty we ask the Mi'kmaq, Maliseet and other Eastern Nations to join with our Nations in making a pledge to live in harmony with each other for as long as the sun may rise. I thank you, my esteemed father and brothers for hearing my humble words. May the Great Spirit always be with you. Lone Wolf, my dear brother, I await your words with great anticipation."

Lightning Bolt, visibly pleased by the course things were taking, without comment, recognized Lone Wolf with a nod.

"Sleeping Bear, your words were like the songs of returning birds in Spring to my ears. Your statement that in the past we have acted foolishly and without consideration for the dignity of our brothers and sisters is the shameful truth. We too, my brother, with pain in our hearts, have spent this Sunrise reviewing the details of the conflict between our Nations and to be brutality truthful we are also hard pressed to find virtue in what has taken place. The shame we share for our follies will be with us always.

"My father, this will please you as much as what my brother said. I've also been authorized by my colleagues to offer our brothers and sisters the Atikitkas our deepest apologies for the ages of hurt we have caused and to accept our share of the blame for the war. In this regard, Sleeping Bear, my brother, you and your citizens have our heartfelt apologies for all wrongs we have committed and we hereby accept our equal share of the blame. And, from this Sunrise forward, we will undertake to live in peace and full cooperation with your Nation.

"It must be so. Just thinking about how many of our beloved brothers have been sent to an early grave fills us with great remorse. How, I ask myself, can a man permit hate to so fully engulf his soul? My brother, you propose holding another meeting here by the banks of the River Goes Backwards; I agree wholeheartedly. We will then ratify our Peace Treaty with you here, if Big Mountain gives permission to use this site, and I know our People will give it overwhelming support. It will be a peace agreement that will withstand the trials of time. I also join with you in inviting the Mi'kmaq, Maliseet and the other Eastern Nations to please come and join with us in this time of healing.

"Lightning Bolt, my esteemed father, the Mi'kmaq have long been recognized as People dedicated to the promotion of peace between Nations. In this instance, you, their son, have found a way for us to escape the trail of destruction that we have so long travelled. In our prayers to the Great Spirit, you shall always be remembered and thanked. We, my esteemed father, as a demonstration of our admiration for the democratic values of the Mi'kmaq Nation, and you personally, intend to learn and adopt many Mi'kmaq customs and laws. In the future, with the help of the Great Spirit, we shall endeavour to live with our neighbours in mutual support, peace and harmony. Thank you, great Chief, for the light you have shown us."

Lightning Bolt was giving silent thanks to the Great Spirit for the change of heart that was so clearly in evidence among these previously warring nations. When Lone Wolf was finished, he spoke. "My beloved sons, you will never regret your agreement to trade peace for war. It will soon cleanse the hate your Nations have nurtured in their souls for uncountable Moons. From this you will learn that forgiveness is the true path to healing, contentment and happiness. With your energies diverted to peace and brotherhood your countries will grow and prosper.

"Peace, my sons, will have many other benefits for your Nations. Already you must feel great comfort in knowing that you can now go to bed at night without fear of an attack from the other. This alone could be reward enough for the course you have chosen this Sunrise, but you will find there are even greater rewards. For instance, the security you will have from knowing that the other side will offer you safe haven and comfort, instead of danger, during a crisis will be something you will forever thank the Great Spirit for.

"As further proof of the benefits peace brings, if such is needed, I offer as an example the beneficial relationship that was established between the Allies and Western Nations after the last war. They have reformed their politics to where true democracy rules and now the elected Western leaders who are in office are loved and esteemed by their People. And, most important, leaders and Peoples from both sides now intermingle with absolute trust.

"My friends, love and respect for one another produces more happiness than all the possessions in the universe. The joy felt by those who give is gratifying to the soul. Being mean and stingy is the way to lose peace of mind. Those who only know how to take spend their lives worrying about the possibility that someone else might take everything they've accumulated. Giving up happiness in order to amass worldly goods is madness.

"My sons, you flatter me by saying I'm responsible for

the peace agreement that you have so quickly accepted this Sunrise. The truth is the seeds of peace already existed in your hearts. Without it, success here would have been impossible. As happens with all good seeds, yours have grown and are about to bloom.

"In closing, I want to say how intensely happy I am about what you did this Sunrise and what you have proposed for the future. Just thinking about seeing all our Nations coming together for a Burying of the Hatchet Ceremony fills me with joy and renews my faith in the goodness of mankind! I believe that the Great Spirit Himself must be rejoicing with us in this time of forgiveness and peace. I agree with joy in my heart, my sons, and thankfulness to the Great Spirit, to meet with you again at this site in the company of all our brothers two Sunrises before the first Moon of Autumn, providing of course, our Maliseet brothers are agreeable. Chief Big Mountain is indicating that he wishes to come forward and speak. My son."

"Thank you, my esteemed father, for giving me the opportunity to speak on this heartwarming occasion. My father, although you may disclaim it, you are truly a Peacemaker. To have had the privilege of seeing you use your wisdom to take these two long-term enemies and convert them into friends is a moment in time that I will forever cherish. The Great Spirit will surely bless you for it.

"My brothers, Sleeping Bear and Lone Wolf, you and your Peoples shall soon begin to reap the benefits of the course you have decided upon this Sunrise. The generosity and wisdom displayed in reaching out for peace will be appreciated by your children and your children's children for all time. My friends, as the Great Spirit is my witness, the trail you have chosen is the correct one. I say this from experience. Our People, like our brothers and sisters the Mi'kmaq, have long accepted the principle that the well-being of relatives and friends comes before individual concerns. When people adopt the principle of one for all and all for one they have taken the first step towards finding contentment. By your actions this Sunrise you've embarked on such a path and you shall soon, with the loving guidance of the Great Spirit, know true peace.

"Lightning Bolt, my beloved esteemed father, our country will be very honoured to host a celebration of peace for all Nations at this site. To take part of the load of preparing for it off your shoulders, I'll look after inviting the Nations of the Eastern Land to come join with us in celebrating this momentous event; you can extend invitations to the rest of the Mi'kmaq Nations. We will also take on the responsibility of coordinating the logistics for the event. Because of the size of it, this should keep our organizers hopping. It's not a problem in any way; in fact they relish this sort of thing and should be happy as larks when presented with the chore. However, I have something I want to add to the agenda. It is my wish, during the conference, after the Penikt and Atikitkas ratify their Peace Treaty, that we all renew our commitments to live forever in peace by also burying hatchets. What a sight it will be to see so many Nations reaffirming brotherly love. My esteemed father, I thank you again for honouring our land by holding this historic meeting here and with your presence. My brothers, may the Great Spirit be with you always."

Lightning Bolt, with a quaver in his voice, replied, "Big Mountain, the kindness and generosity of your People knows no bounds. The knowledge that your country is so enthused to help host the peace celebration and will invite the Eastern Nations causes me much pleasure. I will, on my part, send out runners when I get home to invite all of the Mi'kmaq

Nations. Our celebration shall be the largest gathering of our Peoples in memory. My son, the task of organizing the celebration is of monumental proportions. May the Great Spirit reward you and your People for this act of kindness and generosity, which you so freely give to make this event a success. Until we meet again, my brothers and sisters, may the Great Spirit be with you." They concluded by smoking a peace pipe.

The following Sunrise, after many fond farewells, in weather that was unusually warm for the Season, Lightning Bolt and companions started for home. As the party moved down along the coast of the Basin of High Tides, the Grand Chief began to reminisce and talk to the Great Spirit about many similar trips he had enjoyed in the company of his family or friends. "Great Father, the young warriors are sweating from the effort of rowing. It makes them look so healthy and powerful. Oh, my father, how time flies. It seems as if it were only last Sunrise I was enjoying doing the same. The warmth of a fine Sunrise added to my pleasure then as it does for them now.

"How things have changed. Although these young men find it warm, my old bones find it a little cool. In bygone Seasons I remember coming up this coast in early Spring and thoroughly enjoying the cold crispness of the weather. Now, just thinking about travelling in that kind of weather chills me. I often wish, my Father, that You had seen fit to reward old age with the ability to keep warm.

"Oh, my Father, how travelling this shoreline brings back so many wonderful memories. I see over there the cove where father and I, when I was a young lad of eight Springs, stopped to camp for the night and to replenish our water supply. I can still hear the words he spoke that night, spanning the ages, as if it were only last Sunrise. Seeing the site brings back the night's events so clearly. It began as a beautiful evening. But, shortly after dusk the clouds began to roll in, followed closely by fog. All signs pointed towards a big storm. As we ate supper by our cozy campfire, we could hear some slight echoes. Father told me that the hills surrounding the cove made the area very conducive to repeating, distorting and carrying sounds from some distance. Later that night, when the storm broke in good style, it did so with a vengeance. After we had cleaned up our utensils, father told me to get ready for bed. Trying to impress him with my bravery, I set up my bed some distance from his. After all, what boy of eight Springs needs the close proximity of his father in the dark of night? And was it ever dark. I can still see father extinguishing the fire and hear him retiring to his lean-to for the night. Then the wind started to howl.

"Oh Great Father, the noise that came from it was the most terrifying I've ever heard. It sounded as if every soul of the departed and the living were being subjected to the most inhuman punishment imaginable. I can still hear father's chuckle when I screamed for help and was directed by his voice to his bed. Being embraced and feeling the strength of his naked chest and hearing the beat of his strong heart against my face was the most positive of all my experiences in dealing with fear. And, my Father, my fear that night was so pervasive that it was almost visible.

"Of course, the next morning I was filled with shame about my cowardly conduct, and tried my best to avoid my father's eyes. He pretended he didn't notice my discomfort and restarted the campfire and cooked our breakfast. Afterwards he began preparations to break camp. It was then, with a big smile on his face, he put his arm around my shoulders and said, 'All people, my son, adults as well as children, some-times encounter experiences which leave them in groundless terror. Admitting to it doesn't make one a coward.'

"His statement left me somewhat soothed. To help me fully recover my sense of dignity he told me a story about another young boy who had also experienced a situation that left him terrified. His admission that he was the young boy in the story was the thing that totally dissipated my shame. It takes a man of truly great humility and courage to admit to knowing fear.

"The pleasure of my remembrances must be showing on my face. The young people are giving me knowing smiles. But, so be it, they too must have known at one time or another the feeling of being held tightly in the warm and comforting embrace of a truly great father."

One young man spoke up: "Father, share with us the story that has awakened so many joyful memories in you."

"My son, there are some things that happen to you during your lifetime that they cannot be retold. My thoughts have been with my father and of a trip we had together sixty-seven Springs ago. All I'll tell you about it is that the memories of that special time still bring me great happiness, and until the Great Spirit calls me home will continue to do so."

Another queried, "Would it be too bold, my father, to ask you to share with us a few stories of your adventurous life while we move along?"

"My sons, one would think you would grow weary of hearing an old man's remembrances. However, I'll tell you about Kespek's war with the Westerners. Back when I was a young man of only twenty Springs…" For most of the after-noon Lightning Bolt entertained his young companions with tales of the heroic deeds of the men who had bravely repulsed the invaders of Kespek so many Moons ago. After several such pleasant Sunrises of travel, they finally arrived home. Spring Flower greeted him with a warm embrace. That evening, while relaxing in front of a warm fire, he told her about his successful trip.

As the Summer Moons passed, Lightning Bolt was very pleased to hear about the excitement the approaching peace celebration was generating among the citizens throughout the Mi'kmaq Nations. It was so pronounced that by late Summer many thousands of them were already on their way to the shores of the River Goes Backwards to participate in what they sensed would be the most historic event of their lifetimes. The prospect of seeing the coming together of the leaders and citizens of so many Nations for the purpose of pledging peace and fraternal brotherhood was something no one had dreamed they would see.

To allow them plenty of time to visit old friends and haunts along the way, Spring Flower and Lightning Bolt departed for the River Flows Backwards shortly after the arrival of the second Moon of Summer. The visits were enjoyable and filled with the wonderful memories of the events of past Moons. But camping and seeing once again the many beautiful sights along the shore of the Basin of High Tides was the highlights of their trip. In the comfort of their lean-tos at night, wrapped in their warm sleeping furs, they talked about the past and its happy memories. They also experienced a feeling of building excitement as the Sunrises passed and the time for the peace conference neared.

By four Sunrises before the historic meeting, thousands had already set up camp around the River Flows Backwards and were enjoying the warm embraces of family members and beloved friends. The mood around the meeting area was dreamlike. People looked on in awe and wonder as the citizens of the two former enemy Nations met and embraced and bemoaned the hurt and anguish they had caused each other. Their contrite and honourable conduct promised great things to come for their new relationship.

Late in the morning of the Sunrise before the celebration was slated to begin, Lightning Bolt's delegation and their escort of young warriors arrived. It generated a wave of excitement among the People. But if someone had told Grand Chief Lightning Bolt he was the star attraction at the upcoming event, he would have reacted with utter dismay. He saw his role only as that of a minor player and a presiding officer. After settling in, Lightning Bolt met informally with most of the leaders who had already arrived for preliminary discussions. His heart filled with warmth as he listened to their sincere and enthusiastic expectations for the peace celebration. From their reports of how well their Peoples had reacted to the news of the peace celebration, he knew that the Great Spirit would truly be pleased by the intentions of those gathered. Later that night, wrapped in the arms of his beloved Spring Flower, in happy anticipation of seeing a dream come true, he slept the sleep of a contented baby.

The next morning the sky was blue and the sun shone brightly. It appeared that the start of the peace celebration would be blessed with beautiful weather. It seemed to those present that the Great Spirit was so pleased with the event that He was assuring them pleasant conditions to celebrate. The night before had been bathed in silvery moonlight and the stars had flickered brightly. The Sunrise over the Basin of High Tides was one of the most spectacular ever seen; the beauty of its colours would in future defy adequate words and was viewed by many as a sign that the Great Spirit had been extremely pleased that His children were healing their wounds.

After breakfast, Lightning Bolt asked some of the young warriors to call the People to gather round. Within a short period of time the huge crowd, estimated in the thousands, was brought to order. Speaking through a conical moose caller Lightning Bolt opened the peace celebration. "Brothers and sisters, welcome!"

The crowd responded spontaneously with a mighty roar, "Welcome to you, great Chief!"

Lightning Bolt, visibly pleased, continued, "Thank you! I stand before you this Sunrise my friends in awe at the wondrous event unfolding among us. For me this sunrise is a lifetime's dream come true. In fact it is so awesome that I pray to the Great Father that if this is a dream, He will spare me the pain of ever waking up! Now my friends, before proceeding, I'll ask our brother Chief Big Mountain to come forward and lead us in a prayer of thanks to the Great Spirit for His benevolence."

A thoroughly involved, smiling Big Mountain came forward and replied enthusiastically, "Lightning Bolt, my esteemed father, brothers and sisters, I bid you welcome to the land of the Maliseet!"

The crowd again, as if on a cue, responded spontaneously, "Thank you, Big Mountain!" They then gave the leaders and citizens of the Maliseet Nation a mighty roar of appreciation.

After the noise had subsided, Big Mountain, more pleased than before, continued. "When we first gathered here two Sunrises after the first Moon of Summer, we beseeched the Great Spirit to show our brothers and sisters from the Penikt and Atikitkas Nations the way to find peace. He, with compassion for His children, heeded our prayers. Now I ask you to please stand and raise your hands with me towards the Land of Souls and give humble thanks for His kindness and generosity. Oh Great Father, accept from us, who are sometimes Your unworthy children, our undying love and devotion. We give you thanks for all the kindness you have shown us. We will try harder to live in the image of your ways. Thanks, dear Father, thanks!"

The People formed hundreds of small Circles and partook in Sweet-grass Ceremonies. The aroma from the smoke of hundreds of smouldering braids of sweet-grass spread through the air a smell that was exhilarating to the senses of the thousands of participants. Afterwards, the Chiefs and Elders smoked pipes of peace. Then Lightning Bolt resumed speaking, calling for consensus on the proceedings of the peace celebration, which would resume the next Sunrise. After the sacred pre-meeting rituals were respectfully carried out, Lightning Bolt began his historic address.

"My brothers and sisters, sons and daughters, we have gathered this Sunrise to approve an understanding that will further reinforce our determination to live in peace forever. To this end I'll be asking you for approval of the following actions and laws, which we believe will have the power to strengthen our bonds. To start, we have agreed to dig a pit and have Lone Wolf and Sleeping Bear, the Chiefs of the Penikt and Atikitkas Nations, signify the ratification of their Peace Treaty by placing hatchets in it for burial. Then all other Chiefs, as the representatives of their Nations, shall place in it a hatchet to be buried also. This Burying of the Hatchet Ceremony will reaffirm our commitment to the original agreements that ended hostilities forever among our Peoples. After the hatchets are buried, the Chiefs shall form a circle and make gifts of tobacco to each other. Then they

273

shall further seal the agreement by smoking pipes of peace.

"Then the present members of the Wabanaki Alliance will invite the new Nations seeking membership to ratify the terms that the alliance operates under. A new provision, which officially creates an Arbitration Council to deal with disputes among our own Nations will need to be ratified by all. Although we've never needed it before, it will have authority to find solutions and to have them implemented by consensus when found. If a consensus cannot be found then it shall have authority to impose decisions without further consultations as a last resort. This power, I don't envision, will ever be used as stated. However, in case it ever has to be used, the power to do shall be assured by the Chiefs.

"In addition, to assure that the alliance remains faithful to its purpose, member Nations shall agree to meet each Summer to discuss ways to improve and strengthen its effectiveness. There shall also be special emergency meetings when required. The citizens of member Nations shall have the right to travel freely and unmolested through another member Nation's territory.

"There, my brothers and sisters, you have before you the result of our labours. Do you want time for further discussion before signifying your pleasure, or displeasure, with the terms of the proposal?"

The answer came back in one mighty roar, "No, we approve, we approve." The crowd began a spontaneous round of embracing and shouting out their pleasure to the world.

The Burying of the Hatchet Ceremony then took place. With due respect, each Chief solemnly placed a hatchet in the pit and pledged his Nation's commitment to peace. After it was finished, the People again reacted with enthusiastic noise of approval. After allowing some time for them to express their joy, Lightning Bolt asked the People gathered for silence to hear his word.

"This Sunrise, my friends, we have truly become one family at peace. Peace, my People, is the way to realize human dignity for all people and it is a path that I hope will, one Sunrise, be adopted by all of humanity.

"Brothers and sisters, sons and daughters, there is no praise strong enough to commend you for having the fortitude to accept peace as your guiding light. Life, my friends, is precious and you have this Sunrise recognized this as a central truth, because you have honoured life and each other and your children and their children for countless future generations. By your personal and shared actions this sunrise, you have set the path that is much easier to walk than any other because by walking in this way, we continue to honour our inner nature and the nature of our sacred bonds in relationship with each other.

"This bond is made of the sacred beauty of creation. This beauty is given to us by the Creator. This gift is our sacred trust, given within our hearts and extended to each other. In these ways, we each and every one of us are the hands and arms, the feet and legs and the heart, mind and spirit of the Great Spirit. By living in peace, the Creator's will is made manifest within us and between us. By honouring the sacred bond of peace and by taking the honourable and humble path to reconciliation whenever a conflict may arise, including seeking arbitration and the advice of others, we are in fact offering to ourselves and each other the energy of the Creator's touch, His embrace and His forgiveness by the way we live these commitments to peace.

"My children, my brothers and sisters, seeing our agreement come to pass is a mountain of a landmark in my lifetime. I couldn't ask for more. With the help of the Great Spirit and our good will towards others our efforts shall last for uncountable Moons. Go, my People, and celebrate the beginning of a new life. May the Great Spirit forever bless you with His bounty and may peace be with you."

From this time forward the Eastern Nations knew only peace among themselves. Lightning Bolt, as recognition of his historic accomplishments, became affectionately known as the Peacemaker. The People, knowing he would not approve of the designation, kept this sacred name an open secret among themselves. This was the way of things until that fateful Sunrise when the Peacemaker was called home to the Land of Souls.

//

CHAPTER NINE

Lightning Bolt returned to Kespukwitk filled with a deep sense of accomplishment. The pact that bound all the Nations of the East together was a dream come true. To leave an encampment with the sight of old enemies like the Atikitkas and Penikt demonstrating their new found friendship by partying together and passing tobacco back and forth was an experience to remember. His contentment was reinforced by his deep conviction that the new order was permanent.

After a short rest to recuperate from the rigours of travel, he quickly slipped back into his comfortable routine. Sunrises were once again filled with visits from old friends, relatives and people seeking advice and guidance. However, his schedule was not as hectic as it was when he was younger. With the passage of time he had begun to recruit some of the younger leaders to handle many of the responsibilities that he previously took care of himself. This was accepted by the People with understanding and the extra duties were willingly assumed by the younger leaders in the same spirit.

Prompted by the knowledge that their aged and esteemed father needed to slow down and live an easier life, they had worked out a pact among themselves to further ease the load that Lightning Bolt carried. They did so in the knowledge that, in an emergency, his vision and leadership were always there to show them the way.

Spring Flower's Sunrises were also back to a routine she enjoyed, of helping Lightning Bolt with his duties and participating in the social affairs of the community. Top priority for her was getting Lightning Bolt away from duties by persuading him to go on long trips to visit friends more often. This was not hard. In spite of their advanced age they both still loved to travel and Lightning Bolt made sure more time was available for it. They often, during the warmer Seasons, recruited a group of eager volunteers from among the younger warriors and set off for a destination to the far reaches of a Mi'kmaq, or an allied Nation's, territory.

Recruiting warriors to accompany them was not a problem. The only issue was that so many eagerly volunteered it made it difficult to turn away many who wished to experience these very popular trips. Because of this, the competition among the young men to be selected for the purpose by the esteemed couple was intense. This desire to travel with the Chief and his wife was to a certain extent motivated by the honour of escorting them, but primarily it was because the warriors found the companionship of these two warm and interesting people to be an experience to remember. Also, for many of them, the exciting places the Chief and his wife visited were the only opportunity they would have during their lifetimes to travel.

During these journeys to far off places such as the Bay of Cod, or Where the Mountains Touch the Sky, the young men were often entertained around a roaring campfire by Lightning Bolt's stories. They ranged from tales of his personal adventures to legends passed down through the ages by the Elders. He could tell stories in such a manner that people often felt like they were living the adventures themselves. When Lightning Bolt grew tired, Spring Flower, a fairly good storyteller in her own right, often stepped in and continued the entertainment.

The Grand Chief thoroughly enjoyed the company of young people but as the Seasons passed he became aware that time was depriving him of many of his lifelong companions. Already, at his eightieth Spring, he had seen a great many depart Mother Earth and he knew with the certainty of his faith that they were in the Land of Souls enjoying the company of the Father and their ancestors. Although he was happy for them, from time to time he could not help feeling a little lonesome for their company.

Shortly after he began his eighty-second Spring, Lightning Bolt saw his lifelong friend Crazy Moose called home. His passing left a void that could never be filled and Lightning Bolt missed him immensely, far more than anyone knew, with the possible exception of Spring Flower. She knew from her countless Moons with them that together they had known happiness and shared many experiences, and been there to comfort and console each other in times of stress. The secrets of their lives had been shared and guarded with loyalty. Their special friendship was not replaceable.

At Crazy Moose's Feast of the Dead, Lightning Bolt, after the prayers and other rituals were over, was first to speak. "Great Spirit, please welcome home with open arms my beloved brother and friend Crazy Moose. He was a boy and a man with whom I shared a great part of my life. He lived life in an impeccably honourable and humble manner. He was kind and generous to everyone and was loved by all who knew him. My brothers and sisters, sons and daughters, I've been blessed with the honour and privilege of having known many great men in my lifetime. I've known men who performed outstanding feats in war and peace, and men who have overcome great trials and persevered, but none in my mind have been as great as Crazy Moose. To me the companionship he and I shared throughout the passage of our Seasons is impossible to describe. His loyalty and devotion to me and my family were given freely and were never doubted. There is so much to tell about him I don't know where to start.

"Perhaps, when one speaks about the life of a beloved brother and friend such as Crazy Moose, it's best to start with something he would have preferred, cheering everyone up by relating some of the pleasant things we did together. Actually, I have so many of these pleasant memories that I could talk for many Sunrises without running out of them. One of the funniest incidents that immediately comes to mind happened when we were young boys on a camping trip to Kejimkujik Lake. It was very hot and humid as we set off on our journey. Thus, from the rigours of our hike, we were in a good sweat when we arrived at the lake. After shedding our breechcloths and vests we dove into the lake and spent a leisurely and thoroughly enjoyable time swimming and fooling around in the cool water. Upon returning to shore we found a spot to sit and dry off before dressing.

"What happened next I can still see as if it were only last Sunrise. Crazy Moose sat down at his chosen spot and let out a bloodcurdling yell. He took off for the lake with the speed of a bald eagle diving for prey. I stared in amazement as he ran with the swiftness of the wind to try to escape a swarm of thoroughly riled-up wasps. He charged into the lake and dove out of sight, leaving the wasps to buzz around for a few moments before returning to their hive to make repairs. Because the wasps, in their frenzy, were honed in on taking revenge on the rear end that had sat on them, I managed to escape un-stung from the encounter.

"The stings Crazy Moose got on his rear were so numerous that it quickly began to look like a blown up black-bear bladder, ready to burst. Oh, my friends, applying a poultice to his rear end caused me so much laughter it hurt. Nobody I've ever known, including Crazy Moose himself, has ever moved with such speed as when he had to escape the wrath of those disgruntled wasps! I jokingly told him afterwards that he was going so fast when he hit the lake that I fully expected him to run forever on top of the water, with the wasps trailing behind and encouraging him onward. From that point onward he was very careful about where he chanced to sit down."

Lightning Bolt went on for some time recounting his pleasant memories of his friend and ended, as he had started his eulogy, with a prayer. "Oh Great Spirit, I shall miss the companionship of my beloved friend and brother. However, I take solace from knowing that he is with You, and that one Sunrise he and I shall meet again in Your company. He was a great friend and a devoted family man. All of us who had the privilege of knowing him were blessed with a great experience. He devoted his life, Great Father, to his family and community. Please grant him eternal peace and tranquility in Your company."

Over the course of his next eleven Springs, Lightning Bolt, with increasing regularity, saw the passing of most of the remainder of his childhood friends. And most of those who remained became very frail. Also, while he himself remained quite strong and healthy, he saw his precious Spring Flower become increasingly frail and sickly. When the pain from her ailments struck, which came with increasing frequency, it was sad, yet heartwarming, to see him being so solicitous of her every need. Mercifully, during his ninety-third Summer the Great Spirit called his beloved Spring Flower home. If he had not been a man with such a firm belief in a place for humans in an afterlife, the death of his companion of seventy Summers would have been unbearable. Even so, the loss was an excruciating experience. He spent many Sunrises meditating and communicating with the Great Spirit before he again found the courage to face a world without his precious wife.

The passing of Spring Flower brought people from every Mi'kmaq and Eastern Nation to his village to express their heartfelt sympathies and offer him comfort. Throughout her Feast of the Dead and all the celebrations he remained stoic, not once betraying to anyone his inner turmoil. He took some comfort from the People's solicitations; he knew they meant well. But the visit by his old friend Chief Big Mountain was one of the most comforting. The Chief, a widower himself, knew from the experience of his own personal trauma the inner grief his friend was experiencing. He used his knowledge to help ease the pain. They shared many stories of their youths and reminisced about the wonderful times they had shared with their beloved wives. Lightning Bolt discovered that discussing the heartbreak of his grief with his old friend helped him a great deal in coping with it.

As time moved onward, abetted by the passing of his wife and most of his childhood friends, Lightning Bolt began experiencing a sensation in life that is almost always restricted to the very aged. He entered a time characterized by a form of depressive loneliness. In one of these moods he prayed to the Father. "Oh Great Spirit, please give me the strength and wisdom to understand why, even through I'm always surrounded by people who love me, I sometimes find myself with a sad feeling of being all alone. I know in my heart, Great Father, that You love me, because throughout my life Your presence has always been with me, and has guided the way I've lived. But at this time I need a sign from you to help carry on. Please, my dear Father, help me regain my peace of mind."

That night, Glooscap came as a messenger of the Great Spirit to visit with him in his dreams. Glooscap said to Lightning Bolt, "My brother, in response to your pleas for help, the Great Spirit has sent me to tell you that He has heard your prayers. To help ease your mind, He wants me to tell you that your beloved wife and friends are very happy in the Land of Souls. However, they are deeply concerned that you are wasting a great deal of your precious life pining away because of something that belongs to the past. The Father has instructed me to tell you that He is disappointed that your grief outweighs your thanksgiving for His boundless kindness throughout your lifetime. The Father wishes to extend this love to you now, to help you understand. To regain your happy disposition you must accept that the souls of your loved ones are gone forever from Mother Earth. You must be happy in the knowledge that they are safe and enjoying the company of the Great Spirit."

Glooscap spoke with authority and wisdom. "Instead of thinking constantly that you are alone, start counting your blessings. To warm your heart, you have thousands of loving memories of a wonderful wife and friends. And, my ungrateful friend, you have multitudes of people from your village and elsewhere who love you dearly. They are here now to keep you company. You, my brother, are not alone."

This last statement stuck in his heart, awakening his spirit again. It was as if Glooscap's words were calling back Lightning Bolt's spirit from the many places he had been and from the distant shadowlands of grief and loss. "I'll leave you with this advice," Glooscap continued. "When your time comes to leave Mother Earth and join your ancestors in eternal happiness in the Land of Souls the Father will send for you. Until then, use the time you have left to make people happy and to be constructive with your energy. Start feeling happy for yourself. Those, like you, who are given much, are asked just as much from the Father of blessings and beauty. You, my friend, have much yet to give to your People, so give with a good heart and be happy."

Lightning Bolt awoke the next morning feeling a contentment he had not known for many Moons and with a renewed interest in life. In the deepest recesses of his heart he now felt assured that his precious Spring Flower and his friends were contented with their lot in the Land of Souls. He felt with assurance that during some Sunrise in future he would be reunited with them and would be content. He thanked the Great Spirit for opening his eyes.

The villagers were quick to notice the renewed vigour of their beloved leader. To celebrate the turnaround in his spirits they decided to hold a huge party and invite all his old friends and anyone else who wanted to come from the alliance. They set a Sunrise for it, and invitations were sent out. The guests poured into the village by the thousand, in the mood for a happy reunion, bringing canoe loads of food and presents. As the celebrations got under way, Lightning Bolt, with a twinkle in his eye, plunged into the spirit of the party like a man half his age. He stayed up late into the nights listening to and telling stories, smoking pipes and watching dancers and drummers perform their well-rehearsed and polished acts. It was a party of renewal, and by any measurement was an unqualified success. The People returned to their far-flung villages full of warmth and renewed love in their hearts for their brothers and sisters.

Towards the end of his ninety-ninth Summer, several people reported to Lightning Bolt the disturbing news that they had sighted giant canoes off the coast. They reported that the giant canoes appeared to be propelled by the wind catching in enormous blankets rather than by men rowing them. Upon receiving these reports he sent for Flaming Hair to discuss the matter.

Lightning Bolt said, "My brother, thanks for coming so quickly. I've received worrying news that I want to discuss with you."

Flaming Hair, with a sense of foreboding, responded, "I can tell it must be bad, because you're in a very sombre mood. Perhaps I can help to lift the weight from your mind. What troubles you?"

Lightning Bolt, with a sad heart, told him, "Two hunters, who were hunting in separate areas near the coast, came to see me this morning to report seeing four giant canoes that matched the description you gave me of the boats used by your European ancestors. I take this as almost certain proof that the reports are true, because these people have no way of knowing what European ships look like. The only ones who know what they look like in our community are you and I. Unfortunately, the sighting isn't the only bad news, my brother. I've also had unconfirmed reports that the Red

People of the Big Island are under attack by white and hairy strangers. What do you make of these reports?"

Having his foreboding confirmed as the real thing, Flaming Hair commented, "Lightning Bolt, my brother, my heart is heavy with fear for the safety of our Peoples. What you've related is something I've dreaded for a long time, but I kept my council, hoping against hope that it wouldn't come to pass. If what you've been told is correct, then the invasion of our country by Europeans may have begun."

With his hands on his head, shaking back and forth, Flaming Hair continued to mutter words he would long remember. "I fear this spells disaster, that they may come very quickly. Civilizations like theirs have a history of taking from others by force. Just the thought of the horrors the invaders will unleash against our People makes me grieve for what they are about to experience. They will come by the boatload and deprive us of our sustenance and in the end our lives. They will strip the country bare in search of precious metals and other things they call wealth. Our culture will be destroyed and our children will be sold on the slave markets of Europe. We, my brother, are in mortal danger."

"Flaming Hair, my dear and trusted brother, I know the weight of age has slowed you down considerably, but I need your help. The reported invasion of the Big Island has such grave implications for our Peoples that I want it confirmed, or dispelled, by a person whose word I can really rely on. I know it's an imposition, but could you lead a scouting party of warriors to the Big Island to investigate the rumoured attacks against the Red People? If you agree, you must be very discreet about telling the People the purpose of your travels. I've already sworn the two hunters to secrecy about the sightings offshore, for I don't want to unduly disturb the

Peoples' peace of mind at this time."

"Lightning Bolt, my brother, of course I will do this. In view of the seriousness of the situation, I'll get provisions ready, round up a crew and leave for the Big Island at the first light of dawn. Making allowances for unforeseen delays, with luck, we should return within two Moons. Please don't worry about my age, for I feel as fit now as I did when I was passing through my fortieth Summer. But I tell you, my brother, I go with a heavy heart."

The brothers embraced and parted. Flaming Hair then hurried to his wigwam to inform Spotted Fawn about the trip and to prepare. After a restless and sleepless night, Lightning Bolt and many of his countrymen were on shore to see the men paddle off into the light of the coming Sunrise. The People could sense something was wrong, but with their respect for his good judgment, they didn't press the Chief for enlightenment.

Adding to Lightning Bolt's worries, as if he needed more, news arrived from Eskikewa'kik's Chief that a group of ten boys had disappeared without a trace while on a camping trip near where Little Trout Brook falls into the Big Pond. Their camp had been found with supplies intact and there was no sign of a violent struggle, or for that matter, a struggle of any kind. They had disappeared so completely, it was as if the Great Spirit had come and taken them home with Him. Lightning Bolt requested that he be kept informed of any developments.

Three Sunrises before the second Moon of Autumn, Flaming Hair returned from the Big Island. After quickly greeting his wife, he went swiftly to Lightning Bolt's wigwam to deliver the heartrending news of the plight of the Red People. He wanted to fill Lightning Bolt in before his young companions, who were in a high state of agitation, had the chance to unburden themselves to other members of the village. The two men exchanged greetings.

Flaming Hair gave Lightning Bolt his news. "My brother, the crossing to the Big Island was over light seas, which enabled us to reach the island's western shore only two and a half Sunrises after we left. We closely followed the coast to a place I had previously visited a settlement of Red People. We found the place completely destroyed. After viewing the destruction we became more secretive in our movements and travelled towards the eastern end of the island, as close to shore as possible to avoid detection.

"Our caution, my brother, was well grounded. As we rounded the southernmost part of the island, we came upon a sight that almost stopped our hearts. Out on the fishing grounds sat uncountable numbers of huge canoes. We cautiously proceeded along the coast and eventually came to an area being used by the white fishermen as a fish station. Here, they had set up camps and constructed racks for drying and salting fish. The place was a beehive of activity with men coming and going constantly.

"While scouting their camp, I spotted among the ships one which had hoisted upon its spar the flag of my former country. I advised my young travelling companions that we should keep the camp under surveillance until we spotted one of the fishermen drifting away from it. What I then proposed shook my young companions to the bottoms of their moccasins. Their reaction to my plan to kidnap one of the Europeans was almost total astonishment. It was, my brother, one of the lighter moments of the trip. They reacted with even more incredulity when I filled them in on the rest of what I planned. I told them that once we had captured him we would strip him naked and I would don his clothes and go out among the fleet to gather intelligence. They received this news in stunned silence.

"Our moment soon arrived. We spotted a man, approximately my size, walking off towards the forest. He no more than entered the woods than our men were upon him. I stayed out of sight while the boys blindfolded and stripped him. Their reaction to his ungodly stink was one of pure revulsion. I then climbed into his unwashed and smelly things and set out to visit my former countrymen. As it is usual to have men from many nations sailing on one ship I didn't stand out while I was among them.

"My beloved brother, the stories I have to tell you are not pleasant. These men bragged openly about the despicable actions they had taken against the Red People. I saw very quickly that many of these poor souls were being held in bonds on shore and heard that many were already in the holds of ships, destined to be sold to the highest bidder as slaves when the ships returned to Europe. And, most pitifully, many of their women were being used as sex slaves to satisfy the depraved appetites of the ship's crew. Many young children had been slaughtered or, may the Great Spirit have pity on them, used to satisfy the perverted sex appetites of some of the depraved fishermen. My friend, I fear this is just the beginning. More giant canoes will come, and at the rate that the blood of the Red People is running upon the island, they shall soon be only memories."

Lightning Bolt, with tears nearly spilling from his eyes, groaned a mourning cry and lamented, "Flaming Hair, the news you bring chills my heart." He reached out to steady himself against Flaming Hair's shoulder. They both looked down for a time, in silence.

After thinking to himself that this very moment would be permanently etched into his memory and written upon his heart, Flaming Hair reluctantly broke the silence. "Brother, I have more to report and it is just as sickening. After I had gathered all the information I could, I drifted off from their camp and entered the forest once more. I signalled our warriors to be silent and moved them away, out of earshot of our prisoner. Then I told them I wanted them to pretend in front of him that I was also a prisoner. With it arranged we moved back to our canoe and pushed off with the prisoner still blindfolded and gagged. After we had travelled out of the immediate area, I stripped off the filthy clothes and wrapped myself in a blanket. The boys then tied, blindfolded and gagged me before removing the blindfold and gag of our prisoner. Then they removed mine. This was done to assure as much as possible that the prisoner would be convinced that I too was a captive.

"At the time, my plan was to bring the captive with us to the point of the island where we would be moving off the coast to return to the mainland, and then leave him ashore to his own devices. But first I wanted to see if he had anything more to add to the information I already had. Once the gags were removed, I cursed and swore at the warriors in a fashion that would have shamed the most perverted citizens of the slums of Oslo, London or Paris. I also related the hideous things I would do to them in revenge if the opportunity arose. These foul-mouthed vengeful words completely opened the man's heart to me, and he began to speak with great pride about some of the brutal attacks he and his shipmates had made against the People of our lands.

"My brother, he admitted to me that he had a liking for young children. The sex of the child was of no consequence.

He described how he had taken small children of the Red People and performed vile acts upon them before killing them. I managed to contain my disgust and revulsion and kept him talking. This is the part, my brother, that I've kept to myself and would advise you to do the same in kindness to their families.

"He said he had been a crew member on a ship that had recently come to the shores of our land. I knew it was our land because he described landmarks that were true to the shores of Eskikewa'kik. He related how they had stopped at a point where a brook fell into the sea to replenish their water supply. While filling their water casks, out of the forest walked ten young Mi'kmaq boys full of curiosity. They offered them presents of clothes and trinkets, eventually enticing them to come on board where they were overpowered and taken prisoners. They were then crammed into the hold below. It was the captain's intention to sell them as slaves.

"He then related that many of the sailors had been without women for many Moons and were pining for sexual release. Within Sunrises, they had been abused to the point where they died, or became so sick that the sailors had thrown them overboard. Three of the survivors were sold to a ship off the Big Island, the last was kept by the perverted Captain, who had claimed his young body for his own.

"He got this far in his story and I could stand no more. I advised him to prepare to meet his maker for he had just confessed his gory crimes to a full-fledged member of the Nation whose children he had violated. The look of shock that came upon his face when I began to speak in Mi'kmaq with the warriors was some small comfort towards easing my pain at the horrors he had committed.

"I told the young men most of what had transpired

between us and advised them that I reserved to myself the pleasure of dispatching him to the punishment of travelling forever without roots in eternity. He grovelled, wet himself and moved his bowels in the blanket he was wrapped in. I tell you my brother I've never before killed a person in war, or an animal in the Hunt, without feeling some twinge of remorse. However, the pleasure I felt in watching the terror in his eyes as my war club moved towards his skull is without a credible comparison in my lifetime. My only regret, and may the Great Spirit forgive me for this, was that I couldn't bring him back to life in order to repeat it a thousand times over."

Lightning Bolt, his heart breaking, commented, "Flaming Hair, my brother, the news you've related would cause revulsion in the coldest heart. Is their purpose only to cause pain and sorrow? You must leave me now, my beloved brother, for I must grieve in private for a while, for our children, and for the Red People of the Big Island. Please come back in the early evening and we will continue our discussions. Also, would you please be kind enough to spread the word around the village that there will be a public meeting at dawn tomorrow? Thank you, my brother."

Flaming Hair asked young warriors, who had started to gather near Lightning Bolt's wigwam, to spread the word among the People that the Grand Chief wanted to speak to them at the first light of dawn. They immediately scattered to get it done. Upon returning to Lightning Bolt's wigwam that evening, Flaming Hair found a man who had aged many Moons in the space of less than a Sunrise.

After exchanging greetings the Grand Chief began to speak, "My brother, I've seen the passage of almost a hundred Springs. During that time I've seen pain, death, destruction and grief caused by war and disease. I've been fortunate to have known great love. I have enjoyed the loyalty, devotion and generosity of the People, always knowing that these things were theirs to give and not mine to take. Until this Sunrise I thought I had seen all the trials the Great Spirit could bring to test one's faith in his fellow man. But, all my experiences have not prepared me for what we must deal with now. To face warriors from a society that would mistreat their own children, using them as chattels for their own pleasure and for financial gain is beyond frightening.

"My brother, the stories you told me when you first came among us, about the ways of the Europeans, was enough to cause pity in my heart for people denied the right to live in human dignity. However, at that time, the prospect of us ever having to deal with such cruelty, face to face, was only remote. Now, may the Great Spirit help us, this has become a reality. How will we deal with them? Our people have no experience with an entire civilization where the leadership knows no humanity. Although we have legends such as the one about the Dictators, they were simply characters in frightening stories told to help us learn to share. The Mi'kmaq and other great Nations of these lands will probably not be able to learn quickly enough how to deal effectively with the people who are coming. By the time they learn to appreciate the true ways of the white man it may be too late. I hope, my brother, that I'm not being overly depressing in relaying my thoughts."

"Lightning Bolt, my brother, what you've said is only the tip of the iceberg. What we consider strengths in our society will be weaknesses in our future struggle with European nations. What we consider ills in their society will be their strengths if they attempt to subjugate our Peoples. The fact that their leaders can cruelly inflict terrible brutalities upon their own people means they will have no mercy when it comes to having their way with ours. Our People, who mostly know only generosity and kindness in their dealings with their fellow man, will fall like the dead leaves of Autumn from the trees. Lightning Bolt, my beloved brother, our People's civility will be our downfall. I fear that, although they will face many indignities at the hands of the Europeans, the People will continue to try to treat them as brothers. And it won't work because the only thing Europeans understand perfectly is force.

"If at this time we could convince our Nations to mount an all-out offensive and remove by bloody slaughter the few Europeans from the Big Island, before more of them come, we might have a chance. But you know as well as I that this won't happen. To strike a death blow to repel the Europeans would be to suddenly change and become brutal and viscious people. This is not our way."

Lightning Bolt, sadly looking at his brother and knowing his words to be true, replied, "My brother, the wisdom of your words is not lost on me. I hear you with a heavy heart because I know the destruction of our People is near."

"Oh Lightning Bolt, my brother, my friend, our People are poised on the edge of an unknown and bottomless chasm and will very shortly slip over to their doom. I don't really believe there is anything we can do to prevent it. The forces we are up against are very powerful. However, I will pray constantly to the Great Spirit for a miracle."

"Flaming Hair, my brother, you asked me this Sunrise to refrain from telling the People about the fate of the ten boys who were abducted from the land of Eskikewa'kik. I've carefully considered your request and have rejected it. The People must know the truth about the ones that they will have to deal with. Further, I think it may be helpful in my efforts to convince them to adopt the position we discussed. But, deep in my heart, I know as you do that, because of their ingrained civility, a course of brutality will not be adopted. But in desperation, I must try everything possible to stir them into taking defensive action."

With this they parted to prepare themselves for the ordeal of the next Sunrise's meeting. Lightning Bolt spent a near sleepless night and for the first time since his wife's death he cried.

Shortly after dawn the People began to assemble to hear their leader. Their first sight of him since the Sunrise before filled them with concern, for he had aged by what seemed to be hundreds of Moons. But, even in this time of deep concern they performed the appropriate rites of their civilization before the meeting commenced.

Then Lightning Bolt spoke. "Brothers and sisters, my children, the news I bring you this Sunrise is filled with dark foreboding for our future survival as a Nation. I will relate to you, word for word, what has been reported to me..." When finished, Lightning Bolt began to talk to the People about the future, although by now they had a bewildered and shocked look about them.

"There is no question about the fact that many of the people invading our lands are cruel and viscious, lacking a sense of justice and equality. To them we will be like black-flies, a nuisance to be destroyed. With a breaking heart I urge you my children to prepare yourself for the dreadful things to come. Many of the strangers coming to our lands will at first appear to be friendly, but it will be only a ruse. When they multiply, they will turn upon us and in the end seek to destroy us. They will, without conscience, take all that is ours.

Our remaining Peoples will be left destitute and landless.

"To try to prevent this from happening, I'm calling a general Chief's meeting of Eastern and Western Nations to plot strategy. To this end I've already sent runners to deliver to them the news about the invasion and to invite them to a meeting five Sunrises after the first Moon of Spring. My hope is that by that time the leaders, in consultation with their People, can agree to make emergency plans to deal with this menace to our survival. Go, my children, and pray constantly to the Great Spirit for guidance."

The National Chief's meeting got under way shortly after the Great Chief had passed his one-hundredth Spring. After extending greetings, Lightning Bolt urged the Chiefs to meet in small groups, then reassemble the next morning. The next Sunrise, in an air of despair, he called the general meeting to order soon after dawn. "My beloved children, as I told you last Sunrise, I've called this conference to hear your reactions to the news of the European invasion and to try to reach a consensus on the kind of policy we should adopt to deal with the crisis. Before we start, I call upon senior Elder Morning Child to lead us in prayer to our Maker. Morning Child."

"Lightning Bolt, my Grandfather, brothers and sisters, let us pray that the Great Father will shine His light down upon us to fill us with the wisdom we will need to resolve this grave matter. Oh Great Spirit, Master of the Universe, the giver of life to all creatures and things, please show us your poor children the way. Let your wisdom show through in all of our decisions, and…"

When Morning Child had finished offering prayers to the Great Spirit, and the Sweet-grass and Pipe-Smoking Ceremonies were over, Lightning Bolt continued, "Thank you my beloved sister. My children, I'll now ask, in order of age, all the national leaders to come forward and share with us the reactions of their communities to the coming of the strangers. And then, share with us suggestions for dealing with the situation. We'll start with the Chief of the Maliseet Nation, Big Mountain."

Big Mountain gave a detailed report about how his people had received the news, and their reactions. Then the other Chiefs all made their orations. They told of the People's fear and sense of dismay upon hearing the news of the way the people with pale faces had treated the Red People of the Big Island. However, as feared by Lightning Bolt and Flaming Hair, they relayed that many had almost immediately begun to rationalize the mistreatment of the Red People as the actions of renegades, and to espouse a belief that the leaders of these People would be appalled by the actions of the few and react accordingly. After all, they said, "the invaders wore clothes and manned great canoes; they must be civilized." A consensus emerged to acknowledge the dangers that lay ahead but nevertheless to welcome the strangers. The general feeling was that if these people were greeted with civility and generosity, they would react in kind.

To boost their plea for a moderate approach, they brought forward a man called Broken Stone who had encountered some of these people off Eskikewa'kik and traded some of his furs with them. He produced a knife made out of some kind of manmade hard stone and demonstrated how it worked. He then told them of receiving from them a gift of a wondrous medicine called "brandy." He told how it made a person feel so good that he felt no pain, and how it made one forget all his troubles. When he finished, several other instances were recounted where individuals had come in contact and experienced similar treatment.

Lightning Bolt and Flaming Hair, with sinking hearts, continued to listen as their brothers spoke. As they had predicted, the leaders didn't recognize the extreme danger the People were in and instead were going to try to appease the Europeans. With a sense of dismay and desperation Lightning Bolt began to speak. "My beloved children, I beg of you to reconsider the course of action you are advocating for dealing with these strangers. You say they should be treated like brothers. I ask you: Do brothers come into your home and molest and rape your women and children? Do they come into your home and destroy all that is yours and take you and your families and sell them into slavery? Do they take the very young, the aged, the sick and infirm and slaughter them? No, brothers do not do these things. You talk about the possibility that these people may be civilized. I remind you my friends that abducting, sexually molesting, selling, and murdering our children are not the actions of a civilized people. I ask you, my friends, are the beastly actions they've taken against the Red People of the Big Island the deeds of a civilized People? Of course they're not. The ways of the white man are not known to you my friends; I will try to enlighten you.

"I could start by referring to the Legend of the Dictators, but I'm sorry to say that their actions do not equal what the Europeans are capable of. I'll give you a firsthand account of what the white man is capable of doing. Flaming Hair, my brother, has told me about their way of life. They live in a selfish manner and work to acquire property and power at the expense of others. They don't enjoy freedom and the right to select their leaders as you do. Their leaders are born into their positions and retain their power by brute force." Lightning Bolt and Flaming Hair spoke for the rest of the afternoon, enlightening the assembled Chiefs about the ways of the Europeans. Lightning Bolt, showing the wear and stress of his role, concluded by saying, "My brothers and sisters, my children, you talk of trying to establish brotherly relations with a People you don't know. I tell you they will not be accommodated until they have everything that is ours and have driven us into degradation, if we are permitted to live.

"Accordingly, I urge you, my beloved people, please take time and more carefully consider our options. To protect ourselves I have in mind an option that is very drastic. Before discussing it I want to tell you that it is against the values of our traditions. However, in good conscience I must propose it. My friends, our traditions demand that we welcome any stranger that comes among us. But, in this case, if we don't set aside our civilized values and take defensive measures I predict we will be lost! Therefore, I recommend that we unite and with a determined effort drive these people from our lands. If we don't, they will spread like wildfire and consume everything in their path. If we are to act and contain the danger, the time to act is now. Trying to do so a few generations from now will be too late.

"I will now adjourn the meeting for us to reflect upon what has been said so far. We will meet again when the sun has moved to halfway between noon and dusk tomorrow."

When the meeting reassembled the next sunrise, Big Mountain rose to respond to the concerns of the Grand Chief. "Oh Lightning Bolt, our esteemed father, you are a man with whom we have travelled far during the time allotted to us on Mother Earth by the Great Spirit. Your wisdom has always served us well and will continue to serve us well until the Great Spirit takes you home. But father, after carefully weighing the words you've spoken, I must tell you that we've decided to try to make a civilized accommodation with the strangers first. If it doesn't work, then we will follow your wise advice and take the harsh measures you advocate to ensure the survival of our Nations."

Big Mountain continued to rationalize the proposed action for some time and Lightning Bolt sadly responded, "My brothers, I must accept the will of the People. However, I feel obligated to say that when, in the not-too-distant future, you find that the course you have selected is the wrong one, it will be too late to try the one I suggested. Go in peace, and may the Great Spirit love and protect us all."

Over the following four Seasons, no other violent incidents were reported and the people were lulled into a false sense of security. On a warm Sunrise, one Moon after Summer began, Lightning Bolt called family members and close personal friends to his wigwam for an intimate discussion. "My children, as you are aware, the recent passage of Mother Earth's annual renewal was the one-hundred-and-first renewal that this old body has known. With the passage of so many Springs my body has, as happens to all things, withered and lost most of its vitality. Time, my children, has finally caught up with me.

"In witness to this, last night in my dreams the Great Spirit sent Glooscap to me to deliver a message I've long expected. He told me that my time on Mother Earth will come to pass before the passage of another Moon. For this I'm grateful, for I've longed to be in the arms of my Spring Flower again, and to have the company of my many friends who have gone before me. For this long-awaited pleasure I ask you to rejoice with me in happiness. Don't weep for my poor bones, for although we will miss each other after I've gone home to the Land of Souls, our separation is only temporary. One Sunrise we shall all be reunited in happiness for eternity.

"However, as I prepare to depart upon my final journey, there is one thing that troubles me: the fate of our People. With a heavy heart my beloved friends, I must tell you that Glooscap in our talk told me something I already knew. He confirmed that the strategy adopted by our leadership to deal with the Europeans won't work because the European leaders do not understand how to get people to do things without using force. He said they will come like an outbreak of ravenous caterpillars and eventually consume us. He confirmed that many of the first arrivals will appear to be weak and helpless and that our People will assist them in their efforts to survive and establish themselves upon our lands. Then, once established, they will turn upon our People like parasites. And, may the Great Spirit help you my children, He said many of our Nations would come to extinction and not one would be left untouched.

"He said that before it ends, thousands of Moons will pass and the People shall know unimaginable horrors. They will endure extermination efforts, hunger and starvation, and unknown diseases. The hatred of the People that the White Skins shall develop, because of colour and different cultural practices, will degrade and humiliate us for thousands of Moons. He further told me that the future children of the Europeans, to ease their collective guilt about the horrors they have subjected our Peoples to, will begin to pretend to themselves that they have done nothing wrong. To help in this regard, they will create a fantasy that our People were uncivilized savages, comparable to wild animals, when their ancestors first arrived upon the shores of our land. And, because of this lie they will claim that our People were not entitled to ownership of their properties, nor to claim any rights.

"As time passes they will even go so far as to pretend that our People are to blame for our own misfortunes, preposterous as it may seem, because they did not immediately embrace European civilization and happily agree without reservation to the destruction of their own."

Lightning Bolt paused, while those gathered around looked each other in the eyes, hardly believing his words. Those with a sense of wisdom fought tears of sadness for the things to come. Those who were not yet wise felt anger rising up inside, wanting to stave off this tide of darkness that their own most highly respected Elder was saying would come to pass. Lightning Bolt looked to each person with kindness and love in his eyes. The Peacemaker offered these last words as a kind of prayer for his future children's children. "Glooscap left me with one thing that gave me a small glimmer of hope. He said that one Sunrise our People will rise up from the ashes of their past greatness and reestablish their Nations. For this, I give humble thanks."

Lightning Bolt's loved ones spent most of the night in intimate conversation with him, departing just before dawn for their own wigwams. Word spread quickly about the dream of the Grand Chief. The People, with twinges of sadness, began to make preparations to celebrate his Feast of the Dead. The third night before the next Moon Lightning Bolt awoke to find his precious Spring Flower standing by his sleeping place. She whispered softly, "Give me your hand my dear husband."

With her warm hand in his, the Great Chief slipped into eternity.

AFTERWORD FROM DANIEL PAUL

During my work as an historian and writer, I have had the privilege and the burden of responsibility that is associated with reading the source documents arising from the colonial history relevant to this book. While engaging this research and during the publication and revisions of *We Were Not the Savages*, the notion of writing an historical novel came to me as another way to present a small but important part of the history.

It appeared most important, from my Mi'kmaw perspective, to highlight the period just before the first onslaught of European invasion and colonization. The first definitive invasion occurred during the fifteenth century. This was a period that included a successful campaign of genocide that was waged against the Peoples who occupied the northernmost island in northeastern North America, now known as Newfoundland.

By combining the best of the written historical documents alongside trusted oral traditions, including information from oral traditions never recorded prior to the publication of this book, my effort was to draw the reader into the story from Mi'kmaq eyes, ears and heart. With the insider knowledge afforded to me as a Mi'kmaq Elder, my life has given me many moments of clarity and insight associated with the histories of encounter between the European nations and the Mi'kmaq People.

The main character of the story, Chief Lightning Bolt, otherwise known among the People as the Peacemaker, is a fictitious historical figure whom I have living among our People prior to European invasion. While he lived long ago, for the Mi'kmaq, time is somewhat irrelevant, because we today are connected to our ancestors who still come to us in dreams and visions. Through their stories and teachings, we come to know who we are and what is our way in life, and we learn about our values, beliefs and the ways that we are taught to treat others.

Chief Lightning Bolt is a highly significant Elder, typical of those found within our oral traditions, precisely because he embodies the best of Mi'kmaq values, ethics and beliefs. His path through life and his actions toward his family, friends, fellow villagers, members of the other Mi'kmaq territories and Peoples from many other Nations who came to engage with him during difficult times as well as times of celebration and great accomplishment, are all actions that give testament to celebrated Mi'kmaq ways.

These cultural ways highlight courage, honour, humility, service and sacrifice of personal gain for the sake of others. Lightning Bolt carries this story through his exemplary character, which is celebrated not only within the oral traditions of our People, but also within the chronicles of history. But to get to the essence of this story seemed important to me. For this reason, I wanted to reveal the truth about the Mi'kmaq People. To do this on our own terms, without the imperial gaze of colonial influence, is not an easy task, but is one that must be accomplished.

Therefore, basing this story in the period prior to settlement of the French Acadians, and before the British invasion and their expulsion of the French, the intention was to build a sense of the "pre-contact" culture, values, relationships, family life and national politics of the Mi'kmaq during the fifteenth century.

It is to this world that we turn to find the essence of Mi'kmaw cultural identity. It is from these ashes of our greatness that we can one day see the Eagle rising through the Eastern Door, giving hope and purpose to a Nation being reborn. There is this clear purpose in these pages. Giving insight and clarity where there was none. Offering the assurance of a story borne of generations of toil and suffering, but today a story celebrating courage and survival, entitlement and justice-making. These are the spirit and eternal sparks of Chief Lightning Bolt that give energy and life to this story.

Not withstanding, a friend of European lineage who proofread the early draft of the manuscript that became this book stated to me, "The story speaks of an idyllic way of life — people loving their families and community, no greed, no jealousy or other nasty hateful sins. How could this be? We were taught they were savages!"

However, the myth of savagery, as clever a device of colonization and subjugation as the myth tends to be, is also greatly contradicted by the findings of many European chroniclers during the colonial history. They were awed and reacted in disbelief to what they saw practised in the Americas. These cultural ways stood in such stark contrast to what they knew of European cultural practice, their awe comes forward in their analysis of Mi'kmaq contexts. The following are just a few of their testimonials.

A missionary priest, who was abroad in Mi'kmaq country in the late 1600s and early 1700s, attests to the eloquence and civility of the People: "The Mi'kmaq is a poetic child. His distances are measured in rainbows. His words sound the sense. His fancy is illimitable. He is a born orator. He loves justice and hates violence and robbery. He is courteous." The Jesuit missionary Pierre Biard was quoted as saying, "Never had we to be on our guard against them." The use of the word "child" echoes the biblical teaching to "become like children" before the Lord. As such, his words convey a sense of the innocence, directness, honesty and transparency within the Mi'kmaq culture that form the basis of systems of familial and national justice and citizenship.

Another priest, impressed with the legends he heard while in the company of the Mi'kmaq, wrote:

> The story of the Mi'kmaq is one of the most fascinating studies that a person can take up. His legends carry you back from the first sight of the big canoe, as they called the white man's ship, to the dawn of Creation when Glooscap, the master, lay prone on his back, head to the rising Sun, feet to the setting of the Sun, left hand to the South, and the right hand to the North. This wonder worker was not Niskam, "Father to us all," nor Gisolg, "Our Maker," nor the "Great Chief," but he was par excellence, the Mi'kmaq. He was coexistent with Creation.

There is little doubt that the Mi'kmaq carry a long tradition of stories going back to the dawn of creation. That a European priest caught a small glimmer of the importance of the figure Glooscap within the culture and mysticism of the Mi'kmaq

People, can only be testament to the strength of values, beliefs, ethics and morality conveyed by these sacred stories.

Sieur de Diereville wrote about leadership within Mi'kmaq society:

> The cherished hope of leadership inspires resolve to be adept in the chase. For it is by such aptitude a man obtains the highest place; here there is no inherited position due to birth or lineage, merit alone uplifts. He who has won exalted rank, which each himself hopes to attain, will never be deposed, except for some abhorrent crime.

Here we see something central to Mi'kmaq culture and beliefs — that respect is earned through actions. The European writer sees rank and position, which come forward as dominant within their analysis. But the Mi'kmaq sees each person from the heart — how do you live? How do you treat your family? How do you function when you work each day? What is your disposition and character? These are the defining characteristics of leadership. These are what nurture respect between people.

Bernard Gilbert Hoffman relates this description of Mi'kmaq leadership that he had formed from researching colonial records:

> For a young man to rise in the esteem of his people, it apparently was necessary for him to be superior in hunting, to be among the bravest in warfare, to be generous and hospitable to all the people in his camp and to visitors, stripping himself of all his wealth, and seeking only the affections of his people.

Again, the European into the young man's conduct as rising to and seeking esteem, when the Native person acknowledges that each person warrants respect for who they are. What they do is a small but important manifestation of their spiritual being. For the European, A plus B equals C. But for the Mi'kmaq, a deeper philosophy and spirituality is at play that is, for the most part, hidden from the superficial European gaze.

Calvin Martin found, when discussing the Amerindian attitude towards religious conversion, that it was sometimes difficult to distinguish between genuine conversion and a tolerant assent to strange views:

> Such generosity even extended to the abstract realm of ideas, theories, stories, news, and teachings. The Native host prided himself on his ability to entertain and give assent to a variety of views, even if they were contrary to his better judgment. In this institutionalized hospitality lies the key to understanding the frustration of the Priest, whose sweet converts one day were the relapsed heathens of the next. Conversion was often more a superficial courtesy, rather than an eternal commitment, something the Jesuits could not fathom.

These comments ignore and are completely ignorant of the depth of Mi'kmaq cosmology and spiritual beliefs that govern rules of hospitality. Therefore, how can the author(s) ever provide a quality description of what they fail to understand — and that which is essential to comprehending the First Nation perspective on inter-cultural relations? The very notion of conversion must also be decoded and set within a Mi'kmaq philosophy of science and the cosmology arising from eons of relationship with the land, the sea and the stars that made up the universe of the People.

Chrétien Le Clercq, a Recollect Franciscan missionary to the Mi'kmaq on the Gaspé Peninsula in the 1670s and 80s, describes how a Chief would conduct himself at a funeral oration, correctly conveying the civil values of respect, honour and humility that is deeply woven within Mi'kmaq values:

> The good qualities and the most notable deeds of the deceased. He even impresses upon all the assembly, by words as touching as they are forceful, the uncertainty of human life, and the necessity they are under of dying, in order to join in the Land of Souls with their friends and relatives, whom they are now recalling to memory.

Nicholas Denys relates how others spoke after the Chief, "each one spoke, one after another, for they never spoke two at a time, neither men or women. In this respect these barbarians give a fine lesson to those people who consider themselves more polished and wiser than they."

It is fascinating how the civil democracy of the Mi'kmaq was labelled barbarian. But in essence, anything that was not European was barbaric, regardless of the illogic that formed the basis of racism. Regardless, the essence of the comments point to the democratic equality supported and protected by Mi'kmaw cultural ways. These laws within the culture were and continue to be sacred. They prescribe ways of communicating with one another that provide mutual safety and security, means toward increasing mutual understanding, respect and tolerance of differences. Included in these ways are processes of conflict resolution, mediation, reconciliation and peacemaking. That Europeans who viewed the Mi'kmaq as barbarians and savages, still highlighted in their accounts the civil democratic strengths of the People, is quite a strong and robust acknowledgment from external sources. This acknowledgement helps to verify the true nature of the cultural heritage of the First Nation.

Again, Chrétien Le Clercq describes the courtship and wedding process:

> If the father finds that the suitor who presents himself is acceptable for his daughter... he tells him to speak to his sweetheart in order to learn her wish about an affair which concerns herself alone. For they do not wish, say these barbarians, to force the inclinations of their children in the matter of marriage, or to induce them, whether by use of force, obedience, or affection, to marry men whom they cannot bring themselves to like. Hence it is that the fathers and mothers of our Gaspesians [Mi'kmaq from Gaspé] leave to their children the entire liberty of choosing the persons whom they think most adaptable to their dispositions, and most conformable to their affections.

The oddity of these comments is that the writer viewed the Mi'kmaq practices as utter barbarity. But today many world cultures would see the ancient Mi'kmaq approach to nurturing mutual love, affection, respect and gender equality as extremely enlightened. The purpose was to engender a growth of personhood through the central relationship that produces children and family life, by encouraging communications and relational values that nurture maturity, safe self-disclosure and mutual honesty.

Long before the western nations awoke to the

contemporary notions of human rights, feminism, gender equality, gay and lesbian issues and a wide range of similar movements that characterize the past century, the Mi'kmaq Nation was fully engaged with living a system of high social and moral standards that existed over hundreds of centuries — in a sustainable and enduring civil democracy.

We see then, through these quotations, several wonderful revelations about how a participatory society worked. In reality, these things worked very well — and are today aspects of Native cultures that are coming to the fore when people across the world are looking for answers to ecological and socio-political crisis.

However, in spite of the fact that these chroniclers minutely describe, in their diaries, records and manuscripts, the outstanding values of Native American civilizations, European chroniclers still most often believed European society to be superior to what they termed heathen and uncivilized American civilizations. There are many today who consciously and unconsciously carry forward these colonial values. The notion of a post-colonial approach is far from anything near to a universal application.

People hold these views because they use European societal standards as a value measurement. These values do not have human protection enshrined and are almost exclusively based on personal enrichment and technological advancement. Role and status are assigned through birthright or material wealth or power over others. These systems are invariably related to cultures that are swamped with military influence and values, and are bolstered by ever-increasing arms production focused on maintaining or exercising power to control others.

These dominant European values are not a prescription for the development of a peaceful world society. We acknowledge that European cultures contain a wealth of cultural and spiritual teachings that go far beyond what colonial history conveys. Each tribe and nation across Europe holds a sacred tradition that can still be honoured and celebrated. However, sad as the story goes, these traditional cultural values were largely lost in the rush of colonial invasion of the Americas. Europeans who invaded and settled in the Americas and in other locations around the world, as well as their children today, must in some way grapple with the legacy of horror that was unleashed, and is still underway.

Certainly, and with a large degree of humility, surely part of this journey toward righting the wrongs of the past, and correcting the imbalances and injustice of today, will involve the European and the Native person reflecting on this history. Surely, this process will involve remembering and reconnecting with the best in each of our many traditions. By reawakening these strengths, we definitely have one of the sacred keys to unlocking the current crisis of identity.

We also must, each of us, without exception, acknowledge our role and place in taking responsibility for the past by changing our conduct today, so that our children will indeed have a better future. It is our generations now who are awakening the keys to justice-making. These stories we share are a significant part of this social and political transformation.

Of all world cultures, we ought to remember that European excellence arises across the centuries in how to kill one another most efficiently, with least regard for human dignity, and that this characteristic strength is and was pursued by European nations at a tremendous cost to humanity and has spilled an endless river of human blood around the world. The historical record is clear, going back to medieval torture methods, and including the colonial genocide enacted in the Americas over the past centuries. Up to and beyond the Second World War the European national identities are founded on and expanded by notions of war, conquest and desires for power.

At some stage, however, the European nations and their descendants scattered across the globe might indeed grow beyond these dominant and destructive values that are promoted in each generation under the status quo of the times. Unfortunately, I do not see this growth into maturity happening any time soon. But our work nurtures the path toward reconnecting with the best in our respective cultures and traditions.

Mi'kmaq society developed independently a whole system of social and political values that sustained civil democratic methods of leadership, governance, familial and community law, as well as national and international diplomacy. These approaches were completely opposite to the dominant values of the European colonial cultures.

Chief Lightning Bolt is based on how the Mi'kmaq lived and prospered in a society that was dedicated to the principle of the overall community's welfare being the first priority. For the Mi'kmaq, making war was a last and most distasteful resort. For the Mi'kmaq, peacemaking and living in a sustainable culture of peace and beauty was of central importance.

Mi'kmaw Saqmawiey (Eldering) (Dr.) Daniel N. Paul,
C.M., O.N.S., LLD, DLIT
Halifax, Canada, 2017